Before she started w. in I.T. until she came journalism and writin_ _ ..._.. articles for Women's Health & Fitness magazines as well as newsletter content and media releases for a not-for-profit organisation. In 2011 the fiction bug bit and Helen has been writing fiction ever since.

Helen J. Rolfe writes uplifting, contemporary fiction with characters to relate to and fall in love with. Christmas at Snowdrop Cottage is her eleventh novel.

Find out more at www.helenjrolfe.com, and follow her on Twitter @HJRolfe.

ALSO BY HELEN J ROLFE

The Friendship Tree

Handle Me with Care

What Rosie Found Next

The Chocolatier's Secret

In a Manhattan Minute

Christmas at The Little Knitting Box

The Summer of New Beginnings

You, Me, and Everything In Between

The Magnolia Girls

Snowflakes and Mistletoe at the Inglenook Inn

Christmas at Snowdrop Cottage

Helen J. Rolfe

For my husband who never stops believing in me and supporting me along the way.

Chapter One

Belle Nightingale had no problem going away for Christmas. With her family it had never been a big event, at least not since she was little and her gran had run the show.

But that was then, and things in Belle's life had changed. She found herself wondering whether her gran's life had changed too since the last time she'd seen her, more than twenty years ago.

'What time are you leaving?' Belle's boyfriend, Anthony, emerged from the bathroom, his lower half wrapped in one of her fluffy navy blue towels. They'd been to his work Christmas party last night and even though Belle hadn't let a single drop of alcohol pass her lips, she had the type of hangover induced by too much Christmas music, an enormous turkey dinner and an overdose of mince pies.

Belle plonked herself down on top of her suitcase in an effort to squash the contents and make another attempt at shutting the thing. 'Just as soon as I get this to close,' she said through gritted teeth as she tugged the zip all the way around to the front to meet the other zip, already in place. 'There.' She exhaled hard. 'Done. I think eating too many mince pies last night probably helped me weigh enough to flatten all my belongings.'

'I ate way too much as well, although the food wasn't as good as yours.' He winked and rubbed some product through his hair.

'I aim to please.'

Anthony played with his hair in the mirror for a second and then patted his stomach. 'Gym for me tonight – if my head can take it.'

'Bad hangover?'

'Put it this way, it's going to be a long day. But I don't think I'll be the only one suffering in the office.' The aroma of his clean, crisp aftershave filled the bedroom as he pulled on his suit trousers and a sky blue shirt, adjusting each cuff in turn so it was perfectly straight. He turned up his collar, looped a tie around it and fastened it at the front using the mirror to get it exactly right.

'Drink plenty of water; you'll be fine.'

'I'm thinking coffee might be the order of the day. I wonder if where you're going has any coffee shops. It's a bit in the middle of nowhere isn't it?'

'Who knows what changes they've made since I was last in Little Woodville.' She returned his smile tentatively.

'You won't take long to get it all sorted,' he said. He'd picked up on her hesitation to speculate about how she was going to feel seeing the village she hadn't been to in more than two decades, but his assumption was that she was stressing about selling the cottage, when in reality it was so much more than that. 'Give notice to the tenant, clear out some of the old junk, and come New Year it'll sell fast. I'm still dying to find out whether this man is your gran's bit on the side.'

Belle shook her head. 'I've got no idea who he is, I just hope he isn't a stubborn old goat who refuses to go quietly.' The last thing she wanted was a sitting tenant on her hands.

Both being in the estate agency business, she and Anthony knew a winner when they saw one and even though Anthony was yet to set eyes on Snowdrop Cottage, situated in Little Woodville in the centre of the Cotswolds, he'd seen enough photos and profiles of it to

2

know its value. He also knew Belle's feelings about the cottage she'd had put in her name ten years ago by a grandmother she had nothing to do with any more. She felt the same way about the cottage as she did about Christmas: the whole thing would only end up being one huge let-down, so best to avoid it. And in the case of the cottage, that meant getting rid of it.

Sebastian was the tenant in the cottage and he'd been living at the address since Grandma Gillian went into a care home. Shortly before Gran had left Snowdrop Cottage, she'd signed her home over to Belle via a solicitor and the only stipulation was that Belle should allow the current tenant to stay on, keep paying rent, until Belle decided to sell up or move into the cottage herself. Belle already knew the latter was something that would never happen. Little Woodville was a far cry from life in the hub of Cambridge, with everything on Belle's doorstep including work and her boyfriend. Up until now the rental arrangement had been easy. The man always paid his rent on time and it was a nice little bonus for her every month. And now, Belle and Anthony had started making bigger plans and the time to sell up had come.

'Did you get a message back from the tenant?' Anthony looped his laptop bag over his shoulder and picked up his suit jacket.

'He knows I need to get in and have a look at the place, perhaps clear out some of the junk Gran left behind if there is any.' She chewed the side of her lip. 'I don't know how he'll react when I give him notice.'

'Come on, Belle, you're not going to back out are you?' He paused, car keys already in hand.

He had a right to question her, because loyalty was one of Belle's strengths. She was loyal to Anthony, her boyfriend of three years. She was loyal to Sam, her best friend ever since, at the age of thirteen, they'd pulled one another's hair in the playground over a boy and subsequently decided friendship was more important than the opposite sex. And she was loyal to her neighbour Mrs Frobishire, who lived in the flat on the same floor as hers in the converted Edwardian house in Cambridge and who had become a bit of a confidante, a surrogate grandmother in the absence of a real one in her life. But her fiercest loyalty was to her mum. It was what had prevented Belle from forming any kind of relationship with her gran over the years, and Anthony knew family ties could cloud her judgement over any decision involving the cottage.

Ever since she'd received the call from the solicitor all that time ago, the reasons for such a monumentous decision on her Gran's part, had long since baffled Belle. She wondered if putting the cottage in her name was Gran's way of offering some kind of olive branch, or if it was because she felt guilty about something that had happened in the past. Or was she hoping it would bring the family back together again? Belle had no idea. She knew her mum, Delia, wouldn't provide any answers either, the long-standing feud with her own mother being something Delia never talked about. And since Belle's parents moved to Ireland a few years ago, resolving what had gone on before was even less likely to happen.

She hadn't admitted it to Anthony, but Belle had a nagging feeling that perhaps selling wasn't the right thing to do. After all, if Gran had wanted the cottage to go to anyone outside of the family, she would've sold it years ago. If she'd only wanted to convince Belle of her part in her granddaughter's life, she could've easily given her a lump sum instead of going through all the rigmarole involved in handing over a property. And what if selling the cottage finally broke all ties between Gran and her only daughter? It had been years since the two women had spoken or been in touch, but Belle had always harboured a secret fantasy that one day they could sort out their differences and they'd all be together again. Anthony would call it sentimental and there was no room for that in business, and maybe he was right, but Belle sometimes wanted to believe it could happen.

The last time Belle had been to Little Woodville and Snowdrop Cottage was the Christmas after she turned ten. She remembered the entrance, so much smaller than a normal doorway to a home. As a little girl she'd hovered beneath the covered part wondering whether she'd ever grow tall enough to have to duck her head when she went through the door and whether, once inside, she would be one of those grown-ups that needed to stoop when passing under the big beams that ran down the centre of some of the rooms. Anthony thought Belle was going to Snowdrop Cottage today to hand the tenant his notice and get things really moving, but Belle had another agenda she knew she needed to address before she could do anything so final. She felt she needed to say goodbye. She wanted to return to the place she'd spent so much time in when she was little, the village that had almost been a part of her until she was wrenched away from it, the cottage and her grandmother. She wanted to remember her family together, take herself back to the really good times.

Belle put her arms around Anthony. 'I'm not backing out. I'm going to Little Woodville to see what's what, that's all. I'm a professional remember. And I've been working long hours, so I could do with an extended break.'

He pulled her close. 'You're very good at your job.'

'As are you.'

'And that's why we're going to take the real-estate world by storm, you and I, one day in the not-too-distant future.'

'We most certainly will.'

'Prices have gone up a lot in ten years. The cottage should be worth a fair bit by now.'

Belle smiled, although if Anthony had looked more closely and not been so distracted with getting ready for work he'd have seen it was a smile that didn't quite reach up to the corners of her hazel eyes.

Belle and Anthony had gone through comparable properties that had sold recently, not that there was a single one in Little Woodville. Tourist brochures described the village as a jewel in the Cotswolds, idyllic, an area that hadn't lost an ounce of its charm, as one website had said. It seemed to be one of those villages where people bought property and never left, which was great for the people residing there but not so good for anyone who wanted to move to Little Woodville.

'I can't believe the cottage has been in my family for more than sixty years,' said Belle.

'It doesn't happen much nowadays.' He checked his watch. 'I'm going to be late if I don't get going.' He pulled her to him again and kissed her. 'I'm going to miss you.'

'No you won't – you'll go back to your nice warm lounge and brand-new bathroom and I won't be able to make you come here and stay with me in my sub-standard flat that lets in the noise of the main road.'

'I didn't sleep that well last night.'

'I know you didn't.' They usually stayed at his but with Belle going away today she needed to be here to get

6

going at a reasonable hour. Anthony's place was the other side of the city, which was fine when they had to get to work the next day but not when she had to pass through the main streets, crammed with commuters, and get to the other side before she even started on her own journey.

'I'm already looking forward to our trip to Wales.' His eyes shone. 'You, me, champagne, great food, no tacky decorations, no family annoying us. It'll be perfect. We can laze away the days and make more plans. It's going to be one hell of a year, so fasten your seatbelt.'

This time she really did smile, because his enthusiasm for their venture was sometimes off the scale. Starting their own real-estate-agency business was something they'd been thinking about ever since Anthony floated the idea last year. Belle hadn't ever thought she'd head in that direction, but it made sense and they'd be good at it too. They'd been a solid couple from the day they met, at a major UK event for estate and letting agents in London a few years ago. Belle had worked her way up the ranks from an admin assistant on Saturdays at a small high-street estate agent, to a sales negotiator for another agency, and now a senior negotiator at the same branch. Anthony was already the assistant branch manager for a rival agency at the opposite end of the high street, so between them they had the know-how to take their business venture all the way.

'We can dream up what to call our new company,' she beamed as he grabbed his Barbour jacket from the hook in the hallway. 'How about Belle's Beautiful Beach Houses?'

'Thinking of relocating somewhere coastal?' He laughed hard and pulled open the door to the flat.

'All those Bs just sound right,' she shrugged.

'How about Anthony's Awesome Bachelor Pads?'

She hooked her arms around his neck. 'No chance.'

'We'll talk about it in Wales.' He kissed her firmly, once on the lips. 'I'll see you soon.'

And with that he took the two flights of stairs down to the ground floor and she heard the front door click shut behind him. He'd already been outside that morning and scraped his windscreen clear of ice so he didn't have to do the worst when he was showered and smartly dressed. Belle, however, wasn't quite so prepared, and after she'd made the bed she pulled on her inky blue roll-neck jumper, grabbed her bag and hauled her suitcase down the stairs, inwardly cursing herself for not asking Anthony to do it for her before he left.

It was colder outside than she'd expected, although the white coating to the cars when she'd looked out the window at first light should've given it away. Glad of the toasty jumper, she retrieved the scraper from the glovebox of her dove grey Hyundai and got to work.

Passenger side done, she gladly moved to the safety of the pavement to do the driver's side as her neighbour appeared, gingerly taking the front steps from the house, which had been converted into six flats, down to street level. 'Good morning, Mrs Fro.' Belle began scraping the windscreen again on this side.

'Good morning, Belle. Now that looks like hard work.' Years of cigarettes had made Mrs Fro's voice permanently husky. At eighty-seven, Mrs Frobishire, as her full name dictated, was one of the best neighbours you could wish for. Belle had moved in to her flat eleven years ago, a lifetime to be in one place according to Anthony, who had been in four different dwellings during that time, and Mrs Frobishire had already been here for three years when Belle came so had been cautious about her new neighbour but soon realised that she wasn't a twenty-year-old with attitude, a drug problem or rebellious alcohol use but a girl who worked diligently for what she wanted and who desired nothing more than to make the flat her home.

A year after Belle moved in they greeted new tenants to the building – a young couple who moved in to the flat below Belle's and who played loud music not only into the night but all the way through until the next morning. Mrs Frobishire had given them a stern warning the first few times and then one night at three a.m., when the music levels got too much to bear, Belle had stood on the landing outside her top-floor flat and watched Mrs Frobishire emerge from her own, armed with a baseball bat. She told Belle it was for protection and off she'd marched down the stairs. Belle had followed her, terrified that this little old lady would come off worse, but she'd hung back when Mrs Frobishire confronted the couple and recited several noise acts, police acts and laws Belle wasn't sure really existed, the bat all the while firmly in her grasp. The music had gone off, stayed off, and a month later the couple had given their notice and moved out. Belle's best mate, Sam, had joked they were probably terrified of Mrs Frobishire when Belle had recounted the story the next day, but Belle knew it was more likely the threat of the law. That night, Belle had gone back upstairs behind a still determined and very awake neighbour and said, 'Mrs Fro, you were awesome tonight!' and wrapped her in a huge hug. And although Mrs Fro had tried to maintain a stiff upper lip, it hadn't lasted long at all and a schoolgirl-like giggle had emerged as Mrs Fro pumped the air with her free hand. 'I was awesome!' Belle suspected she'd never before used that word in her life, but from that day on they'd become closer as neighbours and the fearsome Mrs Frobishire became fondly known as Mrs Fro.

'Where's the smart suit?' Mrs Fro wanted to know now as Belle continued to scrape the ice away.

'No work today. I'm off on my travels, remember?' Wearing comfy jeans and boots made it a lot nicer to tackle this December weather than it usually was in a tailored skirt with tights and high heels. Belle had filled her suitcase with similar clothing: more jeans, leggings, a woollen dress, several jumpers. She hadn't had a proper holiday in almost a year, with her and Anthony focusing on saving money, and this trip was as much a getaway as it was to sort a house ready for sale.

'Ah yes, off to Little Woodville, then on to Wales. Forgive me, my memory sometimes needs a while to catch up.'

'You remembered the name of the village.' Somehow it pleased Belle. 'I don't think there's anything wrong with your memory.'

'Not losing my marbles yet.' She tapped her temple. 'I've been on my iPad just like you showed me when I got it, been onto Googly and read up about the village. It sounds like a beautiful slice of the English countryside.' Googly was the word Mrs Fro insisted on using and who was Belle to contradict her? 'Do you remember much about it?'

Belle scraped the last of the thicker ice from the windscreen. 'Not really. I was only ten the last time I was there and I expect it's changed, the way most places have. There are probably bigger buildings now, at least in the surrounds – maybe supermarkets, apartments, that sort of thing.'

'Nonsense. Much of the Cotswolds is a protected landscape, very important to this country. Fingers crossed Little Woodville is included in that and time has stood still.'

Belle had to admire the romanticism, but a lot could happen over the years and Little Woodville was just another part of her childhood that had become detached from her life as it was now: ever growing; ever evolving; no clinging on to the past. 'I'll soon find out, I suppose.' Belle smiled at the woman who had been one of the few constants in her life. 'You look warm in that scarf; I haven't seen it before.'

Mrs Fro lifted the emerald woollen scarf so the pompoms at its ends swung. 'I picked this up at the charity shop at the end of the road.' She pulled out a green mitten from each pocket of her oversized woollen coat. 'And I made these to match. Knitting keeps my mind young and my fingers nimble. Since I gave up the fags, my hands need something to do.'

Belle giggled. 'And I'd say knitting is much healthier for you.'

'You're a wise woman for one so young.'

'Not so young anymore. I'm thirty-one now.'

It was Mrs Fro's turn to laugh. 'You wait! When you get to my age and everything starts heading south, then you're allowed to describe yourself as not so young anymore.'

Belle shook off the scraper and slotted it back into the glovebox of the car. She wondered if her own gran was anything like Mrs Fro. Was she, too, eccentric in the way she spoke and the colourful outfits she wore? Was she an old lady who confronted noisy neighbours in the middle of the night? Or was she quiet, preferring to stay away from drama? Was she thoughtful and kind like Belle's

11

neighbour or was she someone who disliked company? Belle had so many questions that had built up over the years and deep down she hoped they'd be answered one day.

'Your dashing young man already dashed off has he?' Mrs Fro interrupted her thoughts.

'He has to work.'

'You're going on holiday on your own?'

'Only the first part, and it's not exactly a holiday.' Belle hadn't mentioned her ulterior motive for visiting Little Woodville. 'I'm going to look at the cottage I own and perhaps think about selling.'

Mrs Fro seemed taken aback. 'That's sudden.'

'We've been thinking about it for a while.'

'We?'

'Anthony and I are going to start our own business.'

'Well that's grand – it'll give you a good future. So he's the one, is he?'

Belle hadn't thought about it that way but, yes, she supposed he was. 'Don't send out the invites just yet, but you never know what'll happen.'

'Ain't that the truth. Well I'll look after your flat while you're gone.'

'Thanks. I'll be back in the New Year, and at least I've no plants for you to water.' She laughed. Mrs Fro was forever trying to encourage her to buy house plants, telling her they made a home.

Mrs Fro tutted. 'I know you haven't. You're away this year, but next year I'm going to make sure you at least have some holly around Christmas time. It's so festive and it looks wonderful. And one day I'm going to convince you to get a real tree.'

'I'd probably end up killing anything I brought in, you know.'

Mrs Fro rolled her eyes. 'I'll bet that cottage of yours has some lovely flowers come summertime.'

Belle smiled because the memory she suddenly had flooding her psyche wasn't the cottage itself but the snowdrops littered out front and at the rear of the property, too many to count. She remembered because her gran had made a big show of the snowdrops every February when they popped up from the ground with a sign of hope, a promise of spring – but, more, a promise of what was to come, a future.

Tears prickled at her eyes and she reached into the car and started the engine. She was getting overemotional, something they occasionally had to warn sellers or buyers about when it came to their own property, not something Belle ever usually had to worry about. She'd learnt a long time ago that it was best to face facts and make your decisions based on those.

'The trees will be bare and frost will have hardened the ground, I expect.' Belle said matter-of-factly. 'I don't think I'll see any flowers this time round.'

'Maybe next time you will.'

She looked affectionately at Mrs Fro. 'I expect the sale to be a reasonably quick one, once I've cleared out any of Gran's things that she left behind. She took a lot of her personal possessions with her to the care home, so I expect there'll be mostly old rubbish.' The letter that had come via the solicitor from Gran had said she'd left a few bits and bobs around the place and when the time came Belle was to do as she saw fit. It was an ambiguous request, one Belle wasn't entirely comfortable with, but she hadn't wanted to make any fuss when their correspondence only came through official channels.

'Well be careful – sometimes a load of old rubbish can be quite valuable.' Mrs Fro tightened her scarf around her neck to ward off the winter chill.

'That's true, I might get to go on your favourite show.'

Mrs Fro grinned. 'I'd love to see you on the *Antiques Roadshow*, but that wasn't what I meant exactly.'

'I'd get the money to Gran somehow, through her solicitor; I wouldn't pocket it.'

Mrs Fro's hand, now encased in the green mitten, landed on her arm. 'I know you wouldn't, Belle, you're a good girl. All I meant was that sometimes something that seems like rubbish to one person may end up being valuable to someone else. So just be careful. I know you're not a sentimental old goose like me, but try to be sure before you get rid of anything. I'm in my eighties,' she smiled. 'I've learnt a bit along the way.'

She hadn't said it but Belle wondered whether Mrs Fro also meant the cottage in her summation. She knew Belle didn't have anything to do with her gran and hadn't in years, and she was well aware of the current of strain running through the generations in her family.

'I'll make sure I'm careful,' Belle assured her. 'You should go back inside – it's freezing.' She was beginning to feel the December chill herself, even through her super-thick jumper.

'I'm walking to the corner shop, dear.'

'I can give you a lift. The car's nice and warm, and look – the demisters have already cleared the windscreen completely.'

Mrs Fro dismissed the suggestion with a wave of her mittened hand. 'Walking is another thing that stops me getting old before my time.' She winked at Belle. 'My daughter is coming to stay with me for a long weekend

14

and if I don't have coffee she gets right stressed and starts snapping everyone's head off.'

'And she's coming back for Christmas?' Belle hated to think of Mrs Fro all alone. Just because she didn't make a big thing out of Christmas herself, someone like Mrs Fro definitely did. She always had a wreath on the door to her flat, always had a real tree delivered and made the most heavenly mince pies that were enough to make a person weak at the knees.

'She'll be back, yes. Don't you worry about me.'

'Well you take care on your way to the shop, it's icy.'

'Don't worry, I will. I have the mobile phone Stella bought me and if I fall I'll order an ambulance. I've paid taxes for decades and never had to use one yet so I'd say they owe me a free ride.'

'Let's hope it doesn't come to that.' Belle had pulled her jumper sleeves over her hands now and couldn't wait to jump into the warmed-up car. They'd been talking so long her fingers had gone numb. She stepped forwards and hugged her neighbour. 'Have a very merry Christmas, Mrs Fro.'

'Merry Christmas, Belle. Send me a postcard from that picturesque little village, photos of the cottage too.'

'I will. You still remember your email password?'

'Of course I do.' She leaned closer to Belle. 'I've written it down with my PIN number for my bank on the underside of my kitchen table.'

'You never did.' Belle grinned. 'You need to be careful getting down on the floor and into funny positions to write on your furniture or read from it when you need to go to the bank.' She shook her head as Mrs Fro laughed, then added, 'And that's a beautiful table – you don't want to ruin it.'

'Still is,' she gushed. 'Nobody looks underneath it.'

Belle climbed into her car and tapped the postcode into the satnav as Mrs Fro went on her way. She waited for her to get to the end of the street and turn the corner so at least she knew the old lady made it safely one way, and then she reversed a little, went forward a tad, reversed a bit more, and then finally pulled out of the compact parking space in the side street and set off on her way to Little Woodville. She stopped off at the petrol station, filled up the tank and took off her jumper, which was necessary outside in the elements but not needed in the confines of her little car.

As she wound her way from home towards the main roads Belle swapped Heart radio station for a playlist on her iPhone. Driving songs blared out, with Prince, a bit of Bruce Springsteen, some Tracy Chapman and plenty of U2, and she sang her way out of the city in the direction of the Cotswolds. As she drove she thought about Christmases past, not that there were many to remember. She had a handful of memories from Snowdrop Cottage with her gran. She remembered collecting big armfuls of firewood to bring inside and stock the basket in the lounge, she remembered snuggling down beneath a crocheted blanket her gran had made for her in all the colours of the rainbow, she remembered late-night cocoa and cuddles, and she remembered the first Christmas they'd had without her, when Belle's mum had blithely announced that Christmas from now on was going to be different.

And she was right. Christmas had never been the same again.

Belle indicated to come off at a roundabout and followed the next part of the main road, winding into unfamiliar territory, travelling to the unknown, and by the time she approached Little Woodville, with a sign announcing the reduced speed limit and a request to please drive carefully, she felt as though she knew what she was doing. She was here to lay her past to rest once and for all. She was here to say goodbye to Little Woodville and Snowdrop Cottage, sell up, and move on to the next stage of her life.

Chapter Two

According to the satnav she would be arriving at her destination in four minutes, and Belle felt an unfamiliar fluttering in her tummy. It couldn't possibly be nerves – she had nothing to feel nervous about. But there was something going on inside her body that unsettled her.

She drove past a boarded-up shop that looked as though it had once been a photography studio, past a bank housed in a beautiful old building on the narrow high street, past a cobbled street to the side and then a dinky post office. She smiled. She was used to the city, big shops, banks, and food outlets open at all hours, but already she got the feeling that things worked a little differently out here in Little Woodville.

The satnav told her to turn left and she followed a narrow road with a hump in the middle that took her over a small bridge. The walls of it were high enough that she couldn't make out what was on either side; she just knew this was a tiny road and she needed to look ahead and keep her wits about her. Belle pulled into a lay-by to let another car pass and then trundled on her way. On either side of the road were quaint houses – some large, some smaller, plenty chocolate-box like – and she wasn't sure whether it was her memories or her imagination, but she could already envisage what the village would look like covered in snow. Sam had always hankered after a white Christmas, even going to the bookies to join in with the fun at betting whether or not they'd get one, but it had never interested Belle. With snow came ice, with ice came danger and gridlock on the roads, and December through to January was a miserable time anyway. All the bad things in Belle's life seemed to happen in December: her grandad Leonard died, her mum took her away from Gran without any explanation, she always succumbed to a cough and cold somewhere along the way, and you couldn't even go to the local for a quiet drink because there was guaranteed to be some idiot in a Santa hat seeking out any woman who'd give him a Christmas kiss.

The satnav was now announcing that in another hundred metres she'd arrive at her destination so Belle turned left at the T-junction and drove slowly along an even narrower road that had now thinned out so much that Belle worried it was in danger of disappearing altogether, when thankfully the cottage came into view.

There it was. Snowdrop Cottage. In all its glory.

Belle gulped. She hadn't expected her mind and body to react quite so strongly, but she felt semi-elated, semi-numb. She was confused, happy and sad at everything this cottage represented in her life, at everything she'd lost along the way.

It had been more than twenty years since she'd been here but the front of the cottage was exactly as she remembered. Detached, with a thatched roof crafted from dry vegetation, the cottage was an enduring symbol of Little Woodville and felt magical in its presence. The front door was painted periwinkle blue but had faded over the years. The window frames surrounding sash windows with six panes of glass at the top and another six at the bottom were painted a bright white and looked as if they'd been touched up recently. Ivy crept up the front of the stone house, trees punctuated the lawn, with wide, curved flowerbeds on the generous allotment and boxed hedges to either side.

Belle slowly pulled up on the gravelled driveway at the front of the cottage and parked to the side where it looked as though there were previous tracks from a car, probably belonging to the man who rented the place. She'd never been told much about Sebastian but she'd often wondered who he was to her gran. Was he a friend? A man she'd had a relationship with? It was hard to ever think of Gran with another man besides her grandad, although she supposed everyone had the right to move on.

Belle immediately shivered when she climbed out of the car. With the heating on it'd been easy to forget the biting winds of December, especially as the frost and ice had cleared along the way on the main roads and the sun had come out briefly. She reached in and grabbed her roll-neck jumper, pulled it over her head and picked up her bag. The suitcase could wait in the boot and she'd check in at the bed and breakfast later.

She crunched her way across the drive. The boxed hedges had a gap in the middle with a low gate painted the same periwinkle blue as the front door and Belle wondered whether the flowerbeds out front would have snowdrops come spring. As she pushed open the gate her fingers touched the little white plaque that said 'Snowdrop Cottage' in curly writing, faded over the years. Perhaps she'd have it repainted for the sale to enhance this place that was almost a part of the fabric of the English countryside.

As she walked up the path she admired the thatch that hung over the upper windows and the porch like a winter hat protecting the cottage from the change in season. She tapped the iron knocker on the door gently enough for an old home like this but when there was no answer she rapped a little harder, then harder still when the tenant still didn't come to the door. If he was elderly he may not have heard, or it may take him a while to shuffle to the front of the cottage.

'I told him twelve o'clock sharp,' she mumbled to herself. She checked her watch and sure enough both hands were pointing directly upwards. She'd judged the traffic and the distance well, had planned to be a little early, but managed to arrive on the dot.

When there was no answer again after a fourth try, and a fifth, Belle went around to the side of the cottage. On the left there was a bench against the wall, then a gate that was all locked up, and on the other side of the cottage she had similar luck. She supposed at least it was secure but she couldn't wait to see out the back. She knew there was a lot of land that came with Snowdrop Cottage and she could vaguely remember Gran picking onions and pulling carrots from the ground in an enormous veggie patch. She wondered if the patch was still there or whether the tenant had neglected it completely and it was either gone or nothing but a pile of tangled weeds.

Belle sat on the bench for a while looking out over undulating fields beyond the side of the cottage. They still glistened with morning dew that hadn't dried enough in the chill of the day, but after twenty minutes she gave up waiting for Sebastian and was about to call him when her phone pinged. It was from an unrecognised number and was a brief message apologising for the delay and asking if she could reschedule for two o'clock.

Deciding it was best not to get the tenant offside this early on, Belle texted to say that was fine. She'd explore the area first and then check in at the bed and breakfast. She'd be here until Christmas Eve so she had plenty of time to get things on track. And she couldn't be too hard on an elderly man – he could be at the doctor's or at church, or simply have lost track of the time.

Belle drove the same way back, winding along the lane, over the bridge and onto the high street, quaint in its dimensions. She turned left this time, drove all the way to the end of the street and found a small car park. After parking, she bundled herself up in her straight black collarless coat with side-zip fastening, pulled on a claret woollen hat and wrapped a matching scarf around her neck, the scent of laundry detergent bringing with it a freshness beneath the winter sun. Anthony had given her the hat last week, a designer brand she kept forgetting the name of, and it was her first woolly hat since she was a little girl. In the winter he always nagged her to wear one and she flatly refused, saying she'd rather be cold, because it would mess up her hair, but she had to admit it was a lifesaver when the temperatures plummeted.

Belle was still getting used to not having to push her hair behind her ears before she put a hat on. For years she'd had the same thick, luscious, shiny hair the colour of black onyx, and she'd never dared to stray from the usual minimal trim and blow-dry she always went for at the same hairdresser she'd gone to for the entire time she'd been in her flat. But ten days ago she'd gone with Sam, a girl who loved nothing more than to change the style and colour of her hair each time she visited the salon, and somehow she'd ended up being talked into making a change. OK, so it wasn't much of a step outside the norm, just a few inches off the length and a straight fringe put in to frame her face, but Belle had walked out onto the high street feeling as though she was walking on air. And the fringe meant the hat went on now without much of a fuss at all.

Belle kept a look out for icy patches but the weather seemed kinder down here in the Cotswolds and the ground looked clear. She made her way from the car park to the end of the high street, noticing the village already had its Christmas decorations up. She guessed she hadn't looked up on her way through the other end of the high street and had turned off towards Snowdrop Cottage before the main part came into view. But now she could see the faint illuminated presents, bells, a Santa, reindeer, dolls and toy cars, which would surely brighten up the sky the second darkness fell over the village. The lights were strung from one side to the other and as she rounded the bend she saw the village Christmas tree, towering above the few shops that stood in front, bedecked with white lights and sparkling over shoppers bustling here and there. She wondered how she could've missed it on her approach to Little Woodville and realised she must've been so apprehensive about seeing the cottage again that nothing else had been able to penetrate her thoughts.

But king of the high street and never to be outdone by anything as mundane as a Christmas display was the bakery she came to. Small in dimensions but powerful in its presence, it oozed warmth, literally, from the front door. The waft of wholesome goodness and cinnamon carried on the air, enticing Belle as well as anyone else in the vicinity. She peered in the double-fronted shop. Lined up in a row were glazed doughnuts shining like coloured disco lights, sugar sparkled like snow on top of jam doughnuts, gingerbread men smiled at her from the tray where they lay obediently in rows, cookies of all flavours filled another part of the other window, and baguettes, wholemeal, white and grainy, stood to attention in a basket just inside the shop.

Past the doorway with its small step was the second window display and Belle was mesmerised by cleverly designed Christmas cakes. There was a layered cake with three tiers: Father Christmas, a snowman, and a Rudolph face on top. There was another cake standing tall like a candle with white icing dripping down the red fondant wick, another of a snowman's face with a marzipan-sculpted nose and piped eyes and mouth. And then there were yule logs in light and dark chocolate and Belle imagined biting into them so that the filling dribbled out.

Belle's tummy rumbled as if on cue and she knew it would keep doing so over and over if she didn't at least grab something now. She doubted there would be any cooking facilities at her accommodation. She would've preferred self-catering for her stay, if only to indulge in her love of cooking, but the bed and breakfast had been the best option and central to where she needed to be.

She ventured inside, passing between the toy soldiers standing tall on either side of the doorway, and found Cornish pasties and sausage rolls at the back of the bakery in the warming cabinet. She grabbed a traditional pasty filled with ingredients of steak, potato and onion, and as she waited behind a tall man in the queue she scanned the selection of drinks.

'On the house,' the jolly woman behind the counter told the customer in front of Belle. He tried to argue but the woman, hands plonked on her hips, shook her head firmly. 'You came to the rescue; my very own hero. Christmas wouldn't have been the same without the boys.'

Belle wondered who the boys were. Perhaps they were his sons? Perhaps they were this woman's grandkids and the family had fallen out, just as hers had done a long time ago.

She shook away her concern at someone who wasn't a part of her life and as the man bid goodbye to the woman Belle moved up to pay for her pasty, but not before the man took a step back and landed on her foot.

She drew in her breath waiting to say 'it's OK, don't worry, I'm fine, don't mind the expensive boots you've put a nice dirty footprint on' but she didn't have the chance because the man didn't turn round and apologise, he simply left. Was she invisible here in Little Woodville?

'Are you OK? He's twice you're size,' the woman said kindly.

'I'm fine,' said Belle.

'Just the pasty?' the woman prompted, as Belle flexed her toes and checked her boot wasn't marked.

Belle put the pasty on the counter. 'I'll take an orange juice as well, please.'

'Large or small?'

'Just the small please.'

The woman took the bottle from the shelf and put it on the counter, rung up both purchases and told Belle the amount. 'I haven't seen you around these parts before.'

Belle smiled. So she wasn't invisible. 'I haven't been here for a very long time.'

Without another customer in the shop, the woman seemed to sense the opportunity to delve further. 'What brings you here now?'

'I've come to look at a house.'

'I didn't know anything was for sale in the village.' She dusted floury hands across her apron and leaned forwards, ready for a good chinwag.

'There isn't, but my grandmother once owned a house here and left it to me when she moved away.'

At that the woman straightened. 'You're Gillian's granddaughter.'

It was weird hearing her grandmother referred to by her Christian name. Grandparents having names of their own is a strange concept to grandchildren, who tend only ever to know them as Gran, Grandad, Grandpa, Nanny, or whatever name has started in childhood and carried through into their own adult years.

'Yes, that's right.'

'Then in that case...' The woman straightened more and lifted her head as though something had got right under her nose. '...I'm glad Sebastian stood on your toe. I hope it hurt.'

Still shell-shocked but glad she'd got some food before the woman had more or less told her with a glare to get out of the bakery, Belle scurried out of the door and into the icy air. What had at first seemed a quaint start to the experience of Little Woodville hadn't ended up going quite the way she'd expected, and if everyone around here gave her the same frosty reception it would be a pretty cold December this year.

Belle guessed the Sebastian who stood on her toe must be the same Sebastian who was renting her cottage because the village wasn't that big, and it wasn't a common name either. And not only had he not shown at the allotted meeting time but he was far from an elderly or infirm tenant who needed to be given any kind of leeway to keep an appointment.

She walked on, anxious to clear her head. She passed a small clothing boutique and watched as the owner, or someone who worked there, added touches of the festive season by spraying the corners of the mullioned windows with white powder as though snow had just fallen. A charity shop next to the boutique had an artificial tree hung with multicoloured baubles standing tall and proud, and there was one of those reindeer made out of bendy twigs and sparkling with lights along its back as it looked out across the street. When she reached the enormous Christmas tree Belle realised it was actually standing on the village green. She couldn't remember this area from her childhood, but maybe it had faded into her memories like so many other things.

She stared up at the tree, impressive in stature. It wasn't often she was wowed by a festive display but here, in a village of what she'd assumed was such simplicity, it stood out as truly magical. The green was sloped and the tree was at the top, looking over the rest of the village, with a pub on the opposite side. Wandering over, Belle found a bench at the edge of the grass and sat there, bundled up warm and with the heat of the Cornish pasty working to stop her from feeling the winter chill at all.

As she ate, Belle looked out over Little Woodville. The pasty, despite the bakery owner's disapproval at Belle, was one of the best she'd tasted and she finished it in no time along with the orange juice, which thankfully wasn't chilled. Her thoughts drifted to Sebastian, a much younger tenant than she'd expected. When the solicitor had spoken about the tenant her Gran wanted to let the property to, Belle had expected another elderly person. Old people tended to befriend old people, and young people tended to befriend those of a similar age. But given the man's rear view, he was very much still in his prime. He'd been wearing a deep blue donkey jacket and dark hair had curled onto the back collar as though it needed a trim, wide shoulders took charge and whether his height or his build had done it, his heavy work boots had trodden on her toe without him even realising, as though she was nothing more than a clump of dirt he may have stepped on outside.

Belle noticed several people passing by carrying fawn-coloured takeaway cups with white plastic lids and an instant craving for a hot chocolate ran through her. Sebastian had suggested two o'clock as their alternative meeting time but after realising he couldn't be much older than her, she thought she'd let him wait for a change and carried on investigating the village in search of the café that had to be here somewhere.

She turned left from the village green and there it was, a little café nestled between a cobbled alleyway and a beautiful red chestnut tree that must have shielded it from view when she approached from the opposite direction this morning. The tree had white twinkly lights threaded through it from bottom to top and as much as she wasn't a big lover of the actual event of Christmas itself, Belle would be the first to admit this village was beautiful in the way it had been decorated for the approaching festive season. It was nothing like some of the tacky window displays on her street back home, or the over-the-top approach in the corner shop that, every year, overdosed on tinsel and garish coloured lights in the window.

She stepped over the threshold of the café, which was busier than the other shops she'd passed, but it didn't take long for Belle to be served. Armed with a takeaway hot chocolate, she went back onto the high street, crossed over and followed the narrow pavement, along the road she driven up earlier, towards the bridge. She paused when she reached the top of the hump. It was built of Cotswold stone and she imagined people perching on it in the summer as they ate ice-creams or sipped from chilled bottles of water, but now she rested against it as she sipped the warm chocolatey liquid from the plastic spout. She looked around. Many of the houses in sight and indeed many of the buildings on the high street were in the same honey-coloured village stone typical of the Cotswold area. Others were white half-timbered structures and just as much a part of the country village feel.

She looked down to the water. It was more of a stream than a river that ran beneath the bridge, shallow enough that you could see the odd rock popping up from beneath the surface.

She gulped and burned the back of her throat, because standing in this exact place she remembered something else about her gran. They'd played Pooh Sticks! Her gran had read a Winnie the Pooh book to her every night when she'd stayed at the cottage as a little girl and as soon as they'd read about the game, Belle had insisted they play it. Her gran had thought she was mad, but as with most other things in her childhood, Belle couldn't remember her ever saying no to her granddaughter. So why had everything changed so suddenly? Belle felt as though she'd been dropped like a pooh stick from the top of a bridge and the current hadn't carried her out the other side at all, but right under, and the special relationship she'd once shared with her gran had never surfaced again.

Belle stood at the top of the bridge and drank her hot chocolate. The wind was colder here, it being exposed and away from the sheltering walls of the high street, so she pulled her hat down over her ears some more, her dark hair loose as it usually was and giving her that extra bit of warmth, and when she eventually finished her drink she walked the other side of the bridge, found a bin and dropped the cup into it.

On the way back over the bridge, heading towards the high street and then the car park, she stopped, because there were two sticks in her path. She bent down and picked them up and, looking around her as though she could be in trouble if anyone saw what she was doing, she made her way to the top of the bridge and leaned against the stone. The water sounded content enough to flow before it got so cold it froze over and she checked there wasn't a single car in sight. She could do it. Drop the sticks, see if one or either of them came out the other side.

She reached over and dropped the sticks into the water. She grinned and spun round, darted across the road and hung over the other wall on the opposite side, and sure enough, a moment later, there came one followed by the other stick. She'd done it!

'You're playing Pooh Sticks.' A voice came from down below next to the water and a man looked up at her. Roughly in his sixties, he had on an old-fashioned tweed cap and a beagle stood obediently at his side on the thin path adjacent to the stream.

'I was, yes,' she admitted to the stranger.

'I've played it with my grandkids many a time. Not too much traffic around so as long as we're careful it's all good fun.'

She smiled down at him and was about to move away when he said, 'Are you a tourist?'

'Would I be in trouble if I was?' A tourist would probably go down better than her true identity, given the reaction it had fuelled in the bakery.

'No, no.' He laughed heartily. 'People say they don't like tourists, that we want the village to stay as it is, but we need visitors to buy things from our shops, visit our pub so it doesn't close down through lack of business, use the post office so we don't lose that and have to traipse all the way to the next town.'

'If it helps, I've been to the bakery and the café, so there's a bit of money spent.'

The beagle carried on sniffing around on the ground beside the stream and the man raised his hand to his eyes as if trying to see Belle a bit better. 'Are you Gillian's granddaughter?'

Her heart sank. 'Yes, I am.' Wait for it, wait for the abuse – although why it had happened she still didn't understand.

'I'm Peter, Betty's husband. And Betty is the lady you met in the bakery. Good news travels fast.' He smiled and Belle hoped it was kindly.

'Oh.'

'Come on, love, don't let her get to you. She's just protective of her friends and folk around here, but she shouldn't have been so rude. I was out back at the time and heard what she said. Don't worry, she'll settle down. Are you staying long?'

Grateful for his friendliness and his advice, she spoke up. 'A few weeks.'

He didn't ask why but tipped his hat and went on his way with the beagle following at his heels. She wanted to call after him and ask whether he thought Sebastian had known who she was and stomped on her toe on purpose, but she suspected she still had his reaction to come because he didn't seem to have noticed she was even there in the bakery.

Belle collected her car and went on to the bed and breakfast surrounded by a white picket fence with a church just up the road and a doctor's surgery opposite. There was space in the car park, although it was a bit of a squeeze, but after she'd checked in and was being shown to her room, the owner told her there were only six guest rooms anyway so the car park wouldn't get any busier than it already was. Belle didn't elaborate on why she was in Little Woodville and the owner had to answer the phone before he'd had a chance to broach the subject so Belle escaped outside once again and made her way back to Snowdrop Cottage.

As she drove she thought about Betty's reaction that day. She hoped the woman wasn't representative of other people around here because the thought of receiving that kind of welcome every time she said hello to someone new over the next few weeks was enough to put a chill through her body that would turn her into Jack Frost. Then again, Peter had been pleasant enough, so perhaps she was being paranoid. Still, she'd try to keep a low profile and not get chatting to anyone else at length if she could help it. She was here to look at the cottage, assess what work, if any, would need doing and clear out any of her gran's junk that she could box up and send to the care home or throw away. Her memories aside, already she was beginning to come around to the idea that selling up would be the best option. At least she wouldn't have to face the wrath of people who knew her gran better than she did. And perhaps getting rid of the cottage would put the past to rest and allow her to move on and stop dreaming of unlikely family reunions, the kind of sentimentality that occupied far too much thinking time.

It was almost three o'clock by the time Belle pulled into the driveway of Snowdrop Cottage but this time there was an ice white jeep parked in the space she'd been in before and she pulled up next to it, noticing it was dirtier than at first glance. Why anyone bought a white car was beyond her, especially out here with all the country lanes and no doubt a lot of mud when it rained heavily.

She trudged the gravel path again, opened the little gate and walked towards the cottage. She knocked firmly but after a minute when there was still no answer she rapped a little harder.

The door flung open and there was the man again, the same donkey jacket still on even though he was inside, ducking in the doorway that restricted him from standing up to full height.

Belle extended a hand, businesslike in her approach. 'I'm Belle; we've spoken via email and text. It's nice to finally meet you.'

He, reluctantly she saw, held out his own hand and shook hers so firmly it took her by surprise. 'I'm Sebastian. I suppose you'd better come in.'

He didn't stand back and let her through the door first, he left it open and let her wander in herself and shut the door behind her. It seemed he was just as unwelcoming as Betty, which didn't bode well.

He'd disappeared and she passed by a room on either side, down along a corridor and into the kitchen. She didn't remember much about it from her childhood, at least until she saw the Aga. She remembered some winter nights when she and Gran wouldn't leave the kitchen because it was so cosy. They'd sit and drink hot cocoa made on the original cast iron stove in a small pan that warmed the milk until it was on the brink of getting bubbles but never allowed to pass that stage or it would spoil. Belle could almost taste the cocoa now and the nostalgia took her by surprise. Since she'd been in Little Woodville she'd had more emotions thrown at her than a soppy Valentine's Day card, and it took effort to

33

separate those feelings from business practicalities and her intentions to move forwards.

She looked around the rest of the kitchen. A modern cooker had been added and it pleased Belle to see it had been done so well it was sympathetic to the rest of the room, which retained its charm with wooden cabinetry and the beam that still ran down the centre of the ceiling. It was neat in here too and Belle was glad the cottage had been left in capable hands.

'Sebastian?' She looked round to where the walk-in pantry was, then to the other side of the kitchen, and was about to go back the way she'd come when the back door opened. 'You were outside?' He was incredibly rude to have let her in and then walked off, but she wouldn't point it out. It was best to keep a calm head.

'Sorry, I'd pulled a few things from the veggie patch and I know there's a fox in the area because he gets into the bins all the time. Didn't want him nicking my sprouts too.'

He seemed amused at his tale but Belle wasn't impressed. He had armfuls of vegetables, roots and all, in his arms and didn't look ready to talk business in the slightest.

'I'm Gillian's granddaughter.' She wondered if the name Belle hadn't been enough of a clue for him.

His green eyes danced with something verging on amusement. 'I know who you are.' He dumped the vegetables on the draining board and turned back to her, wiping his dirty hands on an old cloth. At least she hoped it was old and not what he used to dry his plates, because it was filthy. He took off the donkey jacket and went through to the hall without explanation, where he hung it on a hook on the wall.

'I wondered if we might sit down and have a chat.' Belle unzipped her coat, feeling the warmth of the cottage kitchen seep into her already.

'Sure.' He plonked himself down without so much as a 'may I take your coat?, can I offer you a cup of tea?', or, 'how was your long journey?', but she supposed she wasn't here to give him good news so it was probably better that he wasn't being nice to her.

Belle shrugged off her coat and hung it a couple of hooks away from his in case mud transferred from one to the other. She took her jumper off too and adjusted her black fitted top with a neckline lower than she'd like when she was conducting business. For some reason she'd expected the cottage to be cold and a lot less welcoming than it felt right now.

'So what can I do for you, Miss Nightingale?' He clasped his big hands in front of him along the smooth wood of the table in the centre of the room.

She sat opposite. 'It's Belle, please.'

'Belle. OK, Belle, what can I do for you? I understand you want to look around at the place, maybe clear out some of Gillian's – your grandmother's – things.'

Again, hearing her first name on anyone's lips sounded odd. To Belle she was Gran, to her mum she was Mum. 'I do want to have a clear-out and her instructions were to do as I see fit, so forward things I think she may still want, get rid of anything else.'

'Well that sounds very formal.'

'Does it?' Her eyebrows knitted together beneath her fringe. She was still taken aback by this man who was half the age of the tenant she'd expected, and his lack of preparedness to discuss the cottage niggled her.

'You'll find most of her things in her bedroom upstairs. There's a fair bit in there; it may take a while.'

'I'm here until Christmas Eve.' If he thought she was only going to be here for one afternoon he was sorely mistaken. 'I know you're the tenant, but it would be great if you could allow me to spend some time in the cottage.'

He shrugged, his hands still in the same position. Even with him sitting down she could tell how much taller he was than her. She was only a few inches over five foot and the family's petite build had stopped with her mum so Belle had the curves that Sam told her matched her voluptuous personality. With full lips, often coloured with a deep pink lip gloss, Belle was frequently asked if she was Italian, a claim that she dismissed and laughed at as she pointed out her roots only reached the exotic terrain of the London borough of Lambeth, where both her parents came from.

Sebastian was studying her but still hadn't spoken and Belle wished she did have a cup of tea, a biscuit, or something, to fiddle with.

'How long do you need to be here today?' He looked at his watch. 'I have dinner guests coming at six o'clock.'

'I'll be finished before then. Do you know why Gran didn't sort everything out before she went into the care home?'

'She's *your* gran.'

She'd clearly hit a nerve. 'She is, but we don't…we're not in touch, put it that way.'

He harrumphed, stood up and went over to the vegetables.

The conversation was far from over. 'Sebastian, I'm afraid I've come to give you notice too.' There, she may

36

as well come right out with it. 'I know you've been here for a while but the time is right for me to sell the place, so as well as having a clear-out, I need to estimate a value, get a local real-estate agent in perhaps, seeing as I don't know the area, look at what work may need doing, perhaps even get organised for painting some of the rooms.'

He turned from where he was ripping the heads off some kind of root vegetable. 'I see.' It was all he said before he turned back again.

Belle watched him organise the ingredients, prepare them for the next step. Cooking was her favourite thing to do and even though Anthony claimed she was always trying to feed him up she always felt pushed for time, like she didn't spend enough time doing the one thing she really loved.

'Sebastian.' She wanted him to turn round so they could have a proper conversation but it seemed the only way she would be addressing him now was by talking to his back. 'Sebastian, I'd like to give you the opportunity to buy Snowdrop Cottage if that's what you'd like.'

She expected him to smile and say great, thanks so much. She envisioned him making a cup of tea and talking value, contracts, dates, completion. What she hadn't expected was for him to rest the tip of a knife against the chopping board, hold the other end with his palm flat against it and turn to her with a look in his eye that intimated he knew a lot more about her than even she did. 'You've got a nerve.'

'And what's that supposed to mean?'

'Coming in here, making demands.'

'It's my house!' Incredulous, she added, 'And I know there's no tenancy agreement, although why anyone with any nous would live in a property without one is beyond me.'

'So not only are you going to make me homeless, and you've treated your gran like crap over the last decade or two, but you're also calling me stupid.' He didn't look at her much longer. He lopped the ends off another vegetable and then picked up a small, square scrubbing brush and beneath a running tap briskly rubbed it across the skins to rid them of the soil still clinging on for dear life.

'I think you're overreacting.'

'Am I?' he demanded.

'Yes, you are. I've every right, as the owner, to give you notice. And I'm not unreasonable – I'll give you six weeks when it's normally four, which you'd know if you'd had a document drawn up, and I'm offering you first refusal on the cottage. I can't be fairer than that. Don't you want this place? Don't you want to make it yours permanently?'

'Maybe not all of us have a little nest egg tucked away that will enable us to buy a house just like that.' He clicked his fingers for emphasis. When he turned back to the sink she knew he was taking his distaste out on the vegetables because the tension was visible in his shoulders, in the muscles beneath his T-shirt that bulged every time his arm moved back and forth. 'Now if you don't mind, I need to get on with things. As I've said, I have guests coming over for dinner.'

She wanted to get going on the bedroom but perhaps Sebastian needed time to process all of this, and she didn't want to make this hard for anyone. So she decided to leave him to it. She was tired after the drive anyway. 'I'll come back tomorrow,' she said softly.

He didn't turn round. 'I'll give you a key.'

'That's not necessary, it's your place.'

He turned then but he didn't smile. 'As you said, it's *your* place to do with what you like.'

'I didn't mean to sound such a cow when I said that.' He seemed amused at her personal description. 'It's just been a long day and I'm keen to get organised.'

'And you're sure you want to sell?' It was the first time his voice lost its hard edge.

She didn't answer outright and instead threw a question back his way. 'Are you sure you don't want to buy?'

'I'm not in a position to do so unfortunately.'

She held his gaze a moment longer and then went to get her coat. She shrugged it on and ran a hand around the collar to tug her hair out from beneath. She zipped it up to the top as she went back into the kitchen. 'I'll come over tomorrow about ten o'clock if that suits.'

He nodded. 'Fine by me, I'll make sure I'm here. Sorry about being so late today.'

'Not a problem.'

'You got me back though. I rushed to be here at the new time we'd agreed and you were an hour late, which was why I had to get going with dinner.'

Sheepishly, she smiled at him. 'I was looking around the village.' He didn't need to know part of her had wanted to pay him back and make him wait too. 'I went to the bakery by the way.'

'You did?' He seemed surprised. He obviously hadn't seen her. 'I was there myself, hence why I was late. Betty needed some help with the boys this year – Jack needed his nose fixing after some idiot broke it last year when they stumbled into the bakery after too much mulled wine and Daniel needed a bit of wood fixed to his butt or he'd look very odd indeed.'

39

That was what was odd? 'I'm sorry, who are Jack and Daniel? Are they Betty's grandchildren?'

A symmetrical grin crossed his face and creases on either side of his mouth deepened the more he smiled. 'Oh, I could have fun with this.'

'Fun with what?'

'Jack and Daniel are the three-foot-high toy soldiers Betty puts out on display in the porch of the bakery every Christmas. They're kind of an icon around here, and they looked a bit of a state. Her husband was supposed to sort them out at the end of last year but had completely forgotten, so when I popped in she commandeered my services and I ended up mending them for her there and then. That's why I was late.'

'Wait a minute…Jack and Daniel?' Her eyebrows arched.

'Yes, after the whiskey.'

'Don't tell me, Peter's favourite tipple.'

He leaned in a little as though this was a big secret. 'Actually it's Betty's.'

'I was there you know.'

'Where?'

'In the bakery at the same time as you were. Betty wouldn't take your money for your order and told you it was on the house.'

'Where were you?'

'Behind you.' She took a deep breath and shook her head.

'You're pretty short – didn't see you.'

Only coming up to his mid-chest, she wasn't surprised. 'You stood on my foot.'

He looked down at her boots. 'You seem fine now.'

'Do you make a habit of going round stepping on people who are smaller than you?'

40

Eyes wide, he looked about to make a comeback when there was a knock at the door. 'Let me show you out.' She doubted he'd have been so polite if a visitor hadn't just arrived.

Belle reached for the door handle at the same time as his outstretched hand reached past her to open it. His flesh landed on top of hers and for a moment he had hold of her hand. She laughed nervously. 'Sorry, after you, it's your door.'

He moved in front of her to do the honours but before he pulled it open he momentarily held her gaze with green eyes that didn't look quite as defensive as they had earlier. 'She's doing well, by the way.'

'Who is?' Standing so close to him in the compact cottage hallway, she could see the shadow on his jaw that depicted the pattern a beard would grow in if he gave it permission.

'Your gran.'

His words cut through her. She was doing her best to separate Snowdrop Cottage from its family link. She kept trying to tell herself it was just another property, part of a business deal, a ticket to future dreams, but being here in Little Woodville had had a surprising effect on her already and, coupled with Sebastian's obvious closeness to her gran, she wasn't sure how to react.

'Thank you for telling me,' she said, and when he realised he wasn't going to get anything more out of her he opened the door.

She stepped out, down the little step and past three faces she smiled at before scurrying away in case they should ask Betty-like questions.

The sky was already overcast and the clouds a very deep grey with only a hint of the sun's orange glow that had hung around bravely today. All she wanted now was to fall asleep in the pink-and-cream bedroom in the bed and breakfast, get a good night's sleep, and anything else she would tackle tomorrow. She unlocked the car and jumped in. She raised a hand in greeting at another guest, who walked past the car and opened the gate to go down the path, and she wondered who these people were. They were all older than her and not the sort of people she'd expect someone like Sebastian to be friends with. He hadn't exactly been hit with the ugly stick and she contemplated whether to hang around to see if a younger crowd arrived, perhaps women tottering in heels. But as she pulled out of the driveway and onto the lane she suspected she had nothing to worry about with the cottage because the crowd who'd arrived so far were unlikely to make any kind of ruckus.

She drove along the lane, took the bridge across the stream, and when she turned into the high street the lights glistened with colours that reflected off shop windows and gave a glow to nearby stone buildings. The whole village sparkled and Belle was beginning to realise how far removed she was from her normal city life here in Little Woodville. She hoped the next three and a bit weeks wouldn't be quite as exhausting as today had been, and that Sebastian would be more friendly as she got things done.

Or maybe she was asking for the impossible Christmas wish to be granted.

Chapter Three

Belle reached the high street and instead of turning left for the bed and breakfast, she went right and to the pizza place she'd seen on approach to the village. She hoped she could try to eat reasonably well during the next few weeks, even though she wouldn't be let loose in a kitchen, but the options were few and far between. There was pizza, a meal at the pub, something from the bakery – although she doubted she'd brave that again, given Betty's reluctance at her presence – and other than that there was a big Sainsbury's supermarket a ten-minute drive away but, again, she didn't have much choice with ready meals.

Anthony called as she was waiting for her pizza and, glad of the excuse to avoid chit-chat with the man behind the counter when she was the only one in there tonight, Belle nattered away to her boyfriend.

'What did you order?' He was walking home from work and she could hear street sounds in the background – the odd beep of a horn, traffic rushing past, voices chattering their way through the city. It was different in Little Woodville, with most people tucked away in their homes already, not many out on the high street, and certainly not many waiting for pizza. She hoped it didn't mean the pizza would be dire and she'd wish she'd gone hungry instead.

'Hawaiian, as always.'

'With extra pineapple?'

'You know me too well.' Usually Belle made pizza at home, the base perfectly golden, the topping not sparse with any ingredient.

The bleep of pedestrian lights sounded. 'How did it go with the tenant?'

'I told him I was giving notice.'

'He knows you're selling?'

'Yep. I offered him first refusal.'

'That would be ideal. It'd save on advertising costs, getting repairs done. What did he say?'

'It's not an option unfortunately.'

'That's a shame. Maybe his pension wouldn't cover it,' Anthony went on. 'I suppose if you haven't bought by the time you're a pensioner, you're not likely to.'

Belle opened her mouth to explain that Sebastian wasn't exactly using a bus pass just yet but she shut it again. She'd only be here a few weeks and Anthony wasn't coming to Little Woodville, so there really seemed little need to fill him in on the tiny details.

'Is there much work to be done?'

'I haven't looked around too much yet. There was some confusion with the meeting time so it was getting dark and after I'd spoken with Sebastian I left him to it. I'll go back tomorrow though.'

'It's a great little cottage. It'll fetch a tidy sum.'

'I know it will.'

'Then we'll be on our way, Belle. You and me, our own business. You'll be your own boss – imagine that!'

She smiled. Anthony had always been ambitious and he liked to take the lead. A city boy through and through, he knew what he wanted and Belle had been swept along with his drive and commitment. Anthony put in super-long hours with work and Belle had got into the habit of doing the same. It was how she'd moved up the ranks so quickly and at first she'd really appreciated the unintentional encouragement, but now and then she grew weary of it. It had taken a while to get her head around the idea of committing to a new venture together without relying on employment within a company. Occasionally,

44

if she thought too hard about it, the responsibility was daunting, but she'd soon realised the change would bring with it a lot of perks. It'd taken some convincing to get Anthony to commit to a week away over the Christmas break, even though real estate fell into the same business coma as everything else over the festive period, and sometimes Belle worried how it would be when they were in business together. Sam had told her it would either make or break them, and even though she'd laughed at the time, Belle couldn't help thinking her friend was right.

'How is it being back in the village after so many years?' Anthony asked.

'It's…well, it's —'

'You wouldn't remember it at all, I'm sure. And I bet it's changed.'

Actually it hadn't, and Belle was continually surprised at how much she did remember about Little Woodville and her days spent here with Gran. What was strange was having to match past memories to the present, be a part of the world Gran had been in without her. 'I have to go. Pizza's ready.' It wasn't strictly true, the man behind the counter could've been boxing up someone else's order for a delivery, but Belle's rumbling tummy hoped it was hers.

After they'd said their goodbyes Belle thanked the man behind the counter but she didn't make it out the door before he asked, 'Are you Gillian's granddaughter?'

Peter was right, word did travel fast in this village. 'I am, I'm Belle.'

The man lifted part of the counter that doubled as an access point and came over, extended a hand after he'd wiped it on his apron. 'I'm Andre, I own this place.'

Belle balanced the pizza box on the underside of one arm and extended her opposite hand. 'It's nice to meet you.'

'It's a small village; you'll find there isn't much that goes under our radar.'

She wasn't sure how she felt about that. 'Thanks for the pizza.'

'You're welcome. Come in again won't you? It's lovely to meet a member of Gillian's family – we haven't seen anyone else. Next time my wife Nel might be in; she likes a good chat. She's not been well lately though so she doesn't do so many hours.'

'I'm sorry to hear that.'

'Don't be. She's going to be fine – still talking, that's how I know.' When he laughed his portly belly moved and his jolly demeanour made Belle feel grateful that not everyone would be against her here. She'd been unlucky to pick the bakery first, it seemed.

Back at the bed and breakfast Belle took the pizza upstairs and ate in her bedroom, polishing off six slices in quick succession. It wasn't bad, in fact. A little bit soggy towards the middle, but that could be because it had been shoved in a box for transportation.

She put the television on and flicked through the limited number of channels, unused to not having Sky at her fingertips. Her mind wandered to the meal Sebastian was cooking tonight and all the root vegetables he'd plucked from the garden. Maybe if she hadn't announced she was selling the cottage he'd have invited her to stay for something to eat. Then again, maybe he wouldn't. Maybe tonight was an intimate gathering she wasn't a part of.

With nothing on television to hold her attention, she shut the pizza box and took it downstairs to put in the bins outside. She didn't really want to wake up with the smell in her room. Wearing no coat or jumper because it was warm inside, when she opened the front door and went out goose pimples immediately raced up her arms as she scurried over to the bins. She pushed the box in the one for recycling, which was of course the third choice so she'd had to touch two other dirty bin lids before this one, and dashed back inside.

'It's a bit cold out there,' said a voice as she made for the stairs. 'I'm Audrey, you met my husband Gus earlier.' The well-dressed woman who looked to be a bit older than Belle came over from behind the desk and extended a hand. People sure liked to get acquainted in Little Woodville. In the city you could keep yourself to yourself if you wanted to.

'I don't mean to be rude,' said Belle, 'but I've just touched the bins so I need to wash my hands.'

Audrey laughed, held up an arm and extended one finger decisively. 'Wait there.' She trotted back to the desk, reached behind it and brought over some antibacterial handwash. 'There, pop some of that on. I always have it handy.' She flipped the top open and squeezed some into Belle's palm.

Belle rubbed the gel into her skin and then extended a hand. 'It's really nice to meet you.'

'Gus gave you the prettiest room tucked away at the top, seeing as you're here for a few weeks.'

'I appreciate it, thank you.'

She smiled. 'If you ever need it, we have a small kitchen area for guests where you can use the microwave or toaster and there are plates and cutlery at your disposal. All we ask is that you wash everything up, dry and put away afterwards.'

Relieved she wouldn't have to eat takeaway or find restaurants for her entire stay, Belle assured Audrey she would leave everything as she found it.

'You know, Little Woodville is magical at Christmas,' Audrey smiled. 'You've come to the right place.'

'I noticed the decorations lining the high street, they're quite something.' She tried to sound more enthusiastic about the approaching festive season than she really felt.

'Did you see the lights in the trees along the sides of the roads?'

Belle nodded.

'And the toy soldiers at the bakery – a tradition every year.'

Clearly Audrey hadn't got the memo from Betty to give her a hard time, or maybe Audrey had a bit more sense and knew alienating a paying guest wouldn't be so good for business.

'Oh, and when a dusting of snow falls over the green and the houses beyond,' continued Audrey, still caught up in the nostalgia of Christmases past, 'it's magical. Carol singers come out, we have a huge carol concert on the green – oh, you must come!' She patted Belle's arm. 'You simply must!'

'I'm sure I will.' Belle knew she wouldn't be within ten feet of a carol concert so she didn't bother to press for more details. She'd sung carols with her gran when she was little – it had been one of their favourite things. She'd loved 'Silent Night' and they'd laughed hysterically at Gran trying to teach her not to slur her way from the first half of the word Peace to the second. It was nigh on impossible! After her mum took her out of Gran's life, the only time Belle really sang Christmas carols was when she was at school and she'd had no choice in the matter. Now, the thought of singing carols brought tears to her eyes because all it would do was remind her that she didn't really know her gran at all, at least not the person she'd been over the last couple of decades.

'Goodnight, Audrey.' Belle turned to disappear up the stairs, back to her room. 'It was lovely to meet you.'

'Join me for a nightcap if you like.' Audrey's eyes danced, anxious to hold her guest's attention. Her make-up was almost as bright as her red hair, but she had a gentle way about her that Belle took an instant liking to.

Belle felt the lure of someone to talk to, someone to ask more about Little Woodville, perhaps about the gran she knew very little about. That's if Audrey knew Gillian too, just like other people seemed to. She succumbed to temptation. 'That would be lovely, thank you.' She came back down the two stairs she'd already taken and followed Audrey past the front desk into the lounge, the area where breakfast would be served. At the far side of the room was a small bar and an elderly gentleman sat reading his newspaper with a pint in hand.

Belle settled on a vodka and cranberry juice with ice and Audrey ushered her to a table by the wall while she made the drink and grabbed something for herself.

'So where are you from, Belle?' Audrey sipped from her bottle of beer.

Belle recounted her history, or at least part of it. She told Audrey what she did for a job, about the flat she had, Mrs Fro, and she finished by talking about her gran, giving more detail than she'd really intended. It must have been the vodka. 'Ten years ago she put the cottage in my name. I'm still not sure why.'

Audrey nodded and Belle wondered how much of this the woman already knew.

'I haven't been back to this village since I was ten years old,' Belle admitted.

'That's a heck of a long time. And you haven't seen your gran in all that time?'

'I haven't. But then, I'm sure you know that.'

Audrey held up both hands in defence. 'I'm not here to judge, not like some people.'

'Don't tell me, you heard about Betty?'

Audrey sniggered. 'I heard it from Gus, who heard it from Nel from the pizza shop, who heard it from Benjamin, the pub landlord, who was in the bakery at the time of the incident.'

The way she said 'incident' made Belle giggle. 'She wasn't very happy to see me, but she was more than happy Sebastian stood on my foot and I think she hoped it hurt, a lot.'

'Betty's a kind woman, loves the people she's close to, but on her wrong side? Let's just say she can overreact a bit.'

'I wouldn't mind if she actually knew me but I'm a stranger to her.'

'You are, but Gillian isn't.'

Belle was beginning to understand how things worked in Little Woodville. Near a big city, other than Mrs Fro, people just didn't interact in the same way. People moved in and out of areas as quickly as folk here probably changed their linen, or at least it felt that way.

'Tell me about Gillian.' It was the first time Belle had asked the question of anyone. She knew she couldn't mention it to her mum, and by default her dad probably wouldn't give much away either. But this stranger seemed open and content to share.

With a second drink each, Audrey began to talk. 'I'm not sure I can tell you an awful lot. Betty would be a much better person but of course it may take a while for her to open up to you. Gus and I didn't start running this business until nine years ago, when we took over from his parents, and Gillian was very much a part of the community. With our own business we didn't really have time to blow our noses let alone get in with village life, but from what I saw of her, Gillian was a lovely lady. She seemed kind, caring and inclusive. She wasn't the sort of woman who'd ever turn her back on anyone.'

Belle hesitated, but picking up on Audrey's tone, it seemed the woman wasn't deliberately implying that this was exactly what Gran's family had done to her. 'She was always kind. I loved going to her cottage when I was little, especially in the winter. Mum would drop me off and let me have sleepovers all the time. It was a whole big adventure. We'd marvel at the snowdrops every February and it always made me really happy. You know, the miserable time when winter feels like it will never end, and up the flowers spring, with a little bit of hope.'

'They're still beautiful at the cottage,' Audrey told her. 'I've driven past many a time and when they're out in force it's a sight to behold. Sebastian has done a great job at keeping the cottage exactly the way it should be.'

Belle felt a strange sense of relief to know he'd done the right thing. He could've just as easily been one of those tenants who didn't really care about the property they were occupying. 'Gran and I would do a lot of work on the veggie patch too. We had a list in the kitchen of what needed planting and when, and each time I came I'd check the list to make sure we weren't forgetting anything. Then Gran would make delicious meals and I

51

loved knowing a lot of the produce had come from the garden. Gran loved to cook and I think that's where I got my passion from.'

'You like to cook?'

'I love it. I find it really therapeutic, but I'm so busy at work I don't get much of a chance.'

'You seem to be able to remember a lot of things about your gran.'

Belle toyed with her glass. 'I can, but I know my memories are only part of who she is. I'm scared I'll never know the rest.' The vodka was really loosening her tongue.

'Go on,' Audrey encouraged when Belle felt as though she should stop talking.

'Before coming to Little Woodville and seeing the cottage again, I'd decided that this visit would be closure, a chance to move on.'

'Don't tell me, it's not working out that way?'

Belle shook her head. 'No, it's not.'

'Do you have the address of the care home?'

Belle knew the implication this time was that she could easily visit, face her emotions, her gran, deal with everything that had been missing over the years. But it wasn't as easy as that. It already felt like a betrayal to her mum simply by being here, and the cottage felt like a flimsy excuse for spending so much time in the village Belle had ties to from long ago. Part of Belle also feared that if Delia and Gillian had fought and gone this long without contact, maybe the same could happen to Belle and her mum. Delia knew she was coming here, but they hadn't engaged in any further conversation about the cottage, the village, or their family. It was as though her mum wanted to pretend Belle was simply going away for a mini-break, that emotions played no part in any of this.

'I do have the address.' She didn't need to say much else; Audrey seemed to understand.

'I don't know the ins and outs but Gillian clearly loved the village and she used to come back on and off.'

'Does she still visit now even though she's in the care home?' Her heart leapt at the thought of her gran walking the same streets as her.

'As far as I know, she doesn't visit much anymore, but she was well liked and I still hear people mention her and talk about how much she loved the preparations for Christmas. Betty told me once that Gillian organised carollers for the concert, coordinated people to pitch in at a working bee up at the school after storms damaged the play area for the kids. She really was a big part of this community.'

Belle was about to ask who Sebastian was and why he was living in her gran's house when the customer at the bar lifted an empty pint glass and Audrey had to go over and serve.

She was back in no time but Belle didn't ask the question when she sat down again. Instead they got talking about the bed and breakfast, the refurbishment it had gone through recently. 'It needed something to bring it into the twenty-first century,' said Audrey.

'Was it that bad?'

'It was a shocker when we took over, except we couldn't be too scathing about it because Gus's parents had run the place for years without any complaints – at least none that were voiced in the guestbook. We're talking brown, swirly carpets, patterned wallpaper that did nothing to brighten any of the rooms, a kitchen that nobody would want to cook in let alone have anything served from.'

'Is it safe to come to breakfast tomorrow?' Belle teased, sipping from her straw and watching the cranberry liquid go down a level in the glass.

'Cheeky. Come to breakfast…all mod-cons now, clean and with hygiene certificates to prove it.'

'What do you know about Sebastian?' Belle asked, anxious to hold Audrey's attention before another guest came along.

'Your tenant at the cottage? Not a lot. All I know is that he's been a good friend of Gillian's in the whole time I've know either of them, and he's the son of someone who lives outside of the village. I'm afraid I'm not much of a gossip myself, so I can't elaborate much.'

Belle dismissed the apology. 'Don't be sorry. Gossiping always feels like far too much effort for me too.'

'Betty once tried to get me embroiled in some scandal with the previous owner of the photography shop.'

'I noticed it had shut down. What was the scandal?'

'Something to do with nude photography as far as I know. Betty likes to think the owner had a guilty conscience and left but I think it's more a case of wanting to put her premises in a town or perhaps city, where she could drum up more business.'

'I wonder what will go in its place.'

Audrey shrugged. 'No idea, but the shop has been empty for a while. I think if you don't know about Little Woodville you're not likely to look at opening up a business here. It must seem way too quiet for some people, but not me.'

'You wouldn't leave here?'

'I doubt it. Sleepy village is more my style than the big smoke.'

'I've always loved the city with so much going on.'

'I can see the appeal.'

'I can see the appeal here too.' Belle yawned. 'Excuse me. The sleepy village is making me tired.'

Audrey nodded and smiled to the couple who approached the bar. 'Time I got back to work anyway.'

'Thanks for the drinks.' Belle wasn't sure she had the energy to make it up the stairs now. Exhaustion had crept up on her unexpectedly, probably more from the emotions than the activities of the day. 'It was really nice to meet you.'

'And you too.' Audrey swished away an offer to help clear up the empties. 'We'll chat again, and you let me know if you have any more problems from Betty. I want your stay in the village to be a pleasant one, and not just because you're a paying customer.'

Belle checked the time for breakfast and took the two flights up to her room at the very top. Tucked in the eaves, it was a quaint space with an ensuite bathroom, which suited her perfectly, but despite every intention to enjoy a bubble bath in the Victorian tub nestled under part of the sloping roof, Belle cleaned her teeth and used her last ounce of energy to lie on the bed, pull over the sheets and blankets, and fall back into a heavy sleep.

*

Belle woke the next morning in darkness and it felt as though it were the early hours when in fact it was marching on towards seven thirty already, as displayed on the illuminated clock by her bedside. She switched on the silver lamp, reached out and had a few gulps of water from the glass next to the clock and then, emerging in her tartan pyjamas from beneath the selection of covers, she padded over to the window. Although it was dark she could look out of the small, square pane of glass, over the car park and beyond to the high street. She

55

could just about see the very tip of the giant Christmas tree on the village green and it gave her an odd feeling, as though it made her feel centred, like perhaps she knew where she was.

She shivered, feeling the icy chill from outside already as she was standing so close to the glass, which she doubted was double glazed. When she touched the radiator she suspected it had only just come on and would take a while to get nice and toasty. She turned the dial up to max and went straight to the shower in the bathroom. She climbed into the bathtub and pulled the transparent plastic curtain around the edge to shield the floor from splashes. She wasn't sure how long she stood there but it was heavenly as the water fell through her hair, cascaded over her shoulders and warmed her body right through.

When she was dry, she pulled on clothing she wouldn't mind spending the day in if she was going to sort through junk at the cottage. Dressed in a pair of jeans and an old denim shirt, she looked out over the frosty village scene. The sun had come up and the traffic was slowly beginning to populate the high street. She could see a couple of people bobbing up and down in the distance as they walked the curve of the road, another person scurrying past the bed and breakfast, head down against the cold.

Downstairs she smiled at Audrey, who was with Gus, and at full speed ahead the pair were in breakfast mode, taking people's orders and whipping them up as soon as they could, replenishing glasses at the square table atop which sat a toaster and a selection of breads. Belle ordered some bacon, two poached eggs, a side of grilled tomatoes and some mushrooms. She may as well fill up now and then she wouldn't need to venture out of

Snowdrop Cottage until much later. She didn't want to get to the point where she was so desperate for food she had to go to the bakery again. Not that it would come to that – she'd rather eat alone in the pub or grab another pizza than face Betty's wrath again.

By the time she returned to her room to clean her teeth the rain had come and was hammering against the window pane with a deafening crescendo up here in the roof space. It was a comforting sound, not one Belle minded, and filled up with breakfast, ready to face the day, she collected her bag, put on some lip gloss to make her feel more herself, bundled into her coat and, outside, made a dash for the car.

The wind added a different type of chill to the air this morning as icy patches were obliterated with the downpour, and Belle wondered whether they would soon swap the rain for snow. Perhaps she wouldn't mind it so much out here. It was almost like another world, one she should know better than she did.

She blasted the heating up to full in the car and set the windscreen wipers to as fast as they would go before driving slowly out of the car park and along the high street. The Christmas lights above certainly lifted the mood of the dreary day, as much as she didn't appreciate the full sentiment on December 25th. She wondered had she and Gran come and looked at the lights when she was a little girl? Had they wrapped up in coats, hats and scarves and made the trek from the cottage down the lane and across the little bridge? Perhaps the stream might have frozen come Christmas and they would've walked by, looked over the wall and seen water that barely moved rather than racing along with the sticks they'd dropped from a great height.

Belle pulled up at the cottage, elegant in its presentation. That was the word to remember, one to include in the description when they came to advertise it for sale. She sat in her car for a moment, turned in her seat and gazed at the front of the home between droplets of rain that had got so big it was like somebody was sat on top of her car pouring bucketfuls of water down over the windscreen.

The cottage didn't look any less impressive in the rain than it did beneath the winter sun, or summer sun Belle imagined, which was good for a potential sale. Sometimes something as trivial as the weather could clinch the deal – if a couple looked at the place bathed in sunshine and could imagine sitting out in the back garden with a glass of Pimm's come summer it would make a big difference, or perhaps if they saw it covered in snow the potential buyers might imagine a roaring fire and drinking mulled wine come Christmas, or a big family might see themselves taking autumn walks if the leaves fell around the cottage during those particular months.

But Belle knew there was another drawcard for this place. The snowdrops. She'd seen photographs over the years – not many, but just enough to give her an idea – and she knew snowdrops had once covered the front flowerbeds of the house, extended into the back garden and beyond the trees at the foot of the garden. Carpets of snowdrops come February could make the most impressive photographs if the place was to go up for sale around that time.

She took a photo of the cottage with her phone and emailed it to Mrs Fro with the title 'Beautiful whatever the weather'. She'd have to take another in the sunshine and send that on too, and she must remember to buy a postcard and send that. Mrs Fro was more than just a neighbour and Belle wondered if it was her estrangement from Gran that had done it, because she loved having her neighbour in her life.

As she was considering getting out of the car, Sebastian emerged from the front door and he looked grumpy. He hadn't seen her yet either. He had a big black bin liner bunched at the top and he turned up the collar of his donkey jacket, made a run for it to the side of the house, where Belle suspected the bins must be, and only when he came back the other way did he spot her car to the side, tucked next to his jeep.

With her coat covering her hair, she climbed out and made a dash for it. It would be too much to expect for him to grab an umbrella and come over to ensure she stayed dry, but then again, perhaps it was best they stayed formal and weren't too nice to one another. This was business after all, no matter who this man was to her gran.

'You're early.' He called from where he must have been in the kitchen when she stepped inside the house.

She shut the front door and dumped her coat on the carpeted floor while she stayed on the doormat and tugged off her boots. She picked her coat up, hung it on a hook and was about to ask where to put her footwear when he appeared in the kitchen doorway, ducking at the difference in height between it and the ceilings, and said, 'Put your boots on the mat in the utility room off the kitchen. The Aga in the kitchen heats both rooms up well so they'll dry in no time.'

'They're not that wet, I only ran from the car.' But she did as she was told anyway.

'Then they'll be warm when you leave,' he added. 'Here.' He held out a hand with a key dangling from his middle finger.

She hooked it off. 'Are you sure you're happy for me to have a key?'

'No skin off my nose,' he shrugged. 'I'll come and go as usual and this way we don't have to arrange times. I'm not much of a timekeeper to be honest.'

Now why didn't that surprise her?

'Well don't worry, Sebastian, I'll make sure I knock loudly and I won't let myself in unless I know you're not here.'

He seemed amused that she'd addressed him so formally. 'Whatever, just come and go as you need to.'

'Do you mind if I take a quick look around? I need to think about what work will need doing before I put the property up for sale.' She rummaged in her bag she'd put on the floor beneath the coat pegs and pulled out a notepad and pen. She flicked her hair over her shoulder to keep it out of the way.

Sebastian rested an arm on the top of the kitchen doorway and leaned beneath it to watch her. 'You'll find it's in good repair. I doubt there's anything you'll need to do.'

'I'll take a look anyway.' She stood up, surprised at how close they were but taking a step back would be too obvious. 'I'll start with the lounge.' She hooked a thumb over her shoulder in the direction of the aforementioned room.

'Like I said,' – his voice followed her – 'I don't think there's much to be done.'

It was the first time she'd been in the lounge at the front of the house in more than two decades and she didn't really remember it. But the inglenook fireplace took her by surprise because she knew it had once been an open fire. 'What happened here?'

He ducked beneath the central beam and managed to stand tall in another part of the room. 'What do you mean?'

'The fireplace that used to be there.'

'It's a wood burner now.'

'Did you put that in?'

He tutted. 'Yes, I make changes as I see fit and I don't care that it's not even my home.'

'I don't appreciate the sarcasm.'

'Then don't make the accusations.'

'I wasn't accusing you.' She moved closer to inspect the changes. The wood burner looked new but she could tell it had been used. 'How long has it been here?'

'Gillian asked for it to be put in a long time ago, since before I started living here. She hated cleaning the grate come morning and how much work it took to get the fire going, so this was a better option for her.'

Belle thought of her artificial fireplace in her flat and how easy and clean it was to flick on at the touch of a button and off again at will. 'Does it work well?' She didn't need the detail, she didn't want to know how much this stranger knew about a member of her own family when she had no idea, but she did feel bad for jumping to conclusions.

'Very well, very cosy in the winter.' The twinkle in his eye beneath the messy, tufty dark brown hair had her moving on swiftly to look at the windows next.

The window panes were newer than she'd realised and he must have seen her making a note because he said, 'They were put in about twelve years ago. Your gran wanted the security of the double glazing and the retention of heat, but wanted the windows to look authentic to the cottage.'

'Well they fooled me,' Belle admitted. 'I never would've known. Too many people make changes that aren't sympathetic to a property, but this is really impressive.'

'I'm glad it meets with your approval.'

She ignored his comment and looked out of the window before making a few notes about the front of the property. Parking was always a plus, especially when a property was situated on a narrow lane, so that would work well for potential buyers. And the periwinkle colour on the gate and front door were pluses too, adding character to the property. With a good jet wash they'd most likely come up looking newer and brighter, all ready for the photographs and viewings.

Belle had stood in the shower that morning going over and over in her mind the decision to sell the cottage. On the one hand it would get her new business venture with Anthony well on its way, but on the other hand this was her family's past, and sometimes she wished it was part of the present. All she really knew as she'd dressed that morning was that she needed to put much more thought into selling the cottage, and perhaps somewhere along the way she'd really find the answer to what she should do.

'I have structural reports in a folder somewhere in the loft,' said Sebastian. 'Round about the time Gillian had the wood burner installed, she became concerned about some cracks in walls that she'd been measuring over time. A structural engineer came in and assessed the whole place, carried out a fair bit of work, some of which was covered by the insurance company, and I think you'll find the whole cottage is in a really good state of repair.'

Belle made a note of what he'd said. 'It'd be great if you could dig the reports out for me so I can look at everything that was done.'

'Sure.'

As Belle looked around, there certainly weren't any sloping floors threatening a problem with subsidence, which often affected properties of this age, and although there were a few cracks in walls, they weren't particularly wide or long, which was another good sign. There were no bulging walls in this room either, which could indicate movement, and at first glance the upkeep seemed to be of a good standard.

She turned to Sebastian, who was observing her as she worked. She hoped he wasn't going to do the same the entire way round the house, but she was grateful he seemed to be more helpful than yesterday. Perhaps he'd slept on the idea of her selling the place, calmed down at the thought she'd abandoned her gran and had no family values whatsoever. But he probably hadn't stopped to consider that perhaps it was her family values and strength of relationship with her own mum that had prevented her from ever trying to reconcile with her gran. It was something she didn't really discuss with anyone – not even with Sam, when her best friend thought the decision now was clear-cut: raise money for a new business and move on.

'Can I ask if you got rid of any of the snowdrop beds surrounding the property?' The hope they all remained wasn't solely because it would be a good selling point.

'I didn't fancy making it Daffodil Cottage or anything else like that, so yes, I've kept the snowdrops.'

'Snowdrop Cottage sounds way better.' She smiled, happy at his answer, but looked away when their shared joke made her flush. 'Is the garden a lot of upkeep?'

'Maybe for some, but it helps that I enjoy being out there and keeping it shipshape.'

'Is that why Gran wanted you to move in to her house?' She may as well ask the obvious question. 'So you could look after the garden?'

'If you spoke to your gran once in a while, maybe you'd know something about her life. It's not for me to fill in the gaps.' And just like that the easy atmosphere disappeared and was replaced with disapproval as he left her to it.

She should've known. One minute she'd thought how approachable he was being, how mature, the next, he'd gone back to the way he was with her yesterday when she first arrived. But she wasn't going to pull him up on it. He was making it easy enough for her to get on with her business when he could've put up more of a fight.

She busied herself taking more notes and then returned to the hallway for her laser tape measure, a godsend to any real-estate agent. She took the measurements of the lounge before crossing the narrow corridor to the other side of the cottage, where there was a second reception room. She took the measurements there and it wasn't much smaller than the first one she'd measured, and she could instantly tell it would be perfect for a grand dining set. Perhaps a solid-oak plank table to seat eight, with leather or suede chairs. She could imagine a big feast set in the middle of it, place settings with shiny silver cutlery, a family enjoying a traditional meal together.

She blinked. Sentimentality was rearing its ugly head.

Out in the hallway she measured the space, had a better look at the floorboards, which were in a good state, and with Sebastian still in the kitchen she took the steep staircase up to the top floor. The small square landing had three doors, one marked 'Bath' in black cursive writing on a white wooden plaque fastened to a hook with white distressed string, so she took that one first.

The bathroom suite looked to be about ten years old, given the style, which was modern yet not so contemporary that it looked newly done. But the Victorian taps still gleamed, there was no limescale build-up anywhere, and the black and white tiles on the floor were faded somewhat although showed no other signs of wear and tear.

She took her measurements and then called down to Sebastian. 'Would you mind if I went into the bedrooms?'

He appeared at the bottom of the stairs and leaned on the bannister. 'The one farthest from the bathroom is mine, the other is your gran's. I don't go in her room except to air it once in a while and give it a bit of a clean, and the other should be tidy enough for you to inspect. I don't think I've left anything too untoward lying around.'

'Right. Thanks.' He was back to being friendly again and it had her on edge, not knowing what to expect next.

She walked away when he didn't, and dealt with her gran's room first. It was weird to come in here and know she'd slept here for years, many of those since Belle had last seen her. Belle wondered where she herself had slept when she visited as a little girl, because she couldn't quite remember which room it had been in. Perhaps it had been a camp bed in here, or did she have her own space in the room that was now Sebastian's?

The window in the bedroom was shut and after Belle had taken the measurements she ran a hand along the curved iron bedstead in cream that matched the curtains. When she looked at her fingers there was no dust and it gave her a feeling of unease to know that whatever Sebastian was to her gran, he wasn't only a tenant. There was something so much more between them and she wondered if that would be the case if Gran had had her and her mum in her life.

The rain persisted and Belle didn't hear Sebastian come up the stairs until, ducking in the doorway, he said, 'I'm off out.'

'In this weather?' She sat on the bed. It wasn't made up but was instead covered in a plastic dust sheet to protect the mattress.

'I have work to do – can't turn it down because of a little bit of rain.'

'No, I don't suppose you can.' She looked out at the black clouds lurking above. 'Can I ask you something?'

At home with hands above the beam leading into the room, clearly used to ducking his way around the place to negotiate low doorways and other hazards in the cottage, he said, 'go ahead.'

'Isn't it a bit weird having this room but never using it? I mean, it's been years. I don't think she's coming back.' She wasn't sure why she added the last sentence, but she knew as soon as she'd said it that her eyes had welled up at the thought of never seeing her gran again.

Sebastian bristled but then seemed to have a change of heart. Maybe he'd seen her face, the sheen in her eyes. 'I rent this place for cheaper than I could get anywhere else, and I love it here. I love the village, the

66

cottage itself. It's more than just four walls to keep me warm.'

She knew he didn't pay a high rent, but it was easy to have a tenant already there and when the cottage had been transferred into her name Belle had decided that unless he made a nuisance of himself then it was a case of better the devil you know.

'But I do the upkeep,' he added. 'I fixed floorboards in the hallway and had them sanded and polished, all with Gillian's approval,' he said, pre-empting a potential question. 'I maintain the gardens and the veggie patches, which is quite a job, and in return I don't take liberties by intruding in Gillian's space.'

'Do *you* think she'll ever come back?'

His voice softened now. 'I think when she first left she always thought she would, which was why she left things here. She visited for a while, but hasn't done so in a long time.' He didn't need to say it but Belle felt sure he was thinking the reason Gran didn't visit was because the memories would be painful. Maybe that's why she'd signed the cottage over to someone else in the first place.

Belle continued to stare out of the window, her hand resting on the plastic over the mattress. 'I remember the snowdrops.' He didn't say anything. 'I remember in February I'd beg Mum every year to bring me out here so I could see them. I'd never seen so many in one place.'

Silence hovered until he said, 'Make sure you lock up if you leave before I get back.'

By the time she turned round he'd already gone, and she heard the front door shut behind him downstairs.

*

Belle spent the next couple of hours making more notes, taking all the measurements she needed to and inspecting every nook and cranny she could so she had an idea of what the property would be worth and what kind of marketing it would need. She'd learnt a few tricks of the trade over the years and knowing how to present a property was one of her strengths. She'd clear out the few boxes and the coffee table from the second reception room downstairs that didn't look like it was used anyway, and instead she'd put in the dining table and chairs from a furniture-rental company, perhaps with a table arrangement in the middle. She'd have fresh flowers on the mantelpiece in the lounge, maybe on the windowsill in her gran's bedroom too, and she'd have a white lace bedspread with matching pillows and cushions to show off the bed that stood proudly in the middle and fitted in with the feel of the old cottage.

A lot of the clutter would have to go too, something she frequently advised vendors to do, some of them willing, others less so. But it did present the property in the best way. So now, it was time to get to work.

In her gran's bedroom was a double-doored wardrobe without any clothes but with plenty of jumble, from an old pair of threadbare gloves and an odd earring to piles of bills that were years old and could be thrown out. She went to her car beneath the golfing umbrella she'd found perched in the corner of the utility room and brought back with her a roll of black bin bags and three modest-sized empty cardboard boxes she'd had the foresight to bring. Into those she could put anything she found that she didn't want to throw out but wanted to have sent to her gran to make the ultimate decision.

Belle found that she could only open one side of the enormous wardrobe and figured she'd clear that side out first and then try to open the other door from the inside once she could reach. There was something solid in there, perhaps a big wooden box judging by the look of the side of it when she stuck her head in as far as she could, but she carried on with the bit she was able to access first and by the time she'd done that she had to fling open the window she was so hot.

The sound of the rain increased a decibel or two and Belle took a brief breather before ploughing on. She threw out papers, a couple of headscarfs that had gone mouldy, and when she found a battered jewellery box with a drawer at the bottom that refused to open, she lifted up the lid and put the earring and a bracelet she'd found in there. Gran could sort through the items and decide what was what.

Belle giggled when she found a tea cosy. Whatever was it doing in the bedroom? She threw it out and, with one side of the wardrobe complete, went down to the kitchen. She filled a glass of water that she finished in a few thirsty gulps and stole an apple from the fruit bowl that she ate in the kitchen she hadn't even measured or taken notes about yet. She'd replace the apple after she went to the supermarket later but, for now, it was back to that blessed wardrobe. Her hands were filthy, she felt as though her hair was filled with dust, and she'd even had a sneezing fit mid clear-out because she doubted this stuff had seen the light of day in years.

Back upstairs she felt behind the door now that one side of the wardrobe was clear and, with small fingers, she managed to slide them enough to fiddle the catch. 'Hey presto!' She grinned when the other side of the door fell open towards her but when she saw what she'd thought was a wooden box, a nondescript item, she fell to her knees.

Because it wasn't a wooden box. It was a doll's house. And she remembered it vividly.

Chapter Four

When Belle was nine years old, her mum had dropped her at her gran's to see the snowdrops now they were in bloom. Belle remembered it well because it marked the start of cracks beginning to appear in her mum's relationship with her own mother. Or at least it was the time when Belle was old enough to notice anything was amiss.

It had been late February and snowdrops had flanked the cottage, blanketing the ground at the front as well as the back, and Belle had knelt on the wobbly wooden stool by the low window in her gran's bedroom and looked out to the fields beyond, marvelling at the carpet of white petals that appeared in spring or at the end of a relatively mild winter. Her gran had brought hot cocoa upstairs – which was unheard of, because her mum never let her have hot drinks in her bedroom, especially not drinks that could spill and make a nasty brown mess.

'They're beautiful aren't they?' her gran whispered to her, clutching her own mug of cocoa.

Belle hadn't missed the tears in her gran's eyes. 'Why are you sad?'

'Oh piffle, I'm not sad.' But her sniff gave her away. 'I have a surprise for you.'

When Belle jumped off the stool she narrowly missed knocking her half-full cup to the floor but her gran didn't reprimand her. She made her close her eyes and, with some clattering about and a creak of a door opening, Belle squeezed her eyes tightly shut until her gran announced she could open them.

Mouth agape, Belle stared and stared.

'What do you think?' Gran stood next to a doll's house, painted in pale blue and cream, with mullioned windows just like Snowdrop Cottage. 'It was your mum's once upon a time, but she hasn't played with it in many years.'

'It's for me?' Belle ran and wrapped her arms around Gran's legs. 'Really?'

Gran crouched down the best she could now her body was getting older. 'It's for you, but what would you say to keeping it here? I think it'll be nice if you have something to play with when you visit.'

Belle was already opening the tiny doors as gently as she could. Her friend Millie had a doll's house and she always treated it so kindly, handling the dolls as though they were able to feel when she squeezed her fingers around them.

Now, looking at the doll's house, the memories came flooding back to Belle. She remembered her gran presenting her with it, the hours they'd spent playing together that very same day, the time she came after that and the time after that, and the furniture and dolls her gran had added to it each time. Belle remembered the game Gran used to play too. Every time Belle turned up at the house, eventually without her mother even setting foot inside or saying much of a hello, she'd race into the dining room where the doll's house was set up permanently and see what Gran had done. One day she'd positioned all the dolls along the miniature veranda as though they were a welcoming committee for visitors; another time Gran had put the uncle in the bathtub and the auntie on the toilet and it had had Belle in hysterics. And Belle remembered the most perfect Christmas visit, when Gran had found a small Santa Claus and put him face down in the chimney, his red bottom and black boots in the air and the brown sack too, and inside the house was a tiny Christmas tree waiting for presents beneath.

That was the last Christmas Belle had been here, the last time she'd seen or spoken to her gran.

Now, after finding the doll's house, Belle was desperate to escape the stuffy room. Even the breeze from the open window hadn't helped as memories assaulted her from all angles. Downstairs, she grabbed her coat and shrugged it on, pulled the same claret woolly hat over her head, tugged on her boots, and, grateful to find the back-door key on a discrete hook in the kitchen, she let herself out into the garden. Armed with a notepad and thankful the rain had cleared, she moved around the huge outdoor space. The veggie patches had multiplied and instead of the single one she remembered there were five in a row, and even though it was winter they looked busy with greenery sprouting up and hiding whatever vegetables lurked beneath. She wondered whether Sebastian would tell her what was in each of them, whether he used them every day to add colour and nutrition to his meals, whether her gran had done the same once upon a time.

The grass was neatly mowed but sopping wet and Belle took the stepping-stone path past the veggie patches to the border on the left where flowerbeds ran all the way to the end. She could already see a vast expanse of earth at the foot of the green space and wished they were closer to February so she could see the snowdrops rear their heads with Christmas out of the way. She looked back at the cottage and put her emotions aside so she could think in business terms instead. She was glad this place had been assessed by an engineer and had been well looked after by her tenant. All the shrubs and

72

trees were well kept and nothing was overgrown or neglected. She knew that plants often had a mind of their own with older properties and had the tendency to take over, causing no end of structural problems.

The icy blast on the air made it too cold to linger outside for long and Belle went back indoors to haul down the rubbish bags from her gran's room, plus the box containing the few trinkets she'd found, ready to load into the car. There was a local tip not too far away so she'd dump the rubbish there if the bins here were too full, and she'd ask Sebastian if he'd mind having the box here until she'd finished her sorting out ready to post on to Gran. Really there wasn't as much junk as she'd expected, and the biggest thing to sort out here at Snowdrop Cottage were her emotions.

With a cup of tea made – she'd have to remember to replenish some stock supplies for Sebastian as it was rude to help herself all the time – Belle went back upstairs armed with a duster. She wanted to give the doll's house a good clean, as it was filthy, but it didn't take long to realise she needed a cloth and soapy water instead. It may have been hidden away behind a door that didn't open, but somehow the dust had found its way in through the cracks and some of the dirt wasn't easy to shift.

Back downstairs again she filled a washing-up bowl with warm, soapy water and then, up in Gran's bedroom, took out everything from the inside of the doll's house. It was no longer neatly arranged but thrown in there as though nobody really cared about it anymore. She found a miniscule cooker, a fridge, a table with three chairs, a tiny blue armchair with white stitching that gave a chequered effect. There were little plastic tins of baked beans and soups, the writing so small that Belle had to peer at them really closely to make out what they were. She pulled out character after character but couldn't remember the wooden old lady with the bun at the nape of her neck, or the younger woman with hair as dark as hers and wearing an apron as though she'd just been cooking. But when she found a see-through bag and saw what it was filled with, she remembered it clearly.

Gingerly, Belle opened the bag and tipped the contents onto the carpet in a space away from everything else so they wouldn't be muddled up. Because this was the set she remembered. Her fingers reached for the Santa who'd been going down the chimney that Christmas when she'd last seen the doll's house. Then she touched her hand to the little Christmas tree, the wreath that would hang from the hook on the front door to the pretend house. She giggled when she found the roast turkey, squashed where something had been weighing on the plastic. There were Christmas plates, red glasses as though the only tipple in them could be a festive mulled wine or eggnog. She pored through some of the even tinier things and there was everything from a carrot and a tiny mince pie to leave out for Santa and his reindeer to Christmas cards that would sit on the wooden mantelpiece in one of the rooms. There were three stockings that had to be for the three child-sized wooden dolls, little Christmas crackers in red and gold ready to adorn the table, and even a Christmas cake.

Belle wiped everything the best she could but suddenly remembered something else. 'The cottage,' she said to nobody but herself. She raked through all the tiny items, looking for the one she really wanted to find and had forgotten about until now. But nothing. Her heart pounded as she realised again what she had lost.

When she was little and had first got the doll's house, she'd taken an ornament from Gran's mantelpiece and put it in the kitchen of her pretend home. Gran had told her this ornament, although small, wasn't for that. She'd sat Belle down and they'd looked at it together, this perfect little cottage in Cotswold stone, with a fence at the front, the same windows as were on Gran's own cottage. Gran had asked Belle what she noticed about the cottage and she'd snuggled next to Gran, running through all the features. 'Oh look, the door is the same colour as yours!' she'd exclaimed, 'And the gate has a sign just like yours does.' It was only when she'd looked really closely that she realised the sign said 'Snowdrop Cottage'. This was a replica of Gran's place, made by a talented man in Bath. Gran had put it safely back onto the mantelpiece and the next time Belle visited, she had a second, identical, piece. She'd put it in Belle's hands and told her, 'So you can magic yourself here even if you're far away.' Belle had hidden her miniature cottage in the doll's house as though it were itself a doll's house for the characters in there to play with, and when she was taken away from Gran and Little Woodville for the last time, she hadn't had the chance to grab it.

When Belle heard the front door go she pushed everything into the doll's house and shifted it back inside the wardrobe. The miniature cottage was gone now, like so many things, and she did her best not to be too sad. She tried to shut the door but it wouldn't even push closed this time. She leaned against it and tried again but no luck and eventually reached down to see if there was something stuck in the groove of the door. Her index finger reached into the gap and ran along finding nothing until the very end, where she felt something cold, thin, like a chain. On her knees, she peered closer. Whatever it was, it was shiny, but she couldn't get a grip of it, the gap was too small. She wondered if Sebastian would have anything in the bathroom and crossing the landing without so much as a peep from him, whatever he was doing downstairs, she opened the bathroom cabinet and found a nail kit. A small one, barely used, and she vaguely wondered if someone had bought it for him. A girlfriend perhaps? She selected the tweezers, went back into the bedroom and pushed them gently into the gap between the wooden panels at the bottom and, with a bit of manipulation, managed to grasp the silver chain. When it wedged again she used her finger to free another part of it and pulled out the entire piece.

The silver locket was as beautiful as it was intricate. Her fingers ran across the oval front – no inscription, just the detailed lines of a roaming plant, perhaps ivy or something similar. Her fingers fiddled with the clasp where the two sides met and when she opened it up there was Gran, a much younger version of the woman Belle remembered but there was no mistaking her. There was another woman on the other side of the piece of jewellery and Belle tried to think whether her mum had ever mentioned an auntie but she couldn't remember.

Belle took out her phone from her back pocket and fired off a text to her mum to ask who the woman might be before she lost her nerve to do so, and as she waited for a reply she studied the photo again. The other woman had the same colour hair as Gran but if she'd had a sister, surely Belle would've known about it. Sometimes she'd been tempted to apply for one of those shows just to find out more about her roots, but she knew the phrase about opening cans of worms and it was the perfect collection of words to use when it came to her family.

Belle fixed the chain around her neck and tucked the locket beneath her shirt. She didn't want to lose it or throw it in a box because it felt too precious to do that. She'd take a drive later, out to the next town, and hopefully find a jeweller who could clean it up. It wouldn't feel right to send it back to Gran in the state it was in. The back of it was tarnished and a bit of cleaner and a decent cloth could work wonders.

When Sebastian still hadn't made an appearance Belle decided she'd call time on the sorting out for today and she ventured downstairs. It was only as she got to the foot of the staircase that she realised Sebastian wasn't alone.

'Hello, dear.' An elderly gentleman spotted her the second she rounded the corner towards the kitchen. He was sitting at the table, feet outstretched and grey socks hanging partly off his toes where he'd taken his shoes off and not pulled the material up again. 'You look the spitting image of Gillian, doesn't she, Sebastian?'

Sebastian turned round from where he was making two cups of tea and layering a selection of biscuits onto a plate. 'I'd say she does, yes.' But he didn't look at her for too long, either because he didn't want to or because he had already looked long enough to know the answer.

'I'm Bill and I live at Stone Cottage down the way.' The man pointed in the direction she hadn't ventured towards yet. 'Only a ten minute walk but Sebastian picked me up today. He keeps me supplied with Brussels sprouts.'

'That's…nice.' She wasn't sure what to say. 'I'm Belle; it's lovely to meet you.'

Sebastian took the two cups to the table and she almost laughed at his determination not to make her overly welcome. He seemed to flit between niceness and an ability to make her feel well and truly in the way. It seemed this afternoon it was the latter. She'd rather he chose one response or the other, and if he really didn't want her here she'd stay out of the way until the formalities were agreed.

'I'll be off then,' she said. 'Thank you again, Sebastian, for letting me sort some things at the cottage.'

'No worries.' He sat down next to Bill and Belle suspected every ounce of his kindness was more to do with her gran than anyone else.

'Plenty of biscuits to go around,' Bill insisted, but Belle knew it was best to take her cues from Sebastian.

'Thank you, Bill, but time's getting on and I've got a bit to do.' She retrieved her boots from the utility room and took them to the front door, and once she was bundled up in her coat again she bid them both a goodbye.

Sebastian certainly had a lot of friends. And they ranged in age about as much as Mrs Fro's outfits ranged in colour, with some bright and new, others old and worn but no less in place, and it highlighted how little she really knew about this man and his place in her gran's life. And it really bugged her.

*

Belle found a jeweller a few miles away and had the locket cleaned. She put it back on straight away for safe keeping and went to the supermarket, where she sat in the tiny café and had a bowl of lentil and bacon soup with a crusty roll. In the winter she usually made plenty of soups and stored them in the freezer so she had something nutritious at hand if she'd worked late or been out after a day at the office. She bought a Spanish chicken dish that came with rice and instructions for heating up in the microwave tonight, a box of tea bags and a selection of fruit. The grapes she'd keep in her bedroom at the bed and breakfast to grab whenever she needed, the apples she'd take to Sebastian's and put in his fruit bowl so he couldn't accuse her of stealing from him. She'd take some tea bags along to the cottage too, and she picked up a packet of fruit shortcake biscuits as a goodwill gesture.

After she left the supermarket and dumped her purchases in the car, Belle decided to wander down the high street. She needed to have some time away from Little Woodville. She hadn't been there long but already she felt bombarded with facts, emotions and decisions she wasn't sure she felt ready to make. Being apart from Anthony, she also found she was enjoying the break and the solitude in a way she wasn't entirely comfortable with. There was no constant pressure to talk about the business they were planning, which seemed to be all he could think about, and she could mull over her emotions without needing to explain them to anyone.

She walked past a gift shop, customers jostling along the tiny aisles choosing gifts, the lady behind the counter wrapping a present in ice-white paper with a big navy bow. Even though her family didn't have a big Christmas, they always bought each other a small gift, and this year Belle had been exceptionally organised. She'd wrapped and posted presents to her parents and left a gift with Anthony, and, likewise, her mum had already sent her a couple of parcels to open on December 25th when she was in Wales.

Belle hovered outside and looked in the window at the display, which had an old-fashioned train set going round in circles – the sort of thing you'd put beneath your tree for the kids. The next shop along was a florist, where floral creations reflected the season. Wonderful arrangements of snow-covered pine cones teamed with flaming orange roses, and green pine foliage stood out against bunches of white carnations with holly berries, held together by a yellow satin bow. There were flowers of all colours in one bouquet, peppered with sparkly silver leaves, and even when the door only opened briefly to let one customer out and another in, the perfume was mind-blowing.

Belle found the post office and bought a postcard for Mrs Fro from the selection of winter scenes depicting a number of Cotswold villages. She wrote it there and then and sent the picture of Little Woodville covered in snow to her neighbour. She went to the library next and spent some time running her fingers along the spines of cookbooks she longed to take with her, stocking up on ingredients and losing herself in the joy of cooking.

Back at her accommodation Belle found Audrey, who let her put her microwave meal in the fridge telling her she was welcome to do so any time, and not wanting the confines of her own room just yet, Belle went for a walk around the village. All the walking was another change from the norm – she usually raced to and from work with little time to do anything else in between.

She passed the bakery and the scent of gingerbread snaked its way out and tried to grab her, but she wouldn't cave in this time and walked straight past, half suspecting Betty would come out and reprimand her, but she didn't. She continued on past the post office and on to the village green, and was about to head to the café for a hot chocolate when another aroma swirled towards her. She stepped onto the grass, followed its slight incline, and sure enough she found a cart serving mulled wine.

'What can I get you, love?' The man, blond, tall and with a booming voice that echoed all around, wasted no time in grabbing the next potential customer to arrive at his stall, with signs above denoting what it sold along with a string of multicoloured fairy lights and sprigs of holly and ivy. The sweet smell of the mulled wine with its cloves, nutmeg and other festive spices was so overwhelming that Belle almost overlooked everything else on offer. There were fresh doughnuts lined up at the front and a teenager was making more at the machine at the back. There were pasties warming in a glass-fronted cabinet and soft drinks for sale too.

'One mulled wine please.'

The man did the honours and ladled the rich liquid into a cup. 'Christmas in a glass, that's what my wife says.' He handed it to her. 'Well, Christmas in a polystyrene cup at any rate.'

'Thank you.' She smiled back at him and let the warmth heat up her hands, cupped around the drink. 'Merry Christmas.' It felt right to say it. She wasn't distracting herself with work, darting from one appointment to the next. Out here she was beginning to take a breath and notice more and more things around her, think about her own feelings.

'Merry Christmas, Belle.'

'How did you...'

'I'm Jonah, I run the café with Trixie. She said you'd been in.' He beckoned her closer. 'But unlike some folk around here, we like to give people a chance before we condemn them.'

Glad of the reassurance that her mulled wine wasn't laced with anything, Belle went over and sat on one of the benches at the top of the green that looked down across the high street. The light had begun to fade and because the wine was so lovely and hot still, a slice of orange floating at the top, she sat there until the day drew to a close around her, the sky blackened and the twinkly lights on the gigantic tree illuminated the entire village. For once she felt calm, centred, like no matter what she decided to do, everything would work out for the best.

When her phone bleeped to indicate a text she balanced her wine on the arm of the bench and took out the device. It was a message from her mum and all it said was that she should send the locket back to Gran along with the rest of her things. At least it was a reply, Belle decided.

She tapped the symbol at the top of the message and then the phone icon and listened to the phone ring until her mum answered. 'Do you have any idea who it is?' she asked after very little preamble and lacking in patience when it came to her mum's stubbornness.

'I don't. Your gran didn't have a sister or a close cousin, but the best thing you can do is send it back to her.'

'Do you think it's special?'

'I wouldn't know, Belle.'

'I still don't get why Gran left me the cottage and not you.'

Her mum sighed across the miles. 'We've been through this. Your gran has her own mind – who am I to question it?'

Like mother like daughter, Belle knew. She persisted. 'Who is Sebastian?'

Her mum hesitated, perhaps suspecting a trick question. 'He's your tenant, isn't he?'

'He is, but who is he to Gran?'

'I don't know, Belle. How's the preparation for sale going?' She was a master at changing the subject.

82

Belle held her mulled wine with her opposite hand for fear it'd topple off the arm of the bench. 'Do you think Gran gave me the cottage because she thought I'd move in there eventually?'

'Belle, I don't know.' Whenever her mum added her name to any part of the conversation, it was a warning she'd almost had enough of talking.

'People here seem to know her really well. They seem to like her.'

'I told you before, Belle, your gran and I didn't see eye to eye about a lot of things. In some families it's just the way it is. How much work does the old place need before you'll be able to show potential buyers round or have another agent do it for you?'

What Belle had started to think about, sitting here on the bench at the top of the village green, was that she didn't want to outsource the sale of the cottage to anyone else. It didn't feel right. It had to be her who did it and not some stranger, and luckily she was in the right profession to know what she was doing. 'Actually, there's very little to do.'

'That surprises me. It's very old.'

'Gran must've been proactive on the upkeep front,' said Belle, 'and Sebastian seems to have kept the place going over the years.' She wondered whether she should mention the doll's house, the most personal item she'd unearthed apart from the locket – but judging by how her mum had clammed up about that, she didn't fancy her chances at finding out much more.

They went on to talk about Wales and Belle's upcoming holiday with Anthony, the potential business they were about to start together. Her mum sounded more excited than she was. She'd always supported Belle's dreams, whatever they were, and Belle couldn't

83

imagine ever falling out with her so badly that they went for years without speaking. Her mum was also fiercely loyal, just as Belle was, and it was Belle's loyalty that had driven her to keep all contact with her gran regarding the cottage strictly business. A handful of times she'd wanted to reach out to the woman who'd played a huge part in her childhood, but she just couldn't do it.

A voice at Belle's side grabbed her attention the second she finished her phone call and put her mulled wine to her lips.

'Belle.' Sebastian nodded in greeting. 'Good to see you.' He surely didn't mean it. 'Is it any good?' He gestured to her drink.

'It's very good.'

Without another word he walked over to the stall. He came back with a mulled wine and a fresh doughnut, which Belle had to admit smelled delicious.

'Mind if I sit?' he asked, although he was already in the process of lowering himself onto the bench beside her anyway.

'I think you already are.'

'Is that a problem?'

She shook her head. 'Not at all.'

'Boyfriend?' he asked, devouring the doughnut in only a few mouthfuls.

'What?'

'On the phone just now.'

'No, my mum.'

'Gillian's daughter?'

Her eyes met his. 'Yes, Gran's daughter.'

He looked over to the Christmas tree. The twinkling lights were beginning to mingle with the stars as they came out to play.

'Is there something going on in Little Woodville that I don't know?' Belle asked.

'In what way?' His eyes were fixed on her now and it made her nervous.

'Betty had a hissy fit about me being here, I've had a couple of people be polite and tell me they don't judge, so what is it I'm supposed to have done?'

'You haven't done anything; we're just a close-knit village, people have lived here years, and Gillian is missed.'

'So why did she up and go to a care home? Was she sick? Was she lonely or scared?' Suddenly she really wanted to know.

He shrugged. 'We were close but I don't fully know the reason why she finally upped and went. All I know is that she made sure the house was in your name first before she did anything else.'

Belle, fully aware that the house had been signed over to her all of a sudden, felt weird hearing it from a stranger. 'Are you in touch with her now?'

'I am.' He looked away and waved over to a group of people Belle hadn't yet met.

One of the people in the group, a girl in her twenties or perhaps a bit younger – Belle couldn't see in the darkness – called out, 'Sunday lunch next week?'

Sebastian put one thumb up on the hand that didn't have his mulled wine. 'You're on. Jessie, you coming?'

Another, much younger, girl said she wouldn't miss it for the world and they filed towards the pub.

'Girlfriend?' Belle asked after they'd gone on their way.

'Jessie? No. She's fifteen. I'm thirty-three.' He shuddered. 'That wouldn't be right.' He seemed amused that she'd jumped to the wrong conclusion.

'What about the other one? She looks about your age.'

'Amy? Again, no. She's twenty-seven, Jessie's older sister, and has a boyfriend.'

She'd wondered how old he was and now she knew, only two years older than her. 'I always thought you were older.'

'What?' He patted his hair. 'I don't think I have any greys yet.'

She looked at the spikes, which were semi-flat and messy but in a style that looked right. 'I can't see any either. But what I mean is that when I knew Gran had a tenant, I assumed you were more…I don't know, her age perhaps.'

'Ah, I see.'

'You're not her toy boy are you?' They both laughed this time.

'You know if Gillian were here now she'd find that hysterical.'

'Then what are you to her? What is she to you?' She didn't mean to sound accusatory but she'd wanted to ask the question for a long time.

'Do you think I'm after her money?'

'No, and I'm sorry if I caused offence. It's just…well, it's just that I don't know anything. Everyone around here seems to know Gran, appears to have an opinion, but apart from that, I'm still in the dark.'

'You hate not knowing what I am to her, don't you?' his voice teased. 'Or what she is to me?'

'Care to enlighten me?'

He smiled, and just when she thought she'd get some answers he stood, necked the rest of the mulled wine with a satisfied murmur, and said, 'Nope. Goodnight, Belle.'

Frustrated, she stayed there. She wasn't going to run after him and ask for answers, and when he went into the pub she made her way across the green, dropping her empty cup with its stained orange peel in the nearby bin, and went back to the bed and breakfast and a microwave meal for one.

Little Woodville wasn't going to offer her any answers tonight.

Chapter Five

Belle had spent almost a week clearing out her gran's bedroom, the loft and the few boxes in the dining room, and apart from a couple more items of jewellery, she'd been able to throw most things away. She'd found a stepladder in the shed and Sebastian had told her she was free to use it – she'd been careful to ask his permission as she didn't want to take too many liberties when he was being abnormally accommodating for a man who was going to have to look for somewhere new to live – and now she was ready to take the next step at Snowdrop Cottage and begin getting it slowly ready for sale. Even in the depths of winter she refused to believe she couldn't make it so beautiful it would lure enough potential buyers to create a bit of competition and get a good price.

The weather had turned in Little Woodville and instead of a light threat of frost on the air and a lot of rain, snow symbols began to appear on the weather forecast with more regularity. As Belle arrived at the cottage she was quickly driven inside by the sudden onslaught of hailstones, her bags hanging off either arm. She'd called Sebastian this morning and asked whether she could start painting the second reception room, which would be perfect as a dining room. It was the most neglected room in the place and she knew it would be a mistake to try to sell it like that. He'd agreed and so on her way here she'd been to get supplies and stocked up on everything she'd need. She had sugar soap, a bucket, sponges, rollers and brushes, paint for the ceiling and a couple of paint trays.

'It's nasty out there,' Sebastian commented as he picked up his keys to go out when she bundled through the front door of the cottage.

'It's horrid. I'll leave the paint till later – it's in the boot and I'm not getting pummelled again.' Belle's hair was wet even on the short dash it had taken to get to the front door, and she let the bags drop from her arms.

'Enjoy yourself. I'll be back around lunchtime.'

She grabbed one of the bags and held it aloft. 'I have some fruit, biscuits and tea bags for you. I can't impose on you more than I am doing already.'

'That was thoughtful of you.' His gaze held hers until he said, 'I'd better go.'

'See you then.'

He nodded to her and it was his turn to make a run for it, but he turned back in the doorway, his head bowed to take account of the difference in height. 'I almost forgot. My friend Jeremy is going to stop by to pick up some vegetables. There are too many for me to eat alone, so he's got a good supply of parsnips in the bag on the kitchen table. If you could give it to him when he comes, I'd appreciate it.'

'Of course. I'll be in there' – she pointed to the second reception room – 'so I'll hear the door no problems.'

'I wouldn't bank on it with these hailstones.' He grimaced. 'Here goes…' And with that he ran from the cottage over to his jeep.

Belle shut the door to keep the heat in and wrestled off her boots, which she took through to the utility room to get them out of the way. In the hallway she stopped in front of the mirror above a small mahogany table upon which sat the telephone and used her fingers to comb through her thick hair. Using the band wound round her wrist she pulled it into a high ponytail out of the way.

As she unloaded the carrier bags she tried to work out why Sebastian was so willing to let her come and go as she pleased. He'd even told her to go ahead and paint the room she was in now and even the hallway if she wanted to, because he could go in through the back door, but she'd stick with the rooms that could be closed off to make it easy all round. The only areas Sebastian said were off limits here in the cottage until he was out of here were the kitchen and his bedroom, which Belle could understand – the latter for obvious reasons and the former because anyone in your kitchen space would get in your way on a daily basis. The only reason for his generosity that Belle could think of was that Sebastian was close to Gran, and he was doing this for her. Belle knew for sure that if she had been renting her flat in Cambridge and was given notice by the landlord, she wouldn't be letting anyone in her space until the day she left.

She stood in the soon-to-be dining room, assessing the job ahead. She'd done some decorating in her time, first her bedroom when she was a teen and suddenly wanted everything red and white, then again when she bought her flat. And faced with this place, especially because she couldn't do it all in one go with a tenant still living here, she was looking forward to it. Working in real estate, she had an appreciation of how you could transform a tired, old property without too much expense.

She grabbed a cloth and dry dusted the walls first, coughing more than she'd anticipated as the dust induced a couple of sneezing fits that made her wish she'd bought a dust mask at the DIY shop. It was amazing, dust lying dormant hadn't bothered her at all but now she'd stirred it up it was out for vengeance.

When there was a knock at the door she answered it to Jeremy, an older man, probably close to Gran's age. He had a ruby red Robin Reliant parked next to her car in the driveway and he didn't want to talk much, but he was pleasant enough. She handed him the bag of parsnips and with barely a couple of sentences exchanged, one of which was a message for Sebastian about the pub, he went on his way and she got back to the job in hand.

Once she'd dry dusted everything it was on to the ceiling. She got the stepladder from the shed – Sebastian had thoughtfully dragged it from the very back behind lawnmowers and other gardening bits and pieces and left it by the door – and got ready to tackle the cobwebs around the vintage pendant shade hanging in the middle of the room. Belle only hoped the guilty party who'd weaved them had long gone.

The next step was to make up the sugar-soap solution and with marigolds covering her hands she got to work. She started with the ceiling as it was hardest being up the ladder, and then took each of the four walls in turn. There was a smaller fireplace in this room that looked unused and after she'd cleaned the walls and left them to dry she found some Jif – or Cif as it was called these days, even though she couldn't get her head around the different name – and a brush from beneath the kitchen sink, and gave the tiles on the fireplace surround a good scrub. It made a huge difference and by the time Sebastian came in through the front door and poked his head around the doorjamb to investigate, she was smiling at how much better it looked.

'Wow, so those tiles are actually a bright turquoise, not a dull, dishwatery blue.' He nodded his approval. 'I've never turned this room into anything since Gillian got rid of the dining table.'

'What happened to the table?' she asked.

'It's in the kitchen. When Gillian had the units refitted and the built-in cupboard was done out to be a pantry so the utility room actually became usable again, she liked to have the table in the room where she cooked. She said cooking and eating were some of the most joyful things in her life, they brought everyone together, so she refused to put everyone in a different room if she was at the stove or seeing to something in the oven.'

Belle swallowed hard. She'd said similar one day to Anthony when she'd cooked dinner for him, Sam and Sam's boyfriend. 'I need an open-plan house one day,' she'd said, 'so you can all keep me company as I cook and we can enjoy a nice glass of wine.'

Belle stood and opened the front window as a sudden hot flush invaded her body. 'Sorry, I'll close it in a second. It's all this physical work when I'm used to an office, it's making me hot.' She was rambling now and wished she could shut up.

'Go stand outside, that'll cool you down.' His mouth twisted into a smile.

She looked out of the window. The hail had stopped but she could still see the stones lurking on the ground so it had to be cold or they would've melted. She leaned on the windowsill and breathed in the icy air. 'It's so quiet out here.'

By now, Sebastian had ducked beneath the door frame and was standing in the room to one side of the low central beam that ran from one end to the other. 'Bit different from what you're used to is it?'

'I live in the city.' She looked out across grass dappled with moisture as well as hailstones. 'A nice short walk to work.'

'But not much of a getaway come the weekend I'm guessing.'

'It's a quiet flat, but no outside space – this is something else.'

'It sure is.'

Goose pimples got under the cuffs of her long-sleeved shirt and shot up her arms. She put her hands on the iron fixtures at the bottom of the window pane and pulled it straight down to close the gap until it clicked shut.

'Did Jeremy pop in?' Sebastian shrugged off his coat and went out to the hallway to hang it on a hook.

Belle followed him. 'Yes, I gave him the bag of parsnips. He said to tell you he'd see you for a pint later on.'

Sebastian grinned. 'He never misses an opportunity for a drink. I'm surprised he didn't invite you down the pub there and then.'

She looked at the front of the scruffy shirt she was wearing, an old one of Anthony's she'd worn when she painted her flat a few years ago. Apart from paint splatterings that hadn't come out in the wash, the cream material now had a great deal of dust and dirt across it as though any particle lying around had made a beeline for her. 'I don't think I'd be smart enough, do you?'

He regarded her longer than was necessary. 'Oh I don't know, you look all right to me.'

Embarrassed at his assessment, she turned and went back to the room to tackle the skirting boards next. She'd already dusted them but they'd need wiping down now

93

so the dust didn't float up to the walls and ruin the paint job when she got going with it. 'Jeremy's car's cute,' she said.

Sebastian's laughter filled the room. 'It's almost as old as he is. I'm not sure he should even be driving, but he only makes his way around locally. Did you watch him drive away?'

Belle turned to face him. 'No, why?'

'He drives a little bit faster than a snail but has a habit of drifting from the left hand side of the road over to the right whenever he feels like it.'

'I'll watch out when I'm driving around Little Woodville then.'

'I would if I were you. I'm just thankful he's so content here he never wants to tackle a motorway.' He leaned against the doorjamb. 'Mind if I ask you something?'

'Go ahead.' She'd turned back to focus on her task. She spotted the grubbiest marks and tackled those first with the scrubbing brush, knocking her ponytail back when it fell forwards over her shoulder. 'I'm listening.'

'What made you come to Little Woodville for such a long time? I mean, why didn't you give me notice from home, then come when I was out of the way?'

She stopped a moment but then kept scrubbing. 'I wanted to spend some time getting to know the village again.' She shouldn't have to explain anything to him. They weren't friends, they weren't family. They were landlord and tenant. But knowing he had a connection with her gran made her want to be at least a bit open.

'Does that help, when you push a sale through?'

She didn't look up, she kept working. 'Sometimes. I always think it's important to not only show the house but also the local area. You know what they say about location. Sometimes it's more important than a property.'

'I'd say this place and the village are equally important.'

She turned now. This was a subject she was comfortable with. 'You're right. You have to get a feeling about a property, know that you can make it a home, imagine yourself and your family there, and then you need to imagine yourself living in the village, town or city where it's situated – because both things will become your life.'

'But you still didn't really answer my question. Why not give me my notice and then come back after New Year's when I'm gone? You'd be able to get the job done so much faster, free to do whatever you wanted, get people in to look at the place quickly.'

'I was due some time off, so it made sense to do it now.' Truthfully, as soon as she'd decided to raise some money for her and Anthony's new business venture by selling the cottage she'd been compelled to come here, to know what her own feelings were, to work out how happy she was to sell up, to deal with it herself and take ownership. She needed to do it without anyone else's voice in her head, without any distractions. She knew it was the only way she'd be able to come to terms with whatever she decided. And now she was here, she was absorbing a part of her gran's life that had once been hers too. And deep down – although she hadn't given this impulse much thought - she'd wanted to come here before Christmas because those were the times she'd treasured the most. It also meant that with the pressure of New Year and new promises, resolutions and the depressing months of January and February to follow, she and Anthony would have the business to throw themselves into, and perhaps, once she did that, she'd never look back.

Belle didn't have to say anything else because there was a knock at the door and Sebastian went off to answer it. This time the person came through the hallway and Sebastian introduced her. 'This is Anne – she teaches at the local school.'

'Nice to meet you,' said Belle. 'I won't shake your hand, I'm filthy.'

Anne smiled. 'You look as though you're working hard. It'll be wonderful when it's finished. What colour are you painting the walls?'

'I'm not sure yet. It'll be white for the ceiling and then I'll see what I can find. Something light and neutral will probably work best.'

'Good idea. People can add their own stamp then.' Anne moved towards the kitchen, where Sebastian must have disappeared to.

Belle hovered near the doorway wondering what this woman had come for. Was she here for tea and a chat? Parsnips? Or maybe some other winter vegetable or something else entirely? But when she couldn't hear anything she realised Sebastian had shut the door to the kitchen. She'd never seen it shut before but clearly this was something private that she wasn't a party to.

She got back to the scrubbing, having finished all along one side. Sebastian had a lot of callers of varying ages and for a brief moment Belle wondered whether he was a member of the clergy given how many visitors he had. She shook the thought away quickly though, when she thought back to his effing and blinding yesterday morning when he dropped a mug on his foot, using words that would make any churchgoer blush. He'd cursed even more the morning before when he'd gone to put more rubbish out and found that a fox had been into the bins at night and pulled out whatever it wanted, leaving the remnants littered everywhere for someone to clean up. It had made her snigger at the time because up until then he'd kept his cool and it was a bit like hearing Elmo from *Sesame Street* yell out a swear word, it was so out of place.

Belle finished scrubbing the skirting boards and after Anne said goodbye and went on her way, she dusted the front of her shirt and went through to the kitchen, where she pumped soap into her palm and gave her hands a thorough wash. Sebastian was out in the shed but came through soon after.

'Are you working again today?' she asked, glad she had the good-mood Sebastian again today, not the ratty one who resented her presence.

'Not with this weather. I'm a caretaker part of the time, up at the school. I've done the inside work I was needed for today but the grounds outside will have to wait. They're pretty self-sufficient in the winter months anyway so I don't need to do much, and I won't do anything with the threat of giant hailstones over my head.'

'Good idea. Anne seemed nice when I met her before.'

'She is. She wanted to discuss the landscaping requirements for next year once the new playground goes in at the school.'

Ah, so not so secretive, but business. For some reason she felt relieved. 'You'll get the work?'

'It looks like it. People are generally good around here and try to keep things local.'

She had a sudden flurry of guilt that she could potentially be making him move away from the community, but Anthony's voice was in her head again reminding her there wasn't much room for sentimentality in this business.

'Do you mind if I make a cup of tea?' she asked.

'Sure.'

She opened a few cupboards before she remembered the mugs were on a mug tree at the side of the kitchen near the sink. 'Would you like a cup?'

'That would be lovely, thank you.' He washed his hands and got the milk from the fridge as she did the honours and poured the water. 'Sugar?' she asked.

'No thanks.' He topped up each mug with milk and they took their steaming drinks over to the table.

'I'll get started painting the ceiling tomorrow if it suits?'

He shrugged. 'As I've said, you do what you want whenever, just not in here or my bedroom.'

She knew her skin had coloured at the unwitting suggestion of her doing something in his bedroom and she glossed over it. 'I appreciate it. Painting always takes longer than you think so it's good to get started before Christmas. You didn't have to let me do anything at all really.'

'I don't get much of a thrill out of being awkward.'

'Still…'

'Will you finish before you advertise?' He moved the conversation on.

'I hope so. January and February are usually quiet months, but I'm hoping this place is unique enough to warrant a bit of interest.'

'I'm sure it will.' He blew across his tea. 'So what do you do, when you're not here annoying me?'

She ignored the ribbing. 'I'm an estate agent.'

'Now why doesn't that surprise me?' He put his mug down. 'From the moment you arrived I could tell you knew what you were doing by the way you made notes, the kinds of questions you asked, and I had you pegged the second you brought out your fancy tape measure.'

'The tape measure always gives me away.' She grinned. 'And what do you do? Apart from caretaking at the school or landscaping jobs?'

'Right now, plenty of different things to keep me busy. I'm part gardener, part handyman, school caretaker, village helper.'

'You have a lot of job titles.'

'Yeah.' He sighed.

'You don't enjoy being that way?'

'I like the variety; I want to be busy and active. You know, I've heard that sitting is as bad as smoking in so many ways, and the last thing I could see myself doing is sitting around on my butt all day.'

'So what don't you like about what you do?'

'It's not my dream, put it that way.'

'Does anyone ever match their dreams to their work?'

He looked directly at her. 'I think so. Don't you?'

She thought about how much she'd enjoyed making her way up the rungs from a junior to a senior negotiator, and now to someone who had the plans for an independent venture. 'I love my job, I enjoy it, but I would never describe it as a dream. I think dreams are more hobbies aren't they?'

'I think finances can dictate what we can do, but I'm a great believer you should follow your heart,' he batted back. 'Your working life spans so many years that the thought of doing something you don't have a passion for is daunting.'

'Where would your heart go if you let it?'

'Before I started my life as an odd-job man – which I guess is the only all-encompassing job title I feel fits what I'm doing – I was the manager of a bookshop for a major retailer. I thrived on it. I loved being surrounded by books all day every day, making decisions, being in charge.'

'I'm surprised.'

'Why?'

'Because you said you didn't want to sit around all day, and reading requires a lot of sitting surely.'

He grinned. 'Reading does, but owning your own business, any business, requires a lot of dedication and time and keeps you incredibly busy. You become the person who takes all the risks, does everything – whether it's selecting books and ordering stock, carting around heavy boxes of book deliveries and returns, dealing with budgets and advertising, or physically arranging the books on the shelves and keeping the premises clean and in good repair.'

'I suppose I never thought of it that way.'

'Anyway, my time as a manager gave me a taster of the bigger picture I envisage one day. My dream, if you like.'

'So what's your dream?'

'I'm not sure I can tell you. You said you didn't believe dreams and jobs could ever be the same thing. I don't need any extra doubt. If you're starting a new business, there's no room for that.'

'I don't know. Doubt often makes us question things and gives us answers we may need along the way. It stops us being cocky and assuming everything will work out fine. It helps us be prepared.' For those reasons she'd come here, to Little Woodville.

He gulped back more of his tea. 'I think you actually have quite a point there, Belle.'

'So come on, what's the dream?'

'Isn't it obvious? I want to own and run my own bookshop.'

'What's stopping you?'

'Finance.'

'Ah. Finance is the reason I'm here in Little Woodville.' At least it was a major part of it and, as far as Anthony knew, the only real reason for her trip so close to Christmas.

'You're selling because you want to buy your own place?' Sebastian asked.

'I already have a flat, but the sale here would generate finance to set up a real-estate agency. Anthony, my boyfriend, and I have been thinking about it for a while and we're forever drawing up parts of plans, ready for when we can get going. That's what's behind my sudden decision to sell this place. I'd not thought about it much before and the rental income was an investment, but when Anthony's grandad left him some money in his will I knew if I sold this place I could match the amount and our dreams could become reality.'

'So it's your dream? To do what you do, but for yourself?'

'Sure.' The warm tea slipped down slowly and she realised how nice it was to be off her feet for the first time in hours. 'I feel lucky I enjoy the job.' When he looked unconvinced she said, 'I do.'

'I'm sure you do, and from what I've seen you know what you're doing.'

'But…?'

'There's no but,' he insisted.

'Oh there's a but – come on, out with it.' She was laughing now, although a little nervously because she wasn't sure she'd ever told anyone what she really wanted to do, because nobody had ever questioned the business plans until now. They'd all commended the idea, known how good she and Anthony would be at it, their experience an excellent foundation.

'The "but" is that it doesn't seem to me that you have a great burning desire. I can tell you *want* to start up your own business, and you *like* what you do. But, come on, if you could pick one thing to do if money were no object, location no problem, in fact, if nothing could stand in your way, what would it be?' She hesitated and it was all the ammunition he needed. 'Do you want to know what I think?'

'Do I have a choice?' she smiled.

'I think you want your own business, I can see enthusiasm for that, but I'm not sure real estate is your passion.' He paused. 'Tell me, if you think things you love can only be hobbies and not jobs, what are your hobbies?'

She swirled the dregs of her tea around in the bottom of her cup and took it over to the sink, where she rinsed it out, located the dishwasher and popped it in. 'I love to cook.'

'Now we're getting somewhere.' He leaned back in his chair, hands clasped behind his head, and suddenly she felt as though she were under interrogation. 'What sort of cooking?'

'I love to cook anything, but mostly savoury. I'm not much of a cake or pastry person.' She looked around the kitchen that had the same yellowy walls from her childhood years here. It had probably been painted since but perhaps her gran had picked the same shade to keep it just as it always had been. 'Gran loved to cook too. My mum doesn't, so I think the passion skipped a generation.'

'Gillian was a brilliant cook.'

Her head snapped up. It seemed such a personal thing to say, especially when she was related to the woman and could never have offered the same depth of knowledge.

'She cooked all the time,' Sebastian confessed. 'You must take after her.'

Uneasy at the comparison, Belle found herself asking, 'What is she like?'

He held her gaze. 'Kind, approachable, friendly, a bit of a laugh at times. She's probably a lot like you remember – I doubt she changed and she certainly hasn't in all the time I've known her. You could also never accuse her of being a pushover.' He laughed. 'She definitely has what I'd call a stubborn streak.'

'Actually, stubbornness is something that runs in my family. Mum has it in spades, and I know I do too.'

'She's also fiercely independent,' he went on. 'She began to struggle with the garden. It's a generous-sized plot and the upkeep is time-consuming as well as hard work, and eventually I managed to persuade her to let me help too. I was allowed to mow although she insisted on paying me – something I didn't like, I might add, but it was either that or she'd try to do it all herself or hire someone else who'd charge the earth. I got away with charging her less but she wasn't daft. She'd investigated costs and was ready to pay me more as she saw fit. It was actually exhausting trying to get your gran to do something when she didn't want to.'

'I can imagine. If she's anything like Mum, you give up because there's no talking her round.'

'Exactly.'

'Gran sounds like she knew what she wanted.'

'She always did. She wouldn't hand over the upkeep of those veggie patches for ages.'

Belle almost giggled with an impromptu picture in her mind of an old lady hanging on to one end of a parsnip and this younger man holding the other, fighting over who would maintain the winter vegetables. 'How did you end up winning?'

'Again, she insisted on parting with cash, and she was onto me, not charging her the going rate, so she'd make up batches of food and send me away every afternoon with enough to feed the five thousand.'

Belle smiled. It was nice hearing things about her gran, because for so many years she'd had to rely on her own patchy memories. 'All this talk of food is making me hungry. I'd better get going.' She checked her watch. 'I'll get some lunch before my tummy starts to really protest.'

'Are you going to the bakery?'

She stood up. 'I can safely say I'd rather keel over with hunger. I'll drive out to the supermarket.'

'How does soup sound?'

'Is there somewhere near here that does good soup?'

'I have a few batches in the chest freezer out in the utility room. There's nothing like it in the winter, especially when it's made from veggies out of the garden.'

'You made it yourself?'

He nodded and went off to the utility room. She heard him call out, 'Mushroom and winter vegetable, or chicken noodle and pumpkin?'

She called back, 'Mushroom, please.'

He reappeared, carrying two Tupperware containers. 'Last couple of the batch.'

'I can't believe you make it yourself. I'm impressed.'

'You haven't tasted it yet.' He put both containers into the microwave and set it to defrost.

'True,' Belle quipped, but she was distracted by her own memories of standing in this very kitchen, on a stool, stirring soup as it cooked on the stove. She'd made it with Gran plenty of times and, even though she couldn't remember the flavours they'd used, she wondered if her ability to make up soup recipes in her own kitchen had stemmed from Gran in the first place. She had her own recipe for chicken soup, another for beef and barley, and a vegetable one that Mrs Fro, a bit of a stranger to fresh goods unless it was the two veg that went with her Sunday roast, declared was better than anything that came out of a can.

'Could you cut some bread?' The timer pinged and Sebastian took out the Tupperware containers. 'It's in the bread store in the walk-in pantry.'

Before she disappeared in that direction she asked, 'Why are you being so nice?'

'Sorry, is that bad?'

She shook her head. 'No, but sometimes you're not exactly happy I'm around and other times, like today, you're welcoming me with open arms.' She blushed when he looked at her and knew he must be thinking about holding one another in a hug. 'You know what I mean.'

He took out a pan from the cupboard, pulled a wooden spoon from the utensils pot by the cooker. 'Gillian is special to me. When I'm being nice to you it's because I suspect it's what she'd like me to do, and when I'm not being very polite it's because I have to consider leaving this place.' He turned his back as he emptied the partially defrosted soup from the containers into the pan. 'I've lived here a long time and it'll be hard to find somewhere else. I'm not saying this to make you feel guilty – I'm renting, this could've happened any time – but perhaps it'll make you see that this isn't simple for me.'

She was beginning to realise this wasn't only a cottage he left his things in and returned home to every night. It had once been owned by someone he was close to, he put love and care into the upkeep of the place as well as the garden, above and beyond any duties of a normal tenant. She wanted to ask him more, delve further into what he and Gillian were to each other, but instead she turned and went to the pantry to get the bread. Perhaps the family stubborn streak stopped her asking too much, or maybe she was afraid of what she might hear.

Inside the walk-in pantry she called out, 'When did Gran put this in?' Seeing the door before, she'd assumed it was a normal cupboard with shelving, but here she was almost in another room filled with so many ingredients it was like a mini supermarket.

From the kitchen he called back the reply, 'Before the renovations it was an old cupboard so she pushed it back a bit, taking part of the dining room, which is why that room is smaller than it once was. Your gran and her cooking took up a lot of space.'

She stood rooted to the floor of the pantry. The tiny little details were gradually emerging to make Gran more of a vivid person in Belle's mind than she'd been in years. Over time, her gran hadn't existed for real unless she'd let her, but here in Little Woodville she could no longer ignore the woman who could be a large

106

part of her life. She turned round on the spot, looking at the shelves lining the walls up above and down below, the space where more ingredients would fit if you needed them to. Gran may not have lived here for years but her spirit lived on in the walls through Sebastian's clear shared love of cooking and his enthusiasm to keep the country kitchen operating as it once had before. Or perhaps all of these things were out of date and, like some of the junk upstairs, needed to be sorted through and thrown out.

Back in business mode, Belle knew this pantry would be a good selling point for Snowdrop Cottage. Walk-in pantries were really popular these days and she'd be sure to add it to the listing description, she decided as she pulled the loaf from the bread storage jar and took it into the kitchen.

'Thick or thin?' She came out of the pantry holding a loaf and tried to locate a bread board.

'Thick, always,' he answered. He stirred the soup as the blue flame on the gas stove flickered gently beneath. 'The butter dish is on the table and plates are in here.' He lifted a foot covered in a thick woolly sock to gesture to the cupboard on the right at the end of the group.

Belle took out the crockery, found knives and cut bread for each of them, and as the soup warmed and garlic coiled into the air, Sebastian plucked some fresh parsley from the plant growing in a tin pot on the windowsill. 'To garnish,' he explained before turning off the gas and pouring the soup into the little navy blue bowls already waiting.

Belle buttered a doorstep of bread. 'What ingredients are in the soup?'

'Onions, a bit of red wine, mushrooms – obviously,' he grinned, 'carrot…' – he thought for a moment –

'pumpkin, and I can't remember what else. I'll let you know when I make it again.'

'Did all the ingredients come from the garden?'

'Yep.'

'Those veggie patches are so big you could probably keep the whole village in vegetables for a year.'

'I do give a lot away – I don't want to waste it.'

'You seem popular with the neighbours.'

'What can I say? Must be my charm.' Bread buttered, he dunked a generous piece into the thick mixture and when the wholemeal turned a rich brown colour, popped it into his mouth.

'It's a good way to be.'

'What about where you live? Do you know many people?'

She explained all about Mrs Fro and how they'd got to know one another, she told him about noisy neighbours and how new tenants soon knew to toe the line when the formidable old woman introduced herself. 'The night she emerged from her flat with a baseball bat gave me a new respect for her.'

'I'm sure it did.'

'She's almost like a surrogate granny in many ways.'

His attention seemed to pique at that. 'Sometimes it's not always family we're closest to is it?'

She tucked in to her soup. 'This is good.'

'You know, you could get in touch with her – it's never too late.'

'Mrs Fro?'

'You know I don't mean her.'

'Maybe I will.' She smiled tentatively. 'One day.'

'How long has it been?'

'Too long.'

'Don't forget she left you this place. She wouldn't have done that if she didn't care.'

Belle ate more of her soup before she said, 'Sometimes I wonder why she did it. I wonder why me and not my mum. If she'd left it to Mum, maybe Mum would've got in touch with her, but skipping her and giving it to me always felt like I'd betrayed Mum.' She was babbling now. 'Sorry, it's family business – I shouldn't talk about it.'

He buttered a second wedge of bread. 'It is family business, and I should keep my nose out.'

'That wasn't what I meant.'

The way he looked at her, she knew he wasn't annoyed.

'I know it wasn't. It's just that, well, there are two sides to every story as they say.'

'How do you know Gran?' There, she'd asked the ultimate question. Now maybe she'd get to the bottom of something.

He shook his head. 'I don't want to feed information to you; I want you to get in touch with her and get to know her for yourself. I don't feel it's up to me to fill you in, but let's just say she's been someone special to me for a very long time.'

'You have a lot of friends who are older.'

'I do, yes. I don't see friendship as something that has to be defined in a particular way.' He started to laugh. 'God, I sound like a total idiot. I don't mean to. And I don't mean to be secretive, but I'm close enough to Gillian to know that you not being in her life left a gaping hole. Maybe she doesn't feel she can ever close it, but perhaps you could.' He stood and took his empty bowl over to the sink as Belle finished her soup.

'Thanks for the soup, it's pretty good.'

'I'll take that as a huge compliment if you're a cook yourself.'

When he dismissed her offer to help clear up she dried the Tupperware and put it away instead. She reached over to put the last lid away but accidentally knocked his wallet onto the floor. Sighing at her clumsiness, she picked it up, but the flap fell open to reveal a photograph.

'Who is she to you?' she asked again, a little more determinedly now she'd seen the picture of her gran with Sebastian. You didn't carry a photograph in your wallet or purse unless it really meant something.

He dried his hands on a tea towel and gestured for her to sit down again as he relented and shared what he knew. 'I don't know everything about your gran. All I know is that she was very good friends with my grandparents, who died when I was little. Gillian, your gran, worked for my dad for a time and she became a bit of a surrogate grandma to me, like Mrs Fro is to you, I suppose. But I can't tell you anything more. I know she was estranged from her daughter, and you as a result, but she never explained the reasons why.'

Belle wasn't sure how to feel. Part of her was overwhelmingly jealous thinking of her gran with a grandchild she wasn't even related to; another part of her thought she should be happy that her gran had had other people in her life. In the early days Belle had worried herself sick that Gran was all alone. It had upset her for nights on end, disrupted her schoolwork for a while, but as her memories slowly began to fade, so had her concerns. Perhaps she should be glad she had gone on to have someone special in her life.

'Excuse me.' Belle left the kitchen all of a sudden, unable to process what she'd heard, but Sebastian didn't follow her. She went up to the bathroom and pulled herself together. She wasn't an overly emotional person but it was as though this cottage had power over you from the minute you let its thatch draw you inside, and she was dealing with feelings she didn't even know she had.

When she went downstairs again Sebastian was looking out of the kitchen window. 'The hailstones are back, bigger and better than this morning.'

She joined him, glad he wasn't quizzing her about her reaction. 'They're enormous. It'd hurt if one landed on you.'

They stood a while longer before he said, 'That's pretty.' He nodded to the locket she hadn't realised she was fiddling with until now.

'It's Gran's.'

'I know, I recognise it.'

'I found it in the wardrobe. It must've fallen in the gap by the door. I didn't want to put it in a box in case it got lost or damaged.'

Her fingers lightly brushed the silver jewellery. She wanted to ask him more questions, get to know the woman who'd been a stranger for so long she wasn't sure she could ever make up for the missing years.

'Belle?'

She shook herself out of her reverie. 'Yes?'

'Would you be interested in coming to the pub tonight? A few of us are meeting up. I assume Betty won't be there,' he said cheekily, 'so you'll be safe. It might be nice for you to get out of the bed and breakfast.'

'Are you sure you want me to?'

'I'm being nice, remember. Gillian would give me a clip round the ear if she thought I was being horrible.'

111

She smiled. 'You might decide when I'm there that you resent me being the person who could ruin everything for you.'

'Or I might decide you're not so bad after all.'

Each time Belle thought she knew the exact path to follow, thoughts and feelings came along to cloud her judgement and she had no idea which way to go. She was beginning to be drawn in to Snowdrop Cottage in a peculiar way, and her involvement with Sebastian was doing little to help her think straight either.

Chapter Six

Belle left the cottage and went to the paint shop to choose a colour for the dining room walls. She settled on something called Oyster, which was neutral yet soft and not stark. She didn't want to detract from the charm and cosiness the home exuded by making any of the decor too modern. She thought she may even choose a painting to hang on the side wall that you'd see the second you opened the door to the room, but reminded herself that this wasn't supposed to be for her – it was to sell, which was a different thing altogether.

Belle dropped the paint tins at the cottage, using her key with Sebastian gone for the rest of the day. She thought about their conversation earlier, the nerves that fluttered through her insides when he suggested he might not, after all, dislike her as much as all that. He'd been flirting – whether intentional or not she had no idea – but while she could handle flirting from colleagues at work who had no intention of anything ever happening, with Sebastian it felt different. She was drawn to him and wondered whether it was because he was undoubtedly attractive, or was it because she knew how close he was to her gran?

She finished at the house and then returned to the bed and breakfast to call Anthony before she got ready for the pub tonight. She didn't mention the outing to her boyfriend. She still hadn't told him that Sebastian wasn't quite the pensioner they'd assumed he must be, and if she said where she was going it'd only encourage him to quiz her about who this man was, ask her whether she was letting sentiment get in the way of their venture. But Anthony had clearly assumed she wasn't doing anything much with her time other than working at the cottage and sleeping at the bed and breakfast, because all they really talked about was the cottage itself. He was excited at the prospect of selling something so charming and unique, a manoeuvre that would open doors for the both of them, and Belle wished she could feel more certain about it. She wondered whether her loyalty to him was the main driver of this move and she contemplated whether there was any way she could keep the cottage and the rental income and still go into business with Anthony. It wouldn't seem quite so final then. It wouldn't sever even more ties with Gran.

She showered in the sloped-ceiling ensuite bathroom and washed away any doubts for the time being but by the time she emerged she'd added in a slightly different piece to her plan. She scrolled through her phone contacts and found her gran's care home address. She'd put it in here once, on a whim, in case she ever wanted to get in touch. She hadn't told her mum she had the details, but now Belle took out the complimentary notepaper and pen on the bureau in her room and prepared to write a letter.

Or at least that was her intention. Instead, she stared at the paper, then out of the box window at the top of the property, then she listened to doors in the bed and breakfast open and shut, low murmurings of voices as they moved past beneath, the gentle dripping sound coming from a drainpipe somewhere near the window now that the hailstones had passed and even the rain had eased off. She tapped the pen against the paper but had no idea where to start. What were you supposed to write to someone you hadn't seen or spoken to in more than two decades?

She kept seeing her mum's face, her reaction if she were to know what Belle was planning to do. On the one hand it was a betrayal, but on the other, if there was any hope of mending whatever bridges had been broken, perhaps this could be the first step.

When she thought about the doll's house again, the way she and Gran had played all those little games, and her fingertips fell on the locket still securely fastened around her neck, she had a change of mindset and, instead of struggling to find the words, Belle now knew exactly what she wanted to say. She had the sudden urge to convey how much she wanted to make Gran a part of her life, of their lives – and what was the worst that could happen? Gran could ignore the letter, tear it up, or she could write back angry at everything that had passed. Or her mum would find out Belle had sent the letter and end up telling her everything anyway.

Or maybe Belle would be lucky and this would work out exactly the way she wanted it to.

Putting all thoughts of the sale of the cottage out of her mind, she began to write.

Dear Gran,

I know we haven't spoken in a very long time, but I hope this letter finds you well.

I want to thank you again for putting Snowdrop Cottage in my name all those years ago, for thinking of me and my future.

I'm still not sure what happened between you and Mum. She never talks about it with me so I don't know whether she is angry, upset, or simply wants to forget everything that went on. It appears I inherited her same stubborn streak and up until now I haven't wanted to get in touch with you for fear of upsetting her. She's been by my side my whole life and I can't imagine it any other way. You should know that she has always been a good mum, and I've been happy.

My sense of loyalty also extends to you, and because you left me the cottage, I didn't want to sell for a very long time and, as requested, I kept the tenant you found. However, things for me are moving on and I'm hoping to start a new business, which is why I'm in Little Woodville now, preparing the cottage for sale. I have met with Sebastian and given him notice and he has been more than accommodating in letting me speed up the process.

I'm still in the village, staying at the bed and breakfast, and would love to hear from you, so if you can find it in your heart to write back to me you can do so at the cottage address. I'll be there most days, clearing things out and painting. You should see the dining room - it's going to be oyster walls in there with a fresh white ceiling and I'll carry on a neutral theme in the hallway too.

Thank you again, Gran, for everything you've done for me, even though I'm somewhat of a stranger. I hope that someday you or Mum can tell me what happened all those years ago and, who knows, perhaps you can both open your hearts and let one another back in.

I'm rambling on now so I'll sign off.

Your granddaughter,
Belle xxxx

P.S. I found your locket! I have it safely on my person and will wrap it up to put with your things and post to you. I'm curious as to who the other lady is? Mum didn't offer any answers.

In writing the letter Belle wasn't at all sure she'd done the right thing by her mum, but this feud had gone on long enough and being here in the village to see what her gran meant to these people, to Sebastian, to hear so many people fighting her corner, Belle knew she needed to get to the bottom of this once and for all. She took the locket from her neck, wrapped it in tissue, and slotted it into an envelope with the letter. It felt right to return it now. She'd box up the remainder of her gran's things and put the letter with it in the morning to take to the post office.

She pulled on her coat, scarf and hat, and, bracing herself for the cold, left the bed and breakfast. The Christmas lights strung from one side of the high street to the other lit the way, a golden bell above, a coloured Santa, white twinkly lights as far as the eye could see zigzagging their way across the road, pausing above shop fronts. The giant Christmas tree served as a beacon and led Belle past the shops, on to the village green and up towards the pub. She was almost at the door before she again felt the flutter of nerves in her belly and was surprised at the reaction. But she didn't think it was worry about meeting Sebastian – it was more her concern she'd bump into Betty or anyone else who shared the same opinions.

The pub was a welcome sight, and the setting at the top of the village green was idyllic. Sparkling lights were strung all around the eaves and the doorway, highlighting its olde worlde feel, its mullioned windows,

117

its tiny door. The windows glowed a soft buttercup yellow from the lights inside. Voices murmured, the odd laugh bellowed out and the chinking of glasses left no doubt as to what was inside.

Belle pushed open the door and made quite an entrance when she stumbled down the step because she didn't see the 'mind the step' sign until the very last minute.

There were two types of pub in Belle's opinion: the pub where you could enter, buy a drink, sit around and not be noticed at all; and then there was this type of pub, clearly a local dwelling, where whenever anyone new walked in all heads turned and punters swivelled on their stools to see what the interruption to their lives would bring. Belle recognised Audrey, much to her relief, and waved, and she saw Anne over on the other side of the bar and smiled at her too.

Sebastian rescued her pretty quickly from having to deal with meeting anyone new. 'I've got a table in the far corner. What can I get you?'

'I'll have a gin and tonic, please.' She passed by faces that pretended not to be looking and found a seat at the table where he'd pointed, his half-full pint of Guinness awaiting his return.

Sebastian fended off anyone else for now and brought her drink over. 'I thought it best you get a bit of Dutch courage before I unleash the village residents on you.'

'I appreciate it.'

His eyes danced with mischief. 'Actually, I should've got you a double.'

Audrey was with them in seconds. 'Belle, it's good to see you out and about, getting to know everyone.'

'Nice to see you, Audrey.'

118

Audrey introduced her friend and they dashed off to make it to the movies and Peter took their place. Belle was only halfway through her gin and tonic so Sebastian's plan hadn't really worked, but with him sitting opposite she didn't feel such an imposter.

Sebastian asked Peter whether Betty would be in tonight but apparently she was busy knitting a jumper for their grandson and already stressing it wouldn't be finished in time to give it as a gift for Christmas. 'Honestly, she spoils that kid rotten, and he's only four – he's not going to know whether he got the jumper on time or not, he'll be too busy with everything else she bought him.'

Next up were Andre and Nel, who had a night off from the pizza place with a young apprentice taking the reins, and Sebastian also introduced her to Bill again.

'Won't Bill want you drinking with him?' she asked when they were left alone for the first time. 'He did invite you.'

'I've sat with him already, and he knows everyone in here. He'll be fine.'

'Did you brief them all?'

'In what way?'

'Well no one's mentioned Gran, so I wondered if you'd asked everybody not to.'

He laughed. 'Not at all, but I think word got around about how Betty reacted.' He lowered his voice. 'She's a lovely woman but sometimes she speaks or acts before she thinks. She was close to Gillian and they saw a lot of one another when Gillian was still at the cottage, so I guess the hackles went up when she saw you.'

Belle wondered what Gillian had told her friend. Betty probably knew more than she did and although she didn't blame her gran for confiding in someone else, it made her sad to think that she was part of the family who had turned their backs and left her no choice.

Sebastian finished his pint and got another. 'So how long do you think it'll take to sell?'

'The cottage?' It seemed an abrupt turn from a relaxed conversation about the locals. 'There's nothing else for sale around here and it has character and charm, definitely a drawcard for somewhere like Little Woodville.'

'Who could you see buying it?'

It was harder to think about another owner than she'd thought it would be, but she played along the best she could. 'A couple, probably with grown-up kids, maybe people who have worked in the city and are taking a step back from the busyness of life in the big smoke.'

'That's quite a profile.'

She smiled. 'You kind of get to know which sorts of buyers suit a property.'

'Maybe a young couple would buy it, you never know.'

'I doubt it. There's no train station around for miles, not much of a bus service, and not a whole lot of local businesses either. Younger couples want a bit more.'

He shook his head. 'I'm not exactly past it and it suits me just fine.'

'I'm sorry, I didn't mean to be rude.'

'No offence taken.'

'All I'm saying is that typically most people of your age wouldn't be interested in a village like this. You've got work, but could you honestly say there's much around for anyone else unless they're already employed here?'

He smiled. 'You're right.'

'It's a shame you can't buy the place – you obviously love it, you've kept it in good condition. And it kind of suits you.'

'In what way?'

She felt herself colour. 'I suppose it's because you're living there and I've never seen you anywhere else.' Her explanation was coming out all wrong and her words reeked of someone who'd been thinking about this man too much. And Belle could tell by the curve of his mouth, the way his eyes didn't look away from her for a second, that he knew it too.

'No, I don't suppose you have.' Silence lingered between them until he said, 'You'll have to have a meal in here one evening. Benjamin, the landlord who just served you, cooks the best chicken roast you've ever tasted. It's even better than my soup.'

She looked over at the man behind the counter, rushing this way and that. 'He doesn't look like he'd have much time to cook.'

'He normally has help – Jackie, another local girl, usually works behind the bar in the evenings and his wife Kiara too, but both of them have come down with the winter flu.'

'No way,' she sympathised. 'Still, better than getting it for the Christmas holidays. That happened to me a couple of years ago and it was miserable as anything. I just stayed holed up in my flat feeling sorry for myself.'

'It's definitely better they get it now. This place will be even more crazy come Christmas Eve, then Christmas Day they're open all day and offer a full Christmas lunch.'

'Ever come here for Christmas?'

He shook his head. 'The food's lovely, the company would be great, but there's something about Christmas at home that just feels right. Don't you think?'

She murmured an agreement but really she was desperately trying to think of the last time she'd had a proper Christmas at home. She'd never hosted one at her flat, and her mum seemed to let the season pass by without much fanfare – the year Belle had gone up to stay with her parents in Ireland there'd been about as much Christmas cheer as there was in a lump of black coal. They'd had steak for lunch, there wasn't a tree and the gift exchange had been brief before the television went on, marking an end to the festivities. Whatever had made her mum dislike Christmas had slowly rubbed off on Belle and she'd stopped bothering with it so much either. She didn't hate it. She supposed she was just indifferent to it.

'What do you usually do for Christmas?' Sebastian interrupted her thoughts.

'I'll be away this year with my boyfriend.'

'Where are you off to?'

She told him all about the cottage in Wales and he waxed lyrical about snowy Christmases, the fact he'd already placed a bet that they'd have one this year. 'We haven't had one for a while, so you never know.'

'You sound like my mate Sam. She always puts a bet on. It's crazy.'

'Does she bet for a white Christmas or against it?'

'Always a white Christmas, so she's only been right once in the last decade. I think she just bets that way because she's afraid that if she bets it won't snow then it'll tempt fate and there won't be any kind of cold Christmas. What did you bet on?'

'A white Christmas of course.' When he smiled she suspected he probably thought along the same lines as Sam.

'What do you do for Christmas?' The question was out before she could consider she didn't want to be asked too many details about her own schedule.

'I'll be holding Christmas at home. Well, the cottage.'

She tilted her head to one side. 'I'm not a complete bitch. I know it's your home, and you should call it that.'

'Talking of which, I have a proposition for you.'

'Hold that thought.' She sipped and moved her straw between the slices of lemon lurking at the bottom to get the last dregs. 'I'll get another round in and we'll talk.'

She hurried off to the bar, wondering whether he'd managed to come up with a financial plan for the cottage. Maybe she wouldn't have to go through marketing and advertising and viewings after all. Then again, as she waited for her drinks, she didn't know whether to be happy about that or not. It would be a done deal if he could buy the place – the process would be speedy, she'd be free to leave the village sooner rather than later.

She ordered another gin and tonic and a Coke for Sebastian, who was only halfway through his second Guinness. It seemed talking business was something he wanted to do with a clear head.

She took the drinks over to the table and, opposite him, poured the slimline tonic onto the gin and ice, and confidently prompted, 'What's the proposition?'

'I've been accommodating in letting you get started with painting and clearing the place out. So, I was wondering, if in exchange for how nice I've been, you'd consider extending my tenancy until the cottage is sold.'

123

'So, if I sold, the moment the buyer completes, you'll be out?' The extra income would definitely help, and it was as good as a chain-free sale when a tenant could vacate quickly.

'The very second you needed me to, yes.'

'I didn't mean it quite like that.' She rolled her eyes.

'You're an easy target to wind up. You need to relax a little, chill out, drink up and get another.'

'I'm not that bad!'

'No, you're not. I'm teasing. But what do you think?'

'I'm not sure.' She bit down on her bottom lip. 'I'd thought it might be easier to sell if I can hire a bit of extra furniture, have the house completely uncluttered.' She thought about it some more. She had no doubt the cottage would be popular but, then again, real estate didn't always move easily and buyers could drag their heels whenever they felt like it. She could be looking at four to six months if someone had another place to sell, longer if they decided to then haggle the price moment before completion, an act she despised and wished legislation could put a stop to.

'I'll continue to pay the same rent,' he added. And you could move in some more furniture if you thought it would help. And I promise I'll keep the place tidy. I could even time any cooking to add to the feeling of cosiness in the cottage. Imagine buyers walking in to the smell of freshly baked bread.' He raised his eyebrows jovially.

'Wouldn't you rather get settled somewhere else, start moving on?'

'I'd love to be in my own place, but all the work I do is in Little Woodville and, as you've said yourself, there's not much around to buy or even rent.'

'I guess it could work.' Sebastian looked as though he intended to say something but stopped. 'Go on, say what you want to say.'

He looked at her. 'I also have another proposition, slightly different, and I'm not sure what you'll make of this one, which is why I started with the other first.'

Bewildered, she said, 'Out with it then.'

'As I told you, I'm not in a position to buy the cottage now. But that doesn't mean I won't ever be. I have other intentions for the finance I have at the moment but I've spoken with my bank manager and if the new venture I have in mind gets under way and goes well, then along with income from the other jobs I'll have to keep doing alongside for a while, I should be able to raise enough for a deposit and be eligible for a mortgage application. I'm not sure what Snowdrop Cottage is worth, but I've looked around at sold prices of similar properties in comparable areas and based on those, the actual mortgage itself would be more than the rent, but it's doable.'

'So you want me to hold on to the cottage indefinitely?'

'Not indefinitely, but for a while longer. It's a huge ask, I know, and you don't owe me anything at all.' He swigged his Guinness. Obviously the Coke hadn't give him the guts he needed for this conversation. She wondered what Anthony would make of this man's request. On the one hand it could hold them up on their plans but, on the other, Belle had the buyer there in the palm of her hand and so they wouldn't have to go through the rigmarole of sale.

'So you want me to stop everything I'm doing, leave Little Woodville and the cottage, then when you're ready you'll let me know and I'll sell.' She wanted to be clear.

All of a sudden this was moving at a speed she wasn't entirely comfortable with.

'I wouldn't put it quite like that. You could give me a timeframe, although I'd like twelve months if I can.'

Her brain was working overtime. From a business point of view it was a no. She'd be saying stay there, pay rent, and then if I don't find a buyer in twelve months you can step in. But she wondered what her gran would make of this, which way her gran would want her to play the situation, and if she went one way and not the other, would her gran hate her for it?

'Belle?'

She hadn't realised but she'd gone quiet, off into a world of her own. 'Can I have a chance to think about it?'

'Sure.'

'Wait a minute.' She suddenly fitted the pieces together. 'When I first showed up you were not impressed and you were quite rude to me. Can I assume the sudden politeness and welcoming into the cottage to let me get on was all part of the master plan? Did it give you time to see the bank manager and sort out where you stood?'

He looked a bit afraid to answer. 'I told you before that part of me was welcoming because of Gillian, and that was all true. But yes, I also decided I should be polite because I had this crazy idea I might somehow be able to keep the cottage.'

'I really don't know, Sebastian.'

'It's OK, I didn't expect an answer tonight. Go away and think about it.'

'I will do.'

His gaze lingered on her a moment longer but then he knocked back the remains of his drink. 'Come on, time I went home.' He collected their glasses and deposited them on the bar even before she'd had a chance to stand up and get her coat. 'I've got a job on at the church in the morning.'

'Right.' She had one arm in her coat and put the other in as she followed him out of the pub.

'I'll walk you home.'

'There really isn't any need.' She wrapped her scarf around her neck as he began leading the way.

'Gillian would never forgive me if something happened to you.' He didn't turn back.

Belle walked after him, her shorter strides making her struggle to keep up as she buried her face deep in her scarf to ward off the evening chill and stuffed her hands deep in her pockets. He'd certainly given her plenty to think about tonight. There was a lot of preparation she and Anthony could do to get their business venture off the ground, so maybe if Sebastian could commit to a twelve-month plan before he'd buy the place, perhaps if he could give her some assurance that at that time he'd be able to move forwards with a sale, then it could be best all round.

They marched down the high street, past shops shut up for the night, past a restaurant filled with customers laughing and chatting, a few passers-by meandering on an evening walk, another man walking a dog. When the man nodded a hello to Sebastian, although Belle didn't ask who he was, she knew she was slowly being drawn into the village more than she'd expected, and this last suggestion of Sebastian's had left her with a big decision to make. If he was as close to her gran as she suspected, it could also be a move that would keep her on side and go some way to helping the family move past their differences.

They reached the bed and breakfast and Belle went in the front gate and shut it behind her. 'Thank you, Sebastian.'

He leaned against the gate. 'You're welcome. And think about what I've asked. No pressure at all.'

She suspected he meant it too. 'I promise I will.'

'Your family, if you don't mind me saying, seems to be good at holding grudges and I don't want to alienate you in any way.'

'You won't, don't worry.' Before he could say it, she added, 'Gran wouldn't want that.'

'No, I don't suppose she would.'

When he turned to go, she called after him. 'I wrote her a letter you know.'

He turned back and returned to the gate, where she met him on the other side. 'You wrote to Gillian? When?'

'This afternoon. I haven't posted the letter yet.'

'Are you going to?'

'I'll send it with a box of her things.'

'I saw her last week.'

His revelation took her by surprise and she didn't know what to say. Instead she looked at him, he looked at her, and neither said a word for what felt like forever.

'Why didn't you tell me?' she asked.

'Like I said, I want you two to sort out whatever happened in the past – I don't want to be the go-between. She's well,' he offered when Belle didn't say anything.

Tears sprung to her eyes. 'Really?'

'Plenty of years left in her yet.' He reached out a hand and put it on her shoulder. 'Send the letter, Belle. She didn't talk about you or your mum last week, but I know she'd love to hear from you.'

'Did she ever talk about me before?'

'She hasn't for a long time. Around about the time you turned eighteen she wondered whether you'd find a way of getting in touch, then again when she put the cottage in your name she talked about you some more, but, other than that, she keeps that part of her life quiet now.'

'You've known her for ages.'

He nodded.

'I didn't realise.' Tears threatened to overflow this time. 'I have to go.'

'Goodnight, Belle,' he called after her as she turned towards the front entrance of the bed and breakfast.

But she didn't turn around. She didn't want him to see how upset she was.

Chapter Seven

Belle stayed away from the cottage for the next few days. Somehow she couldn't face seeing Sebastian again now she knew how very close he was to her gran – it was too much to process, too much emotion to make her way through.

She kept a low profile in the village and went to the post office in the next town to send the parcel rather than risk having everyone in Little Woodville know what she was doing. The last thing she needed was another Betty-like encounter along the way. She took herself off on day trips too. With the weather cold but no sign of snow or ice just yet, she went to visit the charming Bourton-on-the-Water, another picturesque village in the Cotswolds, where she meandered along by the waterside and took herself in and out of little gift shops, marvelling at trinkets she found and enjoying the complete anonymity.

By the time Belle made it to Snowdrop Cottage she felt ready to see Sebastian, ready to be in the cottage again. Her mum had texted last night and avoided any talk of the cottage or Little Woodville, and Belle didn't mention the letter to Gran or Sebastian's proposition in her reply either.

Sebastian's jeep was in the driveway when Belle pulled in next to it. She unloaded the paint tins she'd picked up that morning ready for painting the skirting boards in the dining room and took them up to the front door. She knocked a few times but when there was no answer she used her key. Perhaps he was out the back or had gone for a walk, so she quickly brought the tins inside and shut the door on the cold. She went down the hallway, took off her coat and turned to get to work, when she heard footsteps on the stairs.

She was prepared to see Sebastian but what she wasn't prepared for was to see quite so much of him. 'Oh no, I'm so sorry!' She held up her hands, shut her eyes as a very naked Sebastian rounded the bottom of the staircase and gasped in fright.

He swore and she heard his footsteps as he ran back upstairs. But she wasn't going to open her eyes yet. 'I thought you were out!' she called after him. 'I knocked!'

His footsteps announced his return. 'It's OK, you can open your eyes now.'

She opened one and then the other, still a bit embarrassed that his top half was exposed, and a sight she didn't mind at all. 'I'm really sorry. I should've knocked louder, shouted, I should've…' She tried to think of what else she should've done but after not seeing the man since the pub the other night because she felt awkward around him, this had certainly broken the ice and both of them burst out laughing.

He gripped the towel. 'The bathroom fan was on, I didn't hear you. But all my boxer shorts are in the utility room so I was running down for a pair. You kind of get used to living on your own after a while.'

'Go get dressed. I'll make myself a cup of tea; just give me a shout when it's safe to come upstairs and get on with Gran's room.'

He grinned. 'I will.' He paused before he got halfway up the stairs. 'Did you post the letter?'

Relieved he'd asked her that instead of whether she'd thought about his decision, she said, 'I did, but not at the post office here.'

'Wise move.' He disappeared the rest of the way.

Once her tea was made and Sebastian had gone off to an appointment, she took up some cleaning products and got to work on Gran's bedroom. She gave the windowsill a bit of a scrub, cleaned under the bed, which was much dustier than the rest of the room, and then tackled the wardrobe inside and out. She pulled out the doll's house and put it at the side of the room, careful not to let any of its contents fall out. She got a bowl full of hot soapy water and on her hands and knees sponged the shelves at the bottom of the wardrobe, cleaned up the sides and the dust jammed into any groove it could find, and lastly she wiped the exterior of the white-painted wooden doors that were crying out for a repaint to distract from wear and tear.

She picked up the doll's house to return it to the wardrobe because she had no idea what else to do with it. If her gran ever wrote back, perhaps she'd ask her. Nursery schools or doctors' surgeries often wanted children's toys, but she didn't feel right making the decision without someone else's input. If her gran didn't write then she'd have to ask her mum, and if her mum showed no interest, she'd have to make a judgement call.

She rested the doll's house on her knees and shifted it into the wardrobe, nudging it back on the shelf, but with the final push she heard a sound that couldn't be anything good. The thing had gone in there once upon a time so it couldn't be that it didn't fit, but when Belle dragged it out again she saw the chimney at the top had snapped right off and damaged part of the roof with it.

She sank to her knees. How had that happened?

She looked in again and saw what was to blame. There was a wooden support beneath the shelf – a big, solid block that had met with the old, and far more delicate, house. She left the doll's house at the side of the room. She needed to not see it, a reminder that it could be too late to salvage her relationship with her gran. Perhaps by not getting in touch with Gran when the cottage was put in her name, it had already thwarted any chance of getting their family through whatever had happened years before.

She went downstairs and got to work there instead. Now that the paint on the walls was dry, she removed the tape she'd fixed along the trim of the skirting boards to protect them, prised open the tin of white paint with a knife and got to work giving the fresh wood its first coat.

When the front door went, Sebastian appeared. 'It's freezing out there – I think it's going to be a white Christmas. Something in the air tells me so,' he babbled.

'Maybe.' She didn't turn round. She ran the brush along and coated another section in white.

'You can turn round, Belle. I'm fully dressed.'

His attempt at a joke fell flat. 'I want to get this done.'

'What is it?' He moved in closer behind her and she got a waft of aftershave. 'Have you heard from Gillian?'

'No, not yet. I'm not sure I ever will.' Her voice trembled and it was hard to disguise. Yesterday on the phone to Anthony he'd picked up something was amiss but she'd claimed she had her period. Women's problems always seemed to unnerve men so they didn't ask any more questions. Perhaps she should try that now, or at least she would if she thought she could speak without falling in a heap on the floor.

'Whatever makes you think that?' His voice was close now and she felt his presence over her shoulder.

She shrugged but said nothing.

'Is it me? Did I upset you by asking you to wait and sell the cottage to me?'

She shook her head and still said nothing, and this time his hand made contact with her shoulder just as it had the other night and when she shuddered and the tears came, he crouched down beside her and put an arm across her shoulders. With his other hand he took the paintbrush and rested it on an empty tray nearby, then put the top on the paint.

'Come on, you've got to the end of the section,' he said. 'The rest can wait till later. I think you need a decent cup of tea and maybe a gingerbread man. I picked them up from the bakery, so with every bite you could think of Betty.'

She giggled.

'That's better. Come on.' He stood and went through to the kitchen.

After she'd blown her nose and dried her eyes she joined him. 'Why are you dressed so smart?'

He hesitated. 'I went to the bank to get moving with some of my plans, ask again about a mortgage for the cottage, should I need it. I'm not making any assumptions, but I like to be prepared.'

'Fair enough.' She pulled out a chair and thanked him for the tea. It was odd to see him in a shirt and tie for once rather than old gardening clothes.

'She'll write, you know.'

Her hand stopped before the gingerbread man made it to her mouth. 'Maybe.'

'I could've taken you to see her.'

Belle shook her head. 'It would've been too much for both of us. Neither of us would know how the other was going to react, but a letter at least softens the blow, lessens the shock.

He smiled. 'You like to know what's coming round the corner don't you?'

'What's wrong with that?' She bit off the gingerbread man's head.

'Nothing at all. You'll be good in business; your new venture will thrive.'

Funny, she wasn't concerned that it wouldn't. She was more concerned that it would and that would be it. A business for life. Her path lined out and one it would be hard to veer away from. Not that she'd ever considered a change of career but when you worked for someone else there was always the possibility and these days people tended to change career somewhere along the way.

'These are good.' She bit off an arm and then the other.

'Betty probably wouldn't have sold them to me if she'd known one was for you.'

'Did she mention me?'

'She asked if you were still around.'

'And what did you say?'

'I told her on and off. I said she should give you a fair go.'

'I bet she loved that.'

He grinned. 'Not really, but then nobody can ever tell Betty what to do. Apart from Gillian. She was a match for Betty and never took any crap from her.'

'I can imagine. She was a lovely gran and we had so much fun, but she wouldn't let me be naughty – she had standards she expected me to follow.'

'Like what?'

'Like helping with the clearing up after dinner – I remember that well. She said youngsters should get used to it and parents shouldn't mollycoddle them, thinking they weren't capable of washing a bit of cutlery or plates. She'd have me set the table too, and at Christmas I'd go with her to the bushes at the churchyard, where she'd ask permission and we'd cut sprigs of holly to bring back here and decorate the cottage.'

'She loved holly, everywhere,' said Sebastian. 'There's some growing in the garden now. Every year with Christmas approaching she'd get some to decorate the sides of picture frames, over doorways, an arrangement on the mantelpiece, another on the table.'

'She bought mistletoe one year too.'

'Really? Hoping for one of the locals to come by was she?'

Belle laughed. 'I was too young to think anything of the sort. But she always told me it was magic and if you ever kissed someone properly beneath a sprig of mistletoe, you'd be partners for life. You know, I always remembered that. Every Christmas party I've endured offers of kisses from men twice my age or with wandering hands, and I've steered well clear of the stuff for fear that what she said might be true.'

Sebastian finished his gingerbread man and lifted up his mug of tea, his elbows on the table. When Belle sniggered he asked, 'What's so funny?'

'Your elbows. Gran had a thing about elbows on the table.'

He removed them immediately. 'You're right, she did. I'd better behave then.' His eyes danced with mischief and then settled. 'What was wrong earlier?'

He didn't miss much. 'I broke the doll's house. I wasn't careful enough when I shoved it into the wardrobe and the chimney, as well as part of the roof, came off. I guess it was the memories that got me. Gran bought the doll's house for me to play with when I came here, and damaging it, well it was almost like ruining another part of our relationship.'

She took a few more gulps of tea as she realised she'd bared more of her soul than she'd intended. She got up. 'Thanks for the tea break, it really helped. I'd better get back to it.' She left Sebastian sitting in the same place and went back to the dining room to finish painting the skirting boards so she could come back and do the second coat tomorrow.

*

The next day when Belle returned to the cottage she knocked extra loud so she didn't get a repeat performance of surprising Sebastian when he was naked. Not that it had been a terrible sight – far from it – although it was quite disturbing how much she could remember about him. He had a defined chest from all the outdoor work, arms shaped like someone who wasn't afraid of physical labour, and his broad shoulders gave him a solid presence.

Sebastian seemed amused when he opened the door. 'Didn't want to risk catching me without any clothes on?'

'I thought you'd appreciate me knocking.' She went inside, glad of the warmth. 'It's freezing this morning.'

'I know. I was out first thing gritting paths at the church and the school. The roads round here can be bad so take care when you drive.'

'I drove slowly, don't worry. I didn't want to risk bumping into Jeremy.' They exchanged a smile before she hung her coat in the usual spot and took her boots straight through to the utility room. It was odd having a routine in a house that wasn't yours. 'I'll get started then. I want to give the skirting boards that second coat.'

Sebastian hovered in the hallway. 'I'll be around here today, I hope that's OK.'

'It's your place, of course it is.' She went into the dining room but stopped before she'd even reached the space where she'd left her painting equipment.

'I hope you don't mind.' Suddenly Sebastian was right behind her. 'I took a look at the doll's house after you said it was broken, and managed to fix it up.'

'I don't know what to say.' She stared at the house, the chimney on top once again, the roof intact as though nothing bad had ever happened to it. 'Thank you.'

'It was my pleasure. I'll be in the kitchen if you need me.' He left her to it.

Belle got to work. The dining room was looking good with the oyster paint on the walls, the ceiling far brighter with its fresh white coat, the light fitting cobweb free and a real centrepiece to the room. The fireplace was quite something now it was clean, and Belle envisaged a bucket of coal or basket of wood beside it, perhaps a companion set housing a group of fire tools.

The skirting boards took longer than she'd anticipated, and it was slower than using the roller on the walls, arduous to crouch down and peer so closely to ensure the brush strokes didn't mark the walls. And by the time she'd finished, the music from a playlist on her iPod echoing out around the room, a wonderful cooking smell found its way to her despite the fumes of paint.

She wandered into the kitchen and Sebastian turned round. 'How did you get on?'

'All finished.'

'You've done a lovely job.'

'Thank you. And I want to say again that I appreciate you fixing up the doll's house. You didn't have to.'

He shrugged. 'It wasn't difficult and I had some decent glue, so I'm glad I could help.' He put down the spoon he'd used to stir something in the pot on the stove and wiped his hands on a cloth. He came over to her. 'You've got paint right there.' His finger reached out and touched her gently on the end of her nose.

A tingle sparked its way through her body and she scurried off to the hallway to check her reflection in the mirror. She had a nice blob on the end of her nose and used a nail to scrape it away, wiping the rest with a tissue. It hadn't completely dried so it was off in no time.

'How do you get paint on the end of your nose?' he asked when she went back into the kitchen.

'I've got it on my arms too.' She spotted it on the underside of her left forearm and then on the right as well, but the paint was well and truly dry.

'I'll get you something.' He ducked outside, an icy blast leaping into the kitchen even though the door was only open briefly, went into the shed and was back moments later with a bottle. 'Here, this will get it off in no time.' He gestured for her to go over to the sink.

'What is it?' She rolled her shirtsleeves right up as he opened the bottle and tipped a little of the liquid onto some tissue.

'White spirit.' He began wiping the tissue gently along the back of her right forearm. 'See, it's coming off already.' He was dangerously close to her now and she inhaled the heady scent of shower gel he must've used this morning. She could see a faint glimmer of stubble on his jaw as it tried to come through. 'Other one.'

'Sorry?'

'Other arm,' he prompted.

She'd been thinking too much about this man, this stranger, this person who was tangled up in her family's lives for whatever reason. She lifted her other arm and he took care as he cleaned it up before screwing the top back on the liquid.

Sebastian ran the mixer tap, checked the temperature and then handed her some soap. 'Now wash your arms to get rid of the chemicals.' He plucked a fresh tea towel from a drawer. 'Dry yourself on this.'

As Sebastian went back to check on whatever he was making, Belle cleaned herself up. All dry, she turned and asked, 'What are you cooking? It smells pretty good.'

'Thanks. It's beef stew.'

'Yum.'

'It certainly is.'

'And you've made it from scratch?' She moved towards the cooker as he lifted the lid and released the powerful aroma into the air. She picked up a hint of garlic, the richness of the beef, the herbs and vegetables he'd used. 'Is it your own recipe?'

'It's Gillian's.' He put the lid back on.

'She taught you how to make it?'

'I taught myself, but from her recipe book.' He went over to the bench nearest the window and from the corner picked up a fawn book that Belle recognised at once.

'May I?' She reached out for the book, which he handed to her. In her arms it bulged with pieces of paper sticking out from what seemed like every page; some were notes, others had photographs on them, but all were recipes her gran must have collected over the years. Belle remembered her gran buying magazines, cutting out recipes, gluing them into the notebook or sometimes writing them out with little suggestions for how she could tweak each one to be even more delicious.

'Do you remember her using it?' Sebastian screwed the top on a bottle of red wine he must've used in the stew.

'I do. We did a lot of cooking together.' Belle sat at the table and began to flick through the pages of recipes for Victoria sponge, tea loaf, chocolate and peppermint squares, flapjacks and peanut butter cookies. She stopped when she reached the recipe for ginger snaps. 'These were a particular favourite of mine as a little girl.' She flicked through some more, remembering standing at Gran's side as they made sausage rolls, lemon cheesecake with an assortment of berries, baked rice pudding and Swiss roll. Then came the more grown-up recipes that she'd helped with too, her gran increasing the amount of responsibility for her gradually. They'd made French onion soup, spaghetti Bolognese using a recipe Gran had made up herself with peculiar ingredients Belle had thought at the time, including apple, celery and leeks. As a little girl she hadn't wanted to eat all those vegetables in their natural state and Gran had devised the Bolognese recipe so some of the more daunting vegetable colours and textures were puréed as a sauce and then stirred into the meaty mixture.

'Spaghetti Bolognese, one of my favourites,' Sebastian commented, looking over her shoulder. 'Gillian made it for me plenty of times over the years.'

Belle was torn between relief at the assurance that Gran hadn't been on her own, as she'd always feared, and discomfort at knowing Gran had treated this man as the grandchild she'd never had, or at least the grandchild she'd fostered a relationship with when her own didn't want to know.

Over at the sink, Sebastian filled a colander with potatoes and turned on the tap to shower them in water. She watched him get his hands into the cleaning process, tiny splashes flicking upwards, a few landing on the bench beside.

'This book brings back a lot of memories,' said Belle.

He finished washing the potatoes and was about to talk to her when there was a noise at the front door. Belle looked around the doorway. It was only the post landing on the mat. 'I'll get it for you.'

She walked down the narrow hallway, picked up a wodge of envelopes and took them through to Sebastian. 'Someone's popular.' The first few were coloured envelopes and clearly Christmas cards.

He laughed. 'I'd better start putting some up I suppose.' He took the pile and opened the first few and Belle, done for the day, went to get her coat.

'I've got something for you.' His voice followed her before she had a chance to get her arm in one sleeve.

She was about to ask him what it was when she saw his face, his hand outstretched in the doorway passing her an envelope.

She didn't need to ask who it was from.

Chapter Eight

Back at the bed and breakfast, Belle sat on the edge of the bed toying with the envelope, turning it this way and that, looking at the writing her gran had penned. She hadn't wanted to rip the letter open at the cottage. Sebastian had offered her dinner tonight, which was nice of him, and she'd been tempted by the smell of the stew, knowing it was one of her gran's recipes. But this letter was waiting to be read and she wanted to be alone to deal with whatever it said in her own way.

Belle's hands trembled as she put her finger beneath the stiff paper at the back of the envelope and began to rip it open slowly. She pulled out the letter and, still in her winter coat, her gloves and scarf beside her, she began to read.

My dearest Belle,

Words will never be able to express my delight in hearing from you for the first time in what feels like forever. I want to thank you from the bottom of my heart for reaching out to me and I have read your letter more times than I can count.

Thank you for returning my locket. I thought it had gone for good and I lost many a night's sleep over it and became more upset than one probably should over a piece of jewellery. The other lady in the locket is a dear friend of mine. I shall tell you about her someday, but for now you should know that she had the kindest heart and a very special place in my life.

Thank you for sending on all my belongings. Did you find the doll's house? I always kept it you know, because I always hoped that someday you and your mother would come back to see me. It never felt right to get rid of it, but now it is up to you what you would like to do with it.

I would dearly love to meet up with you, Belle, but I don't want our contact to come between you and your mother so you would need her blessing. I don't come to Little Woodville much anymore but I miss it greatly, and I want to see you, to put my arms around my granddaughter and tell her how much I've thought about her even when she wasn't present in my life. Let me know what your mother thinks of this...she always did have an opinion, much like myself, and I'm thinking much like you too. Am I right?

I hope you write back very soon.

Much love,
Your Gran xxxx

P.S. Do you remember Pooh Sticks? I do!

Belle read the letter three times, absorbing every word. She was surprised her gran had written back and although the writing was a little bit shakier than any in the recipe book she'd seen today, she could tell her gran was in good spirits and, she hoped, good health.

Her phone rang and when Belle saw it was Anthony, she let the call go to voicemail. She couldn't deal with anything other than this letter for now. Her gran wanted to see her, she hadn't ignored the letter and, most of all, she remembered little details from her childhood. And words could not express how much it meant.

A tear snaked its way down her cheek. Gran's only request was that she clear it with her mum first, but that was easier said than done.

When her phone rang again Belle picked it up this time, determined not to let Anthony pick up on anything out of the ordinary.

'I've finished the dining room,' she told him. 'It looks great. I'll email you some photos if you like.' She'd already sent a couple of the pristine fireplace to Mrs Fro, because her neighbour had always longed for an open fire.

'That would be great. Could you also email me all the particulars about the cottage, the room dimensions, the plot size, any alterations, the structural reports you told me about?'

'I don't think we need to rush into getting the listing ready.' She knew how his mind worked. Hers worked in a similar way on a professional basis. But she still hadn't told him about Sebastian's suggestion.

'You know how I am, Belle. I like to be prepared.'

'I'll send the tenant a text and ask him to email me the structural report. I'll forward it on to you.' Handing over some of the details would placate Anthony. She knew she was going to have to discuss Sebastian's proposition with him at some point, but perhaps he'd see it as a good opportunity, one that made sense. And hearing from Gran, Belle knew how good it would make her feel to do this good deed, let Sebastian have the opportunity to stay in the home he loved, in the village that was as much a part of him as he was of it.

After Anthony hung up, Belle emailed Sebastian and asked for the reports. He forwarded the copies of the

145

pages pretty quickly. He didn't mention his offer, he didn't ask if she'd decided against it, and she respected him for giving her space and time to fully consider the implications.

When Belle put the television on in her room, if only for a bit of company, the Christmas film told her the festive season was fast approaching, and this year she had hope in her heart that she'd get a chance to reconcile with her gran.

And with that thought she drifted into a pleasant, heavy sleep, forgetting for now that she had any other concerns in the world.

*

The next morning Belle woke with a sudden determination to call her mum and let her know she'd written to her gran. Her heart pounded against her chest when her mum picked up, and she let herself be drawn into small talk for a while.

'Do you really need to stay in Little Woodville so long?' her mum asked when Belle told her over the phone that she was still in the village, still booked into the bed and breakfast for another week. 'I thought you'd have everything sorted with the cottage by now.'

'It's not so bad.' Belle waited for her mum to reply but she didn't. 'It's gearing up for Christmas.' She could just about make out the top of the Christmas tree from her window at the top of the bed and breakfast but of course it wasn't lit up like it was at night so was not nearly as impressive. 'Did they always have the giant tree on the green?'

Her mum hesitated and then said, 'No. There used to be a nativity scene and a small tree.'

'The one they have here now is huge.'

'How's the painting coming along?'

Belle told her mum about her progress but eventually she had to just come out with it. 'I wrote to Gran.'

Silence.

'I wrote a personal letter.' She wanted to clarify it wasn't formal in any way, shape or form.

'Belle, I'm not sure —'

'No, Mum. You have to let me talk now. I made the decision to get in touch with her, because being back here in the village and at Snowdrop Cottage has brought back so many memories. I bet it would for you too.'

'I told you before, I won't go back there.'

'You did tell me that, and I never thought I would either, but whatever this thing was between you and Gran, can't you just bury it in the past and move forwards?'

'You can't ask me to do that, Belle.'

'She wants to see me.' When her mum said nothing, she added, 'And I want to see her.'

'Well it's up to you; you're old enough to make your own decisions.' She was blunt and programmed in her response and Belle had no idea what she was really thinking.

'She said she wouldn't see me without your blessing.'

'What would you do if I said I didn't want you to see her?'

'I've stayed away from Gran all these years because I didn't want to hurt you.'

'That isn't what I asked.' She paused. 'Have you thought about her much over the years?'

'I did, especially at the start. I worried she'd be on her own, not have anyone. I've been thinking about her a lot more recently too and now I'm here I see she has a lot of friends, she has people, and I think, despite everything, she might even have been happy.' Her mum stayed quiet. 'Mum?'

'I'm still here.'

'What are you thinking?'

'I'm thinking you're definitely my daughter.'

Relaxing at the tender tone in her mum's voice, she asked, 'What makes you say that?'

'You have the stubborn streak your gran and I both have.'

'Thanks…I think.'

'When will you see her?'

Belle gulped, grateful her mum was actually talking rather than shutting the subject down as usual. 'I'm hoping in the next couple of days. The residential home isn't far, but I'll need to find out if they have particular visiting hours.'

'Is she…is…' Her mum's voice wobbled.

'She's in good health apparently.'

'I'm glad.'

'Me too. And mum…'

'Yes?'

'Just because I'm going to see her doesn't mean I've taken sides. I'm just trying to make sense of everything in my own way.'

'You don't need to apologise, Belle.'

Her relief was immense and after she put the phone down Belle gathered her things together. She wanted to go for a walk through Little Woodville, buy a hot chocolate, peruse the gift shop to buy something for Gran. And after that she'd walk over to Snowdrop Cottage to see Sebastian because she wanted to tell him the news the letter had brought.

She would soon be seeing her gran, and she hoped it was the start of bringing her back into her life.

Belle started at one end of the high street, treading carefully on the pavements in case of icy patches. There were a few about but the grips on her boots stood her in good stead. She passed the newsagent, an Italian restaurant, and wasted no time going into the gift shop. She had no idea what to buy and only hoped inspiration would strike. She walked up and down the short aisles, bombarded with glass vases, embroidered pillows, sets of festive coasters and more sturdy versions in silver or china, past framed photographs and mugs with funny or crude slogans. She came to the candles and undid jar after jar to inhale the claimed scent printed on the fronts: cookies, the ocean, wild mint, plum. And when she picked up a bright red candle she inhaled a scent that enveloped her in nostalgia with its tangy sweetness, the fruitiness of cranberry bringing back memories of her gran's Christmas dinners and the homemade cranberry sauce she'd let Belle help with every year up until she left.

Belle bought the biggest of the candles and, to hold it, found a warm-brass vintage candle holder with criss-cross patterns around the outside and intricate flowers on the edges. She had the gift wrapped at the front desk and then went on her way along the high street as Christmas music pulsed from a car parked nearby, shoppers buried their faces deeper into their coats, council workers gritted the pavements outside the café, where it was particularly icy.

Belle ducked inside the café and bought a hot chocolate. When she emerged into the December chill again, she looked across at the former photography place, still with the sign that said 'for sale' pinned to the inside of the window. She crossed over to take a better look. A couple of the windows were boarded up but there were enough covered in only a weak coating of Windolene for her to see inside. The place was compact yet still spacious and it could, with a bit of work, be someone's dream premises. Belle thought back to her conversation with Sebastian that day, about dreams versus real-life work. She wondered, could you ever really have both? And as she sipped on the rich, chocolatey liquid from her takeaway cup, suddenly ideas for a potential food business came flooding into her mind as if a pipe had burst. Just seeing her gran's recipe book yesterday had conjured up a desire for cooking and Belle had begun to reminisce in her mind about recipes they'd tackled together, others they'd talked about, some they'd made and vowed never to bother with again when they hadn't turned out quite right. If she bought this place, Belle could turn it into an ice-cream shop with homemade flavours, a pie shop even though she rarely ate pies herself, a fancy sandwich outlet, or a second bakery to topple Betty off the top spot. She could sell chocolate if she so desired, or run a cookery school for kids and anyone else who wanted to learn.

She could do whatever her heart desired. There was an endless list of options – and, more so, each one ignited a bigger flame in her than the real-estate venture did. But that was probably because it was the dream, it wasn't reality, and with that thought she shook away her daft notions and walked back down the high street to the road that would take her over the bridge and on towards Snowdrop Cottage.

'Mind if I put this in the bin?' she asked when Sebastian opened the door. He hadn't had one of his off, antisocial days for a long while, and it was getting more and more pleasant to be in his company each time.

'Be my guest. The bins were frozen shut first thing this morning but they should be fine now.'

Belle dumped her rubbish and then ducked inside the warmth of the cottage.

'I thought you'd finished doing work here for now,' he quizzed.

'I have.' She paused before taking off her coat. 'Am I interrupting you?'

'Not at all. I'm just surprised you're here, that's all. What's that?' He noticed the gift bag she was carrying.

'It's a present, for someone I'm going to see.' When she smiled she pulled out the letter from her coat pocket. 'I wanted to show you this.'

He took the letter when she nodded that it was OK to do so, and when he walked towards the kitchen she followed.

Belle watched as Sebastian leaned against the worktop near the Aga. She tried not to try to read his face too closely as he absorbed the same words that she'd done many times already.

'It's a nice letter,' he said when he'd finished. 'I had no doubt she'd want to see you, Belle.' His eyes held hers. 'Did you do as she asked?'

Belle nodded, more comfortable in this man's company than she knew she should be. 'I spoke with Mum earlier.'

'And how did that go?'

'Better than expected. She didn't put the phone down, which is a good start. I've always chickened out whenever we've talked and I've never pushed anything because I was wary of upsetting her.'

'What changed?'

She shrugged but then admitted, 'You made me realise how much I've missed out on.'

151

'Oh come on, you didn't need me to tell or show you that.'

'I know, but hearing little bits of what you said and things you shared with Gran made me realise just how little I know her, and it made me really sad. Then it started to make me a bit jealous that I was the grandchild yet there she was treating someone else's kid like she would've treated me. I felt pained at how much I'd missed out on, guilty for keeping my distance.'

'You were doing it for the right reasons.'

'I guess so.'

'So where to from here?'

'I know Mum won't follow in my footsteps and get in touch with Gran, but she told me she suspects I'll do exactly as I want and I don't think she'll be overly upset because I told her first. I'm going to go. Tomorrow.'

He whistled, sat down and leaned back in his chair. He clasped his strong hands behind his head. 'How do you feel?'

'Honestly? Scared, excited, nervous. This wasn't something I ever planned on doing.'

'It might not be the right time to mention this, but have you made any decisions about my proposition the other night?'

She knew he'd have to ask eventually and she didn't mind the timing. 'I haven't. I've forwarded the structural report to Anthony – he likes to be organised – but getting my head around Gran being in touch has taken my mind off your request. I need to give it more thought, but it could work. It'll mean a sale for us eventually after all. It's just that we'd have to wait a little longer. I promise I'll consider it carefully.'

A symmetrical grin spread across his face and reached his eyes. 'Thank you, Belle. It's all I ask.'

'You having people over for dinner?' She nodded across at the collection of vegetables and a packet of meat on the benchtop, another containing pasta next to it and a bottle of olive oil waiting to go.

He smiled mischievously. 'Go over, see what there is, work out what I might be making.'

'OK.' She rose to the challenge, amused at what he was plotting. She picked up an onion and moved it aside to find an apple, celery and some carrot. As she went through the ingredients Sebastian plucked some fresh herbs from their containers and put them on a chopping board nearby ready to be included: basil, thyme, and a couple of bay leaves he found in the pantry. When she saw the meat was mince, she knew for sure. 'You're making her Bolognese.'

'Not only that,' he grinned. 'I'm also making dessert.'

'Really?'

He began listing ingredients: raisins, dark chocolate, double cream, but it wasn't until he mentioned rum that Belle yelled, 'Rum truffles! I'd forgotten about those. Gran loved them!'

'She made them every year. When the letter arrived yesterday I knew it would be good news from Gillian and I suspected you'd want to see her as soon as you could. I had nothing much else to do today because the grounds at the church and the school are frozen over and will definitely wait until another time, so I thought perhaps you could cook here. I know you don't have access to a proper kitchen.' He shrugged as though what he'd done was something anyone would do, but Belle didn't think it was. His kindness this Christmas had extended beyond belief and every time she thought it, he did something else to raise his profile.

'I'd love to. Thank you, Sebastian.'

He opened a drawer and pulled out a navy and white striped apron that he threw to Belle. She deftly caught it and put the neck loop over her head then fastened the ties around her waist as he found another black apron he put on himself. She giggled when she saw the design, with a caption about men liking their pork to be pulled.

'Sorry, I don't usually have company when I'm in the throes of cooking,' he said by way of explanation. 'I won it in a raffle at the pub one year. Thank goodness I did, or some woman could be walking around wearing it.'

'No, she'd have given it away I think.' Belle joined him by the cooker. 'What can I do?'

'Chop the onion, the garlic and the carrots. They go in the —'

'In the blender once they're cooked. I remember.' She smiled, happy knowing she would soon be seeing her gran and could even tell her about cooking in Snowdrop Cottage.

She got to the task he'd given her as Sebastian grated apple, chopped celery, made up some stock and sought out a bottle of red wine. Belle added olive oil to the pan and Sebastian let her take over. He was merely there for decoration now, he said. He could pass her what she needed, find anything she still required, and she was able to request salt and pepper, the jar of passata to be opened, the mushrooms to be finely chopped.

By the time she'd sautéd the vegetables, Belle found she was loving every second of this. She and Anthony operated on such high speed she didn't do enough home cooking, and being in such a spacious country kitchen rather than her tiny one at the flat was an added bonus.

She scraped the vegetable mixture into the blender. 'Are many of these from the garden?' She'd have to tell

Gran all the details later, and the excitement threatened to bubble over.

'The onion, the garlic, the carrots too. And all the herbs are home-grown.'

She whizzed everything on medium speed before moving on to browning the meat, adding more ingredients – the passata, stock, vegetable mixture and finally a third of a bottle of wine as per Gran's recipe.

'Can I tempt you?' He took out two wine glasses from the top cupboard.

'Bit early isn't it?'

'You know what they say, it's always wine o'clock somewhere in the world.'

She didn't hesitate for long. 'Go on then. I'm assuming if you're letting me cook this, I'm allowed to eat some when it's ready. Otherwise I don't think my stomach is full enough for wine.'

'Of course you'll be having some, if you want to stay.'

She had begun to get used to him being kind, but staying for dinner was another thing entirely. She wondered if he was doing it because it was what he wanted or because he thought it was what Gran would approve of. 'I'd like that.' She watched him pour the wine. 'How long does the sauce need to simmer for?'

He passed her one of the glasses and then checked the recipe, running his finger down to the appropriate section. 'A couple of hours.'

A couple of hours was a while to sit around not doing much apart from talking, but then she remembered the rum truffles they still needed to make and felt more comfortable.

With the wine going down a little too well, especially as it was only early afternoon, they got to work on the truffles. Belle chopped up the raisins and Sebastian did the honours by pouring the rum over the top of them.

'It's a powerful smell.' She inhaled the contents of the bowl. 'Imagine how drunk you'd get if you just ate it like it was now.'

'Dare you.'

'No way,' she giggled. 'What's next?'

He consulted the recipe. 'Now we put it in the microwave, then we let the mixture soak for a bit.'

After they'd followed the appropriate steps they sat at the table and talked more about Gran. 'She and Betty used to do a lot of baking together,' Sebastian told Belle. 'They were very close.'

'That explains Betty's reaction.'

'Her age makes her stubborn too, but she'll come around, I'm sure of it. She once asked your gran to go into business with her.'

'Really?'

Sebastian took a long sip of wine. 'Your gran wasn't interested. She said she'd already retired and all she wanted was to cook for the people she loved and those closest to her.'

'Sounds like the gran I remember.'

He leaned back from the table and plucked his phone from where it was resting on the bench. 'No time like the present.'

'What, you're calling her?'

'No, I'm bringing up the website of the care home and you're going to find out all the details you need for tomorrow, so you don't back out. It's a residential care home, so the visiting hours are quite flexible.'

The wine didn't dampen her nerves this time. Seeing her gran was now a reality and the website was right there when Sebastian passed the device across. She picked it up and scrolled through the menus, found what she was looking for. 'Going by this, tomorrow morning would suit.'

'Would you like me to go with you?'

'You don't need to.' She fiddled with the stem of her glass.

'I know I don't need to, but even now you look worried and with all the ice on the roads you don't want to lose concentration thinking about something else.'

She looked from her wine glass to Sebastian. 'I'd really like it if you took me. We could take Gran some rum truffles.'

'Sounds like a good idea to me.'

The raisins had soaked up the rum and it was on to the next stage – melting chocolate, combining cream and sugar, and more waiting around for the mixture to set.

Belle stirred the Bolognese on the stove. 'This smells so good.'

'Put the spoon down; time to make the truffles.'

She grinned. 'Now this part, I remember.'

Using a melon baller, they each scooped out a sphere of the mixture and then rubbed it round and round between clean palms. Each one was placed on the greaseproof paper Sebastian had used to line the baking tray, and then put into the fridge to set.

'Hang on a minute, don't we decorate them with chocolate sprinkles?' Belle was confused. 'I'm sure that's what Gran used to do.'

'She tweaked the recipe.'

'Now why doesn't that surprise me?'

Belle grew impatient waiting for the truffles to set so she could find out what Gran did with them now, but finally it was time to take them out of the fridge. Sebastian melted white chocolate in a Pyrex bowl over a pan of water and with the chocolate in a piping bag, passed it to Belle to do the honours as he found more ingredients from the pantry.

'Just pipe a little on top so it oozes down the sides of each ball.'

'We're not coating the entire thing?' She began to do as he'd asked.

'That's it.' Alongside where she was standing he put down a tub that, when opened, had some tiny, pre-rolled red balls the size of small peas and some carved-out fondant holly leaves.

'I know where we're going with this,' she smiled. 'They're Christmas pudding truffles.'

'Got it in one. Now, your gran liked to put the leaves like this.' He fashioned three leaves on top of a truffle and put three berries in the centre of them. 'She made these every Christmas Eve. Now, I know that every time Betty goes to see Gillian she takes something, so you taking your gran her favourite truffles should put you in a winning position.'

'You mean I have to compete with someone else for her affections?' She gulped when she realised part of her felt like she was doing that when it came to Sebastian, but if he'd picked up on the underlying meaning too, he was nice enough not to mention it.

'Just keeping you on your toes.'

With the Bolognese almost ready and the truffles hardening in the fridge, there was a knock at the door. 'Expecting someone?' she asked.

'I apologise – this isn't a cosy meal for two but a gathering of five, now six with you.'

'Oh, I didn't mean to intrude.'

'Belle, you're not. And if I'd told you others were coming you may not have stayed. Am I right?'

'They're people from the village?'

'Yes.' He moved away towards the door and, before she could ask the question, she heard Betty's voice and prepared herself for what may not turn out to be a pleasant evening after all.

Chapter Nine

'Hello again.' Betty's ample bosom led her into the kitchen before the rest of her appeared and she immediately saw Belle hovering beside the cooker, stirring the sauce that didn't need any attention at all.

'Hello, Betty.'

Peter was next to come through and, surprising Belle – and probably his own wife – he enveloped Belle in an enormous hug. He rubbed his hands together when he let her go. 'It's freezing out there.' He brought the smell of the chill of the outside, easy to forget when you were toasty warm, inside. 'Are we first to arrive?'

'Apart from me, yes.'

'Oh, you're different – this is your cottage.'

His remark wasn't meant with any intent other than merely pointing out she wasn't the same kind of guest. 'I'm glad you're joining us tonight, Belle. We can get to know you a bit more.' He patted the table beside him and, not wanting to be rude, Belle took the seat next to him. Betty was fussing with her cardigan, undoing the buttons, trying to take it off without dislodging her blouse beneath.

'Sebastian invited me and it's nice to have a proper home-cooked meal rather than anything from the microwave, or a takeaway.' When Sebastian reappeared he looked anxiously her way but she neither gave him a look that said she was fine nor one that said she wanted to sprint far, far away from this table and the entire evening. 'Who else is coming?'

Peter answered the question. 'Nel and Trevor.'

'Wait, I thought Nel was married to Andre from the pizza place.'

'She is, but one of them has to run the business, so she'll be along tonight and Trevor offered to escort her.'

'Escort?'

'Oh, I know, it's an old-fashioned word for you youngsters nowadays, but for anyone over the age of seventy, we remember what it was like back in the day. He's been on his own since his wife died so it's nice he's got someone to come along with.'

Sebastian handed out glasses of water, offered wine, but still Betty sat at the table without saying a word. Maybe it was weird for her, being in the cottage with Belle's presence rather than Gran's. It had been said many times before that Belle looked a lot like her gran, especially when her gran was around the same age. And maybe the same hazel eyes, the apple cheeks they both had – well, perhaps they were too much of a reminder. All Belle was grateful for was that Peter seemed to be able to talk for England and showed no signs of letting up as they moved on to discussions of Christmas, whether it would snow in Little Woodville, when Sebastian was going to get a tree up and give the cottage what it deserved.

'Snowdrop Cottage without a tree in the window in the front room would be like our bakery without Jack and Daniel, or the pub without roast turkey on Christmas Day,' said Peter.

'I'll get to it.' Sebastian turned off the meaty mixture, which would wait until they were ready to cook the pasta. 'I'll go tomorrow or the day after.'

'Usual place?' Peter enquired.

'Always.'

'Where's that?' Belle wanted to know.

'I go to a Christmas-tree farm and choose one. Gillian used to be so bossy when we went there together. Trees were deemed too tall, too short, too fat, too skinny, too misshapen, too perfect looking. She had an answer for everything. But when she found the tree she liked…' He shook his head, remembering. '…her eyes would light up and she'd be like a little girl, almost jumping up and down as Dad or I tried to wrestle it onto the roof of the car. I've been going to the same place for fifteen years now and as long as they're in business, I won't ever go anywhere else.'

'And how about you, Belle?' Peter turned to her as she became more and more uncomfortable, as though every time Gran was mentioned, Betty's anger would bubble up some more. 'Will you have a big tree this year when you go home?'

'I won't be at home for Christmas. I'm going to Wales with my boyfriend.'

'Well that's lovely, but you'll have a tree won't you?'

'I don't tend to bother. We'll probably spend the day relaxing, cooking nice food. Anthony's not big on turkey, so maybe steak or pork.' She was babbling now so decided to stop.

'What about a fake tree? Not as good, mind,' Peter went on, 'but at least it's festive. Romantic too.' He nudged Belle and it made her smile.

'My family has never been big on Christmas.' She should stop talking! Justifying it only made things worse.

'But Gillian loved Christmas.' Peter didn't know when to stop and when Belle looked at Betty her mouth was set in a hard line and she was looking right at her.

'Excuse me.' Belle's chair scraped as she shoved it back. 'Bathroom,' she announced, and escaped into the hallway, up the stairs, and closed the door behind her. The cool tiles beneath her feet returned a sense of calm to her and when she felt ready to face the guests again she went back downstairs. She gladly answered the door when she heard chattering outside and saw the automatic porch light flicker on.

Nel introduced herself enthusiastically, Trevor too, and Belle returned to the kitchen, happy to go and find the pasta from the pantry, grate some Parmesan and Cheddar – another of Gran's preferences – for the Bolognese and line up the plates on the benchtop. Guests chattered and although Betty didn't directly say anything to Belle, her disapproval was diluted by the new arrivals.

'Here, have this top-up.' Sebastian handed her a large glass of wine.

'I really shouldn't. I don't want to be hungover to see Gran tomorrow.'

'Are you OK?'

'Sure.'

They were interrupted by Nel asking if there was anything she could do.

'We're all good, thanks, Nel,' said Sebastian. 'You take it easy, enjoy the night off from work and take care of yourself. You know what Gillian would say if she was here.'

Nel shook her head. 'She'd have me lying on the sofa in the other room and people waiting on me hand and foot.'

'She would.' When he smiled Belle didn't miss the affection between him and all of these people in the room. They all seemed to get one another, understand each other, accept and welcome a varied crowd that had come together to eat good food and catch up.

'Are they close?' Belle asked Sebastian after he'd drained the pasta and begun dividing it between bowls.

'Nel and Gillian? Not overly. But Nel's a friend and when she fought her leukaemia Gillian and many other people in the village rallied round. Nobody in the village gets forgotten about, Belle – everyone is included.'

When he moved on to the sauce and ladled it into the bowls on top of the beds of pasta she wondered if his implication was that she should give these people a chance, and she also couldn't help but think that he'd said something similar to Betty while she was up in the bathroom before because when Belle sat down at the table Betty asked her to pass the plate of cheese. It was only a few words but it was a start.

'This is wonderful,' Trevor complimented. 'Hats off to the chef, or was it chefs?'

'It was mostly Belle's hard work,' Sebastian graciously replied. 'It's one of Gillian's recipes and Belle mentioned it was something they used to make together when she was little.'

Belle knew he meant no harm in his comment but she almost burst into tears – whether from the loss of all those years without Gran or the daunting prospect of seeing her again tomorrow she didn't really know. Thankfully Trevor saved her from having to say anything or from further interrogation.

'It must be my turn to cook soon.'

'You guys do this a lot?' Belle asked, grateful to change the focus of the conversation, but they were soon back to Gran again.

'Gillian started it.' Betty looked directly at her but when Trevor spoke again Belle could at least look at him instead.

'Years ago, when my wife passed away, I was on my own for the first time in fifty years. And I don't mind saying, it was a struggle. I came from the generation

164

where the wife did the cooking; I was hopeless. I'd burn toast and pans of water, anything I could lay my hands on. Gillian came over one day to see if I needed anything from the shops – secretly I knew she was checking up on me – and I was eating my dinner: tuna from a tin with a piece of bread and butter. We got to talking and I don't know how she got the details out of me but she found out the dinner was pretty much my regular meal and at once told me to come over to the cottage for a second meal, a proper one. She put on no pretence, didn't spare my feelings if I was sensitive about it, because, to her, I wasn't doing well.

'Gillian started quite a routine,' Trevor went on. 'I would go over once a week, and she'd cook meals for me to put in the freezer. Then when Nel became unwell she got everyone doing the same, so Andre's freezer was constantly full. She even gave me a few cooking lessons. She taught me how to make vegetable soup, chicken casserole, shepherd's pie.'

'It's lovely you're all so close you help each other out.' Belle had made dinner for Mrs Fro a couple of times but not with regularity.

'Gillian insisted the meals happened once a month.' It was Betty who spoke to her now. 'She said otherwise we were in danger of forgetting each other – particularly those that were on their own, like Trevor, or Moira down the road, who sadly passed away earlier this year, and Anne, who was single and quite lonely when she first arrived in the village.'

'I met Anne the other day,' said Belle.

'She's very together now, but she went through a nasty divorce before she came to Little Woodville. She cooks a lovely lemon drizzle cake too.'

Belle smiled at the additional information, the feeling Betty was slowly warming to her. 'So you each take it in turns to put on the dinners?'

'That was what we did originally,' said Betty, 'but somehow it became the tradition to come to Snowdrop Cottage. I think Gillian liked to fuss over everyone and spoil them. And, lucky for us, Sebastian has carried it on. The only complaint we all have is that he never wants much help. You should be honoured he let you help today.'

Belle wondered if her cheeks had coloured to the same shade as the lip gloss she habitually wore. 'I enjoy cooking.'

Betty ended up being conversational with Belle as they discussed recipes Gran had made, what Belle liked to cook now, and the shared interest helped smooth things over between the pair. The dinner ended up being a lot of fun and, after the pasta bowls were cleared away, sumptuous New York cheesecake from Betty's bakery was served as Belle got to know more about the residents of Little Woodville. Trevor had a son who lived in Wales, Nel and Andre had been in the food industry for almost twenty-five years, and Betty and Peter had three children, all of whom had flown the nest, with one living in Sydney, another in Toronto and the third in Scotland. Every autumn, after the flurry of tourists had settled and before the next influx around Christmas time, Peter and Betty took three weeks away from the business, shut shop – literally – and off they went on their travels.

'Last year we went to Sydney,' Peter told Belle. 'A beautiful city; we fell in love with it, didn't we?'

Betty smiled sheepishly. 'I did love it. I don't think I've ever felt sunshine quite like it as we walked around the harbour. We went on one of those boats you see on postcards, took the grandchildren to the aquarium and so many beaches I can't remember the names.'

Trevor had travelled a lot too – but many years ago, before he and his wife had settled for the quieter village life. He extolled the virtues of travelling while you were young. 'You should do it, Belle, there's lots to see.'

'I don't think I'm the backpacking kind.'

'You don't need to be. Just make sure you do something different each year, and your travel portfolio will build up. Sebastian will tell you – he's been to enough places.'

'It's true,' Sebastian admitted, 'but I really did backpack and stayed in hostels.' When she screwed up her nose his laughter filled the room. 'I was in my early twenties. I think my standards were pretty low.'

'Where did you go?' she asked.

'America, Australia, New Zealand, France, Spain, then finished up in Ireland. How about you? Where have you been apart from Little Woodville and Cambridge?'

'I've been to Ireland. Mum lives there.'

'And?'

'Majorca, Paris, Zurich.'

'Let me guess, in a plush hotel each time?'

'Not really. Just self-catering apartments. But I'd love to go away again.'

'When was the last time?'

She thought about it. 'Just over a year ago – a weekend in Paris at Christmas.'

'Romantic.' This time his eyes challenged her and it took Belle a while to realise they were in a room with other people, all of whom seemed to be looking at them expectantly.

'Yes, I suppose it was,' she said self-consciously. 'Apart from when Anthony and I both got food poisoning and had to take shifts in the bathroom.'

The whole room burst into laughter, even Betty.

'Now that's romantic!' Nel wiped beneath her eyes, more than amused at Belle's tales. 'Pass the toilet paper, love.'

'I can laugh about it now,' Belle agreed, 'but it was awful at the time.'

'I'll bet it was,' said Peter, patting the top of her hand in a grandfatherly way.

Belle finished the last of her cheesecake and realised what a good time she'd had tonight. She gathered up the empty dishes and took them over to the sink.

'I'll do those.' Sebastian joined her. 'There's no room in the dishwasher.'

'I don't mind.'

'You're a guest.'

'No, I'm not. And I don't mean that in a horrible way – just that I'd really like to help out. I've had so much fun tonight.' Hands thrust into soapy suds, she wiped around another bowl and put it on the drainer before going back for the next.

'Me too.'

'You could have a bit more fun,' said Nel, pulling out a cluster of mistletoe from her bag. Its white berries and green foliage dangled from a red ribbon. She held it over Trevor's head and kissed him on the cheek, then moved on to Sebastian and then Peter.

Belle kept her distance from the mistletoe and hoped the washing up would take her a while. Nel was trying to hand the bunch to Betty but Betty was having none of it and came to stand beside the sink too.

'Sebastian tells me you're still thinking about what to do with the cottage,' said Betty.

'I am, yes.' She shook the suds from her hands and wiped them on the tea towel hanging from the door of the oven. Sebastian had disappeared over to the table to refill glasses, and Nel, leaving the mistletoe on the side of the table, had already moved on to setting up a cheeseboard with a vast selection Belle doubted anyone here could tackle after the feast they'd already had.

'It would be nice to see Sebastian stay here. He does love the place. And Gillian would be pleased.'

Belle wondered how annoyed she should be that Sebastian had even mentioned anything to Betty, but she guessed they were friends, it was inevitable. She smiled at Betty but before Betty could walk away Belle said, 'I never did it maliciously you know.'

'Never did what?' Betty lowered her voice, for which Belle was grateful.

'I always thought Mum would be upset if I got in touch with Gran; even as an adult it was what worried me the most. I didn't want to hurt her but, in doing so, I know I hurt Gran. I can't change it, but —'

'Dear…I overreacted in the bakery when you first arrived because I am close to Gillian, as everyone in Little Woodville is. And I'm very fond of Sebastian. He reminds me of my eldest son, with the same crazy hair that doesn't have a proper parting, the way he's so strong. I would hate to see him hurt too.'

'Please know that whatever I decide, it won't be something I take lightly.' She wanted this woman to know she wasn't some vulture who'd flown into the village to pick at the pieces she could get and leave a mess behind.

169

Sebastian put on Christmas music and Peter immediately grabbed Nel to dance. Trevor held out a hand to Betty and she accepted, leaving Sebastian and Belle with very little choice.

Sebastian held out a hand and Belle, fuelled with enough red wine for extra confidence, let him lead her to the side of the kitchen where the others were showing their moves. They worked their way through 'All I Want for Christmas Is You' sung by Mariah Carey, a rendition of 'Feliz Navidad', the more melancholy 'Christmas Lights', and one of Belle's favourites, 'Fairytale of New York'. And when Elvis's 'Blue Christmas' bellowed out, Sebastian leaned in and said, 'For the oldies – they love it.'

Belle looked around the room and realised he was right. They all seemed ten years younger all of a sudden and she was mesmerised by the scene, so different from what she was used to. She wondered if this was what Christmas Day could be like for some families; did they all get so enthused with the season they totally lost their inhibitions and danced together like never before?

Nel was back to doing the rounds with the mistletoe and Belle's insides plummeted when she came to them next.

'Kiss her!' Nel encouraged Sebastian.

Sebastian laughed off the comment and twirled Belle over to the opposite side of the kitchen. 'They're not going to be quiet until we do,' he whispered in her ear.

Butterflies fluttered in her tummy when she realised he was going to kiss her, and although when he bent down he only met her lips briefly before he said, 'Merry Christmas, Belle,' it sent her head and body into an unexpected spin.

'Phone's ringing!' Peter yelled, his arms pumping side to side, his feet trying to keep up. 'It's not mine! The black one on the bench.'

'That's mine.' Sebastian had been looking down at Belle but the moment was over. He quietened the music and took the call.

'What is it?' Belle asked when he finished his conversation and turned the music off completely.

'Nothing to worry about, folks. Bit of a family emergency, so I need to get organised. Sorry to cut the festivities short.'

Betty was the first at his side. 'Anything we can do?'

'Nothing, thank you. Just get yourselves home safely, watch out for black ice.'

'Don't you drive anywhere,' said Nel when he refused to elaborate on what was wrong, but Belle could see he was shaken up. She hoped it wasn't his mum or dad, something terrible at Christmas, but his face betrayed the fear he tried to disguise in his voice.

'I'll get a taxi if I need to go anywhere, don't worry about me.'

Nel put the cheese away in the Tupperware box and Belle ushered her away. 'I'll stay here, clear up, you get going.'

Sebastian saw the guests out as Belle wiped down the table and took half-empty glasses to the sink.

'I'll leave you to it,' she said when he came back to the kitchen. 'Unless there's anything I can do to help?' She wasn't sure what their boundaries were.

'Belle, sit down.'

'You don't need to tell me anything.' She swished her hand dismissively, not wanting to intrude, but when he told her to sit down again the truth began to dawn. 'Is it Gran?'

He crouched down in front of her and held on to her hands, their closeness at a whole new level after just one day of sharing the task of preparing a meal, having guests over. 'That was the care home calling – I'm Gillian's emergency contact. I'm afraid Gillian has had an accident.'

Chapter Ten

The care home wasn't what Belle had expected. She'd thought of it as a place where old people sat around in a circle in wing-back chairs, barely saying a word, ignored by staff, and generally waiting until their time came to walk into the bright white light. But it was a residential care home, which meant it was almost like an apartment complex that had a central dining room, a lounge, and residents were as independent as they needed to be.

Sebastian and Belle had phoned for a taxi to go to see Gillian after the call and the second they got there Belle knew she couldn't fly in and see the woman she hadn't laid eyes on, heard from or spoken to in years. Sebastian went in alone but here he was, rejoining her in the lounge where Muriel, one of the staff, had made her two cups of coffee. She'd felt quite irresponsible with the smell of alcohol on her breath, although Muriel had asked her if they'd been at a Christmas party and she'd found herself saying yes, because it had been just like one. Nothing like a work function, but very much like the sort of get-together she could imagine Gran being a part of.

'She's going to be fine' was the first thing Sebastian said, taking a seat next to her, putting a hand on her arm. 'The medics have seen to her wrist. She has a bad bruise where she stumbled and fell but she's not concussed as they'd suspected. There's no need to even take her to the hospital, although I'm pretty sure the medics may have done if she hadn't argued with them and told them not to make a fuss.'

Belle didn't say much, just nodded in acknowledgement. To say it was a shock to hear her gran had been hurt was an understatement. Sebastian hadn't got many details in the initial call, just that first thoughts were that Gran may need to go into hospital. Sebastian had insisted they make their way over there and if the venue changed they'd divert the taxi as and when they needed to.

'Why didn't you tell anyone else at the dinner?' Belle asked.

'That Gillian hurt herself? I knew they'd worry, they'd panic, and they'd all want to be here. That's not what she needs, or you, or me, or any of the staff.'

She smiled. 'Can you imagine Betty making her demands?'

'Oh come on, things didn't seem too frosty between you tonight.'

'They weren't in the end. Maybe she's realising I'm not a total cow.'

'I could've told her that.' His gaze lingered until he added, 'Do you want to see her?'

'Does she know I'm here?'

'She almost ran out here herself until I said I'd get you.'

Belle's heart thudded against her chest. She took a deep breath. 'I'm not sure I can do it. What do I say?'

'Start with a hello, take it from there.'

Belle stood, her legs shuddered beneath her, but when she saw the tinsel around the reception area as they walked past, the tree in the corner with colourfully wrapped gifts waiting beneath, it instilled a sense of calm. Christmas had always been their season when she was little, her and Gran's. She could still remember racing downstairs on Christmas Day to find her stocking pinned to the fireplace and stuffed full of little novelty presents, and the delight on Gran's face as she opened them.

'Belle?' Sebastian had stopped at the door of Gran's apartment. 'Are you ready?'

She nodded.

'Do you need me to come in?'

She shook her head.

Sebastian said he'd wait in the lounge and she knew the staff down there would spoil him rotten. Bravely, Belle lifted her hand and knocked on the door.

A nurse came out and called back to Gillian that she had another visitor.

Belle stepped in and let the door fall closed behind her. Silence.

'Is that you, Sebastian?' A voice came from the room to the left of the compact entrance hall where she now stood. 'Is Belle with you?'

Belle took a couple of steps towards the voice that sounded no different from how she remembered it and when she stepped into the room where her gran was propped up in bed, she froze.

Gran put her good hand across her mouth, tears in her eyes. 'Belle? Oh, Belle. Come here,' she said when she dared to take her hand away.

Belle went over without a word and let her gran hug her, trying to make up for twenty years of absence in a single gesture. Belle cried as she pressed her face against her gran's skin, more papery than it was once upon a time, age spots peppering the surface, but with the same scent of Anais Anais perfume she'd worn ever since Belle could remember. She still recalled giving Gran the perfume as a gift, wrapping the flowery box and tying a green bow around the red paper to make it look pretty.

'You don't know what this means to me,' Gran managed between sniffles. 'Oh, would you look at me! Pass me a tissue would you?'

175

Belle found the box on the sideboard at the far wall and passed it to Gran, who plucked one, wiped beneath her eyes and then blew her nose. Belle took a tissue and wiped her own eyes as she sat on the edge of the bed.

'This wasn't the way I envisaged our first meeting after so many years.' Gran reached out and covered Belle's hand with her own.

'Me neither.'

'You're so big.'

'I think that's a compliment,' Belle laughed.

'And I'm so old.'

'You're the same person to me.'

'Well it's kind of you to say, even though it's a lie.'

'You gave us quite a scare.'

'I didn't mean to. Damn legs have a mind of their own sometimes. I lost my footing on the stairs and stumbled, landed on my arm.'

'Does it hurt?'

'It aches, but nothing too bad.' She leaned closer as though there were hidden cameras or tape recorders in the room. 'If they had their way in here, they'd have me carted off for a long stay in hospital, but there's no way I'll be doing that.'

'It might be the best thing if you're really hurt.'

She used her good arm to wave away the suggestion. 'Rubbish. I'm not missing Christmas, and once you're in those places, getting out would be harder than escaping from prison. I would have to bash my way out, like in that film.'

'What film's that?'

She took a while to think of it. '*The Shawshank Redemption*, that was it.'

'Doesn't seem like your kind of film, Gran.' Belle loved how animated her gran was – she'd always been the same – and even though she was finding out new things about this woman, she felt grounded that some things hadn't changed at all.

'Sebastian got me into it one night. And I have to say, I'm glad I gave it a go. It had me hooked. Talking of Sebastian, is he still around?'

'He's downstairs, said he'd wait until I'd seen you first.'

'He's very considerate, probably knows we need a bit of space. He's a lovely lad.'

'He's nice.'

Her gran didn't miss a thing. 'Oh yes?'

'Gran,' she admonished, squeezing her hand. 'I have a boyfriend, Anthony.'

'I'm not surprised. You're beautiful.' Her gran's smile lit up hazel eyes the same colour as Belle's and a little twinkle of mischief reminded Belle of Christmas Eve when they used to make mince pies and leave a couple for Father Christmas. They'd always pour him a glass of wine too and leave a carrot for the reindeer. Gran had loved it just as much as Belle had.

'I like the blanket.' Belle admired the crocheted piece, multicoloured and folded across the back of an armchair in the corner.

'It's the one I made for you.'

Belle swallowed. 'I can't believe you still have it.'

'Some things are too precious to do away with.'

Belle cleared her throat to stop her voice from catching. 'My neighbour would love it.'

'Your neighbour?'

'Back in Cambridge, where I live, I have a neighbour, Mrs Fro, and she loves colourful things. She has a patchwork coat not too dissimilar to your blanket, and

177

she's forever buying clothes in all colours of the rainbow.'

'Do you know her well?'

Belle didn't miss the sadness in her eyes, the knowledge she'd missed out on so many years of her granddaughter's life, the thought that someone else may have stepped in. Belle knew how she must feel – it was exactly what had happened with Gran and Sebastian and she'd been jealous at the start. 'I've known her for a number of years, and we look out for each other.' She recounted the story of the baseball bat and the noisy neighbours, and had Gran in fits of laughter. 'Honestly, I'd be scared if she confronted me in the middle of the night!'

'She sounds like a lovely neighbour to have.'

'She's forever trying to convince me to get a Christmas tree.'

'Don't you ever have one?'

Belle shrugged. 'There never seemed much point. It was only me there, and I'm older now.'

Gran hid her surprise well. Or was it disappointment? 'You loved Christmas as a little girl. You'd help me collect wood for the fire, then when it was lit and the tree was bare and waiting in the lounge, you'd help me lay all the decorations out on the big table. We'd thread cotton through any baubles that no longer had anything to hang them with, we'd untangle the lights and test they worked, and you'd do it all with tinsel wrapped around your neck like a scarf, another two pieces on your wrists as though they were bangles, and you'd make sure you had a tinsel headband too.' Her eyes danced. 'The only thing you didn't like was holly.'

'But holly is pretty.'

'You liked it once it was up, when I'd decorated the house, but when you were six or seven we'd gone out to cut holly from the bushes at the churchyard and you tripped, fell, and scratched the side of your face on the prickly thorns. When you reached out to pull yourself up you grabbed more. Oh, your hands were so sore, you were crying, there was blood on one of your cheeks. You were not my happy Belle that day.'

It all came back to her. 'I remember. I had a red woollen coat on and a green beret you'd bought for me, and I remember clinging onto the bannisters at the cottage saying you couldn't make me do it. I think you left me there in the end.'

Gran shifted on her bed and Belle adjusted the pillows behind her. 'Thank you, Belle. I did leave you but I was only a few minutes and by the time I came back you managed a smile and we forgot all about it with a tall glass of milk and a big Christmas cookie.'

'You know, that sounds an awful lot like bribery,' Belle smiled.

'Hey, if it works…'

Belle saddened. 'I remember my last Christmas with you; I remember being driven away from the cottage and told that things were going to be very different from now on.'

'Your mother was very angry.'

'She's never done Christmas the same way since. Neither of us have.'

Her comments provoked tears this time and Gran plucked another tissue from the box still on the side of her bed. 'I'm sorry, this is hard for me, Belle. My daughter walked out of my life and never came back. It breaks my heart even more to know neither of you ever did Christmas again. It's all my fault. I should've tried harder. I blame myself.' Tears flowed freely, her body shook and Belle had to put her arms around her to calm her down. She was about to go and find the nurse, panicking this was all too much, when her gran settled down again.

'I've been happy, Gran. That's what you need to know.'

'And your mother?'

'She's stubborn, something I think I got from her, but life hasn't been all bad.'

'And she knows you're here?'

Belle nodded. 'I'm not sure how she felt about it, but she didn't go mad, and I think she knows I have my own mind and she wouldn't be able to change it.'

Gran hesitated and then said, 'Have you really never bought your own Christmas tree?' She looked as though she hoped the answer the second time round might be different.

Belle shook her head. 'If I'm at Mum's, she sometimes has a small tree, but when it's just Anthony and me, neither of us is that into Christmas so we usually avoid the fuss.'

'Fuss?' she was beginning to settle into the Gran that Belle remembered, unafraid to put her views across. 'There was a time when you loved the fuss, and before you say it's a kid thing, it's not. I still love Christmas and wouldn't dream of not having a tree, decorating it, having the big meal.'

'Maybe it's not an age thing,' Belle admitted. 'Maybe it's a me thing. Mrs Fro does Christmas well. She always decorates her flat, always has a wreath on the door, usually a different one each year. For a time she used to go and make one with friends of hers, but now I think she makes it at home. She's on her own, but she has a daughter she sees often.'

'That's nice; it's awful to be alone.' She noticed Belle swallow. 'I was never alone, my darling Belle, I promise you.'

Belle felt happy hearing her say that. 'It sounds as though you had quite the social life in Little Woodville. You have some nice friends.'

'It's a wonderful place. I'm glad you like what you've seen of it.'

'I do, and it's had quite an effect on me.'

'In what way?'

Belle wasn't sure how honest to be. 'It's made me question my decision about selling. Mrs Fro was most concerned I take my time thinking about what I'm getting rid of when I told her I was clearing out the cottage. She was very surprised I was selling the place. And now I'm here, I can see that for myself.'

Gran toyed with the tissue on her lap. 'I have to admit something to you.'

'Is this like one of those huge deathbed confessions and I'm going to find out something awful?'

'I hope not! I've hurt my arm – I'm not knocking on death's door just yet!'

Belle grinned. 'Glad to hear it. So come on, what's the confession?'

'Over the years, I've kept an eye on you.'

'What do you mean?'

'Sebastian helped me track you down. When I decided to put the cottage in your name, it didn't take long to find you. The internet made it easier – he was onto it straight away. I found out an address and that was how my solicitor corresponded with you, but I did something else too.' She covered her face.

181

'Go on, Gran.'

'I came to the address. I made Sebastian drive me to Cambridge and we sat outside your flat.'

'You did?'

'I waited and waited; Sebastian was really patient with me. We waited for hours at the end of a weekday because I was convinced I'd see you return from work. And then there you were. It was six thirty on a summer's evening, the sun was high in the sky, and when you climbed out of your car in a floral skirt with a white blouse, your dark hair cascading down your back the same way as it had when you were ten years old, you didn't even have to turn round. I knew it was you. And when you did turn, to lock the car, well it was like watching Delia. You were, and still are, the spitting image of your mum. Oh, I know you have parts of your father too but, to me, you were her all over again.'

'Why didn't you say hello to me?'

'Honestly? I knew you'd sided with your mother. I wasn't sure what she'd told you and I didn't really want to know. I wanted to see you, know you were well, and I'd done that. It wasn't my intention to upset anyone.'

'Why did you leave the cottage to me, Gran?'

'I knew if I tried to leave it to Delia then I could risk her moving even further away from me. She's been angry for so long, I thought she might refuse it and even take legal action to stop me contacting her. You and I were always so close and my last hope was that you were as loyal to me as you were to your mum, and that you'd keep the cottage. Part of me hoped it would be the key to us all eventually reconciling, but that was just a silly dream.'

'It wasn't silly,' said Belle.

'I thought maybe you'd get in touch after everything was sorted through the solicitor, but you never did. I had a little spark of hope that you'd go to the cottage, remember all the good times, and you'd want to find me. But then when you didn't, I consoled myself with the thought that you having the cottage in your name would at least give you time to think; it would make me closer to you in a different way.'

Belle smiled and her voice, when it came out, was soft. 'It made me think about you a lot. I let you put the cottage in my name because I felt the same way. It linked us together and in a way that didn't make me feel as though I was betraying Mum, because I hadn't seen or spoken to you.'

'That day outside your flat, I waited for you to go inside and then Sebastian sat patiently beside me until he was so desperate for me to eat something that he left me there and scooted off to the nearest shop for a meat pie and some cold drinks.' Gran managed a nervous smile before adopting a more serious tone again. 'It was while he was gone that I had the courage to get out of the car.'

'Did you knock at the door?'

'I didn't. I stopped at the entrance and then lost my nerve. I began to cry and slumped down on the steps, partly hoping you'd come out and see me, but at the same time not wanting you to because I'd be so embarrassed and mortified if you told me to go away.'

'Did Sebastian find you?'

'No, but Mrs Fro did.'

Belle's eyebrows knitted into a frown. 'You've met Mrs Fro? Did she know who you were?'

Gran nodded. 'She did after she'd comforted me – I think she thought I'd escaped from the nearest loony bin – and the whole story poured out. She urged me to come in or to come back another day, and then she offered the biggest act of kindness I could ever hope for.'

'What did she do?'

Gran gripped Belle's hand. 'She agreed to keep in touch with me, let me know about my granddaughter.'

'You mean…'

'She's been doing it ever since, for the past ten years. Oh, Belle, I feel like I've been with you half the time. I saw photos of you with a brand-new car, your picture with your boyfriend all dressed up ready for a New Year's party. I've had letters saying how much fun you were when you came home after a late night and you and Mrs Fro would chat over her infamous mince pies. She told me about the meals you cooked for her. And I know she's always trying to talk you into being a bit more festive, although she kept the lack of a Christmas tree to herself.'

Belle wasn't sure how to feel.

'Are you angry with us? With Sebastian and me?'

Somehow, imagining the pair of them in cahoots warmed Belle's heart. 'No, I'm not angry. I just wish I'd known.'

'I'm glad you didn't. It meant I could know all about you and you'd never have to feel guilty about betraying your mum.'

The nurse knocked on the door and Belle excused herself for a break, but not after she'd reassured Gran that she'd be back. Belle found Sebastian in the reception being plied with sausage rolls left over from a pre-Christmas party.

'Thanks for rescuing me,' he whispered. 'I think I was about to be involved in some kind of Secret Santa event, and I'm not sure whether there were gifts or if I was supposed to be the prize.'

184

Belle giggled. 'Maybe I'll leave you to it and watch. It could be amusing.'

He ushered her past a couple of little old ladies, who looked ready to pounce, and out of the front door. 'I need to get some air.'

Belle gasped. 'It's freezing out here.'

He took her hand. 'Come on, there's a side entrance.'

She trailed after him, the cold biting every piece of skin it could find, until they pushed through another doorway. 'Are we allowed in here?'

'I think the kitchens are through there.' He pointed down a corridor. 'We won't be long – I just want to know how it's all going.'

She smiled, suddenly not cold at all. 'Really well. We're talking. The nurse is with her now but I'll go back if that's OK. If you want to get a taxi home, I don't mind.'

'I'll stay if *you* don't mind. I've seen her myself, but this is a big thing and you're still drunk.'

'I am not!'

He shrugged. 'No, but I think I might be a little bit. Someone offered me some punch in there and I'm pretty sure one of those old biddies has tipped something very potent into it.' His eyes widened.

'You never told me.'

'Told you what?'

'That you took Gran to see me at my flat years ago.'

'She dropped me in it, huh? Does that mean I'm in the bad books again?'

She thought about it, then let him off the hook. 'Not at all.'

'I was worried this would all be too much for her today, but it sounds as though she's coping.'

'She did have a moment where I almost called the nurse in, but she settled down soon enough. I haven't told her yet, but I'm going to call Mum later and tell her I'm here.'

'Is that wise?'

She took a deep breath. 'Not only is it wise, it's about time.'

Sebastian and Belle made their way back around the building and inside he found a newspaper and a quiet corner to hide in while Belle went back up to see Gran.

With a tray table over her lap, Gran seemed to have a bit more colour in her cheeks than earlier and her eyes lit up when Belle entered the room.

'That looks nice. What've you got?' Belle asked.

'Mince pies, of course.'

'You know, if you hadn't had the fall and made me forget, I was going to bring you some Christmas truffles over. And I bought you a beautiful candle too – one that smells just like Christmas at Snowdrop Cottage.'

'Well, you can bring it next time.' Her words hovered between them and Gran wiped a pastry flake from her chin with a little smile. 'Did you buy the truffles from the bakery?'

'No, I'm avoiding that place.'

'Why?'

'Betty took a disliking to me as soon as she knew who I was.'

'She never did.' She only paused briefly before carrying on chewing. 'I'll have a word.'

'She's fine now. She came for dinner tonight at the cottage, along with a few others, and actually managed a few words to me.'

'You were at one of Sebastian's dinners?' Her eyes sparkled.

186

'You make them sound legendary.'

'They are! Well, the legend started with yours truly' – she patted a hand against her chest – 'and he carried it on. He's a good man.'

Belle avoided the clear mention of Sebastian again and all his attributes. Funny, Gran hadn't delved much about Anthony and she wondered what information Mrs Fro had been feeding her.

'So, where did you get the truffles?' Gran asked. 'Not a big supermarket chain?' She turned her nose up.

'Gran! How bad would you feel if I had?'

'I'm sorry, love. It's years of home cooking that's done it; I'm a terrible snob sometimes. I apologise.'

'Well no need, because these truffles are homemade.'

Gran's gaze left the cup of tea she'd lifted part of the way towards her mouth and she put the cup down again. 'You mean, you made my truffles? From my recipe book?'

Belle nodded, delighted she could tell Gran this much. 'Sebastian uses the book all the time and so after we'd made the Bolognese, it was on to the truffles.'

'You've been cooking in my kitchen? With my old recipes?' Her eyes glazed over.

Belle nodded, her eyes doing the same – she couldn't help it. 'I let it slip that I enjoy cooking and I guess Sebastian felt sorry for me being stuck in the bed and breakfast with limited food options.'

'He's —'

Belle pre-empted the remark. 'Don't say he's a good man again, you've already told me, and I know he is. He was kind enough to let me cook.'

'And was the Bolognese as you remembered?'

'Exactly the same. And it was a hit with the crowd.' She recounted who had been there tonight, what they'd talked about, the laughter and warmth in Snowdrop Cottage.

'I do miss the place, you know.'

'What made you move out?'

'Company.'

'But you have a million friends.'

'I'm slowing down now.'

'Sorry, Gran. That answer doesn't cut it I'm afraid. Why leave a village and a home you love?'

She took a while to answer. 'Because I knew as long as I was living at Snowdrop Cottage, neither you nor your mother would ever come near it or Little Woodville again. And I wanted to be settled somewhere else before the move became too difficult. I see men like Trevor on his own after years and he's too stubborn and set in his ways to try anything like this for himself. He's fine for now, but what about as he gets older? I wanted to make friends while I still had all my marbles, know where I was, feel at home.'

'I can understand that,' said Belle, although she was astonished by the banger of guilt that fired off inside her chest at not having been there for her. 'You know, I think Mum never talked about you because it was all too painful for her. Maybe she has her regrets now.'

A sobering smile passed across her gran's lips. 'How about we avoid all the heavy talk for now?'

'Sounds a good idea to me.'

'Tell me about this young man of yours.'

Belle smiled. At last, she was asking. She'd thought about this moment many times, wondering if her gran was at the age where she'd lost interest in the love life of someone of a different generation, but it seemed she'd underestimated her.

188

Belle told Gran how she'd met Anthony. She talked about their work life, their social life, the holidays they'd taken and their plans to start their own business. She told Gran about their upcoming trip to Wales.

'So you won't be in Little Woodville for Christmas – that's a shame.'

'I check out of the bed and breakfast on Christmas Eve. I figured a few weeks would be enough to get my head together, sort things at the cottage.' She hesitated. 'Sebastian has a proposition for me.'

'Oh?'

'He wants me to hold off with a sale, give him time to save up the money so in a year's time he can buy it himself.'

'Well that sounds like a fine plan to me. I have many fond memories of my cottage, you know.'

'Me too,' Belle confessed.

'It's time for it to move to the next generation now,' Gran concluded. 'And I'm not saying this to hurt you, but Sebastian is family. We're not blood-related, but he and his family mean a lot to me. It would mean the world if he got to keep the cottage.'

Belle smiled, because on the way over here, seeing how worried he was and how supportive he'd been over her reuniting with her gran, she'd come to a decision. 'I've decided I can delay my plans, so it'll give him time to buy Snowdrop Cottage.'

'You're going to sell it to him instead?' She covered her mouth with both hands, hardly daring to believe it.

'Yes, Gran.' She let herself be hugged, relished the warmth and nostalgia it evoked. When they pulled apart she said, 'By the time Sebastian moved out and I got the place advertised, it could take months to push the sale

189

through. This way could be better, because we know the buyer, we know he wants it, he's unlikely to back out.'

'Have you told Anthony yet?'

'Not yet. I haven't told Sebastian either.'

'He'll be thrilled! Will Anthony mind?' She asked a little more cautiously.

'I think he'll see it's a good idea. He's got a good business sense, a passion for it.'

Gran's head tilted to one side. 'And is it your passion too? To set up this business you told me about?'

'I think so.' She felt she could be really honest. Her mum hadn't questioned the move at all. It made good sense, she trusted Belle knew what she was doing, but perhaps all along Belle had needed people to second-guess what she planned to do, to challenge her to really think about what was driving her in that direction. 'I love my job, I could see myself being my own boss, but I do have my doubts. Then again, if I didn't have doubts that would be bad, wouldn't it? It would make me rush in and possibly regret it?'

'Are your doubts about the business, or about Anthony? Or both?'

'You always had a way of getting to the point, Gran.' Belle couldn't help but grin. 'I haven't told anyone this, not even my best friend Sam, but sometimes I wonder if Anthony and I fell into a relationship because it was so easy. We work in the same industry, we're on the same wavelength, there's nothing he does that irritates me too much – unless it's talking about work a bit incessantly. We seem to fit.'

'Just tell me, Belle…' Gran pulled a face when she sipped her tea to find it had gone cold. 'Have you kissed him under the mistletoe yet?' She put both arms up and wiggled her fingers as if sprinkling magic.

190

'You and your mistletoe.' Shaking her head, Belle took the tray table and put it on the floor to avoid everything being spilt with her gran becoming so animated. She ignored the zip of anticipation she felt at the thought of her brief kiss with Sebastian earlier on at the dinner.

'So have you?' Gran persisted.

'We've kissed plenty of times.'

'Belle Nightingale, have you kissed him under the mistletoe or not?'

'Not everyone believes those crazy ideas.'

'But you do.' It wasn't a question. 'I'm right, aren't I?' She clapped her hands together and winced.

'Mind that arm, for goodness' sake,' Belle admonished. 'Anthony and I are fine. We don't do Christmas like you do – I don't know anyone who does.'

'Sebastian does.'

Belle started to laugh.

'What's so funny?'

'You! I haven't seen you in years and I'm thirty-one years old but here you are, trying to set me up with the boy next door. Or, in this case, the boy in your cottage.'

'Forgive me. I'm old, I need to live vicariously through you. And it's *your* cottage, remember.'

Belle grinned, and when there was a knock at the door and Sebastian called out to announce his arrival, Belle put a finger to her lips. 'Not a word, no matchmaking – I'll be very embarrassed.'

'You two look like you're hatching a plan,' Sebastian observed, entering the room.

Gran's eyes widened in innocence. 'Not at all. Now come here and tell me about the dinner – Belle says you cooked together.' Belle didn't miss the hint dropped like a meteorite into the conversation. 'I hear you made Bolognese.'

*

When Gran seemed as though the only thing that could keep her awake any longer would be if each of them took an eyelid and hooked it up so her eyes wouldn't shut, Sebastian and Belle took a taxi back to Little Woodville.

'She was the happiest I've seen her tonight,' said Sebastian as the taxi pulled slowly into the village and down the high street.

Belle couldn't stop smiling. 'I can't believe I've seen her. I'll bet I wake up tomorrow and think I've dreamt it all.'

'Straight on please,' Sebastian told the driver. 'We're heading to the bed and breakfast first, then Snowdrop Cottage.'

Belle clocked the time. 'It's almost midnight.'

'She could talk for England, your gran.' His eyes dazzled as though he'd been just as mesmerised by their meeting tonight. The taxi pulled up outside the bed and breakfast. 'Actually, I'll get out here too. I could use the walk.' Sebastian took out his wallet and only after a lot of insistence took some money from Belle to pay for her share of tonight's fare.

When the taxi departed, they stood at the side of the road, in front of the gate separating the path leading up to the front door from the pavement.

'Thank you for tonight, Sebastian.'

'You're welcome. I think I delivered your gran the best Christmas present she could ever wish for.'

'I think you're right.' Her breath hovered white against the air, although bundled up in her coat and scarf she didn't feel the cold on the clear winter's night. 'Is there something else?' He didn't seem in a hurry to go anywhere.

'When I was with your gran, I noticed her wearing the locket.'

'I sent it back to her.' She wondered where this was going.

'I know you did. I asked her whether there was a photo inside and she opened it to show me that there was one of her and one of someone else. I realised who it was.'

'Who?'

'It's my gran. She died a long time ago but she and Gillian were the best of friends, which is how I came to know your gran. I don't know all the details, and I hope she'll tell us more one day. But it got me thinking.'

'In what way?'

He shrugged. It was his turn to breathe into the night air. Wrapped up in his donkey jacket, he turned and rested against the little fence as Belle did the same. 'There's obviously something I don't know either, something that was kept from both of us.'

'Blimey, I feel like I'm on one of those TV shows and I'm about to find out some deep, dark family secret.'

He didn't see the funny side. 'You don't think...'

'Don't think what?'

'I don't know...you don't think we're somehow related or something do you?'

Belle's laughter echoed around them until she clamped a gloved hand across her mouth in case she woke the whole of Little Woodville. 'I really don't. How exactly would that be possible? Gran had Mum and that was it. I think we'd know if Gran had any more offspring.'

'I never questioned Gillian's existence in my life until now, Belle. I knew she was a close friend of my gran's but a lot of people are close, it doesn't mean their family lives become one like ours seemed to.'

'I think Gran didn't have her own family around her, for whatever reason, and yours stepped in. But there's no way we're related. I'm pretty sure if we were, Gran wouldn't be making suggestions left, right and centre.'

'Suggestions?'

It seemed the effects of the wine at dinner earlier hadn't let up at all, or maybe it was her elation at seeing Gran, the tiredness from all the emotions of the night as she reclined here and the church bells began their chime announcing midnight.

She let the bells quieten. 'She loves you to bits, and you should probably watch your back.'

'In what way?'

'Gran clearly enjoys a spot of matchmaking. Not something I experienced as a ten-year-old, but I'd not been with her an hour tonight before she eluded to the fact that you were a lovely man.'

'You don't think I am?'

She leaned towards him to give him a shove. 'That's not what I mean and you know it. My point is, if we were in any way related, she wouldn't be doing it would she?'

'You're right. That would be sick.'

'Very sick.' Belle laughed. 'I've had a good time tonight. And I don't just mean seeing Gran again. The dinner was really wonderful; thank you for making me a part of it.'

'It's a tradition started by your family, and one I'd hate to see go.'

'So would I.'

They rested side by side on the fence looking out across the village. The air whipped across their cheeks – there would be a frost come morning – and the Christmas tree in the distance twinkled knowingly.

'Thank you for letting me cook tonight,' said Belle. 'I told Gran all about it.'

'Maybe tomorrow we could take her the truffles,' Sebastian suggested.

Belle stood and brushed her behind in case debris had clung to her coat. 'That sounds like a good idea. And I need to give her the candle I bought – she'll love it. Do you want to drive over together?'

'I'd like that.'

'Then it's settled. After lunch?'

He nodded. 'Perfect. I'm fetching a tree in the afternoon so that fits in well.'

'I've thought about your proposition too.'

He looked hopeful. 'Dare I ask?'

'I think it's a good idea, easier all round, so it's a yes from me.'

He punched the air with his fists. 'I need to go now or I'll cry like a big girl.'

'I'd like to see that.' Their laughter mingled as she hovered at the little gate after she passed through. 'Goodnight, Sebastian.'

'Goodnight, Belle.'

By the time she got to her room and went over to the window to look out at the village one more time, Sebastian's figure was but a small outline disappearing into the distance and, warmed all the way through after what was an eventful day, Belle drew the curtains across the tiny window and climbed into bed.

It was the happiest she'd been in ages.

Chapter Eleven

Frustratingly, Belle couldn't get hold of Anthony the next morning. Now she'd made the decision and she'd told Sebastian, she needed to make sure Anthony also knew which direction they were heading in. This was her part of the financing, he had his share ready to go, so they needed to sit down after their holiday in Wales and work out a timetable for what needed doing and when. There were so many things to think about and Belle's head spun with thoughts of where to set up their office initially, website design, licences, logos, insurance. She hoped Anthony would also see the delay in selling the cottage as a positive thing.

Belle had a sumptuous breakfast at her accommodation, something she'd have to stop if she wanted to fit into her clothes for much longer, but filled with scrambled eggs, bacon and mushrooms and already vowing to skip lunch, she decided to walk it all off by heading to Snowdrop Cottage on foot.

She'd only been here just over a fortnight but walking along the high street wrapped in her coat and with knee-high boots on over dark leggings, she said hello to so many people she felt as though she really had a place here in Little Woodville and had to remind herself that this was only a holiday. There was Betty, who was polite enough to greet her as she passed the bakery – probably more on-side after seeing Sebastian's acceptance of Belle; there was a hello from Anne as she jumped into her car, parked outside the gift shop; and when Belle turned to walk over the little stone bridge, Peter drove past and tooted his horn.

When she arrived at the cottage and knocked on the door, Sebastian opened it and glanced out. 'No car?'

'I have to work off the breakfast.'

'Say no more, I've heard Audrey and Gus put on a mean spread. Come in – it's freezing. I keep looking out of the windows to see if there's any sign of snow.'

She shook her head. 'You still think we'll get a white Christmas?'

'You bet I do. Right, I'll just get those truffles and we'll be on our way.'

'About the truffles…do you mind if we —'

'Wrap them?' He proffered a square red box with white satin ribbon tied in a neat bow on top. 'I went to the gift shop and got a suitable package this morning. I thought it would look nicer than shoving them in a Tupperware container.'

He'd thought of everything, and it was sometimes the little things that made Belle realise there was more to this man than his rugged exterior and occasionally snappy attitude. Not that she'd seen that lately. Already she was wondering how today would go when she turned up to see Gran with him alongside. Gran would no doubt be meddling, drop the odd comment. Funny, Belle had forgotten so much about her gran, but had quickly got to know again how she'd react in certain situations.

They drove the short distance over to the care home, where they found Gran out of bed and sitting in the lounge socialising with other residents. Of course as soon as Belle arrived Gran insisted on introducing her to everyone, including each member of staff.

'Sebastian's parking the car,' said Belle as she and Gran settled themselves into the chairs beside the big bay window and left the other residents to it.

'You came together?'

Belle ignored the hint. 'It seemed the logical thing to do.' She passed her gran the wrapped scented candle.

'Belle...' Gran took off the lid the second she'd peeled off the tissue paper. 'It smells glorious.'

'You like it?'

'I love it.'

'And these are the truffles we made.' Belle handed her a second present; Sebastian had told her not to wait for him.

Gran's face lit up and slowly she tugged at the edge of the bow on top and watched its satin uncurl so she could open the beautifully gifted box. 'They look delicious, Belle. And you made them?' She put a hand on her chest. 'I'm sorry. It brings back memories, that's all.'

Belle took the truffles and put them on the side table. She sat opposite her gran and took both her hands in her own. 'I remember making truffles with you, but you changed the recipe on me.'

Happy tears were swiped away and Gran nodded. 'That's right, I made them Christmas-like with the white icing to look like Christmas puddings. You've done a good job.'

'All your recipe, Gran.'

One of the staff brought them some tea over as they reminisced about cooking in Gran's kitchen, about the snowdrops littering the property in Little Woodville, the beauty of the seasons as they came and went every year.

'Little Woodville is a lovely village,' said Belle. 'It's kept its charm too.'

'It comes alive at Christmas, you know. Every year there's a carol concert on Christmas night, quite late in the festivities for many people but not for Little

Woodville. I'm not sure if anyone has organised it for this year yet. I haven't heard anything.'

Sebastian caught the tail end of the conversation as he came over. He kissed Gran on both cheeks. 'Of course it'll happen again. I can't imagine Christmas without it.' He pulled up a chair beside them and Belle made sure she didn't look at him long enough to give her gran any more ammunition. 'I think Anne was in charge of sending out the details. She's been busy at the school but I'll give her a nudge.'

'It used to be me, you know,' Gran told Belle. 'I kept everyone on their toes. I miss the organising sometimes, but it was getting a bit much. If I was back in the village I'd want to do things like that again, I'd fuss around people, but my mind and body need a bit of a rest to tell the truth.'

Belle smiled. 'I'm sure they do.

'Did you ask her?' Sebastian wanted to know.

'Ask me what?' said Gran.

'Sebastian and I were wondering about your locket and the other lady.'

'My gran,' Sebastian added. 'You must've been really close friends.'

'We were the best of friends. She included me as a part of your family.' It seemed hard for her to say all this. 'I'm sorry, Belle, I'm not trying to make you feel guilty, but I need Sebastian to know how I will always treasure her generosity, his father's and his own.' She put one hand on Sebastian's, the other on Belle's.

'It's funny how things work out,' said Sebastian. 'Perhaps I need to get to know Mrs Fro, now Belle has you in her life again. I'm not sure how fair it is for her to have two Supergrans when I only have one.'

199

Gran's head tipped back as she laughed, the wrinkles beneath her chin wobbling in amusement. She looked genuinely happy in the presence of them both.

'I have to make a quick call,' Belle announced. 'I'll be right back.'

'Boyfriend?' Gran's voice followed her but she just smiled and carried on her way. She walked along a corridor to the end, where she wouldn't be disturbed, and tapped her contacts to bring up the name and number.

The phone rang five times before her mum answered.

'I'm there now, yes,' Belle told her mum after announcing she'd seen Gran. 'She had a fall.'

'A fall? How bad? Is she all right?'

Belle wasn't sure she should be so happy at her mum's concern, but she was. 'She's fine. She's out of bed now and chattering away, you know, just like she used to.'

'Well, that's good.'

'It's lovely to see her.' Silence from the other end. 'She's in good spirits.' Still nothing. 'Mum, don't you think all this has gone on long enough? I can tell Gran regrets neither of you having anything to do with the other; perhaps this could be the Christmas we sort it all out.'

A big sigh sounded over the phone. 'Belle, it's gone on so long, and it's complicated.'

'Is it?' Fed up with excuses, she couldn't even be bothered to be nice. 'Sebastian isn't even her grandson and he's had more of a relationship with Gran in the last two decades than I have. They're so close that I'm jealous, I admit it, but I'm also glad Gran wasn't on her own all that time.'

'A lot happened back then, Belle.'

'So you say. But I can't help thinking you'll regret this one day. One day, when Gran dies, you will wish you'd at least spoken to her to see if you could put the past behind you.'

'I wish you wouldn't lecture me, Belle.'

'I'm not lecturing you, I'm trying to make you see sense.' She smiled at the man who passed by in the corridor, going to his own apartment she assumed. 'Do it for me, if not for Gran.'

'I wish you hadn't opened this all up.'

'It wasn't my intention. I thought I was coming to Little Woodville to say goodbye, to move forwards, but the place kind of got to me in a way I can't explain. All these years it's been like a veil over part of my life and gradually the material has been pulled back enough for me to see clearly. I remember little details about Gran, about being at the cottage or Little Woodville, and the more I remember, the more I know she was a huge part of our lives. When did that all change, Mum?' Never before had she been so demanding, so questioning, so desperate to find out the truth.

'I don't want to talk about it anymore.'

And, just like that, her mum clammed up.

'Boyfriend trouble?' Gran asked the second she went back in the room.

Belle rolled her eyes as if Gran was spot on. 'Just the usual ups and downs.' She couldn't bear the thought of Gran knowing she'd tried to talk to her mum and her mum, as usual, hadn't wanted to know.

'Any chance of a rum truffle?' Belle eyed the box.

'I thought you'd make me wait,' Gran grinned. 'Sebastian, you do the honours and hand them round. I should rest my arm – I used both hands to undo the pretty bow and I shouldn't have.'

'No, you shouldn't,' he reprimanded, opening the box and handing them round. 'You need to look after yourself. It'll soon be Christmas Day.'

'Well I look forward to you waiting on me hand and foot,' she said cheekily.

'Do you always have Christmas together?' Belle tried not to feel put out.

'Not always.' Gran looked fondly at Sebastian. 'Last year Sebastian went to his parents' and I went to Betty's, the year before I was here because I felt it important to be a real part of the community, the year before that I had Christmas lunch at the pub courtesy of Benjamin and Kiara when Sebastian was away, and the Christmases before that I've always had the extended invitations, many of which Sebastian was a part of.'

Belle let herself relax and helped herself to a truffle. 'It sounds like you get around, Gran.'

'You watch your words, young lady.'

Belle laughed. 'So it's just the two of you this year?'

'Sebastian is continuing my tradition that I started…now, when was it?' Gran looked up in thought. 'Must've been a good fourteen years ago. Anyway, I started a tradition whereby anyone in the village who was on their own or who wanted a bigger gathering at Christmas could come to the cottage. I was doing the dinners anyway so I thought, why not Christmas dinner as well?'

'I was there the first year.' Sebastian dismissed the offer of another truffle and Belle suppressed a giggle because it looked as if Gran wanted to force-feed them to him. 'I was visiting and she told me her idea and asked whether it was OK with me. I didn't mind at all and we ended up with a party of ten.'

Gran's eyes sparkled a little more, almost a match for the tinsel across the fireplace at the side of the room with white twinkly lights weaved in. 'Let me see, there was Stan – he's passed away now, God rest his soul – Dot...' She thought hard.

'Also dead,' Sebastian whispered, leaning close to Belle, and she caught a waft of his shampoo, zingy and fresh and familiar now.

Belle stifled her laugh but her Gran didn't miss a thing. 'I heard that, young man. Don't be disrespectful.'

'Sorry, Gillian.'

Gran reeled off all the names of the other guests that first day, a few familiar, the rest people she didn't know and hadn't heard about.

'Did you make the full turkey dinner?' Belle asked.

'Of course! With all the trimmings. Sebastian came back the next three years in a row, his parents too one year, and after I left Sebastian carried the tradition on.'

Belle looked at Sebastian. 'So every Christmas you invite random people over for Christmas lunch?'

'Not random people, people who are on their own or who want the company. It's not too different from the meals I share with friends throughout the year, like the meal you were a part of.'

She gulped at how much she had become a part of village life in such a short space of time. 'Christmas is much bigger,' she said, wondering if he could surprise her any more. 'Have you ever been tempted to do your own thing?'

'One year I went away with a girlfriend,' he said, 'but I must admit I really enjoy putting on the dinner at the cottage.'

'You do kind of fit there.' She wasn't sure she'd meant to say that out loud. Gran was looking at her

203

expectantly so Belle thought it only fair to update her. 'I've told Sebastian the good news. We just need to sort all the details out.'

'That's marvellous, Belle. Did Anthony take it well?'

'It's all good, Anthony knows it's a wise decision.' It was only a small white lie; she'd tell him soon.

'Well, you've made my day.'

Belle loved the praise. She remembered her gran saying those very words to her many a time when she was little. 'He's looked after the cottage really well. I couldn't have asked for a better tenant if I'd put him in there myself,' she said without meeting Sebastian's gaze.

'I'm a good judge of character, Belle. But tell me, has he put a tree up yet?'

Belle giggled. 'You know you could always ask him yourself, right?'

Gran looked at him, shook her head, and waited for Belle's response. 'No, I need a straight answer.'

Belle told her, 'There's no tree yet, he's getting it this afternoon.'

Gran shuffled in her seat. 'You always leave it so late, Sebastian.'

'That's because you aren't in Little Woodville to nag me.'

'True.'

'Don't worry, it'll get done.'

'Don't you panic they've sold out?' Gran was most concerned.

He shook his head. 'They always have lots there and I've called and checked that's still the case. Believe it or not, I'm not the only one who leaves it until the last minute. I'll get it today, don't worry.'

'Make sure he does,' she told Belle. 'And make sure he puts other little touches around the cottage.'

Anyone would think they were living together! 'Gran, I can't get on his back about —'

'Nonsense. I'm not there, and Snowdrop Cottage deserves Christmas.'

'You're talking about it as though the cottage has feelings.' Belle began to laugh but soon stopped. 'OK, I'll make sure.'

'Thank you. Now, you say the cottage is well looked after. How about the veggie patches? Did you see them, Belle?' Her eyes lit up. 'They'll spring into action come summer. How's the greenhouse, Sebastian?'

'I didn't see a greenhouse.' Belle tried to think where it might be.

'It's a lean-to, against the other side of the shed,' he explained. 'It's not very big. And it's still helping me grow enough produce, thank you, Gillian.'

Belle vowed to check it out later. She must've overlooked it before now. 'What do you keep in there?'

'I tend to grow carrots, winter salad vegetables.'

They talked about the cottage some more, about the seasons that came and went, but before long Gran declared herself tired and announced she'd like to take a nap.

'Everything OK?' Sebastian took her arm and although she didn't really need it, she hooked hers through his.

'I'm fine. Lots of us residents take regular naps. We call it a power nap.'

'Mrs Fro often talks about having a power nap,' said Belle. 'She said it's one of the joys of getting older.'

'You know, one day I might like to see Mrs Fro again,' said Gran after she'd kissed them both goodbye. 'I'd love to thank her for everything she's done.'

Belle knew she'd be doing just that when she saw her neighbour next.

As Sebastian and Belle drove back to Little Woodville, Sebastian asked, 'So Anthony is fine about your decision, is he?' He turned into the lane leading to Snowdrop Cottage.

'Pardon?' She'd been looking out of the window up at the sky wondering if, as the forecast suggested, they would get a snow flurry later. Sometimes she wondered if the weather forecasters just said that to keep things interesting when it came to bets for a white Christmas.

'You didn't tell him, did you.' Sebastian wasn't asking. He shook his head. 'You need to tell him. If he thinks you're here to sell up and you've put a halt to any plans, he's not going to be happy.'

They pulled into the driveway outside the cottage and Belle gazed at the property that had been hers for ten years but that she hadn't fully appreciated until now. Not just the thatched roof and brick walls, but the emotional ties behind it. 'It's no big deal. I'm just slowing part of the financing up, that's all. We can still go ahead with plenty of things. There's so much to organise.' She was about to reel off a list when he stopped her.

'You know that's beside the point, don't you?'

She pulled the inside door handle to escape his jeep. 'I don't need you as my moral compass thank you, Sebastian.'

'Take it easy, Miss Hoity-Toity.' He laughed as he climbed out after her. 'No need to get your knickers in a twist.'

She turned to have a go at him but decided against it. 'Goodbye, Sebastian. I'm going to untwist my knickers.'

His hand landed on her arm and when she looked up at him his eyes danced beneath messy dark hair. 'Belle, would you like to come and fetch the Christmas tree with me?'

She'd been ready to storm off, across the little bridge, down the high street ignoring the ridiculous decorations. She wasn't sure why she was so bothered. Maybe it's because she knew Sebastian was right. She did need to talk to Anthony but she'd been putting it off, telling herself it could wait until they were in Wales together. 'I will tell him, you know.'

'So why haven't you done it yet?'

'It's just, well, I thought it could wait until we're in Wales in a few days' time.'

'Is that because he'll take it badly?'

She didn't want to talk about it anymore. 'How far's the tree place from here?'

*

'You should've said so at the cottage,' Sebastian admonished on their drive when Belle announced she was really hungry.

'Sorry, but the huge breakfast and the rum truffles carried me through until now.'

He pulled into a pub car park. 'I know this place, you'll like it. We'll eat, then drive on to the farm for the tree. Women.' He shook his head but Belle suspected he was happy enough in her company.

They found a table inside and perused the menus. Belle ordered the chilli con carne with fluffy rice, sour cream on the side and tortilla chips, while Sebastian ordered the chicken, ham and leek pie.

'I may as well eat something proper now,' he said. 'Then I won't have to cook tonight.'

'My thoughts exactly. There's a limit to how many microwave meals my body can take.'

'The body looks just fine to me.'

Glad the waitress had appeared, Belle ordered a big glass of Diet Coke and Sebastian went for the same. 'This is a lovely pub.' She looked around at the cosy decor, the log fire crackling away gently, the garlands twisted around pillars along with white lights that faded in and out in a constant rhythm. 'I hope your tree isn't as fat as that one.' She nodded to the Christmas tree at one end of the room, wide enough to spread its girth through the whole lounge room at the cottage.

'I go to the same place every year and they have a good selection: wide, thin, tall, short.'

'I know a few people who have an artificial tree instead,' said Belle.

'I've never gone for one myself, but I can see the attraction. No needles to clear up, kinder for the environment, no trying to wrestle the thing into a stand and get it at the right angle or dispose of it when Christmas is over.'

'I sense there's a but…'

'You know me already.'

She took the cutlery from her napkin, put it on one side and fanned out the material to put across her lap. It was scary to realise she was forming a connection with a man other than Anthony. Last night she'd gone to bed and dreamt about Sebastian, about them as a couple, doing exactly as they'd already done – cooking a meal, laughing and talking together. And she knew that her hesitation to speak to Anthony wasn't only because she didn't want to tell him about the decision she'd made. It was because Sebastian was becoming a bigger part of her life with every passing day. Belle watched Sebastian now and she knew she needed to get to Wales, soon, to be away from him and the village before it swallowed her up whole. She had to get back to being Belle, the estate agent, the business woman who knew what she wanted, or at least thought she did.

The waitress brought over the main course and conversation lapsed into safer topics. They talked about the garden at the cottage, the vastness of it, the managing of the space and the snowdrops that appeared every year.

'They've been photographed for one of the Cotswolds magazines,' Sebastian announced.

Belle glided her fork beneath some rice and chilli and used her knife to top it with a little sour cream. 'That's amazing. I have some photographs from years ago but not many. It's not like now where we snap away with our phones and don't care how many images we have or that half of them may be rubbish.'

'The photographer came at first light and the sun across the snowdrops is striking. I've had the article framed to give to Gillian for Christmas.'

Belle's jaw slowed. 'That's an incredible gift.'

He didn't miss a beat. This was where he understood Belle so intimately that it scared her. 'We could give it to her together if you like.'

She shook her head. 'No, don't be daft, it's your gift.'

'How about we make a deal?'

'Another one?'

Smiling, he said, 'You bake some Christmas cookies for her and we'll give everything to her in one. We could do it Christmas Eve, if you're not leaving for Wales too early.'

'If you're sure?'

'Of course.' He grabbed the waitress's attention and requested another couple of drinks.

Belle crunched her way through a tortilla chip but felt she had to explain. 'I feel as though I've been out of Gran's life for so long, it's difficult to catch up.'

'I'm not sure I follow.'

Cutlery down, she put her face in her hands and shook her head. 'I feel like I have to compete.' She parted her fingers enough to see him. 'There, I've said it.'

'You're jealous of me?' He looked amused but quickly righted himself and she assumed he was wary of upsetting her. 'All jokes aside, you really don't need to be. I have been a big part of Gillian's life. When I was younger I called her Gran.' He reached out for her wrist when she moved to cover her face again and held it gently. 'But grandparents don't always have the one grandchild, they usually have many, and as well as being in Gillian's life for a long time, I also saw exactly what she was missing by not having her own family around her. She was sad a lot of the time and I think we got on so well because I was there to make her feel better. I'm not saying it to make you feel guilty in any way, but to explain that there's room in her life for us both. Unless of course you want me to stop spending time with her.'

He still had hold of her wrist and she cautiously took her arm away when the waitress delivered their second round of drinks. Carols played softly in the background, and every time the door to the pub opened the icy air whipped around their legs. 'I don't want that, she'd hate it. I think she loves you as much as she could love anyone.'

When Belle's phone rang she saw it was Anthony. 'I'd better take this. I'll nip outside.' She grabbed her coat.

'Hey,' she said once she was out of the pub. 'I tried to call this morning.' She wasn't sure it was an explanation or a justification for her lack of contact.

'Sorry, I've been flat out trying to get everything done before I leave for Wales.'

Belle leaned her head closer to the front door of the pub. Sebastian wasn't looking her way but she could see him, scrolling through something on his phone as he waited.

'I have some news,' Anthony announced.

'Sounds exciting.'

'I've found a buyer!'

'A buyer for what?'

'The cottage.'

'What cottage?'

'Well, der…your cottage, you know, the place where you are now, getting it ready for sale. Well, no need. I've found the buyer and let's just say he's offering way above what we think it's worth. He's attracted to the parcel of land it comes with, thinks he can build on it perhaps, so you can go on holiday knowing it's all sorted. Belle? What do you think?' he prompted when she said nothing.

Belle watched Sebastian nonchalantly looking at his phone, sitting in a country pub on their way to choose a Christmas tree for the cottage that should, quite rightly, be his.

'I need to talk to you about the cottage,' said Belle, but Anthony interrupted her by telling her the price the man was offering. 'There must be some mistake.' She swallowed, hard.

'There isn't. I'm telling you, this man wants it bad. He says it's unique, one of a kind, and it'll be years before anything else like that comes up again.'

He was right about one thing. It was certainly unique. Belle could understand the man's desperation even before Anthony spoke again.

'My client says Little Woodville is *the* place to live in the Cotswolds because it has all its old charm, a great community, yet tourists tend to converge in the surrounding areas rather than there.'

'Right.'

'I thought you might sound a little more enthusiastic, Belle.'

'I am enthusiastic, it's just that I've kind of found a buyer here, too.'

'Oh? You never mentioned it.'

'I've been in talks with him.' He didn't need to know it was the tenant just yet. All she wanted to do was stall the purchaser his end, although was there really any point? He was offering an over-the-top ridiculous price, money that would get their business off to a flying start. Sebastian would never and could never match the amount.

'Do you think he'd be able to match the offer I have?' Anthony turned all real-estate agent rather than boyfriend. 'Is he a cash buyer? Or will he be waiting for finance?'

'He lives in the village already and it'll take a few months to get the finance, but no, the offer is nowhere near the amount your client is offering.'

Anthony's voice softened. 'I think we both know what makes sense, don't we? I know you have ties to the cottage and I imagine that's what's making you consider this other offer, am I right?'

He was, kind of. 'It's making me consider the options, yes.'

'This client could settle as soon as possible. You'd go from getting the rental income to suddenly having the price of the cottage.'

'I saw Gran.'

That stopped Anthony in his tracks. 'I didn't realise you had any intention of contacting her.'

'I didn't.' She bristled at his reaction. 'But being here made me decide it was about time.'

'Right.' He hesitated. 'And how did it go?'

Over the years she'd said enough about the family situation for him to know the strain they'd all been under. 'It was strange to see her, but she's just like I remembered. She's lovely. I wish you could meet her, you'd think she was lovely too.' She was kind of like Anthony's Aunt Rose except without the beard or the moaning, but she didn't say that.

'How was she about selling the cottage?'

'She's happy where she is, she is happy for me to sell up.' At least she was when she thought Sebastian would be the person buying it.

'Well then, that's settled. I know what you're like, you're kind, Belle, but let this other buyer down gently and tell him we've had an impossible-to-resist offer. There'll be other places for him, I'm sure. Listen, I've got to go.' She heard jingling keys in the background. 'I've been checking out offices in the city.'

'Already?'

'I know you're not here, but when this client made his offer I couldn't resist seeing what we'd be able to get. Oh, Belle, I can't tell you how excited I am.'

She should be excited too, but of course she wasn't. She almost wished she hadn't come to Little Woodville, she almost regretted seeing Gran and making anything in her life so difficult, because with Gran and Sebastian in her life, suddenly things were about as clear as the muddy puddles in the pub car park that she looked out on now, rain collecting between uneven stones, any

213

footprints that went in coming up much dirtier than they were before.

She'd wanted to move on when she first came to Little Woodville but now it felt as though she'd been turned upside down, shaken sideways and then dumped on the ground from a great height. And she had no idea where to go from here.

Chapter Twelve

'What's going on, Belle?' Sebastian led the way along a collection of Christmas trees, cut and leaning up against the fence inside the shed at a nearby farm. They'd left the pub shortly after Belle finished on the phone and she'd barely said a word on the drive here.

'I've just got a lot on my mind, that's all.' The fresh citrusy pine of the trees was overwhelming and she hadn't realised how powerful a smell could be at conjuring up visions of the past.

'You're not reconsidering are you?'

She spun round. 'What makes you ask that?'

'I don't know, maybe you think the idea of a framed magazine article is naff, although even though I say so myself, I think it's a pretty original gift for your gran.'

Relieved he wasn't referring to her decision about selling the cottage to him, she said, 'It's a very good gift and I'm happy to be a part of it.'

He didn't push it. He seemed to sense when it was time to stop, and Belle was glad. Choosing a tree should be fun, a happy time, and she didn't want to take that away from him, not when in all likelihood she'd soon be taking away much more.

'What about this one?' She stood next to a beautiful specimen, not too tall for the cottage, wide but not as fat as the one in the pub. 'I think it'd fit in the lounge in front of the window, don't you? What? Why are you grinning?'

'If your gran could see us now.' He shook his head, smiling as he inspected the tree she'd suggested. 'She'd have the wedding march playing, a priest booked and us married off in seconds.'

Belle looked around at families choosing their trees, couples doing the same. 'Are you picking her up on Christmas Day?' He didn't seem to blink that she'd changed the subject and she wouldn't look at him in case he found her squirming in any way amusing.

'I will do, yes.' He nodded, firmly. 'I think we have a winner.' He hauled the tree from its spot and took it over to the counter, where it would be wrapped before they took it back to Little Woodville.

'Do you have decorations?'

He paid the cashier. 'What do you take me for? Of course I have. In fact, I seem to remember there's one your gran always insisted on. It's a painted Christmas tree decoration with the centre cut out and a photo of a little girl in the middle.'

Belle wondered who that could be. Then it dawned on her. 'Oh no, not the one I made in primary school.'

He lifted the wrapped tree and rested it against his shoulder as they made their way to the jeep. 'Belle. Mrs Olsen's class, year five, all written on the back in —'

'Red glitter pen,' she finished, covering her face with gloved hands. When she dared to look up she pushed wisps of fringe out of the way. She'd have to have another haircut soon before her bangs were falling into her eyes.

Sebastian heaved the tree onto the roof rack of his jeep. 'I decided I'd put the decoration on the tree every year, even if your gran wasn't at the cottage, because it was so special to her. I guess a part of me felt the cottage without it wouldn't be right.' He looked across the bonnet at her as he fastened one side of the tree. 'You weren't physically a part of her life, Belle, but she never forgot about you.'

Belle gulped and with the air frosty around them, Sebastian told her he'd nearly finished and she should wait in the car.

'We need to make a bet, you know.' He'd climbed in and with keys in the ignition he turned to her.

'About what?'

'The white Christmas.'

She shook her head. 'Oh no, I don't go in for any of that.'

'Just a bit of fun,' he shrugged. 'There's a bet going up at the pub, and it's far nicer than betting at the bookies. It's a bit different. Everyone pays one pound and a little ticket with their name goes into one of two boxes, one marked "white", the other marked "boring".'

Belle giggled into her scarf as he negotiated his way out of the car park. 'You're kidding, it's really called boring? You should call it practical, or sensible.'

He shot her a look that said she was being ridiculous. 'Come Christmas morning at about eleven o'clock it's nice to say Merry Christmas to one another and the pub is the perfect place to meet after a walk before lunch. If it's snowed, a name is drawn out of the white pot and if it hasn't, a name is drawn out of the boring pot.'

'So the person whose name is drawn out gets to take home all the money paid in. Makes sense.'

He indicated down another lane and a sign came into view for Little Woodville. 'Not quite. If it's a white Christmas then the name comes from white and the winner gets all the money to do with as they wish. If the name comes from boring, meaning we didn't get the white Christmas, then that person also gets the money to do with as they wish. But…and here's the twist…if it's a white Christmas then not only do we have a winner from the white pot but also two names are drawn from the boring pot. Those people have to club together to buy a round for the house for being so pessimistic.'

'No way! That's not fair! Why would anyone want to bet against a white Christmas then, and risk buying everyone a drink?'

'Because, as you know, we never get a white Christmas. We've had one in the past ten years – so all the other years someone in the boring pot has walked away with a decent amount of cash. Last year it was almost two hundred quid.'

If Belle could whistle she would have. 'Why two people from the boring pot?'

'Kiara and Benjamin thought it a little unfair to have one person buy everyone a drink. It's usually a full house in the pub on Christmas morning, rain, hail or shine…or snow…so it's a fairer way to do things. Anyway, it's an age-old tradition and something I think makes Little Woodville the place it is. Your gran was always into it.'

On the winding country lanes, careful of ice, Sebastian drove back towards Little Woodville and Belle found herself saying, 'Well, if it was good enough for Gran…'

'That's the spirit.' He grinned.

How was she ever going to tell him she'd have to go back on their agreement? The other buyer was offering substantially more and Belle knew it would be crazy not to take it. Wouldn't it?

*

Kiara, resplendent in a multicoloured dress as she endured the warmth of the pub, busy in the lead-up to Christmas, served them the second they arrived. 'What'll it be?' she asked.

'I'll have an orange juice, please,' said Belle. 'No more fizzy drinks for me or my tummy will burst.' What was supposed to be a quick trip to choose a tree had turned into lunch together, a lot of time browsing at the farm, taking the tree to the cottage to put it outside in a bucket of water, and now cosy drinks for two.

Sebastian opted for an orange juice as well. 'This young lady wants to place a bet,' he told Kiara.

'Ah!' Kiara seemed happy to indulge Belle. 'The White Christmas bet…he's convinced you, has he?'

'I've never bet on it before. My best mate does every year.'

Kiara brought out two plastic containers, one labelled 'boring'; the other 'white'. 'So, what's it going to be? White?' She wiggled the container and Belle could see little pieces of paper inside. 'Or boring?'

Belle didn't know which pot to go for. She wrote her name on a piece of paper, told Sebastian and Kiara to turn round so they couldn't see what she did with it, and slotted it into one of the tubs.

'What did you bet for? Come on, tell us!' Sebastian sounded like a schoolboy who hated secrets.

She tapped the side of her nose. 'Just you wait and see.'

*

'Thanks for today,' Belle said when they left the pub. They'd chatted to Audrey, Peter and Nel, who had informed Belle that their deep-pan pizza with the works was the one to try. 'No more of that poxy pineapple and ham stuff,' she'd told Belle, 'you want some real flavours.'

Sebastian took out his keys to the jeep. 'You're welcome. Where are you going?' he asked when she lifted a hand to wave.

'Er…to the bed and breakfast. I assume you've had enough of me for one day.' And she couldn't look at him knowing she could be about to break his heart when she told him about the other buyer.

He leaned against the car roof, defined forearms she'd seen before hidden beneath his coat. She wasn't sure but she thought she saw a snowflake drift down and land on his fringe. Had she imagined it?

'I can't say I love decorating a tree, at least not on my own,' he said, 'so I figured you could muck in. Your gran will see it Christmas Day and it'd be nice to tell her you helped.'

'Typical man.'

'Eh?'

'You're using Gran as an excuse, just because you need a woman's touch.'

He didn't deny it. 'Come on, as a favour. Please. I promise I'll untangle the lights, the worst job.'

Getting into the jeep again, she said, 'You do know if you'd put them away properly in the first place you wouldn't have a problem.'

'Yes, boss.' He grinned and pulled out of the pub car park.

Back at Snowdrop Cottage Sebastian gave Belle the task of making the tea while he wrestled the tree into its stand.

Handing him a mug, she admired his handiwork. 'How did you get it so straight? I'm pretty sure Gran always said it was next to impossible, that a bent tree was a natural tree.'

'Let's just say stands have come a long way so it's easier, and it helps they wrapped it.' They looked at the tree that appeared to have several layers of cling film wound round it. 'No branches poking into my eyes or catching in my hair.' He picked up a pair of scissors. 'And now for the unveiling.' He sliced up one side and then tugged off the wrapping to allow the branches to ping out.

'It's beautiful, Sebastian.'

'Very beautiful,' he acknowledged. He slurped a few gulps of tea before he went out to the shed for the decorations, and it wasn't long before he came back with two huge cardboard boxes.

Belle knelt on the floor and between them they emptied everything out and unwrapped each tiny piece. Laid out on the floor in the lounge room, on top of a white sheet Sebastian had found so they'd be able to see the decorations rather than try to make them out against the darker carpet, were all manner of Christmas pieces from gold baubles and little drummer boys to candy canes, woodland creatures sparkling with glitter, a woollen Santa Belle swore her gran had made and the tree with Belle's photo in.

'I still remember giving it to Gran,' she said, holding it in her palm. 'I was so proud.'

'You're getting all melancholy again.'

'Melancholy!' She burst out laughing, leaning back on the floor clutching her tummy. 'You sound like a complete arse using that word.'

He threw a piece of tinsel at her and turned his attention to the lights. 'You wait till these are on – you won't be a miserable cow then.'

'Hey, rude!' She sat upright.

He turned from his position on the floor as he tugged the final piece of wiring free from the rest and declared himself finished. 'Don't sound like an arse any more though, do I?'

Belle's job was to walk around the tree and ensure the lights were resting on the branches as Sebastian wound the wire around from the top. She adjusted them as needed, made sure there was even coverage, and once they'd got all the way to the bottom she tucked the switch behind the tree so it couldn't be seen.

'Ready?' Sebastian had his hand on the plug switch as Belle stood back to get a good view.

'Ready.' Hands pressed together in front of her lips, she took a deep breath.

The lights went on.

'It looks perfect.' She froze for a moment but then remembered where she was and put a stop to her emotions taking over. 'Come on,' she ushered, 'we've got a lot of work to do now.' It'd been years since she'd done this, decorate a tree from scratch. Once or twice Mrs Fro had persuaded her to go over to her flat under the pretence she wanted Belle to keep her company but she usually had at least a few decorations she mysteriously hadn't put on yet and had somehow forgotten about. She'd always made cups of tea and asked Belle casually to put the few leftover decorations on the tree. Knowing now about Mrs Fro meeting Gran and keeping in contact with her, Belle wondered, had Mrs Fro been yearning for Belle to fall in love with Christmas all over again just like Gran probably did? She wondered how much Gran had talked about the years gone by, when Belle was a little girl and the pair were so much closer.

'You know…' Belle could hardly believe what she was about to say when she told Sebastian to go ahead and put the angel on top of the tree. '…Gran has a really great recipe for mulled wine, I'm sure she does.'

He stretched to the top, which actually wasn't much of a stretch – he wasn't even on tiptoes – and when the angel was in place, her wings backlit by one of the lights, turned to Belle. 'You were a little girl the last time you were here, how could you possibly know anything about a mulled wine recipe?'

Belle giggled. She'd only remembered earlier today when they were in the pub and Audrey was talking about how she made mulled wine herself every year, and she rated it as much better than any takeaway you could get. 'I'll let you into a secret. Gran loved the stuff, she'd make it and let me stir, and once or twice I *may* have tried a little bit.'

'She gave you some?'

'No, I helped myself.'

'Tut, tut, Belle. Naughty girl.' He winked. 'But I like it. Let's go see if we can find the recipe.'

They laughed their way out to the kitchen and Belle grabbed the recipe book. They went through soup recipes, pages bulging with cut-out pieces from magazines, recipes for cakes, another for quiche, plenty for winter salads and roast-dinner accompaniments, another for apple pie, one for summer punch, and then, bingo! They found the one for mulled wine.

'What's in it?' Sebastian hovered over Belle's shoulder and the proximity had butterflies doing a merry dance all the way through her body.

Belle listed each ingredient as Sebastian went into the pantry to check them off as she called them out. They had everything.

'Are the spices still in date?' Belle asked when he brought a collection of jars into the kitchen. He had allspice, cinnamon sticks, a packet of bay leaves.

He did the necessary checks. 'We're in luck. We're good to go.'

'And the red wine?'

He returned to the pantry, their teamwork effortless. Belle thought back to the grumpy man who'd opened the door to the cottage the first time she came, who barely spoke to her, a contrast to the man standing here now with two bottles of wine held out so she could read the labels and make a decision. She wondered how they'd get on if he knew Anthony had found another buyer, if he knew her head was muddled trying to decide whether she should accept the higher offer. There was a lot more than money at stake now.

'That one.' She pointed to one of the bottles. 'It said in the recipe to use something bold, which' – she turned the bottle over as it was still in his left hand – 'this one is.'

Belle looked at the recipe again to check the method but she noticed another item under the ingredients, scribbled in pencil with a question mark beside it. 'What's SG?'

'SG?' When he moved closer his forearm brushed against hers and sent tingles cascading up her skin. She wondered if he could tell she was holding her breath. 'Ah, I remember.' He returned to the pantry and came back with a bottle. 'Sloe gin. It was years ago, but we tried it as an extra ingredient and it was damn good.'

'I'll take your word for it,' Belle grinned.

They got to work, unwrapping and spooning out spices, slicing oranges, pouring and dropping ingredients into the pan on the stove, and before long the entire cottage kitchen was filled with the scent of Christmas.

'It smells so potent it could floor a man at fifty paces,' Sebastian declared as Belle washed some ruby

224

red glasses, ideal for mulled wine, and he added the final touch. The SG.

'I tell you what,' said Belle. 'If it tastes as good as you say it does, I think we should rub out the pencil SG and write it in pen.'

'OK, but only SG, not the full wording. It sounds better, more secret.' With the heat switched off, Sebastian ladled out two generous glasses and they took them into the lounge room.

The sky outside was completely black, barely a star to be seen, and with the lights of the tree Belle was beginning to feel the magic of Christmas work its way into her. They chatted about anything and everything, taking turns to return to the kitchen and top up their glasses. They talked about her childhood in Little Woodville, about Ireland and what she'd seen when she visited. They discussed his younger years and the adventures he'd had with his dad on their annual camping trips. Apparently Gran had told them she was fun, but not that fun – and she wasn't going to sleep beneath cloth for anyone.

'All gone,' said Sebastian as he knocked back the last of his wine.

'Jeez. Really? I'm going to need some water.' She was already up. 'Shall I bring you some too?'

She didn't wait for an answer. Her head was swimming and not just from the alcohol. Her mind was all over the place with thoughts of Sebastian, Anthony, the cottage, the business she was supposedly going to start. She had no clue which direction she was going in.

When she took two glasses of water through to the lounge, Sebastian was lying at one end of the sofa, eyes shut. She gave him a nudge and he sat up.

'That stuff is powerful. I was about to nod off,' he admitted.

She smiled and handed him one of the glasses. 'Here, drink this.' She did the same, gulping the liquid to try to achieve some level of sobriety. 'I'd better get going,' she announced.

She went to the hall and unhooked her coat, shrugged it on, looped her scarf around her neck and took out her gloves. 'What are you doing?' she asked when Sebastian took his boots from the cupboard and pulled them on.

'Walking you home of course.'

'Don't be daft, I'll be fine.'

'Belle, just let me walk you home.'

She nodded, because it wasn't that she didn't want him to. It was more that she did. And that made things more complicated than she could've ever imagined.

Chapter Thirteen

It was the day before Christmas Eve and Belle woke with more excitement than she had in years. But it was soon forgotten when she remembered everything she had going on right now, and, more than that, she had to wrestle with the fact that tomorrow she would be leaving Little Woodville.

It was already light outside and her room at the top of the bed and breakfast was bathed in an early sunrise glow. She yawned, stretched, climbed out of bed and padded over to the window. When she wiped the condensation she could see more frost than they'd had so far and instead of making her tut like it had during so many winters before, a huge grin spread across her face. Little Woodville at Christmas was more than a picture-postcard scene, it was utterly perfect.

She texted Sam and sent a photo of her view, knowing her best friend would fully appreciate it, and then she showered and made her way down to breakfast, this time choosing two poached eggs on toast with a side of grilled tomatoes. She sat at the table and began to make a list of everything she and Anthony would need to get from the supermarket to take to the cottage in Wales. Funny, every year when they shopped before Christmas it was as though everyone was going underground for weeks on end, the amount people bought. The shops would only be shut for two days at most!

Last night Belle had fallen asleep with ease after the mulled wine and in the shower this morning she'd reasoned with herself that despite a little bit of sadness about driving away from the village tomorrow, Wales would give her a chance to sort her head out. She wasn't going to mention the other buyer to Sebastian, not before

Christmas, because it wouldn't be fair. She'd go to Wales with Anthony and they could talk things through there, she'd air her doubts, they'd see one another's points of view, and then after the week was up she'd move things forwards, however that might be.

After breakfast Belle put on her lip gloss so she felt more herself, and took a walk. She was due to go to the cottage and bake Christmas cookies ready to take to her gran tomorrow to give alongside the picture Sebastian had had framed. It still felt funny giving her a joint gift when they weren't a couple, but, she supposed, they were in a way because they were both her grandchildren. She was by blood, Sebastian was by other bonds.

It was beautiful outside. Belle had on a pair of knee-high boots with a good grip given how many icy patches there were. When she slipped coming out of the gate and righted herself she let out a little giggle, which puffed white against the cold air. She'd have to tread carefully today.

'Good morning, Belle.' Audrey cycled past. 'Can't stop, just got a supply of eggs. We ran out, can you believe it?' She was calling over her shoulder and Belle only just caught the words.

Belle grinned. She liked Audrey, Gus too. In fact, the people in this village had made her feel more than welcome. Even when she walked past the bakery Betty gave her a nod of acceptance. OK, so it wasn't overly friendly, but it was enough to keep the spring in her step as the church bells chimed nine times on the hour and she made her way to the gift shop. She wanted to buy a couple of scented candles to take with her to Wales. The cottage had a lovely roll-top bath and she'd already packed bath salts from Crabtree & Evelyn especially for the occasion.

Belle didn't take long to make a decision. She'd already smelt most of the candles the day she'd investigated the high street and surrounds. She settled on the same candle she'd bought for Gran, with its tangy sweetness and fruitiness of cranberry that reminded her of the best Christmases she'd had as a little girl.

Next, she nipped into the convenience store and grabbed a block of butter and a tin of golden syrup, the only two ingredients the pantry at Snowdrop Cottage was running short of. She turned and crossed the road opposite the village green and made her way over the bridge straddling the stream. She looked down and was unsurprised to find it frozen over. She wasn't sure it was cold enough to be hardened all the way to the muddy bed beneath, but the top was definitely firm and glistened white in patches.

'We could be in for a white Christmas.' It was Trevor, beside her.

'Hello, Trevor. Lovely to see you again.' Belle rested against the stone bridge, wishing she had a hot chocolate to keep her warm.

'Likewise.'

'You out for some fresh air?'

'I need it at my age. Far too easy to stagnate at home and forget there's a whole world to be seen. Not that I'm seeing much of it anymore, just the village for me and the occasional trip to one of the towns nearby. My wife and I used to walk everywhere.'

'You must miss her.'

'Every day.'

Belle tried to imagine what it was like to lose someone you'd spent a lifetime with. When her grandad died, she'd been devastated. She hadn't gone to the funeral, her mum said it wasn't the place for little kids, but she hadn't minded. The whole idea of putting a body in the ground had terrified her, and if she thought about it too much now, it still did.

'I hear you've seen Gillian,' said Trevor. 'How's she doing? I heard she had a bit of a fall, but knowing her she's bounced right back.'

Belle smiled. 'She certainly has.'

'I'm looking forward to seeing her on Christmas Day.'

Belle had always known she was leaving on Christmas Eve, but today as she'd eaten her breakfast she'd felt as though she was about to miss out on something. Christmas Day at Snowdrop Cottage with the gran she'd spent many a Christmas with, and with people who were very different from her yet had become unlikely friends. She'd been tempted to ask Anthony if they could delay their trip to Wales, spending their Christmas here in Little Woodville, but somehow he wasn't a part of what she had here and if they stayed, she'd only stress it wasn't his thing and he wasn't enjoying himself.

'She'll love being at the cottage again – I wish I could see her face,' said Belle.

'You won't be joining us?'

'I'm off on my holidays.'

'Well that's lovely. Where are you going?'

She told him all about the cottage in Wales, the seclusion, the scenery they planned to see on long walks, and when Trevor went on his way to fetch a newspaper and take it home to do the Sudoku puzzles at the back, Belle carried on over the bridge. Sebastian was working up at the church so she'd have the cottage to herself and she was really looking forward to baking and having her own headspace.

'Damn it.' She realised she'd forgotten her spare key, so instead of turning left at the end of the lane for the cottage, she went right and made her way towards the steeple in the distance.

'What brings you here?' Sebastian's smile lit up his face as he stood up after wrenching some kind of dead plant from the ground inside the gate.

'I forgot my key.'

He shook his head, pulled off his gardening glove, delved a hand into his pocket and took out his car keys. 'Take mine off the keys for the jeep.'

'Thanks.' She took off her gloves and with hands shaking from the cold managed to wiggle the key off. 'How long do you think you'll be here?'

'Another couple of hours probably. Are you OK to hang around at the cottage until I'm back? If not, you could lock up and drop the key here before you go back to the bed and breakfast.'

'I'll be there for a while I think. The cookies take a bit of time and I've brought a book so I can sit and read while they cool ready to decorate. If that's all right with you,' she added hastily.

'Of course. Put the wood burner on if you like, it's ready to go. And the tree lights. I'm spoilt you know, I'll be walking into a cottage smelling of freshly baked cookies. You'd better hide them or I'll eat them all.'

'Thanks for the warning.'

'What did you think to the sloe gin in the mulled wine?' he asked.

'I liked it, definitely an ingredient to write in pen.' She blushed at the memory of their closeness last night. It was friendship but on a level that almost spilled over to something else and she was sure he must have felt it too.

'I needed fresh air today,' he said. 'I woke with a foggy head.'

'Me too. The walk has been nice. And it's good that it's frosty but not raining – this is my last chance to look around the village.'

His smiled faded. 'You won't reconsider staying a bit longer?'

'I can't. Anthony and I have plans.'

'He's more than welcome too. Come on, your gran would love it. She could give him the once-over.'

Belle's laughter mingled with the frosty air. 'No doubt she would, but I won't put him through it. And besides, we need to check into the holiday accommodation at four o'clock; I'm sure the owners have their own Christmas plans.'

He turned and threw the dead plant to one side, where there were plenty of others already waiting. 'Another year, perhaps.'

Belle didn't answer his question. 'What are you doing?'

'Something that could probably wait, but it keeps me busy. I have plans in the New Year so wanted to do as much as I can now. If I clear the ground before the snow comes it'll be far easier than leaving it.'

'What plans do you have?'

He shook his head. 'I'm not telling anyone yet, but I will, don't you worry.'

She left it at that. 'What time do you want to head to Gran's tomorrow?'

'Up to you. You're the one driving to Wales, so I'm flexible.'

'I check out at ten o'clock, so how about I leave my things in my car and come to you, then we'll go over for ten thirty, eleven o'clock?'

232

'Sounds good to me. I think she'll love her presents.'

'I'm sure she will.' Gloves back on and key in her pocket, she left him to it and made her way to Snowdrop Cottage.

There, she unpacked the extra ingredients and got to work, but as soon as she tied on the apron she'd used before, she took out her iPhone and found a Christmas songs playlist. Christmas in a village like this had some kind of magical powers, she decided, and she hummed away, jigged a bit and got really into the spirit as she weighed and measured, poured and stirred, and before long the kitchen was filled with the scents of cinnamon, warm butter, ginger and other festive spices.

With the timer set and the cookies in the oven, Belle went through to the lounge and put the tree lights on. It was warm enough without the wood burner so she left that as it was and read her book as she waited.

When the timer pinged she went through to the kitchen, took the tray of cinnamon cookies out followed by the one holding the gingerbread variety, and after a couple of minutes gently prised the treats from their positions and put them on a plate to cool. She washed the trays and then settled herself back in the lounge with her book. By her reckoning they'd need almost an hour before they were ready for decorating.

When her phone rang she tutted, but turned her book spine up so she wouldn't lose her page and answered it to talk to Anthony.

'How's the weather down there?' was his first question.

She looked out of the window, still not tired of seeing the surrounds beyond the cottage, the little lane where traffic could pass, the flowerbeds that would be a riot of colour in a few months' time. 'It's very cold, a bit icy and frosty, but other than that it's a perfect winter's day.'

'My heating just packed up.'

'No way! Not in your super-duper bachelor pad.' She couldn't help but giggle. His had always been the place to go to because it had more mod-cons and everything seemed to work much better, until now.

'I know, and right before Christmas. Good job I'll be away. They can't get someone out here until the day before New Year's Eve. My neighbour will let them in so hopefully it'll be really warm by the time we get back to Cambridge. What's the bed and breakfast like, nice and warm?'

'It's not bad, but I'm at the cottage again today.'

'Whatever for? My buyer doesn't need it painted or spruced up in any way. Make the most of the easy sale.'

Desperate to change the subject, she said, 'I'm baking cookies, for my gran. Sebastian gave me access to the kitchen.'

'Are you taking advantage of an old man?'

Her giggle was at his assumption more than his joke. 'Actually, he's not that old.'

'Well he can't be if he's living there on his own. Where is he now? Having a lie down?'

'Don't mock. We'll all be old one day.'

'I wasn't mocking. All I meant was that you're quite lively, so it must be a bit of a handful having you around with all that energy.'

'Cheeky git.'

'Talking of all that energy, I hope you've got some saved for me. I've missed you. I can't wait to be together in Wales – it's going to be a great break for both of us before we really get going with the business…Belle?' he prompted when she didn't answer straight away.

'Yes, it'll be a lovely break.'

'I saw the weather forecast earlier though and it looks like there's a chance of a white Christmas. I've put my bet on already although the odds have fallen way down.'

She almost told him she'd put a bet on too but it felt like another slice of the life that was just for her, something she could keep for herself and not have to share. 'Let's hope we get to Wales first, then I couldn't care less if we're snowed in.'

'I thought you hated the snow.'

And so she had in all the time she'd known him, but once upon a time, like every kid, she'd cupped her hands around her eyes and stared out of the window on Christmas Eve, into the darkness, willing to see even the tiniest of white flakes fall from the sky. 'It's fine when I don't have to go out in it.'

'We'd better make sure we get lots of food in. I'll bring down what we discussed, then there's a supermarket eight miles from the cottage we're at so how about we stop there first? We could meet there even, if we get our timings right.'

'Good idea. I'm seeing Gran in the morning to give her her Christmas present, then I'll be ready for the off. I'll load the car beforehand so I can be at the supermarket in the car park by three o'clock. Just text me the postcode to make sure we're going to the same place.'

'Will do.'

They ran through a few of the things they needed to make sure they had: matches to light the fire, firelighters in case the kindling and newspaper wasn't quite enough, steaks or chicken, whatever they decided they wanted on Christmas Day, although seeing Gran's recipes for Christmas had almost given Belle an unhealthy craving for turkey and all the trimmings for the first time in years.

'My buyer will meet with us on the third of January,' said Anthony.

Belle shivered. Maybe she would light the wood burner after all, and then the cottage would be nice and warm for Sebastian by the time he got home. It felt like the least she could do.

'Belle, did you hear what I said?'

She'd crouched down in front of the wood burner and opened it up. 'I did hear you, I'm trying to sort the wood burner, keep it warm in here.'

'Can't your tenant do that?'

'I don't mind.'

'So does that date suit you?'

'What? Oh yes, it's fine.'

'Are you having doubts?' He was being patient but she knew how frustrating it must be for him when she wasn't showing anywhere near as much enthusiasm as he was. 'It's totally understandable, Belle. I'm not a complete arsehole you know. I knew when you went to Little Woodville you weren't only going to sort out the cottage and hand the tenant his notice. It must have been a strange time for you.'

She sat back on her feet, surprised at his understanding. 'It has been a little weird. But Gran and I are good now and she's happy for the cottage to change hands.'

'It's an incredible offer, Belle. We won't find it anywhere else. This man really wants the place and he's shown he's willing to do whatever it takes.'

'He must want it bad.' A log slipped and she repositioned it. 'Actually, I wanted to talk to you about the offer.' She hadn't intended to say anything to him until they were in Wales and she was away from the village to give her a clearer head. 'It's just that, well, the tenant here will be in a position to buy the cottage.'

'Really?'

'He'll be able to pay the market value, and I know it's not as much as the client we've found, but…well, it would mean so much to keep it in the family.'

'But he's a tenant, he's not family.'

It would take far too long to even attempt to explain but she had to try. 'Sebastian is close to Gran.'

'So they are carrying on?'

'No, get that thought out of your head.' She managed a giggle at the absurdity given the actual age gap between Sebastian and Gran. 'What I mean is that they've known one another for a long time and they're very close.'

'So they're friends. I can see why that would make it difficult, Belle, but I'm not sure we can get too sentimental about it.'

She looked over at the Christmas tree, the angel looking down on her, the red bauble that showed her distorted reflection as a twinkly light allowed it to glow. 'This is his home, Anthony. How can I even think about telling him we're selling to someone else?'

She didn't hear what Anthony said next because when Sebastian appeared in the doorway with a wreath hooked over one arm, her gaze locked on his and all she could see was anger and hurt.

'Can I call you back?' she said to her boyfriend. 'I'm having trouble sorting the wood burner.'

By the time she'd said goodbye and hung up, Sebastian had already stomped through to the kitchen. He was at the table fixing a piece of red ribbon to the wreath when she came in.

'Sebastian…' Damn, how had she not heard the front door go?

'No need to say anything.' He didn't meet her gaze this time. 'Business is business, right?'

'No, it's not as simple as that.'

'Did you ever have any intention of letting me buy the cottage, or was it easy to let me believe you did, so you could make yourself at home and get me on side until you'd made nice with your gran?'

'That's a bit unfair isn't it?' Hands on her hips, she knew full well it was her in the wrong and not him. She should've been open about the situation in the first place. Knowing Sebastian, and she felt she did already, he may have even said taking the bigger amount was the right thing to do.

'I don't think so, do you?'

'Sebastian, I'm sorry. A client made a huge offer for this place and it's enough to get Anthony and me started with our business, to tide us over with office expenses and all the other stuff we need to sort.'

'Then you have no choice, do you? I mean, my offer won't be until a year is up and even then I don't expect it comes anywhere close to the other one, does it?'

She couldn't say otherwise. 'I should've told you, but I wanted to talk to Anthony next week, I wanted to see if perhaps we could delay things and keep everyone happy. I've seen what this place means to you.' It had come to mean even more to her than she'd ever expected, and she was quite taken aback by that fact alone.

'Shut the door on your way out.'

Obstinately, she sat down. 'I've got cookies to decorate.'

'Then I'll go.' He grabbed his boots and pushed his feet in without doing up the laces, plucked his coat from the hook in the hallway and the door slammed so hard on his way out that Belle swore the kitchen table shuddered.

What had she done?

She contemplated going after him but knew he needed to cool off. Instead she went back into the kitchen and made up the icing for the cinnamon cookies. She took each one, covered it in icing, then covered the top third with edible silver balls to make the shape of a hat, then black ones for the eyes, nose and mouth of a snowman. Once they were all finished she set them to dry on the plate, washed up everything she'd used, dried it all and put every last piece away.

When Sebastian still wasn't back almost an hour later she was about to give up, lock the cottage and post the key through the letterbox when she heard the front door open.

Sebastian took his coat and shoes off less frantically than he'd put them on and when he came into the kitchen, big woolly socks on his feet, he put a box on the table. 'It's a gift box, like I got for the truffles. I thought you might like it for the cookies.'

'Why are you being so nice to me?' She watched him, standing at the sink, his shoulders tense and rising and falling with each breath until he turned round.

'I'm not doing it for you. I'm doing it for Gillian. Over the years she's been to hell and back with you and your mother pushing her out of your lives. Now you're back, and I think it would break her heart if she thought she'd lose you again.'

'Why would she lose me?' She didn't take long to understand. 'Ah, so you think she'll be angry at me too, take your side.'

239

'You make it sound so simple. God, you're infuriating.' He left the room and she followed him to the lounge.

'It's not definite, you know,' she told him as he sat stretched out on the sofa, arms hooked behind his head, feet crossed at the ankles as though he was either deep in contemplation or had given up fighting.

'What isn't?'

'The other buyer.'

'I'd say, by the sounds of the phone call, Anthony at least thinks it is, and if you're going along with that then I reckon it's only a matter of time before you give me my marching orders.' He held up his hands to stop her saying anything else. 'Look, you don't need to explain. You were selling up and I came to you asking for a favour. You're making a shrewd business move and I can't blame you for it.'

She hated being described as shrewd. 'There are extra cookies if you'd like one,' she tried.

He harrumphed and sat watching the wood burner, pretending he was mesmerised, rather than talking to her.

'I'll package up the cookies ready for tomorrow then.'

He remained silent.

Out in the kitchen, eyes glistening with tears, Belle opened up the dainty box. She lined it with baking paper, put in enough cookies to cover the bottom, then repeated the layers until the box was full, careful each time not to damage any of the snowmen. The last thing she'd wanted to do was upset Sebastian; she didn't want to ruin what she had salvaged with her gran. This was all a complete mess. If Anthony hadn't found a buyer by chance the plan would've all fallen into place, but now it was ruined.

And the worst thing was – Belle wasn't sure she could ever put things right.

Chapter Fourteen

Belle woke up well before her alarm sounded on Christmas Eve, and her room was still dark. She lay there looking at the ceiling, contemplating what had happened yesterday. She'd left the cottage without another word to Sebastian and then she'd driven out of town and had dinner at a dodgy-looking chicken place, avoiding the high street and anywhere she was known. She didn't want to talk to anyone, for anyone to pick up on the terrible guilt she was feeling right now. Guilty about Sebastian, guilty all this could hurt Gran, confused about whether she wanted to start her own business, and, most of all, she knew that hiding the little details about her stay here in Little Woodville – how wonderful it had been, how Sebastian wasn't the old man they'd assumed he was, how she wasn't sure she wanted to say goodbye now – indicated that her relationship with Anthony was in trouble.

In the bathroom, she looked in the mirror as remorse flooded her body. She wasn't this person. She was loyal, someone you could depend on. She wished she could talk to her mum about it. Over the years they'd talked about teenage angst whenever it had got to Belle, they'd talked about boys when they came along, they'd aired grievances – apart from when it came to the subject of Gran – and they'd always been there for each other. Belle often wondered whether being an only child had made her closer to her mum in some ways. She'd never had to share her with anyone. But, now, she didn't feel she could pour all this out to a woman who was dealing with enough stuff of her own. Lord only knew what she thought of Belle and Gran spending time together after all these years.

She showered and dressed. For today she'd saved a silver sparkly jumper that felt Christmassy and she teamed it with her freshly washed jeans – Audrey had kindly let her do some laundry during her stay – and dried her hair. The apple shampoo had a tang that usually woke her up, but with so much dread pooling in her stomach at the thought of seeing Sebastian again today, it didn't work its usual magic. She put on some lip gloss and then packed everything into her suitcase, which was no easier to shut than it had been back at her flat the day she left. She sat on it again and with a bit of effort managed to get the zips all the way round to meet in the middle.

The light crept beneath the curtains so she tiptoed over to the window, always wary of stomping if another guest was sleeping in the room below, and pulled them back.

'Oh my goodness!' she gasped, looking out over Little Woodville, because it was a total blanket of white. Everything was still, nothing moved, cars were little humps in the road, buried beneath the snow – her own was buried in its position in the car park. The trees sparkled with frost, glistened with snow on their branches, and the Christmas tree in the distance towered over everything, resplendent in the morning light.

Grinning, she grabbed her phone to fire off a text to Sebastian about a white Christmas Eve, which could mean a white Christmas too, but her smile faded when she remembered they weren't exactly on good terms right now. Instead she took a photo of the picture-postcard view from up here and sent it first to Sam and then to Mrs Fro.

She hovered at the window, her little square of happiness just for now that nobody could take away. Her phone soon pinged with an excited text from Sam. 'You lucky bugger!' it said. 'Hope we get some this way…there's no sign yet! Can you still get to Wales?'

Belle hadn't thought of that. She googled the weather on her phone and found snow was blanketing much of the UK today. The east of the country seemed to be fine for now, but the west had taken the brunt all the way to where she was in the Cotswolds.

She replied to Sam with 'fingers crossed!' before slumping onto the bed. She wasn't sure how to feel about time away with Anthony right now. In a few short weeks she had become detached from what they'd had at home and she could see now that they'd plodded along in their relationship happily enough, but she couldn't help wondering whether their biggest strength was, and always would be, their joint work ethic. Sure, they laughed together, had a lot of fun, the sex was always great. But Belle knew there was that little extra thing missing. If only she could put her finger on what it was. With Anthony, work had, and always would, come first, and for a while she'd thought she was of the same ilk. But being around completely different people, in a place with so many memories, she'd been forced to consider what her future should entail without the distraction of anyone else in the picture. Anthony moved at full speed – he always had – but by being in Little Woodville, Belle had been able to look at their relationship as an outsider. For Anthony, business had clouded his judgement of anything else, but he wasn't the only one at fault. Belle had let herself be led along, a bit like with her mum and her gran, doing what she thought the other person wanted, when all along her dreams were somewhat different.

She shook her head and then pinged off a text to Anthony telling him about the snow, the road situation and the possibility they may not make Wales after all. Part of her wanted to stay here in this very bed and breakfast and not have to make a decision about anything. She'd make a week's supply of hot chocolate, bring it up here and sit at the window gazing out at the snow.

But life wasn't a fairy tale all wrapped up and cushioned in white, and even if she hid out here, sooner or later the snow would melt and she'd have to face up to everything.

It wasn't long before Anthony FaceTimed her and she could see him, in a shirt and tie, sitting at a desk.

'Don't tell me you're at work – it's Christmas Eve.'

'Just tying up a few things before the off.' He rolled his eyes but already she knew he probably wasn't all that bothered. The thrill of being so busy he didn't have time to stop had made her laugh before and they'd joked that she'd have to tie his hands behind his back on holiday to stop him checking his emails. That had been one of the attractions of the cottage in Wales...no WiFi!

'I take it you haven't checked the weather forecast,' she said, wondering where they went from here.

He turned to the side and she knew he was looking out of the window. He turned back. 'It looks cold, bloody cold in fact, but other than that it's fine. Why?'

She turned her phone camera towards her own window, walked over and gave him a full view of Little Woodville.

Anthony harrumphed. 'So the one Christmas we decide to go away, it snows.'

'The roads are blocked from here over to Wales.'

He turned his head and she heard the tapping of his keyboard. 'I'll just get up some weather reports on the computer.' More tapping. 'Wow, this looks like the worst the UK has seen in years. I'll call the owner of the cottage, see what's what.'

'I can do it if you're busy.'

'Don't worry, I'll talk with them and see if there's any likelihood of getting there and if not, maybe they'll be kind enough to transfer our booking to another week, Easter or something.'

'So I guess I'll drive back to Cambridge.' She watched someone shovelling snow in great big heaps off the bonnet of a car out front. The roads did have some dark patches of tarmac on them so perhaps pootling along at a snail's pace could get them to where they wanted to go, but she doubted it.

'Don't do anything, Belle. Leave it with me and I'll come back to you.'

After her chat she went downstairs to breakfast and found Audrey and Gus full of the joys of winter. 'I thought spring was supposed to make people smile like that,' Belle quipped.

'I love the snow.' Hand on her heart, Audrey smiled. 'It's magical, especially at Christmas.'

Gus butted in. 'She's just hoping to win the bet at the pub.'

'Actually I am,' Audrey whispered so other guests didn't hear. 'I've been trying to persuade Gus to let me try out the day spa in the next village but he always says it's too expensive. A little win could come in very handy.'

'Well I'll keep my fingers crossed for you,' said Belle.

Audrey smiled. 'Did you end up placing a bet?'

'I did.'

'Then I'll keep my fingers crossed for you too.'

Belle perused the little cardboard menu folded in half and standing in wait for hungry guests. 'I think I'll have the omelette this morning, if I may, and a very big cup of black tea.'

'Coming right up.' Audrey bustled off and before long was back with the tea and some water. 'I can't believe this is your last morning with us – I'm going to miss you.'

She wrapped her hands around the mug to warm her right through. 'I may have to stay a bit longer though if this snow won't let me out of the village this afternoon. Do you think there's any chance it'll disappear?'

With a sharp intake of breath Audrey said, 'I hope not. I've got my eye on the prize!'

Belle looked through the criss-crossed window of the dining room at the snowy scene, worthy of any Christmas card, and sensed she wouldn't be going anywhere today. 'Could you fit me in for another night do you think?'

'Let me see what I can do.' She patted Belle's arm. 'We'd love to have you, of course. Gus will have your omelette ready in a flash.'

'Thanks, Audrey.'

Gus didn't take long and Belle tucked in to the breakfast the second it arrived, with its little curls of hock ham at the top, the fluffy egg and cheesy mixture hugging pieces of mushroom and herbs. Belle wondered how she'd get used to her usual breakfasts again, the meagre bowl of cereal or a snatched piece of toast when she was in a rush.

She was about to head back upstairs and clean her teeth when Audrey returned, shaking her head. 'I'm afraid we're fully booked. I made a call to the couple heading down to stay in your room as of tonight, wondering whether they'd be stranded too, but they're already in the village and parked up. They're exploring until check-in time. I'm sorry, Belle.'

'No, don't be. The snow might clear, I could be lucky. Don't you worry about it.'

'Oh, I feel terrible.'

Belle pushed her chair in. 'Absolutely not a problem, really. My things are packed so I'll leave them in the car. I'm off to see Gran anyway, unless the roads are terrible that side of the village too, and this afternoon I can see if the snow has cleared enough to brave going to Wales, or perhaps head back to Cambridge.'

'You'll be the first to know if I get any cancellations.'

'Thanks, I appreciate it.'

The reception area was lighter than usual given the snow glow coming from outside, and excited chatter filled the stairwell as a new family settled into their suite with an early check-in, ready to experience the magical delights – their words, not Belle's – of Little Woodville. She cleaned her teeth, squeezed her toothbrush and toothpaste through a tiny opening in the suitcase, double-checked she hadn't left anything else in the bathroom or in the bedroom, remembering to look under the bed, and made her way downstairs. Gus caught her mid-flight and took the suitcase for her.

'I cleared your car a bit for you,' Gus told her, taking the suitcase all the way to the front entrance.

'You didn't have to do that, but thank you so much.' She put her arms around him and gave him a hug. It wouldn't have felt right not to. 'You and Audrey have been wonderful hosts.'

'Well now, you'll have me all emotional in a minute.' He lifted up the case after he'd put a pair of wellies on, and out he trudged to her car. She followed, opened up the boot, and he put the suitcase in, along with another bag she was carrying containing the candles she'd bought ready for the trip to Wales. 'It was lovely to meet you, Belle. I hope you get away safely today.'

She zipped up her coat and took out her gloves. 'Wales is looking unlikely, but the east of the country seems to have escaped the worst of it so I may end up heading home to Cambridge later on, providing I can get out of the village.'

Belle waved her goodbyes again and trudged her way down to the high street filled with well-wishers, smiling patrons rushing for that last minute gift, people bustling in and out of shops. Kids on a patch of grass just before the stretch of street where the shops began were having a snowball fight and Belle laughed – although soon scurried past when she thought they may turn their attention to her.

The smell of the bakery lured her further on and she was surprised to see such a long queue bursting from the inside to the front steps and onto the street. The scent of cinnamon spiralled through the air as Trixie negotiated the crowd and escaped onto the pavement.

'It's so busy.' Trixie clutched a pink and white striped paper bag.

'Unusually busy,' Belle agreed. 'Is it the rush for Christmas cakes or people thinking they'll run out of bread over the next few days?'

'Neither. It's these.' She opened the bag and let Belle take a peek at the ringed doughnut with a hole in the middle.

Belle was almost knocked over by the scent of what was inside, an amalgamation of the smell that was already in the air and more spices and sweetness than she knew what to do with. 'My mouth is watering and I've only just had breakfast.'

'Betty's cinnamon doughnuts. They are to die for.' Trixie made Belle laugh when her eyes rolled to the back of her head. 'Seriously, and there aren't too many left of the first batch. She only makes them on Christmas Eve, so she gets a right rush on. That's why I'm here early.'

'Why only once a year? She could make a fortune doing them all the time by the sounds of it.'

'Betty is somewhat of a traditionalist. When she sees hot cross buns in supermarkets all year round she has a fit, says it's disrespectful, it's big firms making big bucks. I don't point out that we're British so actually they're making pounds.'

Belle giggled. 'The criticism probably wouldn't go down too well, would it?'

'Anyway, she says she will always do them on this one day of the year, and she's in there now, busy making more, but you wouldn't want her to run out of ingredients.'

'Thanks for the warning.'

'I hear this is your last day with us.'

'I'm afraid so.'

'Will you come back and see us?'

Now she was in contact with Gran, Belle knew she'd be visiting frequently and the care home was only a short drive away from here. Suddenly she was warmed through by the thought that today wasn't really a goodbye, it was almost the start of something. She'd be able to see Gran, perhaps bring her in to Little Woodville. She could buy hot chocolates, an ice-cream in the summer, maybe sit on the village green and laze the day away with a good book. They could even play Pooh Sticks if they liked!

'I'll make sure I pop into the cafe when I'm next down this way,' said Belle.

'Glad to hear it.' Trixie held up the paper bag. 'I'm taking this home now; I'll pick up a coffee on the way and then I'm going to enjoy both and get stuck into a Christmas novel. Goodbye, and Merry Christmas, Belle.'

'Merry Christmas, Trixie.'

Belle hadn't been into the bakery since the day Sebastian had stood on her toe and Betty had given her what for. But, today, she was going to do it. Betty had smiled at her last time she'd seen her and she knew Betty approved of her finally seeing Gran again, so what was stopping Belle now?

'Hi, Jack; hi, Daniel.' She patted the toy soldiers' heads as she stood in the queue, which moved surprisingly quickly. She passed through the doorway, the heady smell of fruit, spices and freshly warmed loaves almost too much, and as she got to the counter she could see Betty arranging another load of the cinnamon doughnuts, laden in sugar and spice. 'Hi, Betty.' She may as well take the super-friendly approach.

Betty looked up and from the moment she opened her mouth, Belle knew she was in trouble. 'You've got a nerve, showing your face in here.'

'Excuse me?'

'Selling the cottage to someone who doesn't even care about it when Sebastian has called it home for a long time.' She didn't seem to mind who was around to hear this.

'I…I —' She was about to say she hadn't made any decisions yet, but, from the little she knew about her, it seemed Betty wasn't a woman who liked to offer the benefit of the doubt.

'I'd like you to leave.' Betty stood upright, hands on hips, her bulk enough to make a person shudder. She was attracting more than a few glances too. 'You're not welcome here. Not anymore.'

'Steady on, Betty.' Peter was by her side and his gaze seemed to be imploring Belle not to take it to heart.

'It's OK, I'm leaving.' Belle didn't look at a single person as she ran out of the bakery, almost knocking the toy soldiers into each other. That would've gone down well – upsetting Sebastian and demolishing Betty's precious Christmas traditions all in one go.

Belle didn't take in the happy scene on the high street, with lights strung in zigzags above all the way along, and the enormous Christmas tree on the village green with all its twinkly lights. Head down against the cold, she trudged through the snow still on pavements, made her way over the bridge in eerie silence as the blanket of snow over Little Woodville made it feel as though the village was far from anywhere. She wanted to see Gran today, but after Betty's reaction she was angry with Sebastian. He'd jumped to conclusions about her decision when she wasn't even sure herself and although all the signs pointed to her selling the cottage to this other buyer for a sum that would make even Sebastian's eyes water, there was still room for her to change her mind. But if he was going to be so ridiculous about it, maybe she was better off dealing with a more level-headed client, someone who didn't have the emotional strings attached.

It took her longer than usual to tramp over to Snowdrop Cottage but, determined not to let Sebastian make her feel bad today, she marched up to the gate. In fact, she marched so fast she lost her footing and slipped on a patch that looked like it was covering snow but had been concealing ice beneath. She fell hard on her bum with a thud and yelped.

Before she had the chance to push herself up again, two strong arms hooked beneath her own from behind and hoisted her to standing. She turned round to meet Sebastian, who didn't look amused; he looked as frustrated as yesterday and Belle knew straight away that today's journey out to see Gran wasn't going to be fun.

'Thank you.'

'Don't mention it.' He walked through the gate. 'You need to be more careful. It may look all pretty but there's a lot of ice around.'

Glad she had something else to talk about, she followed him through the gate. 'Do you think we'll still be able to drive to see Gran?'

He kept his back to her as he ducked and went into the cottage saying, 'The jeep can handle it. You don't need to come with me today, you can wait here and we'll give Gillian the presents when we're back. I didn't want to risk her missing the Christmas lunch tomorrow if it snows again, so she's packing an overnight bag and will spend the night here at the cottage.' He picked up his keys from the side table.

Belle clutched her hip, which was already throbbing even through the bulk of her coat. 'That sounds like a good idea.'

When he turned he noticed what she was doing. 'Did you hurt yourself?'

'Only a bump, it's fine. But I'll hang around here if you think that's easier.' She winced again.

'I'm not a complete bastard.' He dropped the keys on the table again. 'Come on, get some ice on it and it'll stop it being so bad later.'

He'd already gone through to the kitchen to do something and so Belle had no choice but to follow him in. She noted the Christmas tree in the lounge as she passed by, the lights off, ready to be desserted in an empty house. Seeing it made her sad; it reminded her of how kind Sebastian had been before he'd overheard her on the phone talking about the other offer.

'Here.' He handed her a tea towel into which she'd seen him put half a dozen ice cubes.

She laughed. 'What, you want me to pull my jeans off here in the kitchen?'

His eyes sparkled and he shrugged.

'Oh, just give it to me.' She turned. 'I'll do it in the lounge if it's OK with you.'

'Fine by me,' he grumbled as she walked gingerly down the hall and flopped onto the sofa beside the tree. She unzipped her jeans and already she could see her left hip was a deep red, hinting at the bruise that would shine through before too long. She touched the makeshift ice pack to it and gasped. It was cold, and painful. But once it was there properly, it began to help and she lay back on the sofa gazing into the branches at the tiny ornaments.

'Keep it on for fifteen minutes.' Sebastian's voice boomed into the room and made her jump. His arms above the doorway as his body pushed forward just inside, he watched her ice her hip and she was conscious her tummy was on display.

She did her best to pull her clothing around the ice pack to make it more inconspicuous. 'I think it's helping.'

'Good.'

He didn't hang around but after fifteen minutes – she'd timed it on her watch – she heard the jangle of keys he must've picked up again. 'I'll get going,' he told her. He wasn't exactly smiling but at least he was talking to her.

'Have you made up her bed?' Anything to make conversation.

'I'm not stupid. I know she's not going to be sleeping on the sofa.' He didn't even look at her and it hurt.

'Sebastian, can't we be civil to one another, just for today at least?'

This time his eyes met hers. 'It's not the fact you're going to sell the cottage to someone else, Belle, it's that you didn't tell me. What, you think I'm a simple country bumpkin who just wouldn't get it? I wouldn't know that business is business and you need to make a strategic decision? I've made a few of my own in my time.'

'I don't think you're a simple country bumpkin…in fact, I think it's been years since I've heard anyone use the term bumpkin.' Her smile and attempt at a joke didn't work on him at all. 'You should go.'

After he left, she walked a little more easily to the kitchen, where she poured the remains of the ice cubes into the sink from their pouch and left the soiled tea towel in the utility room before returning to the lounge. She put the Christmas tree lights on to make the room more cheery, knowing how much Gran would appreciate it when she arrived.

*

255

'Merry Christmas!' Gran came through the door before Sebastian and her voice, echoing around the walls of her own cottage, almost made Belle fall apart with joy. When she met Belle in the hallway and gave her a big hug, Belle could see she had tinsel around each wrist and a bit through the buttonhole of her cardigan.

'You look like Mrs Claus,' Belle beamed.

'Cheeky thing. I like a bit of sparkle at Christmas, gets me in the mood,' she winked.

'What's in the bag?' Belle noticed Gran clutching a carrier bag, unwilling to reveal its contents.

'Never you mind, young lady. All will be revealed.'

Sebastian came through the door with Gran's overnight bag and after she'd stuffed the carrier bag inside, he took it straight upstairs without much of a hello.

'Are you going to be all right with the stairs, Gran?' Belle took her coat from where it lay in her arms and hung it on one of the hooks.

'Sebastian will help me up and down them – I'll manage.' She looked around her. 'Oh, you've no idea how good it is to be back.'

'Are you all right, Gran?' Belle didn't miss the wobble in her voice.

'Just getting sentimental,' she sniffed. 'I have a lot of memories tied up in this cottage.' She put a hand against Belle's cheek. 'Plenty wrapped up with you in them, and it means more than I can say to see you here now.'

'What do you think to the tree?' Belle hooked an arm through hers and led her a few more steps along the hallway, into the lounge room. Gran moved slowly as though she wanted to savour every single inch of the cottage and not miss a thing.

'Why, that's beautiful. You worked on it together?'

Sebastian, downstairs again, answered, 'We did. And all your favourite ornaments are on there.' He pointed out the photo of Belle and for a moment they were back on an even keel, but when he looked away she knew they weren't at all. 'You wait till it's dark and all lit up tonight.'

'About tonight,' Gran began as they filed through to the kitchen. 'Trevor has invited me over for tea and scones and I said I'd go, but I can change my mind of course, if you'd rather.'

Sebastian put the kettle on and Belle sat down carefully opposite Gran. Her hip was starting to hurt again but she wasn't sure whether it was best to be standing or sitting or to keep alternating her position.

'Tea?' Sebastian asked, and both women said yes – even though Belle suspected he'd rather not be making it for her. But it seemed he also didn't want to upset Gran so was playing along for her benefit.

'What's going on with you?' Gran didn't miss a thing and looked at Belle shuffling uncomfortably in her seat.

'I slipped outside on the ice earlier, but it's fine. I've used an ice pack on it. I think it's just going to be a very unattractive bruise for a while.'

'Winter can be beautiful, but treacherous too.' Gran reached across the table for Belle's hand. 'I know you're supposed to be heading off to Wales this afternoon, but I've seen the news. You won't be able to go now, will you? Oh, please say you'll be stranded with us in Little Woodville.'

'I'm not sure what I'll be up to yet. I'm waiting to hear from Anthony and he's in talks with the owner of the cottage.'

'I really don't like the thought of you driving anywhere in this.'

'The main roads might be fine.' She thanked Sebastian for her tea and cupped her hands around the mug, checking her watch at the same time. 'Anthony should let me know soon.' She'd thought he would've told her by now. All her things were still packed in the boot of her car, waiting at the bed and breakfast ready for the off.

'I do love snow at Christmas.' Gran disappeared into childlike mode again and it served as a reminder of Christmases long ago, which Belle wasn't at all sorry about. They had many years to make up for and today was an extra bonus, especially if her departure was delayed.

'I'm excited about my sleepover.'

'I'll bet you are. You get to stay in Snowdrop Cottage again.' It warmed Belle all the way through that Gran was going to get to do this.

Sebastian joined them at the table with his own cup of tea and they talked about the high street in all its splendour, decorated for the festive season with its enormous Christmas tree. 'I'll walk you to see it all tomorrow morning,' he said. 'And we can go to the pub to see who wins the bet, now that it's a white Christmas.'

Gran let out a childlike giggle. 'Oh, woe betide anyone who bet we wouldn't see snow this year. They'll be out of pocket.'

'We could always take a walk now,' he suggested. 'We could pop into the bakery for one of Betty's legendary cinnamon doughnuts.'

Gran clapped her hands together but the smile didn't last. 'You know I would love to, but I think I need a power nap. I'm exhausted with the thrill of all of this, being here with you both.' She had one hand outstretched to Sebastian's, the other to Belle's, joining them all together as one. 'It's a lot of excitement for a little old lady. I think a sleep and then over to Trevor's for the evening will be quite enough. I want to be in top form tomorrow for Christmas lunch.' She beamed.

'Not to worry, power nap it is. How about I go to the bakery and try to get the doughnuts and we'll have them when you wake up?'

'That sounds like a lovely idea. Will you still be here, Belle?'

Belle took out her phone. Still nothing from Anthony. She had hoped he would've been on to the cottage by now and sorted out whether they were going or not. 'I don't know what I'm doing, Gran. But I promise I won't go anywhere without seeing you first. We still need to give you your Christmas gifts, remember. You go for your power nap and I'll get hold of Anthony, see what's what.'

Sebastian helped Gran up to her bedroom, which wasn't a quick task because Gran was reminiscing with every step she took.

'She's glad to be back,' said Belle when he reappeared downstairs but he didn't return her smile. 'Don't worry, I won't hang around the whole time,' she said. 'I'll go now, see if I can get hold of Anthony, and I'll come back in an hour or so. We can give Gran the presents then.'

'You can stay here.' He held her gaze for a moment. 'I'm off to the bakery to get the doughnuts so you won't be in my way.'

He disappeared and Belle, grateful she'd had the omelette this morning to fill her up so she didn't need lunch, washed up the mugs and set them on the drainer. She swept up around the front door where dust and debris had sneaked inside, she iced her hip one more time although silently thanked Sebastian for making her do it straight away because it had already stopped hurting as much, and she lit the wood burner so that when Gran woke up they could sit in the lounge room beside the tree and once again have just a sliver of Christmas, more than they'd had in a long time.

Belle crept up the staircase to check on Gran and with the door ajar she could already see she was out for the count, with a little snore that forced Belle to stifle a giggle. She looked so vulnerable lying there in the middle of the enormous bed – not the full-of-life character she really was – and it reminded Belle that one day she would slip away just like Grandad did, and Belle had to close her eyes tight to scare the tears away.

Downstairs, Belle read the book she'd brought with her and finally Anthony texted. He'd sorted out the cottage and they were booked to go to Wales in February instead, just before the school holidays, because nobody wanted to go away then. It was generous of the owners to do it, and Belle wasn't altogether disappointed. Anthony said in his text that he'd made different plans so could she please sit tight until he got in touch again. He promised he would do as soon as he could.

Strangely, nothing much seemed to overly worry Belle when she was at Snowdrop Cottage. It was as if the world out there existed separately from the world in here, all wrapped up in its own little bubble.

Sebastian came back just as Belle had shut her book and gone upstairs after Gran called her. She helped her pull on her socks, negotiate the stairs, and they both went through to the kitchen, where Sebastian had placed a familiar pink and white striped paper bag in the centre of the table. Belle wondered if Betty had said anything to him at the bakery. She wondered how many doughnuts were in there, whether Betty had refused to serve him if he was going to give one to her, the enemy.

'Betty says hello.' When Sebastian spoke Belle figured there wasn't any doubt that the greeting was for Gran.

'Oh, how lovely, I look forward to seeing her tomorrow. Now, who's for a hot cup of cocoa?'

Belle smiled. 'I'll make it, you sit. And then it's present time.'

If she was going to be leaving the village today, she wanted to make the most of this moment. She'd waited long enough for it to happen.

*

'What do you think to the wood burner, Belle?' Gran was comfortably ensconced on the sofa opposite the inglenook fireplace where the wood burner was housed, Sebastian was next to her on one side and Belle was cross-legged on the floor facing them.

'It's great, much easier than the open fire.'

'I thought so, and I'll bet you use it a lot more, don't you, Sebastian?'

'I use it a lot.' He patted her hand with his own.

'You'll have a lot of winters yet to enjoy it,' said Gran, oblivious of what had gone on between them.

As they'd sat drinking their cocoa and devouring the cinnamon doughnuts that Belle had to admit were a gift from heaven, despite their maker, neither she nor Sebastian had even addressed the small issue of Snowdrop Cottage going to anyone else.

'Present time?' Belle didn't wait for a response; instead, she got up and found the decorated box and Sebastian's wrapped picture.

'I love this part,' Gran admitted.

261

'These gifts are from the both of us,' said Sebastian.

'You went shopping together?' Gran raised an eyebrow. Belle had to hand it to her, she was sharp even at her age.

Gran took the box first and pulled at the ribbon, her arm so much better now. 'Did you make these?' She lifted the box and inhaled the ginger and the cinnamon from the layers of cookies inside. 'They smell wonderful. Oh, have one, go on, both of you.' She proffered the box but had no takers.

'Seriously, Gillian,' Sebastian protested, 'we've had the doughnuts so that'll do. Maybe later if you're home from Trevor's early.'

'Well thank you, Sebastian. Thank you, Belle.'

Sebastian lifted the wrapped picture and put it on Gran's lap. She could tell it was fragile and undid the Sellotaped edges carefully, pulling back the paper to reveal what was inside, and when she did, she covered her mouth with a gasp. 'It's my cottage. Oh, you two.' Tears filled her eyes. 'You don't know what this means to me.'

'You might not be living here anymore,' said Sebastian, 'but if you put this up on the wall in your new room at the care home, you can look at it every day.'

Gran's fingers traced the picture, the thatched roof, the arched thatch over the door, the little fence and gate and the snowdrops out front as well as at the sides. 'It's the best present I could ever ask for, apart from you coming back into my life, Belle.'

Belle reached out and hugged her gran and Sebastian followed suit. They all sat in contemplative silence, admiring the photo, giving in to temptation and eating one of the gingerbread cookies each.

'Could you do me a favour please, Belle?' Gran brushed crumbs from her cardy onto a tissue.

'You can't fit another cookie in, can you?'

'Don't be daft. I won't eat a thing at Trevor's later if I have anything else now. No, could you please go upstairs and on my bed is a shopping bag. Don't look inside it, but could you bring it down to me?'

'Of course I can.'

Gran stood up. 'I'm going to use the bathroom at the back of the utility room to avoid those stairs.' She waved away any offer of Sebastian's help, Belle disappeared upstairs and Sebastian answered the door when someone knocked.

The sound of carollers drifted up the stairs as the front door opened and Belle came downstairs to 'Ding Dong Merrily on High'. It made her insides fizz – the thought of Christmas, the cottage, everything that had gone before, everything that was left to experience. The financial incentive to sell the cottage to Anthony's buyer was enormous, but the emotional stakes in doing so were also high. If Sebastian were to stay in the cottage, her connection with Gran would forever stay strong. If he didn't, Belle worried she and Gran would never be as close again.

Gran joined them at the door on her way back from the bathroom and the sheer delight on her face was enough to melt Belle on the spot as the carollers finished their tune, bid them a Merry Christmas and went on their way.

'They were enchanting.' Gran hovered at the door, watching as the group faded into the distance.

'Shut the door before you catch a chill.' Belle handed her the bag she'd brought from upstairs.

Gran shut the cottage door and Belle made her excuses and went to use the bathroom now. She went to the one upstairs and it wasn't that she really needed to use it, she just needed some breathing space from everything – from seeing Gran here, from Sebastian and the current of tension running between them, from Anthony and whatever he had planned for Christmas. She'd never enjoyed the season, not since she was a little girl, and now she was reminded of why. It brought major emotions to the fore, there was a pressure like nothing else, and if she could run from it all right now she might just do that.

'Belle?' Sebastian's voice called from the bottom of the stairs.

She opened the door, her face fresher from touching it with cold hands after she'd run her skin beneath the tap. 'I'm coming.'

'I need to take your gran to Trevor's soon, so she wants us in the lounge room.'

Belle thought it peculiar but followed him to find Gran by the Christmas tree with a little boxed gift in each hand. 'You didn't think I'd let Christmas pass by without a little something for my grandchildren did you?'

Belle and Sebastian looked at one another, her trying to get used to the fact Gran was putting them together as grandchildren, him with a look of trepidation that Belle suspected was because he was uncomfortable with the terminology.

'You've been in her life for more years than I ever was,' said Belle, meeting his gaze.

When he looked at her it was with a sudden kindness. 'Physically, yes, but you've been in her heart for much longer.'

'Now there's no need to fight over me,' said Gillian, proffering the gifts once again.

Belle took one box, Sebastian the other.

'They're both the same,' said Gran. 'I hope you like them. I picked them up last week when Jenny, one of the staff, took a few of us shopping in Cheltenham. It was a palaver with parking and what have you, Marcel tripped as he got off the minibus, we thought he'd done his ankle…'

But Belle wasn't listening, because what she was looking at was the most perfect present she'd ever been given. It was a snow globe and beneath the falling pieces of white was Snowdrop Cottage, the replica she'd not seen for more than two decades. 'Where did you find it?'

Gran's eyes glistened with tears, and if Belle wasn't mistaken, Sebastian felt the emotion too.

'Remember the jewellery box you found, Belle?'

'The one I posted to you?'

'That's the one. Well, there was a drawer at the bottom that was stuck.'

'I remember. I shoved all the bits and pieces I needed to put inside in the top instead.'

'The drawer was stuck because I'd rammed in both of these cottage replicas. I found yours in the doll's house after your mum took you away from Little Woodville and I put it alongside mine on the mantelpiece for a while. Seeing them together made me think that someday you would come back to me.' Her voice caught. 'And I suppose you did. It took a lot longer than I'd hoped, but you came eventually.'

'What were they doing in the jewellery box, Gran?'

'When I decided the time had come to move out of this place, looking at them was painful. It reminded me that life was changing in a way I didn't want it to, that for more than two decades it hadn't gone the way I really wanted.'

'Oh, Gran.' Belle sat beside her and rested her head on her shoulder. 'I'm here now.'

She put a hand on Belle's knee. 'When you wrote and said you wanted to see me, I was over the moon. I wrote back, I walked to the postbox with Jenny from the care home and posted the letter myself and then I went back and sorted through what you'd sent me in the parcel. Most of the things I threw out, but when I got to the jewellery box I yanked that drawer open, tore the main part, because I wanted those little pieces so badly. I sat with them in my hands and had to explain their significance to Jenny. I put them on the shelf in my new bedroom and then I had an idea. It was Jenny who put me onto it. She'd had snow globes made with photos of her grandchildren in them, so, with her help, we found somewhere that would do what I wanted, and I decided both of you would get a Snowdrop Cottage for Christmas.' Her eyes went to Sebastian. 'It felt fitting to give you the other one because to me you were, and still are, my other grandchild.'

Belle smiled warmly. She had no animosity at the claim, no need for reassurance of her place. 'This is the most exquisite snow globe I've ever seen.' She shook it for effect and stared at the piece, mesmerised by the Cotswold stone of the cottage with its periwinkle blue door and gate, the teeny white sign at the front with the name, the trees sitting to each side now covered in the fragments of snow as it settled.

Gran looked over to the illuminated pine tree dominating the room as the wood burner kept them as warm as they needed to be. 'I do wish you were staying with us for Christmas, Belle.'

Belle had almost forgotten the time. She fired off a text to Anthony, anxious he let her in on his plans soon or she didn't know what she'd do. 'Today has been perfect, Gran. I couldn't have asked for a better Christmas Eve than this.'

'Excuse me, I need to use the bathroom again.' Gran stood and shuffled off down the corridor once more.

Sebastian's brow furrowed. 'Hasn't she only just been?'

'Shush, she'll hear you! She's elderly.'

'So?'

Belle lowered her voice. 'She might have bladder problems.' But as soon as she'd said it she heard giggling and Gran reappeared.

'What are you up to?' Belle wondered.

'Nothing, dear. Sebastian, I think I'd better get over to Trevor's now, if you don't mind. Belle, please don't go without saying goodbye. Sebastian will tell you Trevor's address and if you must be silly enough to drive this afternoon, don't do it without seeing me first.'

'I promise I won't.'

'I'll get your boots from the utility room,' said Sebastian.

'Thank you.' Gran waited for him to go down the hall and through the kitchen to the other side and then said to Belle, 'Oh, could you grab me my handbag? I've left it on the kitchen table. Silly me.'

'Of course I can.' Belle walked along the hallway and was about to go through to the kitchen but passed Sebastian coming the other way.

Gran let out a giggle and they both stopped in the kitchen doorway, him just in front of it and her right beneath.

'What?' they said at the same time.

267

Grinning, Gran pointed upwards and they both tilted their heads to look.

'Mistletoe?' Belle queried. 'Did you put that there?'

Sebastian started to laugh and whispered to Belle, 'She'll try anything. She's lucky the doorways are so low or she never would've been able to reach.'

'Well, come on,' said Gran. 'It's rude not to kiss someone under the mistletoe.'

That wasn't what Belle was thinking. She was thinking about what Gran always said, how mistletoe was magic and kissing a man beneath it meant he would be yours for life.

Before Belle could say anything, Sebastian ducked his head and planted a kiss on her cheek that took her by surprise. The light stubble of his jaw grazed her skin, not unpleasantly, and she was glad she was leaning up against the door frame because her legs suddenly felt as though they wouldn't hold her up for much longer.

'I suppose that'll do,' Gran sighed as Belle brought her her handbag and Sebastian helped her on with her boots.

A knock at the door had Gran clapping her hands together. 'More carollers?' she asked hopefully.

But when Sebastian opened the door Belle could see their visitor wasn't exactly the carolling sort, but someone who would make this Christmas very different indeed.

Chapter Fifteen

'Anthony? Whatever are you doing here?' Belle was temporarily dazed but soon found a smile. 'Come in, out of the cold.'

Anthony wrapped her in his arms and squeezed her tight, a look of surprise lingering on his face when he looked again at the man who'd opened the door. 'I drove down almost as soon as I'd spoken to the owner of the cottage. I figured we'd be stranded in this village together instead, and it would give me a chance to see the cottage for myself.'

'Anthony, this is Sebastian,' Belle clarified, putting him out of his misery.

'Sebastian?' He couldn't hide his surprise but being polite, extended a hand. 'It's good to meet you.' He extended his hand to Gran next. 'I'm Anthony, Belle's partner, in both senses of the word,' he said, putting an arm around Belle's shoulders and pulling her close.

'It's nice to meet you, Anthony.' Gran didn't look like she wanted to go anywhere in a hurry now.

'Gran is staying over at the cottage tonight because of the snow,' Belle explained. 'I still don't understand, are the roads safe for driving?'

'They're fine from Cambridge to here and all the main roads are clear and gritted. It seems it's from Little Woodville all the way to Wales that's the problem, so we'd have no hope of going in the other direction. I parked up before I reached the high street and walked the rest of the way.' Belle noted the bag over his shoulder, a leather holdall as smart as him. She wondered if he'd booked into the hotel just outside Little Woodville, the place that was a bit too pricey for her to justify a few weeks in but one that may do for a night or two. He looked around, taking in the warmth of the place, the tree lights, the kitchen he could see from where they were. 'Wow, this place is quite something.'

'It certainly is.' Sebastian's voice was firm and his gaze moved from Anthony back to Belle.

Belle didn't really want any of this to be discussed in front of Gran and she silently hoped Gran wouldn't delay her departure, but her hopes faded when Gran took off her coat.

'I've got time for another cuppa,' said Gran. 'I need to get to know this man who has my granddaughter's heart. Put the kettle on, would you, Sebastian? Belle, how about fetching a plate of my cookies? You must be starved after your long journey.' She fussed over Anthony and Belle didn't know whether to panic or be relieved she was so attentive.

'Does Anthony take sugar?' Sebastian asked Belle when they'd both made it into the kitchen.

She opened a cupboard and took out a serving plate. 'Er…yes. One sugar, not too much milk.'

'Right you are.'

Belle wasn't sure if he was being snippy or not but she hastily finished arranging the cookies. She wanted to get back to the lounge room before Anthony mentioned anything about the cottage. She needed to keep the subject very clearly on something else.

'Here we go.' She offered the plate to Anthony first. 'Are you hungry after the drive?'

'I am a bit. This is what I call service.' He looked at Gran. 'We usually rush dinner back in Cambridge or we eat out, don't we, Belle?'

'But Belle loves to cook,' said Gran.

'I do a lot of the time,' Belle explained, 'whenever I can.'

'She's a star at work, this one.' Anthony put a hand on her hair as she knelt down beside him, more comfortable on the floor than all sitting in a row on the sofa.

'I do my best.' Embarrassed at the attention, she was grateful Sebastian came in bearing a tray lined with cups of tea. 'Thanks, Sebastian.' She took the one he indicated was Anthony's and passed it to him, then took her own, and Sebastian handed Gran hers, which she asked him to set on the coffee table beside the sofa.

'So, Anthony. I want to get to know you.' Belle would've laughed at Gran's announcement if she wasn't dreading what Anthony would say. She hadn't had a chance to ask him not to mention the buyer he'd found; she hadn't been able to make a firm decision in her own mind yet and talk it through with her boyfriend and soon to be business partner. She hadn't thought about where she and Anthony should really go from here, but she had a feeling this Christmas would give her all the answers she needed. She would just prefer to find them when they didn't have an audience.

Anthony had to cover a lot of ground with Gran. He told her all about where he'd grown up – Tunbridge Wells – how many siblings he had, what he'd done in his career up until now. They talked about the business he and Belle planned to start and skated very close to the subject of the cottage until Belle changed tack and showed Anthony the snow globe Gran had given her. Sebastian walked in and out of the room as he pleased – he seemed as uncomfortable as she was – and it was only when the phone rang and he answered it to Trevor that Gran relented and realised she would have to make a move.

'It was lovely to meet you,' Anthony said genuinely, and Belle could tell her Gran was hooked by his charm and ease. He focused on Belle again. 'Do you think we could stay an extra night at the bed and breakfast? Seeing as we're not going away to Wales now?'

Her heart sank. 'I assumed you'd sorted something already.' She could see Gran's eyes darting between the two of them.

'No, I thought with this being a small village and it being Christmas, the bed and breakfast would be able to extend your stay an extra night or two.'

Belle shook her head. 'I've asked but they're fully booked.'

'Ah, then that puts us in a bit of a tight spot.'

Belle dismissed the concern. 'We'll drive back up to Cambridge later, it's fine. Or we could try phoning the big hotel just outside Little Woodville. What's it called?'

Sebastian gave her the name and she tapped it into the search engine on her phone, got the number and told Anthony, 'I'll call them right now, see what they can do.' She didn't want to return to Cambridge, she wasn't quite ready, but she did need the headspace the hotel could offer.

'What are your Christmas plans?' she heard Anthony ask Gran as she waited for someone at the hotel to answer her call. She waited as it went through an automated menu, giving various selections she wasn't interested in.

'I'm having Christmas lunch here, at the cottage. Sebastian has carried on my tradition of inviting anyone who's on their own, anyone who wants the extra company. Over the years it's become quite a special event.'

'That'll be lovely, last one and all that. It'll be special.'

Gran's brow furrowed. 'Well it may not be my last one – there's plenty of life in the old bird yet.'

Shocked he'd said something out of hand, Anthony said, 'No, I didn't mean that at all. I just meant with the cottage being sold, you wouldn't have Christmas here after this year.'

Sebastian chivvied Gran towards the door. 'Come on, Trevor is getting impatient and it's beginning to get dark.'

But Gran wasn't having any of it. 'Well, unless Sebastian doesn't invite me again I don't see why it has to be my last this year.'

Anthony, perplexed, looked at Sebastian and Belle could tell he'd realised this woman had no idea of the client's offer and Belle's subsequent consideration of selling it to someone else, and as Belle talked as briefly as possible to the woman on the other end of the phone and found out there was no room at the hotel for them tonight, she thanked Anthony silently for having a bit of diplomacy.

When Sebastian and Gran left and Belle hung up, she said, 'No room at the inn, I'm afraid. We'll have to go back to Cambridge.'

But he wasn't interested in accommodation right now. 'Belle, do you want to tell me what's going on?'

*

Even though they had the cottage to themselves, when Sebastian and Gran left Belle realised she couldn't have this conversation here. Instead, they walked into the village and found a semi-quiet corner in the pub despite it being Christmas Eve and punters getting into the swing of things. Slade's 'Merry Xmas Everybody' put a smile on the face of everyone in the room, from the little old man nursing a pint of Guinness in the corner to the family who bustled through the front door in search of a meal. But Belle and Anthony remained sombre as they sat down ready to talk.

'What's going on, Belle?' Anthony cradled a pint of orange juice and lemonade in front of him. He'd declined the offer of a pint of beer or anything else alcoholic because right now their only option was to drive all the way back to Cambridge.

'It's about the cottage.'

'I kind of deduced that from the way your gran was talking. She doesn't know, does she?'

'No.'

'And does Sebastian? Who, might I add, is considerably younger than I thought he'd be.'

Anthony had never been the jealous type and she knew he wasn't thinking about another guy on the scene, he was thinking in business terms as he usually did. Sometimes it was as though he couldn't think in any other way.

'I still don't know what to do, to be honest.' She fiddled with the straw in her glass.

Anthony sat forward a little closer. 'This is a dream offer, Belle – it won't come along again.'

'I know it won't, but I had already promised Sebastian he could have the year to get himself sorted and buy the place, and there's plenty we could do in the meantime, isn't there? We have to deal with licences, find premises – there's so much to do.'

'You're not listening to me, Belle. The offer is incredible. I can't stress it enough. So by giving in to sentimentality – and I'm assuming this is what this is – you're passing up a significant sum.'

She took a gulp of Coke that made her eyes water it was so fizzy. 'It's more than that.'

'What, you think your Gran will disown you if you sell it to someone else? She gave you that place, remember. She said to do with it as you saw fit. If you hadn't come to Little Woodville, you would've accepted the offer – no question.'

'You're probably right. You know, I didn't think about the cottage or the village too much before Gran signed her home over to me, but ever since she did I had this yearning to come back and see it, to close the door on my past if she wasn't going to be in my life anymore.'

Anthony reached across the table and took her hand. 'This Sebastian, can't he buy another place? He's single, I assume, and what would he want with all that land? It'll be a waste.'

Belle couldn't answer that. Explaining to Anthony a person's attachment to a cottage, to a building that could be constructed somewhere else to the exact specifications if you so desired, would be pointless. He wouldn't see it at all. It wasn't that he didn't appreciate beauty in a home, because he did, but his business acumen had always blinkered him and common sense and level-headedness won every time.

'This is more than about the cottage,' she began bravely. 'I'm worried I'm not as behind our business venture as you are.'

'This is the first I've heard.' He took his hand away. 'What's brought all this on? Are you worried we won't make a success of it?'

'I think we will make a success of it, yes.'

'Then I don't understand.'

'Remember when we first met and I cooked you dinner rather than go out to a restaurant?'

'Of course I do. You made beef bourguignon followed by a raspberry cheesecake.'

She grinned. 'I'm glad you remembered.'

'How could I forget? I was amazed how skilful you were and how unfazed you were at me watching.'

'I've always loved to cook, but, apart from a few dinners, I don't really do it much anymore.'

'What does this have to do with our business venture, Belle?' Typically, he got straight to the point.

'All my life I've tried to please people. When I was taken away from Gran I wondered whether I'd done something wrong. I started to think that if I did everything I was supposed to, I wouldn't lose anything else in my life. I got a Saturday job quite young because I knew it pleased Mum to see me taking control of my future. I followed the path as an estate agent after she was so over the moon when I was offered a full-time trainee position. Every achievement of mine has been celebrated and I loved how together it made me feel. When I met you I was sailing on a career I enjoyed, and I never once stopped to think *what if*? What if I'd done something different? Was this really what I wanted to do?'

'I'm still not sure what your point is.' He'd now taken his hands all the way back to his side of the table and Belle couldn't blame him. She was turning his world completely upside down.

'As a little girl I did a lot of cooking with Gran and I always dreamed I'd do it as a job, but that was all it ever was, a dream.'

'What, so now you want to open a restaurant? Make food for a living? Really?'

'I know it's hard to understand, but coming here has made me think about what I want rather than what anyone else wants for me. I may realise that actually cooking is something I enjoy but not something I want to do as a job. But I need to come to that conclusion myself and I need to try it first rather than ignore it.'

'Belle, cooking is great as a sideline, and, as you're saying, you may not want to do it full time. You have a talent for the real-estate business, you do well, and we've got the most amazing opportunity coming our way if only you'll let it.'

'But it's your dream, Anthony.'

'That's funny,' he said. 'Because all along I've been thinking it was ours.'

*

Belle needed fresh air and so they left the pub and found a seat outside on the bench at the top of the village green.

'I can't deny it's an impressive village.' Anthony took in the scene laid out before them like a canvas with plenty of white, the enormous Christmas tree, the lights zigzagging their way through the high street, shoppers bustling this way and that, the sound of Christmas tunes drifting from the pub behind them. 'Are you sure you're not romanticising this new dream of yours? It'd be easy to do on days like this.'

She had suspected the same when she first found her gran's recipe book, when she first searched ingredients in the pantry and memories came flooding back. But since the day she and Sebastian had had the conversation about dreams and jobs, and whether they could ever be the same, Belle had begun to think about cooking in a completely different light. She'd asked herself, if she could cook instead of doing what she was doing, yet earn the same money and have the same financial security, would she do it? And the answer had been yes, of course she would.

'At first I thought I probably was,' she told Anthony now. 'Part of me was caught up in the rapture of cooking in Gran's kitchen, the nostalgia, but I've thought about this a lot. It's not some dream I've come up with since coming here. It's been a part of me for a long time but I hadn't thought it would ever eventuate into anything.'

'I think you'll regret it if you turn your back on your work as an estate agent.'

'I won't do so straight away, but I want to at least try something different.'

Anthony leaned forwards, his elbows resting on his upper thighs, fingers steepled and his chin resting on top. 'You're backing out of our plan,' he said.

'Yes. I am.' She could see it clearly for the first time.

'So where does this leave us?' He turned to face her.

Belle searched his eyes with her own and suspected he already knew the answer. She moved closer and kissed him on the lips, just once. 'It was always more your dream than mine. I think I went along with it because it was the right thing to do.'

'So a cook can't be with an estate agent, is that what you're saying?'

'Don't you see?' She didn't want to hurt him but the time had come to follow her own path and she had to be, for want of a better word, a little bit selfish. 'I've been going along with what I thought I *should* do rather than with what I really *wanted* to do. I think if we stayed together I'd be holding you back, you'd be frustrated that I didn't see the world in the same way as you do.'

'But we're good together.' He took her hands. 'Come on, Belle. What do you say you and I avoid all this

Christmas rigmarole, head back to Cambridge and hide out at your flat with the fire, a bottle of red and each other?'

She touched a hand to his cheek. 'You see, Anthony, I realised something else since I've been here. I don't hate Christmas; I was scared of it.' She shook her head. 'It sounds crazy, I know, but I've avoided it because it was so painful. Traditions only reminded me of Gran and what I'd lost, and I think Mum was the same. But being here, I realise how much I love it. It's as much a part of me as I am of it.' She knew it was a step too far in the wrong direction of sentimentality but she couldn't help it. 'And tomorrow, Sebastian and Gran will host Christmas lunch with anyone who wants to come, people who are alone, people who want extra company.'

'But you hate big get-togethers like that, unless it's work.'

There was nothing else to say. Anthony knew it, Belle knew it, and so Anthony and Belle said goodbye for the final time. They returned to the cottage and he collected his bag, she asked if he'd like her to walk with him but he didn't. Hurting him wasn't what she'd wanted, but, she suspected, in a few days he'd be gunning ahead with his business plans alone and he'd make a huge success of it. She doubted it would even be long before he found someone else to invest in the new business, become a partner even.

Belle couldn't watch Anthony walk away, so instead she trudged through the snow, back to the bed and breakfast. She cleared it with Audrey that she'd leave her car there, tugged a few items from her suitcase and went back to Snowdrop Cottage as the snow began to fall in earnest. She'd have to stay over now. She couldn't bear the thought of leaving Gran, leaving the village, being alone tonight or tomorrow, and her mum was too far away, in Ireland, not that that was an option anyway. Her mum didn't do Christmas in the way they embraced it here, and all of a sudden Belle couldn't stand thinking she'd miss out on it yet again.

Belle wasn't sure what to do when she got back to the cottage. She knew Gran would want her here – she could sleep on the sofa – but first she needed to make peace with Sebastian.

It seemed forever before they came home and her heart leapt when she heard the door open.

'Belle!' Gran held her arms open. 'I knew you wouldn't go without saying goodbye. Now, where's Anthony?' She looked past Belle into the kitchen.

'Sebastian?' Belle wondered what he was doing because he'd hurried up the stairs the second he came in.

Sebastian came downstairs with a bag stuffed full. He picked up his keys. 'I can't do this. I can't play happy families and pretend nothing's wrong.' He turned to go out the front door.

'What's he talking about?' Gran had one arm out of her coat.

'Gran, could you give us a minute to talk alone?' Belle needed to tell him what she'd decided. She helped Gran off with her coat and hung it on the hook, and in those few seconds she heard the door slam shut.

She ran to the door and called after him, 'Sebastian!' But her shout fell on the icy air as he drove away from the cottage. Everything outside was still and quiet and, apart from the few footprints in the snow on the path and the tyre tracks he left in his wake, there was no sign of him. Sebastian had gone.

*

You're freezing – get in front of that wood burner right now,' Gran demanded the second Belle admitted she was far too cold to be standing outside in the snow that persisted when Sebastian was nowhere to be seen. 'Now, care to tell me what that was all about?'

'He's angry at me, not you.' Belle knelt in front of the wood burner but it was too hot up close and so she sat further away, back against the sofa, warming her toes at the same time.

'And why is he angry?'

'Anthony found another buyer for the cottage. A buyer willing to offer almost twice as much as it's worth.'

'And you're taking the offer.' Gran wasn't asking. As Belle looked at her she had to hand it to Gran – she really was supporting her in whatever she wanted to do. Perhaps she was as scared as Belle was that they'd fall out again.

'Actually, no, I'm not.'

A wide smile spread across Gran's face. 'Then why on earth —'

'I never told Sebastian my decision, because it took a long time to think about it. I was going to keep it quiet, about the other offer, but he overheard me talking to Anthony on the phone. I wanted to take Christmas and New Year to really think about what I wanted.'

'You don't just mean who you wanted to sell to, do you?'

Belle shook her head. 'All my life I've tried to please everyone else. I tried to be good for Mum so she wouldn't take me away from anyone or anything else, I kept the cottage when you put it in my name because I thought that was what you would want, I got good grades at school and went into the job I'm in because I

281

knew Mum approved, I agreed to starting a new business with Anthony because it was his dream.'

'But it's not your dream, is it?'

'No, it's not. I thought it was, once upon a time, and I kind of got carried along on the wave of what I thought was right, the success, the prosperous future.'

'And now?'

Belle sighed. 'I will stay doing my job for a while, but I think I finally know what I want to do. I want to cook, I want to set up my own business. I don't know exactly what yet, and it may be ridiculous, but I'll hate myself if I don't try. I'll always look back and wonder, what if?'

'You're stronger than you think. It takes a lot of guts to go after what you want.'

'Oh, Gran. What a mess.' She looked into the flames of the wood burner. 'What will Mum say when she hears about all this?'

'You're a grown woman, Belle. Your mum will know any decisions you make won't have come lightly. Even I know that about you and it's been many years since I've been in your life properly. Has Anthony gone?'

'It's finished between us.' She shrugged off Gran's concern. 'It's for the best. I thought I'd be more upset, but I know it's the right thing, for both of us.' She looked out the window again. 'I wonder where Sebastian has got to.'

'Somewhere to cool off, probably. He'll be back. Did Anthony take it very badly?' she asked more tentatively.

'He's hurt, I know he is, but he puts on a brave face. I know he'll go ahead with starting his own business, though, and I'm certain he'll make it a roaring success.'

'I liked him.'

Belle was surprised. She'd noted a bit of reservation when her Gran greeted her boyfriend, but maybe it was because he was a new face in these parts. 'We were happy for a time.'

'Mrs Fro said you had a good 'un by your side. But she also told me she wasn't sure he was The One.'

'Really? It sounds as though you and Mrs Fro got to know each other pretty well.'

'She took pity on me, probably because she has her own daughter and could imagine how I must feel. And I'm so glad I met her that day. She brought you closer to me.'

Belle's smile faded when she turned to glance out of the window again. 'It's fully dark out there now.'

'Don't worry about him, Belle.'

'Anthony can look after himself.'

'That's not who I was talking about.'

Belle busied herself offering a cup of tea, something to eat – anything to stop Gran seeing her reaction, her longing to sort this out with Sebastian, a man who was so much more than her tenant.

'No food for me, thank you. I'm full after Trevor's scone gathering.' Gran followed her to the kitchen. 'There were four of us, a mountain of scones. That man has no idea about portion size.'

Belle's heart warmed to hear her Gran so animated, so enthused at having people around her. She picked up one of the apples she'd bought a couple of days ago to fill the fruit bowl with. She decided she'd better at least try to have something healthy today – tomorrow's feast was set to be huge, and she doubted any amount of seasonal vegetables could cancel out the fat and sugar load they'd all be hit with.

Gran pored over the recipe book on the side. She and Sebastian had already agreed a menu – Belle had heard them talking about it. She thought glazed carrots, he thought fresh; she thought roast potatoes and Hasselback potatoes, he thought one type was quite enough.

'There's so much to do.' Gran shook her head.

'Do we have Christmas pudding?'

Gran checked in the pantry. 'Got it. Sebastian must have collected one from Betty's, it's got her sticker on it.'

'I'd better try not to choke on it then,' Belle frowned.

'You're fighting again?'

'She started it.'

'I ought to bang your heads together, both of you,' Gran scolded, but she looked sideways in mischief and Belle nudged her with an arm.

'So who do we have?'

'Well, there's me, you, Sebastian, that makes three. Then Trevor, that's four.' She counted off on her fingers. 'Then Anne will be on her own this year – her daughter's in South America with her dad, nasty divorce – and we have Barbara from the church, you'll like her. That makes six…' Her brows knitted together until she said, 'Margaret, Betty and Peter – they're staying in Little Woodville this year – and that takes us up to nine.'

'I've made it uneven, haven't I?'

'Oh, nonsense,' said Gran. 'The table seats ten when we pull the ends out, so there'll be an extra space should we get any strays.'

'Is that likely?'

Gran shook her head. 'We're pretty careful each year to make sure nobody is forgotten, so everyone knew, we had all the replies.'

'It sounds like you plan this well.'

Gran sat at the table, the recipe book abandoned for now in favour of resting her legs and enjoying a cup of tea. 'I always enjoy the planning almost as much as the execution.'

'Tell me what the first Christmas was like, back when it all began.' Belle nursed her cuppa.

'It was the first Christmas after you left.' Her head tipped to one side as she carried on. 'I wasn't sure what I would do all on my own. I'd got so used to having you around, even if it wasn't on the day itself, but with the thought of the festivities stretching out in front of me with nothing but emptiness, well, it didn't bear thinking about.' She stared into her tea. 'It was Betty who encouraged me to do it.'

'How?' Belle wished she and Betty had more tolerance for each other. Well, it was there on her part but Belle knew it wasn't reciprocated.

'I went into the bakery one morning, just before Christmas. I hadn't heard from your mum since the previous year. I'd hoped to at least get a Christmas card, but when that still hadn't come by the day before Christmas Eve, I decided I could either wallow in self-pity or I could damn well get on with it.'

'That sounds just like you, Gran.'

'I think you get your determination from me.'

'And my stubbornness,' Belle grinned. 'Mum has it too.'

'She certainly does.' Gran left her cup of tea alone for now. 'That day I asked Betty whether she had any Christmas puddings left. I didn't know her too well. We'd chatted once or twice in the past when I bought bread or pastries, but had never really taken the time to get to know one another. She was in the middle of lining up Jack and Daniel by the door, as she did every year, but she said she'd check. She found one miniature pudding left. Everyone else had got there first. I said that it was enough for one, so I'd take it. Oh, the look that woman gave me. It was pity, and I knew it, and I burst into tears. She took me out the back and I sat on a stool and told her everything. You see, up until then I hadn't let anyone know you and your mum weren't coming to see me anymore. For all they knew you came and went from the cottage but steered clear of the high street.'

'It must've been awful.'

She nodded. 'When I got up from the stool in the bakery my backside was covered in flour and pieces of dough, and we crumpled into fits of laughter because I looked a right state. I'd never seen Betty laugh and her cheekiness set me off all the more. Anyway, she ended up inviting me for Christmas. She apologised because she was a lousy cook and I turned it around and said they must come to me instead. She leapt at the chance. And then when she remembered she'd invited Fliss because she was on her own – she lived near the church, but she's passed away now – and Gerry from the school, a teacher and a single dad who would probably burn down his flat if left in charge of a turkey, she thought I'd change my mind and withdraw my offer.'

'So you invited everyone?'

'It was a case of the more the merrier. We had Betty's turkey and Gerry drove out to a town not too far from here to find another. We had vegetables from my garden and the rest from what Betty already had, Fliss had made a Christmas pudding, Gerry brought crackers, and we all had Christmas at Snowdrop Cottage. It was the first year we did it and after that I didn't want it to ever change.'

'So who came the year after?' Filling in the gaps in the portion of her life that Gran wasn't a part of meant the world to Belle. It brought her back the missing years.

Gran went through the guest list for the year after, the one after that, and the one after that. Some she could barely remember, they were so long ago, but most she could. When she'd finished talking she looked up at the clock. 'I hope Sebastian is back soon, we were going to make mince pies tonight.'

'I'll tell you what,' said Belle, 'we'll give him until eight o'clock, then we'll make them instead.'

'That would be lovely.'

The clock seemed to tick slower than usual but by the time eight o'clock came around and they heard the church bells faintly chime in the distance, they got to work. Gran hadn't forgotten any of her cooking skills and was a dab hand at the pastry component. Belle cut out the circles and lined the sections in the tart tins. She totted up the number of sections. 'We're making forty-eight mince pies, did you know that?'

Gran sniggered. 'This will be a shock for you if you don't usually cater for many people. Believe me, nine people can get through a lot of mince pies.'

'But that's five each, with three left over!'

'Well done, you know your times tables. And it's not three left over. You and I will need to test one each; Sebastian too if he ever comes back. And anyway, they last for days so whatever isn't eaten tomorrow, we'll eat Boxing Day or the days after. You know, I've always preferred to make too many than too few. I can't bear the thought of someone wanting one and there not being any left.'

'I guess I can see the logic.'

Between them, they put the tops onto the mince pies. Gran used a knife to make a small slit in the top of each and Belle brushed the raw pastry with egg.

They sat by the Christmas tree as the mince pies gradually turned from pale to golden in the oven and when the timer pinged and the cottage was filled with the rich smell of butter and spices, Belle lifted out the trays and set them on the top of the cooker.

'Stop looking at your watch.' Gran caught Belle checking the time again. 'He'll be back, I'm sure.'

'I wish I'd told him about the cottage sooner.'

'But you needed to work it out in your own mind.'

'I really did.'

'If you'd have told him sooner he may have got his hopes up, so it's better you didn't do that.'

'You should've signed the cottage over to him instead of me,' said Belle. 'It would've made things a whole lot easier.'

'Sebastian is very special to me, but I needed something to bring you back into my life. I was desperate. The thought of dying without ever getting to know you again was something I couldn't bear thinking about, and Sebastian understood that.'

'I'm glad you had someone, other people around you, Sebastian and his family, everyone in the village. You deserve happiness.'

'So do you.' Gran's eyes met hers. 'And so does your mother. Is she happy?'

Belle could see Gran twisting the ends of her cardigan around her fingers, something she'd seen her mum do more than once. 'She is happy. She has a lovely place up in Ireland, you'd like it.'

'Do you have pictures?'

Belle smiled and went into the hallway to fetch her phone. 'As a matter of fact, I have plenty.'

They spent the next hour or so trawling through photos of her mum's place in Ireland – not too dissimilar from Snowdrop Cottage. It was hard for Gran to see photos of her daughter and Belle let her linger over those as long as she needed to.

'I'm afraid I might have to leave you to it, Belle, and say goodnight.'

'But we haven't tested the mince pies yet.'

'I'm sure you can manage that part.' Gran tried to stand but Belle had to help her in the end. 'These sofas are a bit low down for me and my old legs.'

'Perfect for me to sleep on though,' Belle smiled. 'If that's OK?'

'Of course it is. Will you be warm enough?'

'Don't you worry, I found a couple of blankets and a spare pillow in the airing cupboard.' She hoped they weren't Sebastian's favourites or he might whip them off her when he got back.

'And you'll tell Sebastian about the cottage the second he gets home?'

'I will. If I'd been a bit faster I might have caught him before he drove away, but he's too fast for me.'

'He's handsome too,' Gran winked.

'You're a bit old for him though,' Belle batted back. She helped her up the stairs, left her to have her bathroom time, and when she heard her shut the door to her bedroom, Belle left the Christmas tree in all its glory and the wood burner that was still warm even though the flames had all but gone now and went into the kitchen. She tasted one of the mince pies, which was as delicious as it looked, and wondered whether she should leave one out for Sebastian. She decided instead to put them all into a Tupperware container to keep them fresh and leave the tub on the side for him to help himself.

After she'd done her teeth in the downstairs bathroom, she snuggled down on the sofa. She had every intention of greeting Sebastian when he came in, hoping he wouldn't meet her presence with any more disdain when he realised her plans for the cottage had changed and he could stay as long as he liked, but she fell fast asleep and stayed that way until morning.

Chapter Sixteen

When Belle woke she groaned. Her neck was sore from sleeping in an odd position and she wondered if she'd even turned over in her sleep, she'd been so tired. She sat up and let the blanket fall off her but it was cold. Checking the time on her phone, it was only five a.m. Sebastian must've been so quiet last night he hadn't woken her, unless he'd not seen her and he still had that surprise to come.

On her way to the downstairs bathroom Belle felt the radiators, but they weren't on yet and probably wouldn't be for another hour or so. She contemplated firing up the Aga in the kitchen but settled for getting the wood burner going again. She found a dustpan and brush in the utility room and, anxious not to wake Gran or Sebastian, she quietly shovelled out the ashes from inside and swept up the debris. She took logs from the basket at the side and before long had everything set up, ready to get going again.

Once the fire was lit and the tree lights on, Belle opened the curtains. The village was blanketed in white and it made her as excited as a ten-year-old all over again.

When neither Gran nor Sebastian was up at six o'clock she began to get twitchy, but at least Christmas lunch wasn't until three o'clock today. They had the pub to go to late morning, to hear the outcome of the betting, and then it would be all systems go as they finished everything.

Out in the kitchen Belle flipped through some of Gran's recipes they'd marked with Post-its: homemade gravy with all her little touches, how to cook the perfect Christmas turkey, Hasselback potatoes with or without bacon pieces, stuffing to go with the meat, and cranberry sauce that Belle could remember dipping her finger into as a child. She looked at the turkey in the fridge and took it out to put it at room temperature as the recipe book specified. Funny, she adored cooking, but this one meal of the year was something she'd never bothered to tackle. Growing up, after she'd left Little Woodville for the last time, Christmas had been a toned-down, quiet affair. They'd had turkey roll some years, chicken pieces on others and even steak on occasion, when her parents chose. And it hadn't bothered her. She hadn't understood all the fuss. But seeing the recipe book now, she got it. She knew why people went to such lengths to make it a special occasion. Talking to Gran had reiterated how special this day was and how important it was to make sure nobody spent it alone unless they wanted to.

Belle checked the weight of the turkey. Five kilograms, which meant, going by the calculations she'd seen in the book, that it would take around three and a half hours – so they had to have the stuffing made and cooled, and the meat in the oven, by eleven o'clock this morning, before they went to the pub.

Belle opened the window in the kitchen and the freezing air bit at her cheeks, but she smiled. It felt like the first day of the rest of her life, here with Gran for Christmas, knowing that in the New Year she might be single but she was, for once, following her own path. She watched as a robin perched on the branch of a tree overhanging the shed, his red breast standing out against the frost and snow that had come to the village just in time.

'A white Christmas,' she said on her next breath. She shivered, the bird flew off and she shut the window just as the church bells chimed half past the hour.

When her phone went in the lounge room she trotted back down the hallway, her ink blue cardigan hugged over her dove grey pyjamas. She'd have to wake the others in half an hour if they weren't already up but she hoped the phone hadn't disturbed them just yet.

'Mum, Merry Christmas,' she said when she answered, never quite sure how the sentiment would be received.

'Merry Christmas, Belle.' Perfunctory in her delivery as always, her mum sounded different. 'I didn't wake you, did I?'

Apart from a quick text to let her mum know that she was extending her stay in Little Woodville because of the snow, the two hadn't spoken since the day Belle begged her mum to give Gran a chance, to put whatever grievances they had behind them before it was too late. 'No, I was already awake. I've got to help make Christmas dinner for nine people today, so plenty to be done.'

'They make you help at the bed and breakfast?'

She hadn't had a chance to tell anyone of her change of location after she'd found out the bed and breakfast was full. 'No, of course not. Long story, but the bed and breakfast had no spare rooms last night so I ended up sleeping at the cottage, on the sofa.'

'Why didn't you sleep in Gran's old room?'

'Because she's here with me, Mum.'

Silence.

'Mum, did you hear what I said?'

Delia cleared her throat. 'Yes, I did. Why is she there and not at the care home?'

Belle explained Sebastian's predicament and the snow. 'So you see, if he hadn't brought her here last

293

night, she might not have made it at all. And besides, I think it'll take three of us to make this enormous dinner.'

'So who have you got coming?' Delia's voice was timid as though part of her didn't want to know at all but the rest of her did.

Belle reeled off names her mum had never heard of, talked about people alone, friends, told her mum how long Gran had been doing this for. 'I like that she had so many friends around her, Mum.'

'You blame me, don't you?' It wasn't really a question.

Belle sank down onto the sofa. 'I don't blame you for anything, but I do think it has gone on long enough. She's sad. She's sad about you, me, and everything that went on. When I arrived she was closer to her tenant than she was her own granddaughter.'

'I doubt that's true.'

Belle's silence confirmed it probably was.

'Belle, I'm here in Little Woodville.'

Her shock announcement came at the same time as Gran's voice called out to Belle. 'Just a minute, Gran, I'll be with you in a sec,' she shouted up the stairs and went into the farthest corner of the lounge room to finish the call. 'Mum, what are you doing here?'

'I came down yesterday and spent the night. Today I thought I might go to the care home and see Mum.'

'Seriously?'

A huge sigh came across the phone line and Belle gave her mum time to gather her thoughts. 'You sounded so upset, so angry, and I feel terrible that in all these years I've not thought about what this has done to you. From that phone call I could tell I owed it to you to at least try.'

'I don't believe it.'

'You were right, it is time. But I had no idea she'd be here in the village.' Her mum's voice faded away as the prospect of what could happen dawned on her. 'I thought I'd have a chance to see you, sort through where I went from here.'

'Where exactly are you?' Belle asked, sensing the trepidation in her mum's voice and her heart.

'I'm at the bed and breakfast, the one where you said you were staying. I booked in with plans to go and see your gran, and when you said you were staying put in Little Woodville I was already on my way and I thought it would be a chance for me to sort things through with you too.'

Belle didn't know what to say. 'I can't believe you're here. Why didn't you find out which room I was staying in and come and see me?'

'Because I wasn't brave enough, Belle. I thought I'd call you first and talk. I was so abrupt on the phone when you called from the care home and I wasn't sure how you'd react. I couldn't decide whether it would be best to see mum first or you.'

She sounded confused but willing to try and Belle felt the tension dissipate at long last. Belle began to laugh. 'You probably took my room, you know.'

Delia chuckled. 'You know, I probably did.'

'Mum, I have to go. Gran's calling. Why don't you come over?'

'No, I'm not ready, Belle. Not yet.'

'Mum, you have to do it, today.'

'But you have guests. How can I do it with an audience? And besides, I think I need to talk to my daughter properly first, don't you? And I don't mean on the telephone.'

'Then I'll come to you,' Belle said hurriedly. 'Give me half an hour. I'll help Gran, she'll stay with Sebastian, and I'll come to the bed and breakfast. Do they know who you are?'

'I met Gus and Audrey but I've not seen either of them before, so I assume they've no idea.'

'Did you see my car in the car park?'

'I did. Just about. There's a lot of snow. I drove at a snail's pace to get here.'

'We'll meet at the car and sit inside and we can talk there.' All she wanted was to get to her mum before she changed her mind.

They agreed, Belle went off to help her Gran down the stairs, and when she managed to stop Gran from pulling out pots and pans and ingredients just yet, Belle went off on the pretence of needing a brisk walk to get herself going for the task ahead.

This was about to be one hell of a Christmas Day that none of them would ever forget. And Belle hoped it would be for all the right reasons.

Chapter Seventeen

'You know, I remember one Christmas I spent here as a child and it snowed even more than this,' said Delia when they were in Belle's car in the car park, the engine running and the heating on full blast.

Belle looked out over the road and beyond at the stone houses glistening in white. 'How could it snow more than this? I'm surprised you made it here without a hefty snowplough on the front of your car.'

'Believe me, it did.'

'How old were you?'

'I was nine and I went to bed on Christmas Eve after a cup of my mum's hot cocoa and hoped that for Christmas my dad would come home.' She looked ahead at a wall partly covered in snow. Some of the brick was still showing where the cars had shielded it from the icy blast. 'Dad worked away a lot. So much so that I used to fear I'd forget what he looked like.'

'I always loved Grandad Leonard,' Belle smiled. She had fond memories of going to his place when she was young. He had all the time in the world for his granddaughter and had, sadly, passed away the year before her final Christmas with Gran. Without Grandad or Gran, Christmas had become a diluted version of what it had once been, with neither the excitement nor the fascination it had once had. Belle put some of it down to growing up, but most of it was because of everything that had gone before.

'I loved him too.'

'He would spend hours with me,' said Belle. 'Do you remember the train set he had in his loft? He'd built it up over the years and we'd spend hours up there. He'd let me touch it, too, even though I worried it might break.

He'd read me stories every night, or sometimes he'd make them up and they were so far-fetched I'd end up giggling and wouldn't want to go to sleep.'

Delia turned to her daughter, her face full of admiration but with an undeniable sadness. 'That's the dad he was, but only when he was there.'

'What do you mean?'

'My dad worked hard, and I mean really hard. He was away a lot, sometimes weeks at a time, months even. When he was home he was attentive and perfect and the epitome of what a father should be, but those times were only a handful in comparison to the days he wasn't around.'

'That must've been hard on Gran. Do you think that's why they divorced?'

Delia looked away. 'Partly.'

Belle didn't press her for more. Instead, she sat and watched clumps of snow slowly slide down the windscreen as the heat from the engine melted what was up above. It was such a waste sitting here with the engine running but they couldn't do this in the bed and breakfast, where they may be asked questions, nor at the cottage, where Gran and Sebastian would, by now, be getting organised.

'I always put my dad on a pedestal,' said Delia. 'He was so high sometimes he could barely be reached,' Delia smiled, 'and to Mum's credit she never once bad-mouthed him.'

'Did she need to?'

'No, not really. But your dad and I, well, we've always been there for one another. We both work, sometimes we put in extra hours, but neither of us goes away for long stretches at a time. I suppose with two incomes we have the luxury of being each other's support system, whereas with my parents Gran was the stay-at-home mum, your grandad was the one who supported the family and we never went without. We bought Snowdrop Cottage and all that land, and after buying a house of my own it's clear that it wouldn't have come cheap. There would've been a sacrifice. Dad always said he wanted to give me the world and, in his way, he was doing that by working so hard.'

'But you would rather you'd seen more of him.'

Delia turned to her daughter again. 'I really would. He missed out on a lot of my growing up. You know when you used to get embarrassed at Dad and me coming to your school assemblies or productions?'

'I hated it when I got older.'

'You certainly did.'

'I'm glad you did it though.' Belle had been lucky, but she'd taken it for granted that they always showed up, never missed an event.

'Grandad saw very little of my school life, Belle. Home life, when he was there, was tremendous and that's what I remembered him for. When he and Mum split up, shortly after I turned eighteen, I blamed her completely.'

'What happened?'

'She fell in love.'

'She had an affair?'

'Of sorts.'

'Either she did or she didn't, Mum.'

Audrey tapped on the window and Belle had no choice but to wind down the glass.

'Everything OK?' Audrey asked. 'You're not going to try and drive anywhere are you, Belle?' She laughed but when she noticed Belle wasn't alone, Belle's

299

assurance that she was just sitting having a chat was enough to send Audrey on her way.

'I wonder if you'll be the talk of the village,' Belle grinned.

Her mum smiled back, but went on with her explanation. 'Your gran had a very strong friendship with someone else for five years before she and my dad split up.'

'So it was an emotional affair?'

'It was with a woman.'

Belle's mouth fell open. 'Gran left Grandad for a woman!'

'I reacted much the same way as you're doing now, Belle.'

'I don't believe it. Gran…a lesbian…'

'You know, I'm not sure if she was or not. But I wasn't interested in her excuses, her reasons. All I knew was that she was splitting the family up. When Dad found out about the relationship, that was it. There was yelling, arguing, and even though I was eighteen I felt eight years old, as though I should be sitting on a too-high chair, legs dangling, in a school uniform and not quite understanding what they were telling me when they said they were separating.'

'But that was years before you stopped speaking to Gran. You gave her a chance, so what happened?'

'Life was hard for a while but I settled down with your dad and we had you.' She smiled fondly at her daughter. 'We both vowed we wouldn't let work take over. We'd rather live in a smaller house, have a poky garden, than miss out on the one thing I never had. The gift of time. It's all a child needs, Belle. Remember that when it's time for you to start a family. You can go on the best holidays, buy your kids everything they want, spoil them rotten, but without spending time with them doing the simpler things like a puzzle on a rainy day or reading them stories, watching a movie together, none of it means a thing.'

'What happened to make you take me away from Gran?'

Delia leaned her head back against the headrest. 'I tried, I really did. You and your grandad had always been close and you stayed that way, something I treasured – especially the time he gave to you, the time I hadn't had with him. I stayed close to him and was glad I was getting his time in a different way. I resented Mum – I knew it was her who had driven a wedge between them. You know, I think I could've forgiven her if it'd been an affair with a man, but when I found out she'd been in a relationship with a woman I felt humiliated on Dad's behalf. It was as though his life had been a lie, the woman he'd loved for so many years maybe hadn't loved him at all.'

'I'm sure that's not true.'

'I don't know.' Delia shrugged. 'I've never asked Mum about it and she's never said anything. Dad smoked once upon a time but when I was little he'd given it up, for me. He wanted to be around for me, he said. After he and Mum split, he went back to the cigarettes. Sometimes when I'd go round he'd have been sitting in a chair for hours on end and I could see how many butts there were in the ashtray.' She shook her head at this. 'Dad died of lung cancer in the end, at Christmas time, as you know. I blamed Mum, because he wouldn't have started smoking again if she hadn't split them both up with what she'd done. All I saw was that Dad had worked all the hours he could, for us, and the thanks he got was Mum giving her heart to someone else.'

'You know, Mum, things are never that clear-cut.'

Delia nodded and Belle saw a tear track its way down her cheek. 'I knew that all along really, but it was how I coped with my grief. It was easier to blame someone, be angry at that person, than deal with his death.'

'Did Gran carry things on with this woman, after Granddad moved out?'

'I've no idea. I never saw her with anyone else over the years. I'm not sure how I would've reacted if I had. I couldn't stand the sight of her when your grandad died, Belle. I couldn't be within ten feet of her without wanting to throttle her.'

'When we left, you never did Christmas properly again,' said Belle. 'You always said tradition was just an excuse not to change your ways if I asked why we weren't doing what other people were doing.'

'I did, didn't I?' Delia wiped a finger across the condensation of her window. 'It was painful to follow traditions, Belle, because your gran had so many. She had her way of doing things and it was beautiful. To do them myself was like squeezing my own throat really tight – I couldn't breathe, it hurt too much.'

The church bells made Belle jump as they chimed. 'You and Gran need to sort this out.'

'I thought I could.' Delia seemed glued to the seat.

Belle switched off the engine and zipped up her coat again. She pulled on her hat and opened her door to let the cold fill the car. 'You're doing it now. Come on, out!'

Belle wasn't sure but she thought she saw something close to admiration in her mum's glance, as she did what she was told and off they set, back to Snowdrop Cottage.

Delia stopped at the front gate.

'Mum, come on. If anything, I've got a dinner to help make so I have to get in there.' Belle willed her mum not to back out now. She'd come this far, further than she had in the last twenty years.

Belle opened the front door and beckoned her mum to follow after her. 'Gran, I'm back!'

'Oh, thank the Lord!' Gran, flustered, bustled out of the kitchen. 'Sebastian isn't here!' Wide-eyed, she shook her head as Belle hovered in the doorway. 'I think we'll have to cancel the lunch. I don't think we can manage to get it all done between us.'

'Wait a minute, Gran. What do you mean he isn't here?'

'He never came home.'

Belle tried to digest what she was hearing.

'Well, come in, shut the door.' Gran stepped forward and when she saw who was hovering at the end of the path, inside the little gate by now, she froze. 'Delia.' Her voice was smaller than Belle had ever known it. 'Is that my Delia?' She dared to take a step forwards at the same time as Delia did the same.

Delia took another step, then another, as Gran hovered in the porch, her slippers mostly dry but partly submerged in the snowdrift that had crept as close as it could to the cottage.

Gran opened out her arms and in the time it took another cluster of snowflakes to flutter past their noses, Delia embraced her mum for the first time in twenty years.

Chapter Eighteen

Belle gave her mum and her gran some space, but all they did was sit in silence in the lounge room holding on to each other's hands as though they daren't let go again. When at last she heard them talking she took in cups of tea, she took mince pies, not caring their guests later on would have to make do with something else if they ate too many. But the tea remained neglected, the delicious festive treats went untouched.

'Tell me about Victoria,' said Belle when she sat with them after her gran began to talk about her relationship back then. Belle was still hardly able to believe three generations of Nightingale women were here, together.

Gran touched her locket with one hand, her daughter's arm with the other. 'She was my best friend. She was there for me in the toughest of times and her family have been with me ever since' – this to Delia more than Belle. 'You see, I thought, well, we both thought, we were in love. Victoria had been through a terrible time with a boyfriend who was one of those men you hope your daughter will never, ever meet. I was content but something was missing from my life, with Leonard away all the time. It was fine when Delia was little because she'd kept me so busy I didn't have time to question anything. As she got older, I put myself through an accounting course and I wanted to work, but your grandad, Belle, well he wouldn't hear of it.'

'That's a bit old-fashioned.'

Grateful for the normalcy in conversation, Gran said, 'It's archaic, not old-fashioned.' They all managed a smile. 'Anyway, I was fed up. Leonard was away all the time, I wasn't working and Delia needed me less and less, and when Leonard came home he had time for

Delia, but we never did anything together. I met Victoria at the local library one day. She got to talking about her waste-of-space boyfriend; I moaned about your father,' she told Delia. 'That's all it was at the start, but when Victoria's boyfriend turned violent I was there to see it. Oh, it was a nasty sight, not one I ever want to see again. I called the police, he was charged with assault, and Victoria needed a friend more than ever.

Around about that time Leonard had been working away in the North of England so much he rarely came home and so I suggested Victoria come and stay with me for a while. I knew that if I were in her position she'd do exactly the same for me. She had nightmares that would see her screaming in the middle of the night, and one night I held her tight and rocked her back to sleep.'

'That sounds terrible.' Belle couldn't imagine what it must've been like to be so scared of a man. Anthony, although not her soul mate, had been a gentleman and never would've hurt her like that.

'It was. But not as terrible as when your father came home and found us in bed together.'

'But you were comforting her,' said Belle, noticing her mum stayed very quiet indeed.

'I was, but he put two and two together and came up with five. He stormed out and I told Victoria not to worry, he'd see sense come morning. Anyway, the next day Victoria went to stay with her auntie in Scotland, she wanted to get away for a while. Truth be told, I suppose I had had a little crush on her. Nothing had ever happened, but she showed me more attention and affection than your father had in a long time. We laughed together, we cried, we confided in each other.' She looked at Delia but carried on when Belle's mum's face remained blank. 'Your father came home and

305

demanded to know how long the affair had been going on. I yelled at him and said she'd been kinder to me than he had in years. I was glad he was jealous, showing some emotion for once. That was when you came home, Delia.'

'I remember walking in on the row.' Delia's eyes brimmed with tears. 'I remember Dad going upstairs and packing a suitcase, telling us he was going to his brother's for a while. I remember looking at you and hoping you'd stop him. I saw precious little of him as it was.'

'I'd run out of steam by then, Delia. I could tell him until I was blue in the face that he was neglecting me, us, and I'd sound like an ungrateful wife who didn't appreciate her husband's dedication to providing for his family.'

'So you let him believe it was an affair?' Delia asked.

'I didn't intend to. He walked out, you yelled at me to stop him, I just wanted to run away myself. A few weeks later Leonard returned to the house and I wondered if we'd be able to talk properly, but I had already decided I wanted to split up. I'd loved him very much once upon a time, but how could I love a man who was never there?'

'Did he want to try again?' Belle asked, sitting cross-legged when her feet went numb from kneeling on them.

'I never did find out what he'd come to say. I made him a cup of tea but when the phone rang he picked it up and it was Victoria. He told her never to call here ever again, she wasn't welcome in this house or around his wife. I'd never seen him so angry and in turn I was furious. She was my only friend, a lifeline when he was away, and he was taking that away too. I told him it wasn't an affair, but by then he'd made up his mind. I was to have nothing to do with her again. I think he really thought there was something physical going on, and I couldn't convince him otherwise.'

'I never realised.' Delia's words came out barely audible, but they encouraged Gran to carry on.

'He was a lovely man and had many good points, but he really did like things to be done a certain way. I had no social life at all without Victoria. I knew Leonard worked hard for us, but he never wanted me to do anything other than be at home. He was a traditionalist and I'd always done what was expected. I was loyal, but everyone has their limits, and that was mine.'

'Why didn't you tell me any of this, Mum?' Delia looked at Gran. 'Why did you let me go on believing you'd had an affair with Victoria?'

'I was embarrassed.' She looked at her hands, clasped together. 'I couldn't get my head around how unreasonable Leonard was being, I couldn't begin to explain how isolated I felt. I thought all my complaints would only make me sound ungrateful. And then I got angry. My anger consumed me and I couldn't see past it. I also knew how hard it would be, Delia, to make you see how any of it was your father's fault. I'd rather hoped he'd admit it himself eventually but then the more time went on, the more resentment you had, and I was scared. I got to see Belle and I was terrified that if we fell out you'd take her away from me.' Her voice caught and Delia put a hand across her mouth, realising she'd done exactly that. 'When Leonard died I couldn't take away your memories. You were in so much pain. And then you left. I almost looked for you but I knew it was no use. I knew I could make it worse with whatever I said.' Gran looked from her daughter to her granddaughter before her eyes settled back on Delia. 'I wanted the cottage to go to Belle because I hoped it would somehow link us all together again.'

Belle felt Gran's pain but she had more to ask. 'Didn't Grandad want to know why you were so unhappy?'

Gran's voice softened. 'He was a proud man, and that pride stood in his way. I'd humiliated him by striking up the friendship in the first place. People would talk, he said, he'd be a laughing stock, he told me. He packed his things, he left for good, and you blamed me.' She looked at Delia. 'And I let you.'

'But why?'

'Because you worshipped him.' Her voice wavered. 'You never saw enough of him and I didn't want to take away the part you had left. You got on famously and it thrilled me to know how much time he spent with Belle when she was tiny. I think that deep down he regretted not spending enough time with his own daughter, and this was his way of making it up to you in some way.'

'It was nice.' Delia smiled, thinking of the way things had once been. 'But he started smoking again, went into his shell a bit.'

'He liked a pint at the pub, a bet on the horses, and, yes, he liked a good smoke.'

'I always thought he started again because of what you'd done to him.'

'He may well have done, but I can't be blamed for his health.'

Delia nodded, no words came out.

'I'm sorry, Delia, for everything your dad and I put you through, but beneath his faults he was a good man and I'm a good woman. We made mistakes, that's all.'

'So did I,' Delia sniffed. She pulled out a tissue and blew her nose. 'I wish you'd told me.'

'You probably wouldn't have listened.' That got a smile from all three of them. 'You're as pig-headed as Leonard and I both are.'

'What happened to Victoria?' Delia asked Gran.

'She died.'

'I'm sorry, Mum.' Delia clasped her mum's hand in her own.

'It was a long time ago, and up until then she had a very happy life. She fell in love with a man shortly after she came back from Scotland and he treated her really well. I had nothing to worry about. And our friendship was as strong as ever. I never told her Leonard made assumptions about us, I didn't want to make her uncomfortable.'

'Did she marry the man?' Belle moved away from the wood burner – it was still so hot even though the logs she'd loaded it with earlier had all but burnt away.

'She did, and they went on to have a son, Paul, who was a lovely lad, and he helped me a great deal. I'd had accountancy training and when I was lost and wondering what to do, he gave me a starting position and I stayed with the company until I retired.'

'Is he still alive?'

'Paul, yes.'

'Does he have children?' Delia asked, clutching her balled-up tissue.

Gran smiled and looked at her daughter and granddaughter in turn, her fingers resting on her locket. 'He and his wife had a little boy, Sebastian.'

Belle's gaze shot up. 'So that's how you two know each other.'

'What am I missing?' Delia looked between both women.

'Sebastian is Gran's, or my, tenant. He lives here, in the cottage.' Belle gave the quick explanation. Her mum didn't know how special this man was to Gran and she wasn't sure how she'd feel about it.

'Talking of Sebastian,' said Gran, looking concerned, 'he's still not back.'

Suddenly aware it was Christmas Day, they had guests due this afternoon and a feast to prepare between one rusty cook and a little old lady who needed her rest, particularly after her emotions had been put through the wringer, Belle stood up. 'We can't let him down, Gran. He already thinks I conned him and he's losing his home. Let's not mess this up.'

Gran stood with Belle's help. 'We'd better get cracking.'

'Mum, are you with us on this?' Belle turned back and looked at Delia, still sitting on the sofa.

'I don't want to be in the way. This is your Christmas, this —'

'Delia.' Gran held out her hand to her daughter. 'This is *our* Christmas, and what I say is – the more the merrier!'

Chapter Nineteen

It was all hands on deck in the kitchen. They had just over an hour to get to the pub for the grand reveal of who won the bet on a white Christmas and who lost. Butter had melted in a pan, herbs were chopped and whizzed in a blender, the stuffing was made and set on the worktop to cool.

'Whatever are you doing with that?' Belle watched Gran unravel some string and take out the scissors.

'You're telling me you've never trussed a turkey before?' Gran frowned.

'My fault,' admitted Delia with a look of foreboding, but then she smiled and looked at her mum. 'Christmas turkey wouldn't have been right without you, so I never made it.'

A look passed between them that spoke of the bridges that were beginning to be repaired.

'Belle, do the honours and stuff the neck cavity, would you?' said Gran.

Belle scooped up handfuls of the cooled mixture, the hint of sage wafting into the air. She pushed it into the appropriate part of the turkey. 'It feels weird in there.'

Not standing for any nonsense that would mean delay, Gran dismissed Belle's hesitation and encouraged her granddaughter to finish. She then began winding the string under wings, around legs, beneath something she called a parson's nose – which, apparently, Belle should know if her love of cooking was as great as she claimed it to be – and before long the bird was neat and compact and sitting on top of a rack in a baking dish. Belle smeared butter over the skin, seasoned it, and Delia covered it loosely with foil before putting it in the oven.

'Right, vegetables are prepared, thank you, Delia.' Gran beamed, totally loving taking charge of a kitchen. Belle couldn't imagine her staying in the care home, but Gran was very happy there, she said, as long as she got the occasional day release. 'Potatoes are peeled and chopped and in water, ready to do what we need to. Thank you, Belle, for setting the table – it looks beautiful.'

In the middle of the room was the long walnut table that had once dominated the dining room, many years ago when Belle was little. Now it set the scene for a day of festivities, a day of welcoming, love and friendship. Down the centre was a deep red runner, upon which sat the place settings, each with two white oval plates of different sizes, the heavy silver cutlery only used for best, a napkin with a sparkly silver ring gripping it in the centre, and a glass with a red body and a clear stem. Candles were positioned at three intervals along the table, ready to be lit when the guests arrived.

'One final touch, Mum.' Delia pulled out three sprigs of holly from behind her back. 'Let's put these as centrepieces, they'll look so pretty.'

'Oh, yes, please do.'

Delia took one, Belle another and Gran the third and they fashioned the holly beside each candle so that when the flames flickered, the berries would catch the light and glow like tiny fairy lights on a tree.

The three of them stood there admiring their handiwork, less frantic now than they'd been for the last hour.

'You go and put your feet up,' Belle told her gran. She looked beat, they all did, but she wanted Gran to be awake enough to enjoy the festivities later.

'You know, I think I will. I don't want to miss the fun at the pub when we know the outcome of the bet and find out who has to buy a round for the house.'

After Gran took the stairs and Delia sat down on the sofa Belle said, 'I'm so glad you came.' She checked the wood burner and it was only partly glowing now. They'd stoke it up when they returned from the pub to make the room cosy and ready for guests to flop after they'd eaten too much.

'Me too. You know, I wish I'd made Mum tell me more back then; I wish I hadn't put my dad on such a pedestal and assumed he could do no wrong.'

Belle smiled. 'You loved him, that's why. You were upset about him leaving, gutted when he died. I think Gran gets it.'

'I'm glad she didn't give up on us. I'm also happy she had another family when her own couldn't be there for her.' When she covered her eyes Belle realised she was crying and she knelt on the floor, wrapped her arms around her and hugged her long enough for them to be interrupted.

'Hi.' It was Sebastian. He'd come in the front door, brushing snow from his collar.

'Where were you?'

He ignored her question. 'I've got a Christmas dinner to make. It's my last – it needs to be a good one.'

'Hold it right there,' Belle demanded, standing up with hands on her hips. She wasn't going to let him go anywhere until she'd said what she needed to say.

'I need to get going.'

'It's all in hand.'

He looked from Belle to the crying woman on the sofa and back to Belle again. 'You found another guest.'

'My mum.'

'Oh?'

'Long story, but she's here, Gran's here, where the hell were you?'

'I stayed with a friend. Keep your hair on. Excuse me,' he said to Delia, who waved his concern away. She seemed to want to stay well out of the domestic that was about to explode. He stalked into the kitchen and promptly stopped. 'You've got everything prepared.' He sniffed the air. 'The turkey's in?'

'Yes it's in, you jerk!' She slapped his arm a little harder than she'd intended.

'Ow! No need for that.'

Belle lowered her voice so neither Gran nor her mum could hear. 'Yes there is. Gran has been worried sick about you. You know what she's like. The weather is atrocious – for all we knew you were in a ditch somewhere freezing to death.'

'I'm a big boy now, Belle.'

'Yes, I know you are.' She blushed at the double entendre and he knew it, she could see in the way he laughed with his eyes even though his mouth stayed in the same solid line.

'Where's lover boy?' he asked, inspecting the range of vegetables that had been prepared, nodding approval at the ingredients set up ready to make gravy, others ready to adorn the potatoes that were waiting patiently in a pan of water.

It was her turn to ignore him this time. 'We did enough for nine people, make that ten now, and you know Gran. She hates to think she won't have enough.'

'Where is she now? I need to apologise for making her worry, but I had to get out, Belle. I didn't want to stay here and listen to you and your boyfriend talking shop, making plans for the cottage I've called home and hoped to continue to do so.'

'The cottage is yours, Sebastian.' She lowered her voice when she realised she'd spoken as though he was a hundred metres away rather than just the one separating them now.

'What do you mean?'

'I'll give you the year you asked for.'

'That's incredibly generous of you.' He stole a slice of raw carrot. 'What does lover boy think of that?'

'Stop calling him that. And he's gone.'

His head snapped up at her revelation. 'Gone?'

'Gone.'

'Because you wouldn't sell the cottage to the buyer?'

'No, because I don't want to go into business with him anymore.'

'Well, that's not what I expected when I came back here today.' He leaned against the worktop.

'What did you expect?'

'You and him, your gran, all playing happy families and me tagging along.' He grinned. 'I didn't expect to find you, your Gran and your mum. How on earth did it all happen?'

When Belle had given him a quick rundown of what went on he said, 'You know this means I was right.'

'How were you right?'

'When you turned up here and said you were selling I thought, this girl is making a colossal mistake and if by the end of her time in the village she can't see that then I was wrong about her.'

Belle didn't know what to say. She certainly hadn't expected such a candid response.

Sebastian shook his head. 'I think I need a pint to digest all of this.'

315

Belle gasped, remembering they had somewhere to be. 'We'd better wake Gran, we've got to be at the pub in twenty minutes.'

'I'm up!' It was Gran, in the kitchen doorway, and she'd already moved over to Sebastian faster than Belle thought possible, enveloping him in one of her best hugs.

'So this bet,' Delia said, joining them, 'explain it to me.'

'I've got this,' said Sebastian as they bundled into their coats, locked up the cottage and went on their way towards the village and the pub at the top of the green.

*

A smile spread across Belle's face the second they pushed open the door to the pub. Celebrations were in full swing and Belle suspected the white Christmas many of them had hoped would happen had added to the merriment. Familiar faces stepped forwards to hug them as they came through the door, strangers weren't shy either and Sebastian bustled his way to the bar as Gran was rescued by Betty and taken to the table in the corner of the room. Belle could relax. She knew her gran was getting tired, and she would've suggested Gran stay at the cottage and keep resting until the big lunch if she thought she'd be able to get away with it.

'Do you want to stay with us at the bar?' Belle asked her mum, who was looking around, taking in the scene.

'I'm a big girl, Belle. I can look after myself. Here goes.' And with that, off she went to join Gran.

'What are you drinking?' Sebastian was trying to get her attention.

She squeezed past a couple of revellers and fitted in neatly by the bar, already too warm bundled up in her coat. 'I'll have an orange juice, please.'

'I'll be on the soft drinks after my pint too,' he smiled. 'Saving myself for later.'

'Exactly.'

Belle managed to wrestle off her coat and when Sebastian had a tray of drinks she cleared a path for him to take them to Gran's table.

Once the drinks were handed out, Sebastian took the tray back to the bar and Belle followed. He put the tray down and let Kiara pull him into a hug across the bar. Belle didn't get away with it though and Kiara was on to her next.

'She's getting into it,' Belle giggled, looking at Kiara's reindeer ears waggling around as she bopped along behind the bar to serve the next customer.

'We all do around here, Belle. You didn't stand a chance if you thought you could have a quiet Christmas.'

'It's pretty special with the snow.'

He nodded, contemplating. 'I thought this could possibly be my last Christmas here, at least as a resident.'

'You jumped to conclusions, that's why.' She plonked her coat next to his on the stool beside them.

'Can you blame me?' He leaned one arm on the bar. 'When it comes to money, I know that when an offer comes along that you feel like you can't refuse, the chances are you're going to take it.'

'I told you, I don't have the same dreams about the business as Anthony.'

'You said that. But the money could be used to pursue *your* dream.'

'I know, and it still can. I'll use the next twelve months to really focus on saving. I don't need to go out for fancy dinners all the time, the mortgage on my flat isn't too horrendous, and when you buy the cottage I'll

317

have more of a plan for what I want to do, and I'll have the finance to make a start.'

'It sounds as though you're thinking seriously about doing something different.'

'I'm not sure about leaving the real-estate world full time, but I think over the next year my plans will evolve, and I'll just know.'

'So you're looking for a sign?' Either he thought she was crazy or he was very interested, because he moved closer and put down his glass as though this was more important.

'Kind of. Does that sound mad?'

'Not really. So, tell me, what ideas do you have?'

'Something to do with food.'

'I knew that already.' He'd remembered and it warmed Belle right through to know he had.

'I don't want to be a fancy chef, open a restaurant and earn Michelin stars or anything like that. I don't want to have a cake shop either, even though I don't mind baking.'

'You could go to Betty for tips if you did,' he teased.

She kicked his shin gently with her boot. 'Watch it, or you could find your Christmas dinner portion is very tiny when I serve it later.'

'Hang on, who says you're serving? That's my job, non-negotiable.'

She shook her head, glad they were friends again. They were both a huge part of Gran's life so it was important they got along. 'OK, I'll give you the turkey.'

'You know it makes sense.'

'You think I can't handle a turkey?'

'Oh, I'm sure you can handle whatever's given to you, Belle.' His eyes locked with hers and she lost all ability to speak. 'Come on then, what's this food project

318

you're going to embark on, if it's not cakes and it's not opening a top-notch restaurant?' Thankfully Sebastian didn't ever seem to suffer from nerves and his strength sent her stomach into all kinds of knots.

'That day I cooked in Gran's kitchen and made the Bolognese – well, the thing I enjoyed the most was that it was hearty home cooking. It wasn't overly fancy, no frills, no designer plating, and I thought of all the cooking I'd done over the years and it's those sorts of meals I enjoyed the most. When I found out Gran had been doing these dinners for decades, and that you carried them on, well, it struck a chord with me. And when I thought back to the vegetable patches at Snowdrop Cottage, the homemade soup you gave me that first day you made me lunch, I knew what I wanted to do. I want to open a small outlet that sells homemade soups, breads and sandwiches, catering for all seasons. I want to have new and exciting flavours.' Usually confident, putting her idea out in the open wasn't quite so easy. 'Does it sound totally naff?'

'Belle, it's not naff. It's your dream, by the sounds of it.'

'Do you think it would be a success?'

'That's for you to find out. You've got the idea, the little seed that is growing in your mind all the time, and you need to do some research next. You've crossed the biggest hurdle when going into business though.'

'What's that?'

'Doing something you like. It's amazing how many people try to start a business but aren't that emotionally invested. I think the more you want it, the more you'll fight to get it.'

She couldn't help thinking about Anthony, and Sebastian was right. Anthony had wanted the real-estate

319

business for so long and there's no way a glitch like his girlfriend backing out would ever stop him.

'Is it going to be a sole venture?' he asked.

'I assume so.'

'Because if you go into business with, or alongside, someone else, you need to be sure it'll make what you're doing stronger.' He seemed to be giving this a great deal of thought.

'I'll try to remember that.'

Sebastian looked around the pub. 'I think people here would love the idea of a soup place, especially in the winter. Take today, for example. I bet if it wasn't Christmas you'd have loads of customers.'

'Somewhere like this village would be ideal.' Belle smiled, looking around her and over at Gran and her Mum, who were laughing together about something or other as though they did this every day and hadn't had a gap at all. Audrey and Gus had joined them and Benjamin had sneaked out from behind the bar until Kiara saw him and ordered him back to help.

'Would you prefer to be back in Cambridge?' Sebastian interrupted her soaking up the atmosphere, these people.

'Not necessarily – in fact, I don't know if it would work there. The rent in the city would be sky-high for a start, but I suppose I could look at the smaller surrounding villages.'

He considered her words. 'I've got a proposition for you.'

She grinned. 'Hang on, didn't you have a proposition for me the last time we were in here together?'

His laughter was almost enough to drown out the sounds of Christmas music, but not quite. 'You're right. It must be a good sign – it means you might say yes.'

'Out with it then.'

'You already know I talked to the bank about buying Snowdrop Cottage. What I didn't tell you was that I'd kind of started making some plans for my own dreams. Remember how we sat and talked about what we both really wanted to do.'

'And you said you wanted to open a bookshop, I remember.'

He seemed touched she hadn't forgotten. 'I've kind of moved on a step from just thinking about it.' A grin spread across his face. 'I've bought a premises. When I thought I couldn't buy the cottage anymore I decided that, rather than sit around feeling sorry for myself, I'd make things happen. I'd found a place, but hadn't made an offer, so that's exactly what I did. The vendor accepted and the legal process is under way. There's a small flat above the premises so I figured I'd move in there for a while – it's tiny, a studio so everything in one room apart from the bathroom, but it'd do me.'

'Sebastian, that's wonderful. I feel like we should be buying champagne to celebrate. But what does this have to do with me?'

He looked around. The pub was heaving, they'd been lucky to stay out of the fray, but in one swift move he grabbed their coats, then took her hand and they wove their way through the crowds and ducked out of the front door.

'Where are we going?' Belle put her coat on and zipped it up.

Sebastian buttoned his own coat and began walking away from the pub, across the village green covered in its white blanket with only footprints marking the surface. 'Come on, you'll see.'

They walked down to the high street, took a left, went past the cobbled streets and the little bridge that led to the cottage, on past the post office and the bank and a sign for the little school she hadn't laid eyes on yet, and then they stopped.

'This is it,' he announced outside what used to be the photography studio.

'This place?' She beamed and stepped forwards to see if she could see more than the last time she'd looked but she couldn't. The only difference now was that instead of looking at it randomly, she was envisaging it with books on shelves, a till on a counter in the middle, perhaps a sofa or a kids' corner. 'Sebastian, that's amazing. I'm really pleased for you. And I'm kind of glad I drove you to make a decision.'

He rubbed his hands together and blew into them to warm them up. 'It's double the size you can see from here. It goes right out back too.'

'You'll need a lot of stock to fill it.'

'Maybe.'

She turned and looked at him.

'My proposition this time, Belle, is that you join in with me. I'm going ahead with the bookshop, but maybe you'd consider opening up your food outlet at the back. We'd need to look into licensing and all the legalities, but there's certainly the room. And if you're renting part of the space from me, or you buy into it, it'll give me enough money to still buy Snowdrop Cottage. There's an entrance at the side of the shop, too, so you could even open it out kind of like a big serving window and take orders from there.'

Belle's dream up until now had been just that, but this catapulted it closer to reality.

'There's a lot to consider,' he went on, 'but I got to thinking when you said you weren't going to start your own real-estate agency business anymore. It's just an idea, but don't answer me now. All I ask is that you think about it, seriously. Maybe give me an answer after Christmas, come and take a look around yourself, do some more research.'

'OK.'

'So it's not a definite no?'

She looked him straight in the eye. 'It's almost a definite yes, but give me some time to get my head around it.'

He nodded, satisfied. 'We'd better get back.'

Belle followed him in silence. She had no idea what to say. Of all the things he could've possibly sprung on her today, she'd never thought this would be one of them. She'd half expected him to tell her he no longer wanted the cottage or the hassle of buying it, that she'd have to find another buyer after all. Another part of her thought he might say he was involved in Gran's life and would be civil to her but, apart from that, wanted Belle to stay well away.

When they pushed open the door to the pub, having already taken off their coats so they didn't have to struggle out of them amongst the crowds, Gran looked up from her table. She nudged Delia and then Audrey and all of them looked their way.

'The gossip mill is starting already,' Sebastian whispered in her ear. She didn't mind him getting so close, but she was aware of everyone looking.

Thankfully they were saved by Kiara ringing the bell usually reserved to announce the pub was calling time and the patrons didn't have long to finish up their drinks and go home to their beds.

'Ladies and gentlemen.' Kiara was loud for a short and very slight woman. The Christmas music was quietened. 'We have a white Christmas!' she announced with glee, and a huge cheer went up around the pub.

'I'm so glad we got one, finally.' Sebastian was applauding with the rest of them, nestled at one side of the pub with Belle. They hadn't even attempted to merge with Gran and the rest of them because it would've meant fighting through too many bodies.

Belle didn't have a chance to reply because as soon as the cheers died down, Kiara was on with the announcement. Because it had turned out to be a white Christmas, it meant whoever's name was drawn from the hat would win all the money.

'The money we've collected this year amounts to a total of…' Kiara paused while Benjamin patted his hands on the table at quick speed to mimic a drum roll the best he could. '…two hundred and twenty pounds!'

Another cheer from the crowd and a few shouts telling Kiara not to keep them in suspense any longer.

'And the winner is…Amy Carlson!'

'Go, Amy!' Sebastian yelled before leaning in to tell Belle, 'Her boyfriend will be happy about that. I heard them talking in the bakery the other day and he's been trying to persuade her to go to Florida with him next year, travelling.'

'Ah, that's nice.' Belle was suddenly struck by her single status, but rather than be scared by it, she felt as though she had a whole new outlook. She'd contact Anthony when she was back in Cambridge, maybe go out for a drink with him when things had settled down. She had the feeling he'd be just as happy to stay friends too.

'And now for the fun part,' said Sebastian.

As the crowd quietened, Kiara couldn't stop smiling. 'As you all know, the winner, if it's a white Christmas, gets to do whatever they like with their winnings, but…and here's the exciting bit…now it's a white Christmas it means we get to draw not one but two names out of the "boring" pot and those people have to buy a round for the house.'

Cheers seemed to be par for the course today. Sebastian leaned over and said, 'I'm lifting my drinking ban in that case. No more soft drinks for me.'

Benjamin did another drum roll and Kiara pulled a name out of the 'boring' pot. 'And the first winner, or I should say loser, is Betty!'

Belle could see Gran falling about laughing and when she looked at Betty she was taking her punishment well.

'Get your purse out, Betty!' Trevor yelled across the pub from where he was talking to someone Belle hadn't met before.

Betty joined Kiara at the bar as Kiara delved into the pot a second time. 'And the person who will be sharing Betty's punishment and joining in to buy a round for the house is…' She pulled out a piece of paper. 'Belle!'

Sebastian's mouth fell open. 'You bet it wouldn't snow! Shame on you.' But he was laughing as hard as everyone else, including her own mum and her gran. 'Get up there then, mine's a large Baileys by the way. It's Christmas after all.'

Belle was hugged by so many people on the way to the bar that it didn't feel like a punishment at all, it felt all part of the fun, but she didn't know whether Betty would see it that way.

But she needn't have worried and when Belle looked over to Gran, Gran winked back. She'd obviously told Betty what was what, perhaps asked her to be a little kinder to the granddaughter she'd got back and didn't want to lose again. Belle and Betty clubbed together. Betty had come armed with a wad of cash that Belle gasped at. Belle put her half of the round on credit card and stood with Gran as she sipped on a double Baileys and Sebastian did the same.

And by the time they left the pub, Belle knew that this Christmas would mark a change in all their lives, for the better.

Chapter Twenty

Back at the house it was all systems go. Potatoes were parboiled and sliced almost all the way down for the Hasselback potatoes, vegetables were put into pots, others in the steamer, Sebastian took charge of making a big saucepan of mulled wine for them to enjoy after the meal, the turkey looked like it was coming on a treat, and Gran and Delia fussed over the gravy to get it as perfect as it could ever be.

Guests arrived in clusters and by the time all ten of them were seated, her mum making up the even number, Belle asked everyone to raise their glasses.

'I'd like to firstly thank Sebastian, for being a wonderful host.' She smiled at him, seated at the opposite end of the table to her like a book end that finished off the shelf that she started. 'Without Sebastian being so amenable in the first place, my trip to Little Woodville probably would've been short-lived, without a very good outcome.' She looked at her gran now. 'Some of you know my gran very well, all of you know Sebastian, and what they do with these dinners year after year I can see now is nothing short of amazing. So I'd like everyone to raise their glasses, not only to Sebastian and to Gran, but to kindness. So simple to execute and achieve, hard to ignore, but absolutely priceless.'

'To kindness!' Everyone raised their glasses, sipped, and glassware met across the table, to the sides, at difficult angles, until everyone had met each other's celebratory toast.

'And a toast to Belle and Betty,' Sebastian began, leaving her wondering what he was about to say. She hoped it wasn't going to ruffle any more feathers. 'I'm sure everyone here would like to say a heartfelt thank you for our drinks in the pub today. Cheers!'

Everyone fell about laughing, even Belle, who exchanged a meaningful look with Betty. 'Thanks, Sebastian. I'm never going to live that down, am I?'

'Nope.' He pulled the turkey plate closer to him, ready to do the honours.

Gran clutched Belle's arm in thanks and then turned the other way to do the same with Delia. Sebastian, armed with carving tools that would impress royalty, got to work on the turkey, crisp and golden and standing proudly at his end of the table. Everyone passed plates his way, passed them back again, bowls of shiny Brussels sprouts were passed along and glazed carrots, potatoes you knew would be crisp on the outside yet melt in your mouth, and the two gravy boats did the rounds until everyone was ready to begin eating. And for the entire meal, Belle couldn't stop smiling. In fact, none of them could. This was what Christmas was all about, and it was just perfect.

Nobody tried to wimp out of the clearing up, and between ten people it took no time at all.

'We'll have to do a Secret Santa next year,' Gran suggested as she squeezed out a cloth and left it by the sink.

'That could be a lot of fun.' Trevor and Anne already had a pack of cards, Delia had the Monopoly out, and the eight people in the house apart from Sebastian and Belle got right into the spirit of Christmas: togetherness, friendship and love.

'Secret Santa would be a great idea, if you fancy it next year.' Sebastian stirred the mulled wine mixture that was being kept warm in its pan on the stove ready for ladling out at will.

328

Belle threw the sodden tea towel she'd used for the last roasting tin into the utility room by the washing machine. 'It would be fun. Hey, maybe I could ask Mrs Fro to come here too.'

Gran, as usual, didn't miss much. 'Oh, yes, Belle. Please do. I'd love to see her again – I've got a lot to thank her for.'

'Mulled wine?' Sebastian used his hand to waft the spices further towards Belle.

'Go on, then. Maybe we'll leave the oldies to it and go sit by the Christmas tree.'

'Heard that,' said Gran. 'Less of the old.'

Belle took out two ruby red stemless glasses and Sebastian ladled in the mulled wine, ensuring each of them had a slice of orange.

In the lounge, Sebastian tended to the wood burner and Belle put on a classical Christmas music CD this time. 'Is this OK?'

'Definitely.' Sebastian relaxed into the sofa. 'I had more than enough loud Christmas music at the pub; my ears are still ringing.'

'I wanted to talk more about your proposition.'

'I told you, no pressure – wait until the New Year. I'll put it to you in a proper proposal, on paper.'

'Sounds formal.'

'It needs to be, it's business.'

She watched the flames lick around the logs, the lights sparkle on the Christmas tree. Was it just business? 'I can't stop thinking about it. I want to leap in with both feet.' She hadn't felt the same way when it came to the business venture she and Anthony had planned. This time she knew it was right.

'Just take your time, Belle.'

'Are you having second thoughts?' Was it punishment for how she'd messed him around with the cottage?

'Not at all, but it's a huge step. You've had a lot going on so I want you to be sure.' He shook his head. 'I should've waited for things to settle down for you, but I'm not the most patient of men, Belle.'

Their peace was interrupted by Barbara and then Delia, each equipped with a glass of mulled wine, and talk turned to the village carol concert due to be held tonight. Belle had forgotten about the event even though they'd been talking about it at lunch when her mind was on the little premises Sebastian had shown her, and whether she should take the biggest leap of her life.

'Gran, do you need a rest before tonight?' Belle asked after draining her glass and leaving it in the kitchen with its stained orange slice. She'd love another. She wanted to curl up in the lounge, doze for just a moment with the tree lights on and the wood in the burner crackling away. But she couldn't miss the carolling. It'd been a long time since she'd sung Christmas carols, let alone done so alongside her mum and her gran.

Gran shook her head vehemently. 'I'll be fine. But I'll be straight up those stairs when we're done. My legs might give way otherwise.'

Belle knew that with Delia by her side Gran would be fine. Her energy probably came from absolute euphoria at everything that was going on.

As soon as she had the chance, Belle sneaked upstairs to the bathroom to freshen up. Her washbag was still there so she ran a brush through her long dark hair, the same colour as her gran had had once upon a time. She added a little bit of lip gloss to her lips, spritzed some perfume and was ready to go.

330

Downstairs, everyone was gathered in the kitchen and Belle went to join them, but Sebastian filled the tiny doorway coming from the other way and Betty was first to notice they were under the mistletoe.

'We meet again.' His green eyes drank her in, the creases at the sides of his mouth speaking of mischief.

Belle was about to take a leap of gargantuan proportions, perhaps alongside this man if she accepted his proposal. She looked up into his eyes and everything else seemed to settle around them. This felt like more than business, or was she imagining it?

'Kiss her!' Gran hollered from the table, and Belle ended up in a fit of giggles.

'Leave them be,' Betty admonished but the way she was looking at them said she was thinking along the same lines.

Sebastian leaned down and planted a gentle kiss on her lips, but he lingered longer than a friend would, hovered close to her in a very non-platonic way.

'Merry Christmas, Belle.' He didn't take his eyes from her.

'Merry Christmas, Sebastian.'

And then just when she thought they'd go on their way, out into the snow and the cold to sing their hearts out on the village green, he pulled her to him and his lips landed on hers as she let him kiss her properly. She wasn't sure who was cheering, it could've been her insides doing all the shrieking they liked, because when he kissed her, it was magic.

Epilogue

It was the end of February. Christmas had been and gone in Little Woodville and New Year had happened in a whirl. Belle had returned to Cambridge the day after Boxing Day, despite plenty of protests by her mum, Gran and Sebastian for her to stay, and she'd wasted no time investigating how to start her own business. Sebastian had carried on with his jobs around the village but had taken the time to put together a more formal proposal on paper, which he emailed to Belle. He followed it up with an hour-long phone call too – totally unnecessary from a business perspective, completely needed from a personal viewpoint.

The premises on the high street had sold to Sebastian in late January and he and Belle had negotiated a rate for her to rent part of it from him once the major renovations were done. And, now, she was here in Little Woodville for the weekend, armed with her laser tape measure, notes and a couple of sketch pads so they could get serious.

'It's going to look amazing.' She sipped from a cup of tea at the table in Snowdrop Cottage. They'd just made an appointment with an architect to draw up the plans for the bookshop and the rear space that she'd decided to turn into a small café. She'd serve beverages including coffee – she had to get to grips with one of those fancy coffee machines, a task she was oddly looking forward to – soups would be her main food in the winter months, sandwiches would be on the menu too, but she knew it would be a matter of adjusting what she offered to meet demand. If one thing worked she'd carry it on the following season; if it didn't, she'd have a rethink.

Belle looked out the window at the veggie patches that would soon have all manner of produce growing in them. She intended to source as many ingredients for her café from this very garden and the greenhouse and already she'd bought some gardening books to find out what else they could grow.

'Come on.' Sebastian opened the back door that led from the kitchen to the outside. He pulled on a jumper because it wasn't yet mild enough to be too minimalist in the clothing department, yet the sun didn't warrant a huge winter coat either. 'Your mum and Gran won't want to miss the snowdrops so we'll do a selfie in front of them.'

'Great idea. I'll send the photo to Mrs Fro too.'

Beyond the cottage, at the foot of the garden, a carpet of snowdrops arced in front of the fence to meet the lawn. They'd begun to come up a week ago, with the weather suddenly so mild, and they'd gone from clusters to a whole bed of the things. Their droopy heads fluttered in the breeze, hanging downwards as though they weren't sure whether or not it was time to look up. Almost like a performer on stage, feeling all alone, they were shy as the first flowers of the season.

'Gran said the flight went just fine.' Belle pulled on a roll-neck jumper and tugged the sleeves over her hands as they walked towards the flowers that had given this cottage its name. Or had the cottage come first? Belle wasn't sure. All she knew was that they were a heady combination and one didn't feel right without the other.

They admired the snowdrops as they got closer. 'She'd never flown before,' she told Sebastian. 'I think she'll be doing it a lot more.'

'She'll love Ireland. Delia will show her how beautiful it is up there.'

333

'I wonder if she'll want to stay.'

Gran was happy in the care home here but when Delia had asked her to go to Ireland to stay with her, she hadn't hesitated. And it sounded as though she was having a grand time. She'd been there almost two weeks, with another three to go.

'Mum did mention to me that she was going to suggest it.' Belle hoped Sebastian wasn't too upset.

'I figured she probably would. They've got a lot of catching up to do.'

Belle bent down to feel the snowdrops. 'I used to love how silky the petals were. I'd hardly dare to touch them though because I knew they were the first flowers to come out after Christmas and I thought if I was too rough with them, they might stop coming altogether.'

Sebastian pulled her to him and, their heads together, they snapped a few selfies with the snowdrops in the background.

'Did the architect include the plans for the flat above the bookshop?' Belle asked as she turned around on the spot. Covering three hundred and sixty degrees, she caught sight of the snowdrops at the sides of the house too and knew they extended beyond the front fence.

'Bookshop slash café.' He always insisted on including her whenever they talked about it.

'You know, that has a nice ring to it. Perhaps that's what we should call it.'

He pulled her to him and kissed her full on the lips. 'You know, there's room for you here at the cottage rather than moving into the flat when it's ready – it's still your place after all.'

'We'll see.' Belle hadn't wanted to rush into anything, but deep down she knew. With Anthony she had never felt unsure as such, but now she was with

Sebastian she knew what completely sure felt like and by the end of the year she'd agreed to give serious thought as to whether she'd retain part ownership of the cottage and he'd have the other part. They'd share a business and a house and the idea wasn't as scary as Belle might have once thought. They'd gone from enemies, to friends, to lovers and business partners all in the space of a couple of months and Belle's feet felt as though they'd barely touched the ground.

Hands around her waist, Sebastian said, 'You know, if you play your cards right, I might take you to the pub and make a third proposition to you.'

'Oh?' She snuggled against him.

'Well, more of a proposal of sorts.'

She grinned. 'Well I did kiss you under the mistletoe and you know what Gran always said...'

'I know...if you kiss someone properly beneath a sprig of mistletoe, you'll be partners for life.'

'Do you think she might be right?'

He grinned. 'You know she's right.'

And, with the snowdrops in the background, Sebastian took another selfie – of them kissing outside Snowdrop Cottage. It was another photo for Gillian, the woman who'd given him more than he could ever have hoped for, and for Gran, who'd always been in Belle's dreams and would be forever in her heart.

THE END

Acknowledgments

Katharine Walkden, editor extraordinaire, did a stellar job with this novel and helped me shape it into the final product. I'd also like to thank my proofreader, Edward, for catching any mistakes that slipped through the net. It was a pleasure working with both of you.

Thank you, Berni Stevens, for your hard work designing a cover that I love. It gets harder with more and more books, but I'm really pleased with what we came up with.

The research for this novel was so much fun thanks to my husband and my children. Investigating the Cotswolds in the summer holidays was amazing. Maybe we'll have to try Christmas one year and find a Snowdrop Cottage of our own!

Thank you to all my readers who support me in my writing journey, who read my books and review them. I'm so glad you're still enjoying my stories and I hope you enjoyed this latest winter trip to the stunning Cotswolds.

Helen J Rolfe x

Christmas at the Little Knitting Box
(New York Ever After, Book 1)

Christmas is coming and New York is in full swing for the snowy season. But at The Little Knitting Box in the West Village, things are about to change …

The Little Knitting Box has been in Cleo's family for nearly four decades, and since she arrived fresh off the plane from the Cotswolds four years ago, Cleo has been doing a stellar job of running the store. But instead of an early Christmas card in the mail this year, she gets a letter that tips her world on its axis.

Dylan has had a tumultuous few years. His marriage broke down, his mother passed away and he's been trying to pick up the pieces as a stay-at-home dad. All he wants this Christmas is to give his kids the home and stability they need. But when he meets Cleo at a party one night, he begins to see it's not always so easy to move on and pick up the pieces, especially when his ex seems determined to win him back.

When the snow starts to fall in New York City, both Cleo and Dylan realise life is rarely so black and white and both of them have choices to make. Will Dylan follow his heart or his head? And will Cleo ever allow herself to be a part of another family when her own fell apart at the seams?

Full of snow, love and the true meaning of Christmas, this novel will have you hooked until the final page.

Snowflakes and Mistletoe at the Inglenook Inn
(New York Ever After, Book 2)

As the flames on the log fire flicker and the snowflakes swirl above the New York streets, maybe this Christmas could be the one that changes everything...

When Darcy returns to Manhattan, she's put in charge of the Inglenook Inn, a cosy boutique hotel in the heart of Greenwich Village. The Inn needs a boost in bookings if it's to survive the competition, so Darcy is convinced that hosting Christmas this year is the answer. What she doesn't expect is to meet a face from the past, which can only spell trouble.

Myles left England behind and took a job in New York. It's a step forwards in his career, and has the added bonus of being nowhere near his family. He's also hoping to avoid Christmas, the worst time of the year. But when his company puts him up at the Inglenook Inn and he recognises Darcy, it isn't long before they clash.

When disaster strikes, can Myles and Darcy put their differences aside to make Christmas at the Inglenook Inn a success?

Made in the USA
Columbia, SC
28 October 2020